# EVERY HAPPINESS

# EVERY HAPPINESS

*a novel*

## REENA SHAH

BLOOMSBURY PUBLISHING
NEW YORK · LONDON · OXFORD · NEW DELHI · SYDNEY

BLOOMSBURY PUBLISHING
Bloomsbury Publishing Inc.
1359 Broadway, New York, NY 10018, USA
50 Bedford Square, London, WC1B 3DP, UK
Bloomsbury Publishing Ireland Limited, 29 Earlsfort Terrace,
Dublin 2, D02 AY28, IRELAND

BLOOMSBURY, BLOOMSBURY PUBLISHING, and the Diana logo are trademarks of
Bloomsbury Publishing Plc

First published in the United States 2026

Copyright © Reena Shah, 2026

All rights reserved. No part of this publication may be: i) reproduced or transmitted in any form, electronic or mechanical, including photocopying, recording, or by means of any information storage or retrieval system without prior permission in writing from the publishers; or ii) used or reproduced in any way for the training, development, or operation of artificial intelligence (AI) technologies, including generative AI technologies. The rights holders expressly reserve this publication from the text and data mining exception as per Article 4(3) of the Digital Single Market Directive (EU) 2019/790.

This is a work of fiction. Names, characters, businesses, places, events, locales, and incidents are either the products of the author's imagination or used in a fictitious manner. Any resemblance to actual persons, living or dead, or actual events is purely coincidental.

Bloomsbury Publishing Plc does not have any control over, or responsibility for, any third-party websites referred to or in this book. All internet addresses given in this book were correct at the time of going to press. The author and publisher regret any inconvenience caused if addresses have changed or sites have ceased to exist, but can accept no responsibility for any such changes.

ISBN: HB: 978-1-63973-300-2; EBOOK: 978-1-63973-301-9

LIBRARY OF CONGRESS CATALOGING-IN-PUBLICATION DATA IS AVAILABLE

2 4 6 8 10 9 7 5 3 1

Typesetting by Six Red Marbles India
Printed in the United States by Lakeside Book Company

To find out more about our authors and books visit www.bloomsbury.com
and sign up for our newsletters.

Bloomsbury books may be purchased for business or promotional use.
For information on bulk purchases please contact Macmillan Corporate and
Premium Sales Department at specialmarkets@macmillan.com.
For product safety–related questions contact productsafety@bloomsbury.com.

*For Dinesh and Madhuri Shah, who are my parents and the best of people*

# PART ONE

# Ruchi

## *August 1992*

Ruchi Mehta and her family arrived late to the Jains' annual beach party, as usual. A sign in Deepa Jain's florid script pointed them around to the back where a wedding-sized tent covered the porch, though most people gathered around smaller tents that dotted the dark sand. The party unfolded like playacting, everyone perspiring and working hard to simulate enjoyment. So many people, too many to greet and too many to notice them, which, in its way, was a relief.

"They've hired waiters. Like this is a restaurant," Naren said.

"Why should this bother you?" Ruchi said, though her husband was right, the waiters were new. They passed dry-looking dumplings, chalky chutney triangle sandwiches, wedges of brie—a cheese Ruchi had never understood, given its off color and smell of old milk. She'd stopped bringing dishes years ago.

She felt sorry for the waiters, who trudged through the sand in long-sleeved button-downs, smiling only when they approached guests. Sanjay, Deepa's husband, was talking to one of them. He looked preoccupied and rumpled, and Ruchi wondered if anyone else noticed. Deepa was nowhere to be seen.

Overhead, the sun was a white-hot disc. "A horrible day for a party," Naren muttered.

"You'll feel better after you eat and drink."

Her husband grumbled unintelligibly. Golden beverages sloshed in clear plastic tumblers. Separate tables for alcohol and soft drinks, just as there was separate onionless, garlicless food for the strict Jains.

Sweat dripped down Moksh's face and into his hoodie. Her son refused to wear anything else. Days passed when she hardly heard her son's voice, though she made a point of seeing him at least once in the morning and once at night. She looked up at him and was shocked anew by his height: almost six feet tall and still four months shy of seventeen. "Dikra, aren't you uncomfortable in this heat?" she asked.

"It's not even hot," he said.

It felt laughable to suggest he eat, so she didn't. As if she never had, as if motherhood was a series of forgettings.

"All the young people are over there," she said and pointed to the rocks. "And look. Anu Jain is home from college. She cut her hair. Very short."

"Stay close by. We're not staying long," Naren said. "I don't want to go hunting for you."

"It's not my fault we're here." Moksh raised his eyebrows and dragged his bottom teeth across his upper lip. He never left his scars alone.

"No one is saying it's your fault," Ruchi said. "We'll have fun." Though really it was her fault. She'd insisted they come to these parties, that it was rude to decline invitations. She took in the tent and waiters, all these guests with their important jobs, their Caribbean holidays and gym memberships, thriving medical practices and healthy retirement accounts, their children with strong biodata, and her resolve wavered.

But how else to see Deepa, to take her aside, to speak, for once, at last?

She watched Moksh lope around the perimeter of the party toward the rocks, avoiding the tents entirely, until he became a thin, dark slash. If only he would eat. Anu tugged at her tufts of hair and pulled at the cuffs of her blouse that clung to her thickened middle. She made room for him, and the two of them sat apart from the other kids.

"We're very late," Ruchi said. She and Naren remained at the edge of the party, like interlopers.

"It doesn't mean we'll stay later," Naren said.

"We have to eat something."

"Then eat first."

They approached the blue food tent. Two banquet tables lined the tent with trays of food that couldn't be passed: soupy enchiladas, deep-red pastas, browned broccoli. AMERICAN CONTINENTAL read a label alongside pale-rose napkins exquisitely fanned.

Where was the cake? At previous parties, there was always a general cake from which Deepa hand-fed Sanjay and Anu while everyone clapped, though it was never anyone's birthday. But today not a single sweet.

"Food and more food. That's all we do at these parties," Naren said, stabbing a spiral noodle. He filled his plate with a little of each item, while Ruchi followed behind him. She was too nervous to eat.

At the end of the table, Ravi Ravichandran was gesturing between bites to Minal and Varun, a couple Ruchi had met at the opening of Deepa's Bharat Friendship Association three years ago. Pious and opinionated, Ruchi remembered.

"You have to get them into the extracurriculars," Ravi said and waved his plate in an arc. Ruchi sometimes picked up files from his practice. At the Association's Diwali events, he made a show of praying to every god and reciting all the pujas, then partner-danced with young girls. Deepa said these were perks she allowed him for being their biggest donor.

"I pay my life for guitar lessons and Latin lessons and this camp and that camp." Ravi tugged his nose, smiling. It was more show. His eldest was an honor society tennis star who trained in Florida during school holidays. With Moksh, nothing had stuck, not the Hindi classes or the baseball or the clarinet, which seemed to signal Ruchi's own deficiency.

Naren sipped his fizzy drink. His eyes went misty as he stifled a burp. "All this spending and then what?"

"Then they go to college. Then they make their own money," Ravi said good-naturedly.

Varun chimed in with, "Ere, boss, then there are no more worries. Then we live the life." He jerked his wrist and didn't notice his drink splash onto Naren's shirt.

Naren flicked off the liquid. What was this "live the life"? There would always be worries, though no one talked about them. Everyone was nice and everyone was rich, with children who would also be nice and rich. Happy children who made them proud.

"Deepaji's Association has such good functions. We are looking forward to Ganpathi Chaturthi," Minal said. She poked at her shiny slab of brie.

"Not just functions. Your dues are for seva, too," Ravi said. "We just sent money for the Ram temple back home. One gold brick!" Everyone nodded in unison.

"We are very involved," Naren said. "My brother in Bombay is a local leader, with my help of course."

Ruchi's body fizzed with irritation. It was all fake piety. She should tell them how Deepa used to detest temple and the stinking swamis and the greasy prasad they were forced to eat. In Bombay, Gujaratis never celebrated Ganpathi Chaturthi as much as the Marathis did, but here all festivals were on equal footing. Ruchi attended in case a vengeful god perceived her thoughts. The old superstitions persisted. Eat plain curd before trips. Never walk out the door in the middle of a sneeze. Mark your child with an eye pencil when you catch him asleep, and press hard because will you get another opportunity? Naren poked fun at the habits, asking what good they did. The question wasn't mean-spirited, was maybe even right to ask, but it stung nonetheless. That was the problem with any precaution. There was no knowing the dangers you missed.

But she wasn't here to give speeches; she'd never been good at them. She was here for Deepa and later none of this talk would matter.

THE BEACH HOUSE was off-limits this year, but who was going to stop her? Ruchi followed the property line around to the front where the heavy door, robin's-egg blue, was unlocked. Inside, every room was ablaze, overhead lights clashing against streaks of sun. Drooped and dry plants in the foyer, thick-stalked, moon-faced leaves begging for water. Out of habit, Ruchi had taken off her shoes at the door; crumbs stuck to her soles. Someone had spilled orange juice across a counter and not bothered to clean it up. Someone had cluttered the coffee table with mugs and granola bar wrappers and a bowl of orange peels. Ruchi ran her hand up the banister, the wood soft as gum. If downstairs was overly illuminated, upstairs was dimly lit, blinds down and curtains drawn. Laundry sat in a pile in the middle of the hall. The mauve carpet needed vacuuming. It should've been satisfying seeing the house diminished and ugly. It should've made her feel better, a sense that some great but imperceptible wrong had been righted.

It would've been easier if Ruchi had come here to coolly witness Deepa's misfortune and insist that all would be fine, the way Deepa had insisted over the course of their long friendship. Next time will be better, next time we'll do this, we'll do that. Lunches. Afternoons. Next time. It would've been easier if Ruchi had come here to relish the mess Deepa's husband had gotten them into. Ruchi had been right, which should've offered a little thrill.

But mostly she felt sad. She'd come here with an idea, a hope.

A choked sob from the bedroom. Ruchi waited but didn't hear it again. She pushed open the door. The bedroom had become shabbier over the years: the dresser sun-faded, the perfume bottles half-filled, lampshades dust-caked, and a bed that probably creaked. The vertical blinds were drawn, one panel flipped wrong. The light was swampy. Sitting on the floor and leaning against the bed frame was Deepa. One bare leg splayed out in front of her, the other tucked underneath. Her dress rolled up past her underwear. She swept tears from her cheek with the heel of her palm.

Ruchi took a single step into the room and swung the door shut behind her. Her whole body ached. She was grateful for it, for the stricture in her throat, her cold hands, a sign that she wasn't empty yet. She was grateful that face-to-face, her pulse quickened.

And still Deepa was a mystery, no more known to Ruchi than she had been thirty years ago. What did it mean to know a person? Really know them on the inside? It was an impossible thing, a person; one could live close to your heart and remain a riddle.

"Ruch." Deepa arranged her face into a smile. A mask of ease with salt-crusted eyes. "You made it. How nice. I'm just getting ready."

"Aren't you well?" Ruchi asked. Slowly she stepped closer. Her red toenail skimmed the wrinkled sole of Deepa's foot, the one folded under her thigh.

"Nothing like that." Deepa patted the spot next to her. "Come, sit with me."

Ruchi slunk down to the floor. She thought Deepa would edge over to make space, but she didn't. Their shoulders and upper arms brushed. She was aware of Deepa's bare thighs and the puckered skin of her knees. A black streak where her calf met her shinbone and a white shine on her forehead and chin. The bones of Deepa's big toes, mangled from too-tight heels, jutted out like peninsulas. Ruchi saw these details in quick glances, careful not to stare, not to take in too much. Then she saw the papers that Deepa clutched in her fist, like a child.

So. Deepa knew.

"The host should always give time for guests to mingle on their own. Is the party going well? Have you not tried the food?"

"Deepa," Ruchi said softly and turned to face her. Freckles had formed under Deepa's eyes, little brown islands in the fragile, smoky skin. Ruchi gestured to the papers and disorder.

"A mess, as you can see," Deepa said. A muscle in her temple fluttered.

"I'm sorry."

"So you also know?"

Ruchi nodded.

Deepa's eyes narrowed. "How?"

Ruchi hadn't expected the question. "I handle Dr. Sharma's billing. I've told you that."

When Deepa didn't respond, Ruchi rambled about how she'd unwittingly come across the bills. Then she lied and said she hadn't told anyone else in the medical suite, not even Dr. Sharma.

Deepa laughed a throaty, spiteful laugh. "And you didn't tell me?"

"I was planning to." She hated that she couldn't keep the quiver out of her voice. Deepa tossed the papers onto the stack beside her.

On the wall behind Deepa and above the bed, Anu's framed pencil drawing of Shiva Natraj hung by a corner. Behind it, the safe was cracked open. Inside were stacks of bills banded together as bricks, more gray than green. The simpleness of wealth disappointed her.

"Let's put all this away," Ruchi said. "Come. I'll help you." She reached for the papers, but Deepa caught her wrist.

"You said you were *planning* to tell me. Planning. Planning what?"

Her grip was tight. Ruchi held her breath but was sure Deepa could feel her pulse pounding.

"Sanjay might be caught. Already the authorities might know," Ruchi said, but it wasn't how she'd wanted to start.

"And so?"

Ruchi stared at Deepa's pruned knee, a crescent scab, the vulnerable patella. Her wrist burned where Deepa held it. "You don't have to stay in this marriage."

Deepa's eyes were tearless and fully awake. "You want me to leave my husband?"

Ruchi whispered, "Yes."

"And then?"

And then? Ruchi didn't know what to say. They lacked the language for intimacies. Whoops and chatter from the party punched through the window. Ruchi had thought it would be simple, that explanations and plans would be unnecessary. Her friend wasn't miles away, inaccessible like an out-of-reach dream. She was just here only, a hair's distance.

# Deepa

## *1962*

Deepa had forgotten about her hunger by the noontime meal. It was 1962, she was twelve, in seventh standard, and the new girl was to thank, or to blame. Her oily braid, her dusky complexion, her hunched posture. But she had answered every question in morning lectures, had raised her hand without hesitation to recite all the correct formulas in maths. Deepa stood on the wooden steps of Our Lady English Medium School for Girls and scanned the chalky, sun-bleached courtyard where every day, for forty minutes, the nuns disappeared and released their charges to their own natures. Girls sat cross-legged in circles of threes and fours and fives, knee to knee, pillows of yellow dirt puffing up from the ground as they squirmed and laughed. But no one made room for the new girl, who retreated to the shade of the withered banyan in the courtyard and stared into her tiffin. A smudged kaala teeka at her temple to ward off the evil eye, a frayed black thread around her wrist. Deepa rubbed clean her own teekas when she found them and stretched the threads until they slipped off or broke. She thought of herself as bold and besharam, while most girls were simpletons. Likely this new one was too. But Deepa, who could join any circle she pleased, who ignored the throngs that beckoned to her—classmates a little fearful that she might join them and then relieved when she walked on—this Deepa took daya on the new girl and approached. The girl's face jammed, and a nervous tongue pushed against her smooth cheeks. Deepa made note of how she shifted just slightly, so that Deepa had to sit on the segment of root still in the sun. When at last the girl looked up, her eyes were sharp and begging. Too much.

"My name is Ruchi," the girl said in a whisper.

"Why have you joined so late in the year?" Deepa asked. "Already you've missed two months."

Ruchi flushed and turned away from her. Down covered her dark neck, and Deepa had an urge to trace it. Instead, she took Ruchi's hand in hers; the girl's face snapped back. Deepa abruptly released the hand, and Ruchi stared at where she'd been touched.

"You say 'service,' not 'toilet,'" Deepa instructed in English. "Or 'loo' if you want to sound posh. Sister Braganza prefers the good girls." She made sure her *t*'s were hard, practicing a private school lilt that would eventually become second nature. She noticed that Ruchi's khaki uniform had been deeply scrubbed, the sign of a mother trying to make old clothes appear new. A faded orange dupatta formed an X over her chest.

Sister Ferrao bustled across with her bell to end lunch. Dust coughed around her inky habit. "Instead of 'ma'am' you must call the teachers 'Sister,'" Deepa went on. She explained that the two nuns ran Our Lady with rulers they wielded as whips and that they'd been banished from the convent in Bandra for praying to goddesses. Ruchi hurried to stack her tiffin, and Deepa feared she wasn't listening. "Sister Ferrao doesn't like pets, so you can stop answering all the questions."

Ruchi gripped her tiffin handle, blinking fast. "I don't answer all the questions."

Deepa stood up. She wasn't used to being contradicted. "You're no good at playing dumb," she said, and rushed ahead to reach the class first. But she was pleased that Ruchi was just behind her, arriving second.

Over the following weeks, they sat together every mealtime, and on Saturdays, after half lessons, Deepa bought them fresh jalebi fafda from the cranky vendors in Gulal Wadi, using the money she stole from her mother's home temple. She learned that Ruchi had known only municipal school until now, was the middle sister of three, that the older one, Aruna, didn't finish ninth and the younger one, Tejas, had no interest in studies. She was twelve like Deepa, the two of them a year younger and inches shorter than the other seventh standard girls, though Ruchi seemed even smaller. She was overly cautious, afraid the jalebi might singe her tongue or the fafda might upset her stomach, but Deepa saw the glow of smartness underneath, how Ruchi kept it at the ready.

Deepa acted like each time she touched Ruchi was casual, weaving lace trimming into Ruchi's unmanageable hair, cupping her hands over her ear. Deepa explained that she and her mother had moved from Aden the year before, narrowly avoiding the collapse when the Gujaratis were kicked out. "Kicked out for good reason" was a phrase Deepa liked to say. Ruchi asked what she meant, but Deepa evaded answers, enjoying her new friend's confusion, her curiosity. She marveled at the dark marble of Ruchi's skin, unlike Deepa's inflamed cheeks with pustules she couldn't help but pick and squeeze, inflaming them further. Ruchi had no inkling of how lovely she was; Deepa kept her admiration secret, as if the knowledge might make Ruchi lovelier still.

WHENEVER SHE COULD, Deepa escaped to Ruchi's flat in a gully off Bhuleshwar Road. Ruchi's mother tutted over Deepa's painted toenails, the father who never returned from Aden, the mother who let her daughter walk about anywhere. "Why does she spend time here when she lives in one of those ugly buildings with sea view?" Deepa overheard Ruchi's mother say. Ruchi's flat was a dingy chawl, three separate rooms at the end of the hall, the kitchen raw, their cooking vessels dried on rags on the concrete floor, all the girls sleeping in one room, shared toilets.

And yet Deepa loved the crowd of sisters and cousins, a dadi who called out at all hours for her legs to be pressed, a flat where privacy had to be stolen, where a whisper could be overheard. It was a flat where Deepa was one more person, not entirely welcome, but tolerated. She pretended she was part of the general chaos and thought the place matched her own largeness of spirit, a largeness that was a hint as yet, not fully noticed or appreciated. In the flat, she was too modern, too forthright, no longer the daughter of a sad and superstitious mother who prayed more than she talked to Deepa, but the daughter of a woman who dared to live separate from her husband—a husband who sent boxes of embroidered silks and linens to tailor into new suits, but rarely enough cash.

Deepa tried to present herself as both mysterious and brave. On the flat's shared balcony with its rickety wooden balustrade, she and Ruchi hid, knees tucked in tight to their chins, thighs grazing, behind a wall of blue crates filled with Thums Up bottles that Ruchi's mother sold to bottlewallas for money to buy tobacco-laced paan. Pigeons swooped so close they threatened to pierce through the bottles and peck at the girls' cheeks. Deepa leaned toward Ruchi's ear, her thigh pressing harder now, and said, "My family lost all their money."

"But how is that possible?" Ruchi said. "You live in a flat with its own balcony. With a lift and a liftman." She seemed to press back, but Deepa couldn't be sure.

"He's there to make sure children don't chop off their fingertips with the black metal gate."

Deepa described the waiting jaw, the flat smack it made every time the liftman slammed it shut. Ruchi's leg stiffened with fear.

"Before the liftman there was this one girl." Deepa shook her head mournfully. Her salwar was damp from sitting too long, even the bottoms of her feet sweating. Her breath was hot and putrid, or maybe it was Ruchi's.

"One girl what?" Ruchi asked.

"Cut her finger clear off. Like, sha-tak! It was hanging." Deepa bobbed her head for effect. Below the flat, an argument broke out, high-pitched gibberish punctuated with slaps. "Held by a bloody strand of tissue."

"What are you talking?" Ruchi said, but her eyes were wide.

"The blood gushed out. You could see the bone." Deepa paused, again for effect. "The digit fell into the black slit between the lift door and ground floor. The crack was just big enough."

The air was only breathable in gulps. Deepa's red toenails flared in the wet light while Ruchi covered her bare, amphibial toes with her hands.

"Did she scream?"

Deepa shook her head. "Pain like that doesn't hit all at once. By the time it comes you are half dead."

"How do you know?"

Her friend was on the verge of disbelief. What did it matter how Deepa knew? "Don't believe me then." Deepa edged her thigh away, and Ruchi nudged closer to touch again. That night Deepa dreamed of the fingerless, pain-stricken girl she'd made up, the ribbon at the end of her braid trembling in shock.

SISTER BRAGANZA AND Sister Ferrao had identical stubble growing on their chins and brows that protruded like cliffs. They barreled like ships across the courtyard and through the halls. They were already ancient in 1962, and as years passed they remained old but grew no older, as if made of metal.

The women lived in a small wooden house at the far end of the courtyard. The banyan tree and main school building dwarfed it. A giant padlock, sea-scoured with rust that flaked off in chunks, secured the front door of the sisters' home, and the curtains of the two windows were tightly drawn so that if a stray girl tried to peer inside, all she would see was herself. At mealtime the women retired there, emerging just before afternoon lessons.

The nuns inspected the girls in the mornings for lice and pink eye. Enrollment dwindled in the ninth and tenth standards, but the school prepared for it by overenrolling younger sections, girls in crisp white shirts that Sister Ferrao compelled to perform rigorous calisthenics in the courtyard as if to ready them for war. They lectured cursorily from textbooks but read from English newspapers about politics, droned on about Indira, Nehru's daughter, how she managed her two sons, her husband, her father, attended Oxford, was appointed the president of Congress. "See how careful she is with her appearance. A Durga in an excellently pleated sari," Ferrao liked to say, glaring at them over the paper. "A lesson to you all!"

The nuns beat the backs of Deepa's hands with first a wooden, then a plastic ruler for wearing her orange dupatta too low or braiding her hair to the side or hitching her skirt to show her newly waxed legs. They chastised her for speeding through exercises. "Slow down, Deepa Bapodra! Slow down," they called out. Still, she wouldn't have hated them if they'd noticed her sharpness, if they hadn't regarded her as insignificant and shallow. She wouldn't have warped them into miniature, monstrous figurines and banished the sisters to a low shelf in her mind had they offered a drop of approval.

"We, too, are sisters," Deepa told Ruchi one Saturday afternoon. As usual, they were on the balcony behind the bottles, which they had arranged in a semicircle around them, enough space to sit face-to-face, legs crossed, knees glancing, fingers still sticky with jalebi syrup.

"I already have sisters. Let's not be like that. They're a bore," Ruchi said.

"When we get old we can go to Sea Club every day for sweet tea and desserts."

"We can stay all afternoon. Eat until we get sick from sugar."

Through the gaps in the bottles Deepa made out slivers of the opposite balcony, women hanging laundry and scrubbing pots on their haunches, water and scum flowing to the gully below, as if the whole bloating city was just this place, a closed loop within which she and Ruchi were cocooned or trapped.

"We can grow fat," Deepa said. "And balloon to the sky, big and swollen." She made a circle with her arms and as she lifted them a crisp cloud of rotten pulp escaped and stung her nostrils, filled her throat. She saw Ruchi swallow, maybe in disgust. It made Deepa hungry.

"You know, we should get rid of this." Deepa licked her finger clean and dragged it across the top of Ruchi's lip.

Ruchi covered the shadow of hairs, embarrassed. Deepa had taken care of her own mustache months ago, and it was lighter anyway, more like fuzz than teeth.

"I can do it for you. My mother showed me."

"Was there blood?"

"What are you, stupid? Do you not know threading? It takes two minutes." They tiptoed from the balcony into the bedroom, where they rarely spent any time. It was strangely empty of people. Ruchi hid her away so no one could drag them down to the gully to play kho-kho or oil someone's feet. Deepa wouldn't have minded playing kho-kho or oiling someone's feet, but she would never admit to her loneliness.

They found white thread in the vanity under the green three-way mirror. The paneled mirror was the one indulgence in the austere room of metal wardrobes and folded mats. Deepa patted the ground in front of the mirror and pulled at the thread. "It will do," she said. The thread was too waxy—her mother's was thinner and easier to wind—but Deepa wanted to see Ruchi's clean upper lip. Strays would appear every week, and Deepa would point them out. It would feel like winning. "Now sit and keep still."

"Are you sure you know how?"

Deepa hated the glimmer of doubt in Ruchi's voice. "Ere, you are a scaredy." She wound the thread, held one end taut with her teeth, and swept it across Ruchi's forearm.

"Ouch!" But it was already over. Thick commas of hair littered the red raw skin. Deepa admired her work before tilting Ruchi's forehead back with her thumb. She searched for an opening and drew close enough that her lips were a finger's breadth away from Ruchi's cheek, eyes level.

"Close your eyes."

"But—"

"Close them. It's better."

She felt Ruchi's shoulder against her chest, the brisk exhale of pain as Deepa motored the thread across the lip, once, twice, thrice. Deepa had smudged the kaala teeka at Ruchi's temple. Her upper lip was now a splotched newborn color. There was no cream to calm it. "Oh, it's lovely," Deepa said, turning Ruchi around so they could peer at her handiwork, the two of them in the mirror, reflected again and again to diminishment.

THE HEAT WOULDN'T ease though it should have after the new year. The sun was in constant rapture. Deepa sat diagonally two rows behind Ruchi and studied her as she lined up her ruler and pencils. Forty girls were crammed into the room for a nonsense exam about Shivaji, the form only slightly more complex in ninth standard than the test in seventh, and in fourth before that. Who was Shivaji? What was the battle of Raigad? How did he kill Afzal Khan? The textbook illustrations were cartoonish, Shivaji barrel-chested in a saffron kurta, the ultimate Hindu warrior. What good were the nuns' strange lectures about politics if the forms were interested only in the textbooks? Deepa answered with no interest, thinking of the film she and Ruchi planned to watch that afternoon, but she saw Ruchi hunched over her blue form book. The delicate movement of her pencil indicated small, fastidious handwriting. So much useless work.

But the following week, Sister Braganza called to them from down the hall, waving a form book in her hand. Deepa assumed that her form had finally received top marks for its precision and brevity. "Sister Ferrao and I would like a word," the woman said, but when Deepa opened her mouth to speak the sister looked through her.

Ruchi froze.

"Chal," Deepa said, "they're calling you."

"But what for?"

"It can't be anything good," Deepa whispered. "Look at how her nose is sweating. Go fast so we don't miss the film. *Sangam* was all shot in Europe."

The nun bounded to the front office where punishments were meted, and Ruchi followed with her hands hugging her elbows. Deepa watched them until they turned the corner and out of sight, then waited among the vines of the banyan. It seemed that hours passed, though it wasn't possible because the sun didn't move.

"Ere, so long you took! What did the two witches do?" Deepa said when Ruchi appeared. She seemed unharmed.

"They said I—" Ruchi flinched at bulbuls squawking in the branches. "They said I have top marks. That I should do Medicine. Houshiyar, they called me," she said in a small voice. "But Ammi will never allow it." Her face was lit with pride, her paper clutched in her fist.

"Houshiyar?" No one had ever called Deepa that and until now she hadn't cared. She tried to speed ahead as she smiled, tried to focus on the steamed milk she'd steal from the chaiwallah at intermission, the scald down her throat.

DEEPA WAS THERE when Sister Braganza visited Ruchi's parents to talk about their daughter. She didn't want to miss it, despite the pain she expected to feel at the prospect of Ruchi's success. The stupid nuns had dismissed Deepa outright, as if she were ordinary.

Braganza sat upright on the plastic seat, sweating in the fanless air. The small room next to the bedroom that served as a sitting area was dark even during the day because on all sides were other, bigger buildings.

Ruchi's mother had instructed them all to stay in the bedroom. "You'll be called if you're needed," she'd said to Ruchi, but Deepa had tiptoed into the hall and hidden in the shadows behind the thin, cracked door, and the sisters and cousins had joined her. Ruchi's mother had enlisted a neighbor to serve tea and biscuits to give the appearance that she had help, while the father praised the school in his false singsong. Braganza slurped from her saucer.

"She looks like a horse," Aruna whispered.

"How much she must be perspiring! Chi, I heard that they tweeze the hairs from their own heads." Tejas giggled.

Ruchi glared at them. "I'll tweeze the hairs from *your* head."

"Oh ho! All because she thinks you can become a madam doctor!" a cousin said.

"At least I'll sit for my exams."

Aruna poked Ruchi hard in the shoulder. "Don't think you are big big just like that."

"Why not?"

"You might fail."

Had Deepa had sisters and cousins she would've won their admiration, but Ruchi was too sensitive. She struggled against them.

Deepa wandered down the hall to the bedroom. Not a single personal item was in view; all belongings were locked in the wardrobes, mats rolled with their bedding. It felt barren for a room where so many people slept, and it made Deepa lonelier still. She had to guess at which bedding might be Ruchi's, and she picked a checkered green mat rolled in a hurry with sheets bursting from the edges. She searched between the folds and found the blue form book. Ruchi had written her name in determined block letters. The paper began like one any student could have written. But on the second page were other Shivaji facts. That at the age of ten he married his first wife, followed by seven more. That he was short. That he had loved intricate mosaic work, domes, Persian swirls, even as he drew up documents in Sanskrit. His father's name was Shahaji—"The name of a Moghul," Ruchi had written. The letters became uneven here, the loops larger and taller and more beautiful. How did Ruchi know these things? Where had she found them out? Deepa's heart twisted but she would never give Ruchi the satisfaction of asking her. At the end, a single word in Ferrao's blunt handwriting—*brilliance*. Deepa folded the form book and tucked it into the hidden pocket of her salwar.

She returned to the hall, where all the girls were quiet.

"And as doctor, she will be working?" the mother asked.

"Of course, what else?" Now Sister Braganza was using the tone she used with children who couldn't understand. A voice like night.

The father thanked Sister Braganza for taking a special interest and wished her a good day. Deepa could see Ruchi's shoulder blades twitching under her kameez.

"Yes, then. I'll be going." But Sister Braganza didn't stand up right away. She looked searchingly at Ruchi's parents, like they were the type of people she railed against as backward. "You do understand that now that the prime minister is dead, there is talk of his daughter."

"His daughter?" Ruchi's mother asked. "Always there is talk." She said to her husband, loud enough for the nun to hear if not understand, "Amari dikri Nehru ni dikri nathi!" The man chuckled.

Deepa drew up next to Ruchi and saw in her profile the ache and repulsion, as if she were seeing her family for the first time, how faulty and cruel the flesh of their love could be. Deepa took Ruchi's hand and held it with no hesitation.

Later, on the way home, she strode through market stalls, wove through men tossing open bolts of chiffons and cottons and silks, and clenched Ruchi's form in her salwar pocket. She rode the lift to her flat, ignoring the liftman's leering small talk. He opened the metal grate and before she stepped out, before she found her mother inside, too lost in prayer to notice her daughter, Deepa let the form slip from her fingers and disappear into the bottomless crack.

# Ruchi

## 1966

After Sister Braganza's visit, the nuns' interest slipped. They no longer looked to Ruchi to answer questions or gave her extra tuitions on Tuesdays. Nineteen sixty-five turned to 1966, the year of their tenth standard final exams, and the nuns treated her like any other girl, except they didn't beat her, which somehow seemed worse.

"Do you even want to do Medicine?" Deepa asked at last.

"Of course. What else is there to do?" Ruchi said.

"That's different from wanting to."

"I'm the one who gives Dadi her golis, who makes sure she swallows them."

They sat under the old banyan in the courtyard where they took their lunches. Deepa picked at the crust of her cheese toast, avoiding the yellow, eggy spread. Ruchi tried not to want the yellow cheese, which was probably from the shop where foreign goods were sold. She tried to focus on her curried potatoes floating in oil. "We are not showy people," Ammi told her when she wouldn't let Ruchi paint her nails. "But we are shokin about our food."

"You don't really want it, Ruchi. All those years just studying," said Deepa. Once the crust was gone, her friend stuck her finger in the filmy center of the toastie and examined it. "If you wanted it, you would do it anyway."

"Ere, how do you know?" Ruchi said, though Deepa had unsettled a doubt. What did Ruchi know about what she wanted? So little. Deepa had a habit of making her feel shaky, uncertain, which Ruchi took as a sign of internal weakness, some lack of decisiveness on her part. She was going on sixteen and all she'd known was what was asked of her.

"In any case, they're witches, the sisters," Deepa said as Sister Ferrao strode into the middle of a group of fourth standard girls, then took hold of an ear and twisted. "They only want to say they sent someone from this horrid school to Medicine. Someone from an easy, 'forward-thinking' family. They don't care about you."

Deepa couldn't have known that this hurt her and made her feel small. Ruchi thought of her precise writing inside the blue form booklet. She'd slept with the booklet under her gadda until it went missing. She blamed Aruna or Tejas, but maybe it was a sign that the booklet hadn't mattered. Any girl could write nicely. It didn't make you special.

At least she had Deepa, though every day she was on guard for when their friendship would end, leaving Ruchi alone again. During recitations, she sometimes saw Deepa whisper and throw smiles to everyone but her. Or some girl would approach them at the banyan tree and mention a film that Ruchi didn't know Deepa had seen and the two would trade plotlines and song sequences like two intimates. It was as if Deepa craved Ruchi's longing, and then Ruchi would worry, what did she really know about the girl? She'd never been to Deepa's flat and had seen her mother only from the school gate where she dropped her daughter every morning, her cheeks orange with rouge, kohl thick under her eyes, diamond studs in her ears. A filmy woman, Ammi called her.

Ruchi wanted to ride in the lift with the liftman to see if he'd wink at her, too, see if the metal jaws were as sharp as Deepa said they were, if the flat was draped in fabrics, if they truly had only atta and rice for food. She had no reason to disbelieve Deepa except that the left side of her mouth curled in a dare. Ruchi wanted to scrub the expression off her face, just as Ammi used to scrub her upper lip to depress the hair follicles, which had done nothing in the end.

But then, as if sensing Ruchi's desire to know her more, Deepa asked her to come to the Mahalakshmi Temple that her mother insisted they visit on holy days.

"What holy days?" Ruchi asked, though she didn't care. Of course she'd go. It was the end of January, two months before the exams, but she'd forgo studying for this.

"Whatever day my mother says is holy," Deepa said. "I hate it."

They followed Auntie up the hill on Bhulabhai Desai Road toward the temple steps where devotees thronged. The heat had finally broken, and a chill threaded the morning. Auntie wore a white kurta that clung to her back and hips, studded chappals over beige socks. Like her daughter, she was beautiful; she had the same deep smoke around her eyes that made people stare. Ruchi detected no great feeling between the two, neither animosity nor love. They hardly looked at each other. Ruchi couldn't fathom it: to live with a person and not be either berated with constant criticism or suffocated by incessant worry.

Auntie had them keep their shoes with a flower vendor at the base of the steps instead of the chappal depot where they charged the price of milk. She then joined the mass of people, but Deepa pulled Ruchi back. "Shouldn't we keep up?" Ruchi asked.

"She doesn't care as long as I'm here. Up front is for all the shaking ladies who pretend a goddess has taken them."

Inside the temple, a statue of Durga's silver-coated lion separated the crowd of men to the left and women to the right. Ruchi could no longer see Auntie, who must've pushed to the front, where a bald, bare-torsoed priest in a flimsy dhoti chanted and flicked holy water into the air at the three disembodied, crowned heads of goddesses. Ammi had told her the heads had been found in the bed of the creek that once divided Worli from Malabar Hill, back before Bombay's islands had been taped together with mud and concrete. Maybe the goddesses' bodies were still down there, trapped in silt.

Ruchi and Deepa sat the way they always sat, their arms touching. Deepa whispered every now and then in her ear as women prayed on either side of them. The white tiles were both cold and damp. Ammi warned Ruchi that it was bad for girls to sit directly on cold floors, that the cold would ride up their legs and freeze their wombs. As she got older, everything became about the viability of marriage, as if her parents might have to disclose on her biodata each time she'd folded her legs and taken a seat on the ground.

Young men with pencil mustaches stole glances at Deepa. Men were always staring; it was nothing unusual. Deepa didn't avoid them, but neither did she return their looks. She simply swept over them as if they were invisible.

"Which ones should we marry?" Deepa asked. "That one for you."

Ruchi felt her neck go hot and turned away from the men. "Don't be stupid. He's so old."

"He's the handsomest one."

"I don't care." She could hear the amusement in Deepa's voice. She focused on Saraswati's gold bust, eyes painted black under a long, flat brow.

"We could marry the same one," Ruchi said. The priest passed around an aarti tray, and people rummaged in their handbags for coins and notes. Ruchi reached in her pocket and crumpled the ten-rupee note Ammi had given her.

"Same one?"

"Why not?" Ruchi asked, though she wanted to scuttle out of the room, away from the odor of feet and incense, the aarti tray now snaking its way toward them. She wanted to keep the note in her sweating palm for a cone of cashews or meetha paan or fresh milk to drink straight from the bag.

Deepa whispered into Ruchi's hot ear, "Why not?"

The ladies around them pressed their hands in prayer, lips muttering mantras. "We could live in a bungalow," Ruchi whispered.

"In the hills."

"Overlooking the ocean."

"A view."

"Every day he'd take us to a different film," Ruchi said, louder now, emboldened. "And he'd buy us nimbu pani and cutlets at intermission."

"You can't eat oily cutlets every day. You'll have loose motions."

"We'll teach him cooking."

"We'll teach him cleaning." Deepa surveyed the men bowing their heads to the floor. "But chi, none of these. Not even your Mr. Handsome."

"No, none of these," Ruchi said, her heart lifting.

"We'll have to see about his height, once we stop growing."

Ruchi shrugged. "Fine."

"Will you feel bad if I make him fair-skinned?" Deepa asked.

Ruchi considered the back of her hands, the darkest part of her. "No problem," she said, but flushed with embarrassment.

"No, no. We'll make him of chocolate instead. Chocolate and rose syrup."

"Oh."

"Don't you like chocolate?"

This was Deepa: say something biting then pull back, pace over it until it was smooth and you couldn't know if anything sharp had been there at all.

The aarti tray grew closer with its wobbling oil lamp. Ruchi thought of the note in her pocket and dreaded giving it up.

"We should give him a name," Deepa said. "A good name. High caste."

Ruchi didn't want to give him a name. She wanted him to be a vapor, or more sound than substance. She loved her father and uncles, though her stomach turned at the grunts she heard at night, muffled but still clear through the walls, their animal efforts, her aunts' silence. Her mother's. Ruchi knew what she was supposed to want, she knew what happiness looked like. It was in every film, and in Ammi's face when she received inquiries about Aruna, Ruchi's older sister. Happiness was a relief, the disaster of an unwanted woman avoided. And yet here was Durga, unwed. Brahma was Sarawati's second husband, but she'd cursed him and lived alone. But Lakshmi. Lakshmi changed forms to be with Vishnu in every incarnation, as if she existed only for him. Ruchi quietly found it all rubbish, but only quietly. She didn't want to provoke bad luck. All she wanted was to be with her friend, not because Deepa was always kind or caring or particularly nice, but because of an inexplicable need.

"Anil," Ruchi said without thinking. "Call him Anil if you want. I don't much care."

"That's an ugly name. An old man name."

"Make him rich with no family so we don't have to live with them," Ruchi said. "But nice so he doesn't get the idea of hitting."

"Your Anil sounds boring."

"Our," Ruchi said.

The stern priest arrived with the tray and held it out. The women around them rose and filled his tray with money, forcing Ruchi and Deepa to rise as well. Deepa gave him her ten rupees, briefly holding her hand over the flame that was supposed to purify them. The notes threatened to spill over, as colorful as candy. Ruchi saw a small rattan bag tied to the priest's waist, where he stuffed the money from the tray to make room for more.

"I don't have anything," Ruchi said. Saris pressed in around her.

"Here, give him this," Deepa said, and slipped her a fresh note. Ruchi took the money in her right hand, her left holding her own bill in her pocket. She nudged the women aside and used both hands to take the fire's blessing.

"Such a good girl," Deepa said, and pushed her way out of the crowd. They were going the wrong way. Now that the aarti was over, they were supposed to follow the women toward the statues where another priest would anoint them with vermilion as the goddesses passed their eyes over them. It's what they were here for, but Deepa held her back.

"Don't you worry what might happen if you don't take the blessing?"

"No," Deepa said.

"Won't your mother be angry?"

Deepa continued away from the goddesses. Ruchi followed.

"Look." Deepa slipped a round metal tin from the pocket of her salwar. Inside, red powder glittered. She licked the pad of her ring finger and dabbed it in the powder, then pressed it first to her forehead and then to Ruchi's. The touch was too firm. "She'll never know."

Deepa's cheeks had broken out again, small oily buds on her pale skin, the white pus inside innocent and sweet-looking. Ruchi wanted to run her hands over them but instead she touched her own smooth cheek and felt something missing there. She was the better student and always would be, Ruchi knew it, but Deepa was the kind of girl you could pin your hopes on, the kind who dazzled no matter what.

"We'll make him a Vora," Deepa said. "Anil Vora sounds a little nicer. Like Rajesh Khanna."

"Whatever, as long as he's made of rose syrup and chocolate." Bells began to ring as people finished their viewing and prostrations, their blessings and absolution. "As long as we can both marry him," Ruchi whispered under her breath.

"What?"

"Anil. God of the wind," Ruchi said.

"Perfect. Invisible."

They remained close to the entrance stairs and now separate from the crowd that formed a single organism around the deities. Ruchi felt self-conscious of the separation, like they were dirty girls with their monthly chums and weren't allowed too close.

Bells rang and Auntie, who was likely among the first to take her blessing, pushed out from the crowd. Her eyes were glazed and bleary. Ruchi felt bad for her, the sadness in her shoulders, as though she were experiencing the world through a thick cotton. On closer inspection, Ruchi realized that she was nothing like her daughter. Ruchi imagined Auntie living with them, with all of them, with Ammi and Papa and Dadi in a flat that grew rooms like tulsi branches. Not cramped with cotton gaddas rolled in every corner, not every inch of wall lined with wardrobes or stacked with her father's and uncles' accounting files and burlap sacks of dals and rice and netted bags of onions from the small dry goods business they ran. The smell of rye and curry patta and drumsticks absorbed into the walls. No, she and Deepa would have a big bungalow. The two of them would run the place like benevolent queens. Not sisters. Better than sisters. Though Ruchi's only example of women living together was the nuns and their cold, loveless air.

"Where had you gone to?" Deepa's mother asked, her forehead splotched with teekas and rice. "Did you take the blessing?"

Deepa nodded. "We snuck in when the crowd was thin." She lied with ease. Arms relaxed. Casual. Auntie was easier to fool than Ammi, who would've noticed that the tint on Deepa's forehead was a different hue. Ruchi and Deepa followed Auntie around to the side of the temple where people lined up in front of gray counters to collect prasad. When it was their turn, Auntie took out a wad of rolled rupees from the leather purse around her wrist and passed it whole through the metal grate to a red-toothed, paan-chewing clerk who pushed back a newspaper pouch tied with white thread. Auntie tore it open and placed sugar cubes in their right palms. God's food. It smelled, musty and chemical.

They left the temple and collected their shoes from the flower lady, who frowned at the change Auntie offered her. Their chappals had baked in the sun. It was not yet noon. The sabziwalla was setting up, jarooing the footpath clear of dirt and sand before snapping open a yellow chadar and arranging his vegetables. A once-a-day barber stared in their direction, at Deepa.

Deepa returned his gaze, and he winked. Ruchi felt a chill run through her, despite her hot feet. Deepa threw her shoulders back in that posture that Ruchi didn't dare try. A tiny smile, the slightest upturn of that long mouth, appeared on her face, her pimpled cheeks glistening in the light. The barber angled a silver knife against his client's throat. Ruchi stepped closer to her friend, and the man shot a glance at her. But this wasn't what she was after.

Ruchi turned to Deepa, blocking her view of the man. "We'll teach Anil Vora to make cha," she said, her voice unnaturally high. "Every morning and afternoon, karak and piping hot. We'll make him press our legs when we're tired."

"Press our legs," Deepa said, focusing on her at last. "How sweet."

But seriously, Ruchi wanted to say. Why not.

"And if he prefers me to you?" Deepa asked.

"What does it matter?" Ruchi said. Her feet were sweating, and she shuddered. What if Deepa preferred him to her? She pictured herself alone among them, floating through rooms in the ever-expanding house. It was a silly game they were playing. Just a game. It was best to cling to her smartness. She could still get top marks, prove to the nuns she was worth their earlier attention. Houshiyar, Ruchi silently incanted. Houshiyar houshiyar houshiyar.

"Ere," Deepa said and elbowed her. "But who says he won't like you best?"

# Deepa

## *1966*

On the first day of exams, Deepa heard Ruchi vomiting in the washroom. She emerged, wiping her face on her scarf, eyes wild. "You've studied so hard," Deepa said. "What are you worried about?" Deepa was taller now by an inch, though it felt like more. They were put in different rooms, and Deepa answered the questions quickly and didn't look back to check. How many soldiers did Shivaji have for this battle? What was his armor? If $x$ in the formula means ____, what does $y$ mean? Name all the generals in Shivaji's army, first and surnames. The questions were on thin, grayish paper and often wrongly spelled. The second day of exams, meant to test logic, was more formulas, things crammed into their brains that were now spilling out. Fewer girls showed up. Again Ruchi vomited and this time Deepa held back her hair. Deepa didn't understand her nervousness, given that it was unlikely that the exams mattered. Ruchi would be lucky to do Commerce or Arts like the rest of them. Neither of their mothers had done tenth, much less college. Deepa worried that her friend might be dying, that the meaningless exams were killing her. On the last day, Deepa filled the extra time—she couldn't help her quickness—drawing stars in the margins and swatting at the gnats that bit her ankles.

A month later, the list was posted in the hall and girls crowded around until Sister Braganza pushed to the front and called out marks from the bottom up. Deepa passed in the 60s, far below the cutoff for any top school, even in Commerce, but, given her deliberate inattention, she felt proud, as if she'd proved a point and managed a spectacular feat.

Sister Braganza reached 70 and had yet to call Ruchi's name. Ruchi picked her nailbeds until they bled, then punctured her sleeve where the fabric was already thin until Deepa pushed her hand firmly to her side.

At last: "Ruchi Gupta, seventy-three percent, with distinction." Sister Braganza didn't look up or pause to let the news linger. Meher, a Parsi girl Deepa had never considered, had done better by a point. Ruchi was second. Neither was good enough for Medicine. Braganza told the girls that the marks would be filed to appropriate colleges, if they wished to attend, and that the top girls could apply to their choices, before walking off, black cloth flapping around her legs.

"You were almost top," Deepa said, though it was an empty comfort. No one was close to the citywide topper whose name would appear in the papers the next day, a Cathedral girl who scored an 83. Deepa peered at Ruchi's pained face and felt a bond in that instant that she thought was unbreakable. The bond of wanting more.

THE FINAL MONTH of school was desultory, like they'd been playacting all these years. Girls entering and exiting classrooms, uniform shirts untucked, scarves wrinkled, shoes scuffed from running in the courtyard dust, the ribbons of their plaits as oily as their hair. Only Ruchi brought her books, scribbling notes from a musty biology textbook that she couldn't possibly understand. In a matter of weeks, Ruchi had rounded—her arms, her breasts, her thighs—and Deepa both enjoyed examining these changes and worried that she was becoming more beautiful. But Ruchi hunched more than ever, hiding herself. She sat in the classroom, wiping sweat from her brow with her orange scarf, picking at her shaak roti. For days, Deepa was patient with her, until her irritation overflowed.

"Ere, Ruchi, what is the point?" Deepa said, standing at her too-small desk. She curled the corner of Ruchi's blue book around her finger.

"We're still in school."

Ruchi lifted her pen and Deepa snatched the form book away, rolling it into a tube.

"Deepa!"

"It's not healthy. Eating like this all bent over. Come outside."

The banyan in the courtyard had begun to die, some of its tendrils collapsed to the ground. Deepa placed Ruchi's tiffin on a wide branch, tore off a fold of roti, pinched a yellowed potato, and brought it to Ruchi's lips.

"I'm not hungry," she said.

Deepa nudged the roti closer, staining Ruchi's lips. She hoped Ruchi might swat her hand away, but she just dipped her chin. "Why are you smiling?" Ruchi asked.

"Because you're a stubborn goat." Deepa laughed until Ruchi also laughed. Then she pushed the food inside.

"Aren't you going to eat yours?" Ruchi asked, scooping the last of her shaak. She side-eyed the little sandwiches and toasts and cheeses Deepa's mother had packed. Store-bought foods they couldn't afford. Deepa never offered and could've explained that she rationed her lunch because there was no telling whether they'd have dinner. But she preferred to keep Ruchi guessing.

"Later," Deepa said, and scanned the courtyard. Younger girls played kho-kho and hututu, ignoring the older ones huddled in circles, a large group around a preening, boasting Meher. Since the exams, the nuns appeared less and less, leaving the school to the assistants and junior teachers. The senior girls no longer mattered to the sisters; none of them were exceptional.

Ruchi stood up to leave. "Where are you going?" Deepa asked.

"Back to my studies."

"Leave it, no?"

"At least it's something to do."

Deepa bit the inside of her cheek. Ruchi's pointless industry frightened her.

She noticed then that the lock on the nuns' house was missing. "Here's something to do." Deepa left her tiffin to bake in the sun and strode across the courtyard, through the kho-kho circles and shrieking girls, to the house. She felt eyes on her back. Her heart pounded, but she didn't turn around to check if Ruchi was following. She decided to be angry if she didn't, an anger she'd carry around for days. But Ruchi ran to catch up, as if she'd been waiting for Deepa's invitation.

"Let's see how the old witches live." Up close the little house was large, the girls in the courtyard reduced to mice chattering, the banyan by the gate a frail old man.

"What will it be? Some furniture. Some beds," Ruchi said. The lock was off, but when Deepa pushed the door, it was bolted from the inside. In a small window to the left they saw their own stubborn reflection against the gray curtains.

"Then why lock the door? Why never open a window?" Deepa asked. She wanted to return to the safety of the courtyard, the girls and their numbers, to shrink the nuns' house back to size. But she also wanted to emerge from the house triumphant, the holder of important, incriminating secrets, something to vanquish the students' collective failures and disappointments in one shocking swell. "It's like a fortress. A jail."

"They might hear us."

Deepa shrugged but whispered, "Maybe they're stealing. Why is this school so shabby when our parents pay fees every month? Why not nicer uniforms? Probably they stole at the convent, too."

"And you are a detective. How nice," Ruchi said, but Deepa saw her excitement.

They circled the house to the back. Black mold rode up the sides and down from the top. Deep knots in the wood that could swallow an arm. How did it survive? A wooden house in this place where saltwater ate everything.

They found a half door, simple to push open. Deepa crouched and her scarf slipped and she was aware that anyone could see down her shirt and she thought of her mother in her housecoat, the dark cave that formed when she bent over. The room inside was dim and a level down from the rest of the house. They heard a gasp, and Ruchi stepped back.

"What are you scared of? They're probably napping," Deepa chided.

"They could wake up."

"So? They aren't bhoots. Come."

The room smelled wrong, like tin. There was no gold. No light fixtures. There were cold stone stairs, which didn't creak.

"What do you see?" Ruchi whispered into the back of Deepa's neck.

Deepa wanted to see the worst, to see the sisters drinking or gambling or, what? What was truly bad?

Gray light filtered through gray drapes that trapped moths. More of them in the cracked lampshades. A fogged-out glass fixture on the ceiling. The floors were the same stone as the three stairs they were standing on, a moonscape. A hard-backed sofa covered in a white sheet. Deepa heard the gasp again, but less like a gasp this time, more like a long, oceany inhale, like a person trying to make something last.

"See? Just napping," Deepa whispered back. Ruchi pushed her way to the top step, their arms glued together. The bedroom door was ajar. A bed and two bodies, four pairs of bare feet sticking out from the covers. The bodies turned toward each other, the feet, two dark ones and two light ones, the light ones caressing the dark. The figures under the cover were breathing together but a kind of breath Deepa had never encountered, an inhale pulling out an exhale. Her heart thudded in her ears.

"They're not sleeping," Ruchi said.

They watched. It felt like they'd been lifted, all four of them, off the earth and suspended in a middle space, a universe that existed next to this one. A bony foot arched back and a darker one pressed against it. The sounds were soft, drowned, and Deepa thought of a warm place filled with small, delightful objects. A place that wasn't supposed to exist.

Outside, the air was soupy and harsh. A bead of sweat traced its way down Deepa's spine. Ruchi's arm skimmed hers, and Deepa stepped aside. They walked around to the courtyard where girls continued to play in the white sun, but nothing was the same. Deepa felt caught, like the banyan was pointing its gnarled roots at them, the girls' shrieking accusations. Every cab, rickshaw, and bullock cart lined up behind the school's metal gate to reprimand them.

Deepa stood up straighter. The nuns' filth had nothing to do with her, no matter the quake in her chest. "Well," she said.

"I have to study," Ruchi said in a small voice.

She wouldn't raise her eyes, and Deepa wanted to shake her. She wanted to know, for sure, if her heart was thudding too. If her undergarments were damp. But girls were taught to appear demure, to hide and cover and pretend to be timid. Deepa refused. She refused to let her shoulders creep toward her sternum, refused to cower, refused to bend her spine in that ugly way. Sometimes she saw other girls walking in front of her on the boardwalk and all she wanted was to kick the space between their scapulae, to thrust them forward.

But about the nuns and their feet and their sounds, Deepa couldn't speak, and she hated that Ruchi wouldn't either.

"We should go back," Ruchi said, and they walked to the banyan to collect their lunches. But while moments ago Deepa felt watched, now it seemed they were invisible. Not a girl glanced at them, as if, by entering the nuns' house, she and Ruchi had turned into ghosts.

"I told you the nuns were witches," Deepa said, though it wasn't what she wanted to say.

"What difference does it make?"

"Chi. They're Sisters. Nuns. *Ladies.* They shouldn't be living together like that." Stray curls framed Ruchi's glistening face.

"Like what?" Ruchi asked.

Deepa wasn't expecting the question. She adjusted her scarf and feigned boredom. "Unnatural." She skipped ahead to the pile of overgrown roots and found her tiffin where she'd left it. The cheese had turned oily, and she dipped her pinkie in it, let it gleam under the sun.

THEY ENROLLED IN college, Deepa at SNDT for Arts and Ruchi at KC for Commerce, far from the best campuses. They saw each other less, though Deepa still came over when she could to show Ruchi the flare pants and short tops she'd tailored. They never spoke of the nuns, though they haunted Deepa. She saw mirages of the sisters everywhere. They were at the dosa counter slurping overly salted sambal. They were floating down Marine Drive. Their habits flashed among the crowds at sabzi mandi, but when Deepa looked closer, they were gone. Or never there. She worried they'd appear at Bandra Fort where she and Ruchi, now seventeen years old, spent a Sunday afternoon. Here the sea was quiet and cowed. They descended the stone steps to the fort entrance, Ruchi a step ahead, arms bent as if prepared to fall. Deepa could've skipped ahead, she could've pushed Ruchi lightly and startled her, but she resisted the urge. It was a clear enough day that they could see the tip of Worli against the horizon. Ruchi's braid was frizzing in the humidity, ends reaching out in every direction and defying the red ribbon tied at the bottom. Deepa wore her hair open and the new flare pants. She lied and told Ruchi her mother had begun collecting proposals.

"But you're still in college," Ruchi said, pausing long enough for Deepa to push ahead.

"Arts is useless." Deepa felt like an actress portraying great cheer. They reached the stone doorframe that opened to the viewing platform and the sea. Deepa wove through families and couples to win them a spot along the wall with a view.

"And marriage isn't? You could do more than the two-year diploma." Ruchi tried to slick her braid and hide her bosom. Each time Deepa saw her, she'd grown fuller, while Deepa remained angular and sharp-edged. "I might sit for the twelfth standard exams."

"Twelfth?" Deepa asked. "To do what? Become a secretary? Work at Air India?" She turned and abandoned the view without warning.

Ruchi called out, scrambling to keep up, "Air India might be good. Or Insurance. Accounting. A CPA."

"All day as an office girl, sitting and typing. No. Not for me." Deepa led them out of the crowds into the garden of looming palms and yellow hibiscus where couples stared out furtively from the shade.

"Then what do you want?" Ruchi asked, as if she'd seen inside Deepa's mind and pulled out the question.

"Something else," Deepa said. "Somewhere else." The thought of leaving the city had just occurred to her. She could become a different woman. "You see in the American films how the girls don't have a care."

"Like the sisters," Ruchi said.

"The nuns? The witches are nothing like that."

"You shouldn't call them that."

"But they were awful. Slapped our hands. The rulers. Have you forgotten?" *Oh, but you were their pet.*

"At least they didn't have to marry," Ruchi said.

"Ere, what are you scared of?"

"It's not that."

She didn't want Ruchi to say anything more because anything she might say could split their lives in two. Deepa led her off the main walking path and into a shadowy grove of empty benches. An oasis away from prying eyes. She wanted to take Ruchi's hand and hold it between her own. Deepa wanted them to sit on a bench like a couple, just for a few moments, just until she regained her footing. She pointed to Ruchi's upper lip. "You haven't been keeping up. Look, you have an ingrown."

Ruchi ran her fingers over the sprouting hairs. "Oh."

"At least let me squeeze it out." Deepa stepped closer.

"It will hurt," Ruchi said, but without protest.

"Oh fo. It's just a prick!" Deepa placed her fingers on either side of the stub of hair and squeezed it between her nails. The skin around the stub filled with blood, and she stepped closer still. She felt Ruchi grip her hip to steady herself. "Almost," Deepa whispered.

"I don't want to get married," Ruchi whispered back, speaking through her teeth.

"Keep still."

"I don't."

"Of course you do. Everyone wants that. There. It's done." The hair popped out with clear pus and Deepa flicked it to the ground and pressed the spot with her thumb to calm it. Ruchi's hand remained where it was, and Deepa thought she felt her rub where her bone jutted out. Their lips were nearly touching; sweat pearled on Ruchi's cheeks. The walking path, just on the other side of the bamboo and palms, receded, the foliage closing rank. It felt like the most alone they'd ever been.

Deepa made the initial adjustment—a small one, a step closer, mouth opening against Ruchi's already parted mouth. The taste of metal, of salt. A color burst, more simmer than shock. Her tongue searched, skimmed an underbelly, pressed a canine. She felt Ruchi's hand slide to the flesh of her hip, Ruchi's tongue lick the corner of her lip. Deepa dared open an eye. The warm brown expanse of Ruchi's cheek, the curl of a sideburn. But behind the palm trees, black habits flapped, then fled. Deepa bit down, blood flooding her mouth.

Ruchi jumped back, cheeks aglow, a siren in the shadows, her lips wet and red.

"It will be like that. Once you're married." Deepa kept her voice firm and final despite the tremor in her chest, a tremor that matched Ruchi's face. Deepa shifted under her hand.

"Sorry," Ruchi said and removed it. Tears brimmed in her eyes. Deepa wanted to suck them dry.

"What sorry? How else would we learn?" But she stepped through the thicket, back into the stream of walkers and the pale sun. She felt the day close.

# Ruchi

## 1972

Ruchi never sat for her twelfths. First there was Aruna's wedding to prepare for. Then a cousin's. Then no money to pay for exam fees and books. Then she was twenty and too old for school.

Deepa, too, was busy. Her mother arranged suitors for her every week. Though occasionally Deepa would steal away, and she and Ruchi would hide on the balcony, their kameezes pulled over their knees, and laugh about the suitor who arrived with namkeen crumbs in his mustache, the one who belched through his tea, the one who passed loud gas without asking Deepa a single question.

"I said no to them all. Mummy gets angrier every time. I'm waiting for a thin, clean-shaven doctor."

*Good.*

They had to fold themselves to fit behind the soda bottles on the balcony but managed to sit without any parts of their bodies touching. A subtle but definite boundary had formed between them not to be crossed. Sometimes Deepa casually brushed her knee, but Ruchi was afraid to do the same, worried she might be swatted away.

Whatever had happened in the shadowy palms was trapped there, not to be discussed.

"Eventually I'll say yes," Deepa said. "When there's one who wants to go to America."

"Always talking of America. My fua's brother's daughter went to California and Ammi says she's sick from the food."

"Or Canada. But not Australia. That funny accent." Deepa swept her tongue across her front teeth. "You should let them look for you. It can take time."

Ruchi was quiet. Her calves spasmed.

"Please don't be like that," Deepa said.

"I'm not being like anything." She might still find a job. But there were many young women who'd done two years of Commerce. She didn't even know where to look. And who to ask? Every day Ammi found another dish for Ruchi to learn only to berate her for learning it wrong.

Ruchi wanted to relax her folded legs and let them fall into Deepa's, but she didn't dare.

AT TWENTY-ONE, DEEPA was married. It was 1971. Four years had passed from the kiss in the palms. The word "kiss" itself made Ruchi feel shy. The wedding was quick, and Ruchi got only glimpses of the trim Jain doctor with a medicine fellowship in the States who smiled like a donkey through the ceremony. He was the same caste, same jati. Deepa looked nothing like herself, eyes downcast, face immobile, and wearing a thick foundation that didn't quite smooth out her stubbornly pimpled cheeks. When the time came for the women to whisper advice in her ear, Deepa stared into her lap as Ruchi draped her arms around her neck. She thought she felt Deepa's shoulders tighten. She wanted to say something sly, something funny and knowing, but managed only "Good luck."

Deepa's visa arrived earlier than expected. Too quickly. It was done and Ruchi was alone.

She received a single letter in January. Six lines about the cold and the lawn green like in the photos and the many kinds of powders to put in milk, not just Bonvita. The milk itself was tasteless, Deepa wrote. "Like cloudy water." Scribbled at the end were the following words, an afterthought: "Marry, Ruchi. Find someone who can apply for a work visa in Connecticut."

Connecticut. A spiked, nettled word. Ammi said, "You're too dark to be so picky," but Ruchi made it her one stubborn stipulation.

ON THEIR WEDDING night, Ruchi and Naren, a twenty-four-year-old engineering graduate, sat next to each other on the edge of the bed, both still in their wedding clothes, tired from hours spent on the reception stage greeting people they didn't know. Now twenty-two, Ruchi had been on the cusp of too old, but her parents had managed it. She was supposed to be grateful.

Her sister-in-law had decorated the bed with cheap roses that wilted upon purchase. Perfumed pink petals stuck to Ruchi's palms, a scent so strong she could taste it.

"Flowers make me sneeze," Naren said, and swiped at them. "A shelf has been cleared for you in the bathroom. For your things."

"Thank you."

In the bathroom, she peered down at the squat toilet and brilliant white tile. Orange light pooled on the ceiling and cast double shadows. She struggled to unhook the dozen pins that held her sari in place. The nightie, a stiff thing Aruna had packed for her, was too long, and she lifted it to keep from tripping.

In the room she found Naren in a bandiyu and loose pajama pants. He was still brusquely sweeping petals from the bed, oblivious to the pink streaks. The room was on loan from Naren's brother, Anoj, until Naren left for America in a month, well before the rains. Then Ruchi would sleep in the hall until her own paperwork was complete and a cheap enough flight could be booked. Her mother had warned that the second daughter-in-law was the powerless daughter-in-law. Another reason leaving was lucky.

Ruchi told no one that from the moment she'd been engaged, all she'd imagined was the flight, the arrival, Deepa.

Ruchi tucked her earrings and choker—everything except the red and white marriage bangles—deep in her suitcase. She said good night, and he also said good night before switching off the tube light once she was under the sheet. The walls turned milky gray. Her dyed hands smelled of grass and mud, a scent that would fade a little each day.

They'd been alone once before. A carriage ride to Nariman Point. He'd talked in short bursts about the job in "Conn-ect-ti-cut" and the visa and the paperwork and the visits to the consulate. "You don't have to wait in line if they do the paperwork for you," he'd said. He'd bought her honeyed cashews from a vendor and tasted one for freshness. Her sisters had warned her against asking too many questions ("Don't act like yourself," Aruna had said, the sister who thought herself too special because she'd married first), but before Deepa left she'd said to pay attention to profiles, whether they were confident and good-looking. "It means he'll make money," she had promised, as if money were a consolation and all there was to be wanted.

Ruchi had agreed to the match, but after the ceremony, she'd sobbed when her father blessed the crown of her head with his hand. She blinked and was here: a body next to hers. She wanted to test it, dig her nail into his skin and watch the half-moon impression lift and disappear. Over the course of the night she felt him cross one leg over another, turn to a side, scratch himself. She heard his breath deepen and catch, a gurgle in his snore.

IN THE MORNING Naren talked of comfort. Did she mind the whir of the fan? The faint smell from the market below? He booked them to see *Pakeezah* at Regal that afternoon. "Meena Kumari's biggest role," he told her as they waited in line for tickets. They stood side by side like a real couple, Ruchi with her arms folded in front of her and Naren with his hands clasped behind his back.

"Always some sad role she plays. Some big drama," she said.

"Her husband made the movie for her. Like Taj Mahal for Mumtaz."

"He must be foolish then." She'd meant it as a joke, but Naren nodded solemnly.

"What can he do? She's a drunk."

The director husband was a jealous old man, and the magazines said she wore three layers of foundation to hide the bruises. But it didn't change her behavior. At home, Ruchi studied Meena's face in Ammi's copies of *Stardust*, the way it gave and held back.

Naren pointed to the *Pakeezah* movie poster, the actress crying red tears. "Her left pinky finger is mangled from an accident years ago. She always hides it."

"Really?"

"You don't believe me?"

She didn't want to spoil things. "Of course I believe you."

Inside, the theater was nearly empty. She was disappointed that there weren't more awed young girls to gawk at them. How many times had she and Deepa sat behind newly married couples? The women's henna still black, the men still skinny and timid. Sometimes she'd caught them with their arms around their waists while exiting the theater, as if the dark still hid them. Sometimes Ruchi had brushed her hand against Deepa's thigh or eyed her kneading a mint in her cheek or licking the salt off her fingers. But she wasn't supposed to be thinking of her friend now.

Ruchi liked *Pakeezah* more than she'd intended to. The film belonged to the heroine, and the camera lingered on her wide, strange face, trying to trap its light. She played a dancing girl but acted like a madam. She was a good dancer, her body spinning on an invisible axis. Sadness lurked in her shoulders. The hand that floated to her face was always her right, which gave Ruchi an inexplicable satisfaction to know her husband had been correct. She was covered in jewelry, like the terraces at Hanging Gardens cloaked in shrubbery. Ruchi had hoped to wear such ornaments for her own wedding, but Ammi had only simple items and saved the largest pieces for Tejas, the youngest, lightest sister. "They don't suit your face," Ammi had said.

During intermission, Naren bought samosas and cold drinks. When the lights went down, he rested his elbow near hers and on the way home he hummed a tune. His voice was not unpleasant.

That night they lay in bed fully dressed. He again asked if she was comfortable, and again she said yes, though the bed was too soft and in the middle of the night she flung the extra pillows to the floor. She crossed her legs, and her sari rode up her calf.

"It was a very good film," she said. "Even Meena Kumari."

"Too many dances. One after another."

"Maybe." The dances were what she liked best.

His hand was softer than she'd expected, and damp. He passed over her chest and paused, ready to pull away, then rubbed the skin just above her blouse.

The flat was quiet, but others were likely awake. She let her fingers roll over his oil-slicked skin, her bangles crashing. She wasn't uncurious. His face was even darker than her own. Black freckles scattered across the bridge of his nose.

"One moment," he said. He locked the door, slipped off his pants, and stood in his underwear. She looked away because he had the legs of a child. He placed his mouth on hers and the taste was sharp, like earth. Here was a tongue, a lip. Her mind traveled to the one closeness she'd known; the memory was a skin for her thoughts.

Naren lightly kissed the bulge of her breast where his hand had been moments ago. Her breath caught. She watched his lips on her skin, and when she closed her eyes, the image eddied around her lids.

"Are you fine?" he asked.

She nodded and worried that her expression was off, that it revealed a desire too close to the surface.

"One moment," he said again, looking strained like he was holding his breath.

"It's okay," she said. "This is fine." She wished she could take off the bangles, but she'd have to squeeze her wrist and thumb and remove them one by one, and in any case this would bring bad luck. He undid her blouse. She watched her breasts fall to either side, and then his hand, how it inched lower.

She knew what sex was. "The man puts his thing inside," Deepa had once whispered while they watched Shammi Kapoor jhatka his hips in *Brahmachari*.

"That's all?" Ruchi had said and felt a momentary surge, a feeling part brass bell, part blinding electric glow. She hunted for the feeling now as Naren moaned into her hair. He didn't lick her nipples and the longing for it grew. Her body was working without her, wanting something she was sure she shouldn't want. She hated the usual, perpetual reproach. She tugged at his undershirt.

"Leave it," he said gently.

He reached down her leg and pulled up her sari and petticoat together. The cloth crumpled on her stomach and formed a pillow between them.

Sex wasn't like his lips on her chest or the afternoon at Bandra Fort. It was an ache in her center, a dazzling pain. She arched toward him, but the movement offered only a fleeting lift. His breath arrived in short, jagged bursts, and he looked surprised, an expression she hadn't yet seen on his face. She didn't understand what she was supposed to feel and worried her face gave away her confusion.

Afterward, he loosely hugged her. In the bathroom she washed between her legs. Pink, luminous blood threaded her pee and she couldn't help but feel she'd committed a betrayal. Whatever had been stirring in her was swimming now, darting about like ghosts.

MOST MORNINGS, NAREN left to study at the Iranian sweet shop, reading building codes and company manuals so that when he arrived, no one could find fault with him. Since Ruchi was in the apartment temporarily, she was asked to do nothing, like an unwanted houseguest. She tidied her suitcases and counted her footsteps from one end of the flat to the other. By noon, the flat smelled of fish from the market.

She avoided being alone with her mother-in-law, who she called "Mummy" as she was expected to, each time startling them both. Sarika, the sister-in-law, offered no companionship. She lorded over the kitchen and addressed Ruchi as "thu" as if she was a girl or servant rather than a relative, though Ruchi made sure to call Sarika "Bhabhi." She was four years married and still not pregnant, a bechari according to Ammi, though Sarika didn't look like a poor thing. Was she secretly taking pills like the lady prime minister advised? Aruna had given

Ruchi some to keep hidden. "Throw them out once you're ready." But what did it mean to be ready?

Anoj, short and light-skinned like Tejas, complained about having to relinquish his room to his newlywed brother and sleep in the hall. He was free of Naren's self-consciousness and marched about the flat proudly scratching himself as if on the cusp of greatness. To Naren he said things like "In America you'll be a big man, eating cheeseburgers and letting your hair grow long," to which her husband mumbled a clipped response about the bank job that Anoj won only through the influence of their father. Ruchi was pleased that Naren would soon be free of this man.

She missed the Brontës and Austens she'd stolen from the school library, items Ammi said were unnecessary to bring with her. She missed the smell of her gadda and the symphony of burps and farts that echoed through the chawl at night. She missed the balcony, and her friend, and did her best not to think of her, as if Deepa were a waning infection.

"What kinds of buildings will you make?" Ruchi asked Naren three weeks into their marriage. She was folding saris, gathering the cloth in arm-length segments and shaking them out, a job that never got faster. She wanted to wear a salwar kameez, but her mother-in-law said a new bride cannot. In the mirror Ruchi could see Naren lying in bed glaring at papers, legs crossed, fingers woven through toes.

"I don't know yet."

She waited for him to say more. She'd expected him to be talkative. "You study so many hours. I'm sure it will be appreciated."

"Hmm."

On the floor, Ruchi laid out the linen sheet that carried the lemon-and-garlic scent of her mother's hands. She placed the neatly folded sari in the middle and wrapped the linen around it into a square.

She lay down on the narrow portion of the bed not covered in papers, the sheets cold from the fan. "Are you frightened?" she asked.

"Frightened?" he repeated without looking up.

"Of leaving here. Going there. The work."

"Silly to be afraid of something that you cannot avoid. Something you want."

Was it? She didn't think of it as silly. Fear was keeping her in place and a safe distance from secrets her body held, that maybe all bodies held, secrets that opened and closed like a sleepy eye. "I, too, can work. Once we are settled, of course," she said. He continued to read his papers. She'd told him on the carriage ride that she'd done Commerce, and he'd nodded appreciatively. She didn't tell him that she could've been a doctor, her waiting room overflowing with sick patients.

"My cousin in New Brunswick has a neat and trim house with thick grass. All the houses have hot water taps. Everything done properly." He placed his hand close to hers and she traced the line where the pale of his palm met the dark of his hand. Since their marriage, only one letter from Deepa had arrived, a simple congratulations.

"Won't we be in Connecticut? In an apartment?"

She and Deepa had liked the sound of the state at first, long and delicate and full of light. Ruchi had studied the state's map, could name the lakes and rivers. The Connecticut River started not in Connecticut but in the adjoining state of Massachusetts. Every state had a flower and a bird and this one's were a mountain laurel and a robin. But Hartford, the capital, sounded like a thick loping animal. No one had heard of it. Ammi said that only New York was like Bombay.

"It will be like New Brunswick. And we'll buy a house quickly. You'll see."

A house. Lawns the color of limbu. She'd only ever lived in a crowded flat. She'd miss the sea.

The fan kept turning. She was aware of every exposed part: her feet, her neck, the small bones of her wrist. From somewhere in the building she could hear a woman's falsetto singing "Chalte chalte yun hi koi," the number that Meena Kumari danced almost entirely with her eyes, her lips hardly forming the words. She waited until Naren was fully asleep, then pulled up her nightie bit by bit, trying to keep her bangles still. The air made her skin unrecognizable.

∼

ANOTHER WEEK PASSED. Ruchi yearned for the street below. Each day she waited for letters that never arrived.

When Sarika ran out of channa flour, Ruchi quickly offered to get it herself.

"But you're not supposed to go out alone," Sarika hissed. "Not yet." Ruchi knew this, of course, but no one could explain why.

"I'll be so quick, Bhabhi. You can have a moment of peace. No one needs to know." It was Tuesday morning and their mother-in-law wouldn't be back from temple for at least another two hours.

Sarika sucked her teeth, like she'd seen an ugly smudge on Ruchi's face. "Up to you."

She thought she'd feel the world anew after so many days under close supervision, the shock of light after a dark room. Instead people gawked at her, a newlywed woman in the streets in the heat on her own.

She bought the flour and wove through the market stalls to the narrow lane with the Iranian sweet shop. The windows were small and dark and the shop inside was crowded. It seemed like a bad place to study, but maybe the noise was a kind of silence.

Men idled around the doorway, shouting and smoking bidis and holding hands. She and Deepa had often seen boys like this, fingers entwined and arms swinging. Sometimes one threw his arm around the other's neck, and they walked that way down the street. She used to watch them and hope Deepa might try it, that they too might walk hand in hand, though Deepa said the men were low class.

She hoped Naren would be with a group of them, arms casually thrown around each other, a rude light in his eyes, a bidi glowing in his mouth. Her father didn't smoke or chew paan and berated Ammi for her betel-juice-stained teeth.

Ruchi stood near a textile stall where an older woman asked to see bolt after bolt of tussar silk, frowning at each one. The woman caught sight of Ruchi's hands. "Itanee achchhee mehendi lagaee hai. Show."

Ruchi opened her palms, and the woman traced the ropes of filigree with her bony finger. She smelled of camphor and bitter gourd. "Are you waiting for your husband?"

Ruchi nodded.

"He left you outside like this?"

The plastic bag of flour cut into Ruchi's wrist between her bangles. The woman sucked her teeth.

"He's buying me sweets. Every day he brings me a whole box," Ruchi said, then added, "chocolates with rose filling."

The woman looked offended by the excess. "How nice." Her smile was a gruesome, too-wide opening. "You should be careful. A young bride alone," the woman said, and gestured to the men around the sweet shop. Ruchi wanted to tell her that in America no one cared if you walked through the streets alone or if you smoked or where your husband was.

The crowd cleared enough for Ruchi to approach the nearest window of the shop. Naren was at a table against the wall, his back curved over his books, a thin hand on the nape of his neck. She was disappointed that he wasn't more part of the scene. That he didn't know how to act any more than she did. If he looked up, he'd see her, and she suspected it would embarrass him or make him nervous. Maybe he'd become angry seeing her surrounded by men. Maybe he'd cause a scene, tip over the table, scatter books, make a show of sending her home. What would she do? Leave? She hoped not. She hoped she'd stand at the window and let everyone stare.

A MONTH INTO their marriage, Ruchi prepared for Naren's departure. She organized his two allotted suitcases splayed open next to hers and was grateful for the task. Dry goods she sealed in double plastic bags to avoid customs. His clothes she wrapped and labeled in brown paper. She made sure a sweater and hat and gloves were in his carry-on.

"The time will pass quickly," he said on the night before he left. He climbed over the bags to join her on the bed where she watched over the packages.

"You'll manage your food?"

"In America there's so much ready-made food."

"But tea? In the morning you'll make your tea? I've packed fresh masala and will bring more."

"I might be too busy for tea every morning."

She placed her head on his chest but her neck ached and she pulled away. Hurt flashed in his eyes, but she didn't know how to address it, and like that their month of marriage disappeared. They were strangers again, and the girl she'd been flooded back.

"You have the number, no? Of my friend and her husband? They must already be settled."

"I'll have no time," he said. Ruchi heard the impatience in his voice.

"They might be helpful." Deepa's name filled Ruchi's mouth, but she didn't dare say it.

"I won't need help," he said, and pulled her sari off her shoulder. He kissed her there. It no longer hurt when he pushed himself inside, and she found that just before he entered, for the briefest moment, she could move in such a way that he grazed a place that shot through her. She was certain that he couldn't know what it was, the way she was certain that he wasn't cruel, because had he known, he'd have lingered there, he'd have stayed and maybe placed his mouth over her breast and she'd have closed her eyes and held the feeling close, held it until it ran through her entire body, until it died.

# PART TWO

# Sanjay

## *August 1992*

In August 1992, a week before the annual beach party at their Guilford house, Sanjay Jain made his way downstairs, the lawyer's letter in one hand, the paper limp from the many times he'd unfolded it to reread it, the other hand on the stair rail. He walked slowly, feeling the grain of the wood. A solid-core banister when most people chose hollow frames. The designer had advised against this detail when they built the house eight years ago. "Why spend so much for a summer home?" she'd argued. "Save the money for upgrades down the line." A Jacuzzi on the patio. A Japanese rock garden around the perimeter. But he'd insisted. He'd wanted to feel the heft of the wood under his hand, as if the heft could root him to this place.

At the bottom of the steps, he eyed himself in the mirror. He wore his ironed jeans, his white linen shirt with the Nehru collar, and a belt with a gold belt buckle. They liked nice things, he and Deepa, which was unfortunate. Had he wanted simpler things, had he not noticed the poor stitching on the Marshall's knockoffs, had he liked sale items, had he bought a timeshare in Florida instead of building a second home on an ugly beach, then maybe he wouldn't be in this situation. Maybe the money would be there, waiting to be returned.

He was well dressed but looked sunken and old, though he was no older than the red-faced man who would likely be the next president and raise his taxes. Sanjay would still vote for him, having made a promise to his daughter, who insisted Clinton was the lesser evil. Anu, the one bright spot among the pressures he faced. He was about to have a whole ten days with his daughter, who previously found excuses every college break not to visit for more than a day, maybe two. Always some test, some opportunity on campus, and always he paid for the extra housing and meals, all overpriced. This summer she had an internship in the city with a bone specialist, and he was proud.

A breeze traveled through the foyer windows, sour at this hour when the fishing boats came into port at sunset. The real estate agent had warned him that the plot, when the wind blew southeast, would be engulfed in "sea scents," the equivalent of Machchi Market in Malad. The seaweed trapped the smell sometimes, but he ignored it as he did most warnings. This was a country that rewarded risk-taking. He stood in the kitchen, one hand on the back of the sleek metal barstool, the cold of it a shock. He held the insurance letter at first behind his back, but then let it fall to his side. He was not here to hide.

Deepa was at the sink liberally dusting pots with Comet. She didn't look at him, but this wasn't unusual. He considered returning to the bedroom, tiptoeing away as if he were invisible. But he hoped, stupidly perhaps, that the revelation might unleash love between them. He pictured his wife stroking his cheek, cooing comforts, laying her hand on his chest, like in that photo they had somewhere from Vegas.

He cleared his throat.

"You'll have to call to get the beach cleaned for the party," Deepa said, pointing with her elbow out the window.

"The party. Yes. I'd like to talk to you about that," Sanjay said. All these parties. Normally he enjoyed them. The admiration they received for their vacation house, for Deepa's taste, for her fusion curries and their new patio furniture and the upgraded grill. The party had become an annual event since the first one in 1984, which had been a modest housewarming. Each year the event had grown, with a separate eggless table for the strict veg, another with no root vegetables for the strict

Jains. Deepa swept through the crowd in a sundress and expensive swimwear, soaking in the guests' flattery, more and more of them programmers and finance workers who talked about their eventual return to India. For them, all this was temporary.

"There's something I need to tell you," he started. He willed Deepa to look at him, to ask what was wrong, to put the pot down, show some concern. He'd lost weight, and people said he was looking fit these days, that he must be going to the gym, doing Weight Watchers, eating pineapple, following some ancient diet. He wanted to joke that all it took was the near-constant threat of destruction.

But Deepa was elsewhere, thinking about god-knows-what. She wore a housedress with billowing sleeves, hair swept up above her ears. Light shone on the craters of her cheeks. He'd never complained about her complexion, never wanted her to feel self-conscious about it. "Anu is taking the twelve fifteen to New Haven on Wednesday."

"The party, perhaps we should cancel?" It wasn't how he'd intended to start out, but now it seemed best to deflect, to work around. "The heat this year."

"Are you well? The party is a week away. Cancel for heat?" She finally placed the pot in the sink and made a show of turning to him.

He had hoped for love. She'd been a grinning, stylish bride, walking quickly around the fire, for which the priest admonished her, though Sanjay had found it charming. She was still admired for her figure, her fashion sense, her posture. He, too, admired these aspects. In their first Northeastern winter, he had hugged her in malls, in grocery stores, at evening parties, and she had enjoyed the attention, he was sure of it.

"There's something that I—that we—need to discuss." He took a deep breath, his heart pounding in his neck. "Some business problems to take care of." He slid the letter across the island. She stared at it before picking it up and unfolding it, as if the letter might bite. Her eyes zigzagged across the page. Then she flung the letter, now wet and stained with scouring powder, back at him.

"What is this?"

"Everything will be fine," he said hastily. "Just, some errors." He told her about the initial mistake. And then how the mistake turned into a little extra, a small thing at first that caused no one harm, denied no one an appointment, a shot, care. Denied no one, he'd denied no one. Ravi Ravichandran, that ridiculous pediatrician, had suggested the scheme to him in the first place. Ravi had put the idea in his head not to report any mistakes, not to return any money. "We work hard enough, do we not, Sanjaykumar, coming to this country penniless?" he'd said, sweating between service games. "Ere, who says we are responsible for other people's mistakes? Why should we not enjoy?" Sanjay had never liked him.

Even then, Sanjay had told Joan in Billing to clear up the mistake. But the checks arrived, and to send them back might have looked fishier, itself prompting an inquiry, and so the money was kept. Sure, they'd engaged in some upcoding for years, claims made for services more expensive than the ones rendered. "A common practice," Sanjay said, though he had no idea. Now they'd submitted more vaccine invoices and had received more insurance checks. And yes, the government had provided the vaccines for free. The money was a trickle and then, well, more than a trickle, most of which he'd invested in improvements like the koi pond, like the state-of-the-art MRI machine, paying off mortgages, saving for Anu. He became used to the ease of having extra cash. And why should he not have ease? Why not, when he had put his money on the line to open the medical suite, had lured in investors, convinced skittish doctors about relocating their practices, joining his "one-stop shop" that the *Journal Inquirer* called "a boon to Central Connecticut"? Him, a skinny boy from Ahmedabad.

He shouted now, as if over a great din. "And, in any case, all the doctors benefited from the MRI machine, no? Sending their patients down the hall quite happily! Enjoying the pond, the courtyard, the upgraded bathrooms! Who is doing everything seedha-saadha all the time? No one!" His body felt coiled, ready to spring. He rolled his shoulders to calm himself. "So, you see, everything is fine. Under control. But this year maybe it's best to postpone the party."

Deepa turned around, picked up another pot, coated it in Comet, and gripped a square of steel wool in her fist. She scrubbed with the intensity of an athlete, the wool likely cutting her fingers. "We're not canceling."

"Not cancel. Postpone." He was again sweating down his back and into his pants. A drop ran down his crack.

"Just give it back," Deepa said.

"Give it back?"

"Return it. The money."

He gestured to the walls, the floor, circling his arms as if to take flight. His legs felt wooden. "Where do you think the money is? Eh? Where? There's no giving back. Give back means we have nothing."

Deepa dropped the pot in the sink, half-scrubbed, where it would remain for the rest of the week. He hadn't cheated, not in all these years, though there were nurses who would've been glad to oblige. He'd done his best to make Deepa happy, though he realized now that she might've been happier had she caught him cheating. He wished for someone, anyone, to blame.

"All these invoices and insurance letters. The paper trail, where have you kept it?" Her wet hands dripped on the floor.

Oh dear. "Honey, the lawyer said it would be fine." The lawyer had said no such thing.

"Tell me where."

The photo of them from Vegas was a mockup magazine cover that the hotel had offered to guests. *Playboy*. Neither of them had understood what that was. That's how newly minted they'd been. Sanjay in a bow tie with no shirt, Deepa in a deep-blue satin jumpsuit, her fingers woven into his chest hair. Where was that photo now? It had once sat on their dresser, but he was glad it was gone. He was glad his daughter was too young to remember the photo or that they'd left her with a sitter while he and Deepa visited the hotel casino where the photo was taken. What a thing, to leave their child with a stranger they had only just met. Anu. He clung to the thought of his daughter.

He was a good father. Everything he'd done was for Anu but now all these headaches, all these letters. How was it shameful? How was he greedy? Look at Mansingh who flirted with the nurses, how much Satish drank, at Ravi Ravichandran who surely paid less than 10 percent in taxes. Look at Naren Mehta, that poor family failing in this country. Naren too quiet, too stubborn to fight for himself. No, Sanjay was better than that. All this Anu must see; he must make sure she saw. He was a good man.

"I told you there's nothing to worry about," he said weakly.

Deepa knocked her knuckles on the island. "Show me."

UPSTAIRS HE TOOK down their daughter's framed drawing of Shiva and scrolled through the combination lock on the safe. The safe had been his idea, one of his few touches in the beach house, which was otherwise his wife's realm. He could've satisfied himself with a lockbox in the back of his closet, but this was better, a cavity easily hidden, close at hand when he was asleep and at his most vulnerable. The safe and its contents keeping watch through Anu's sketch, infusing the pencil scratchings with life.

Deepa rummaged through the letters, then the invoices, and finally the falsified tax documents he had meticulously maintained. She read through a few items carefully, then skimmed through the rest and tossed the documents over her shoulder. "How nice," she said. "It goes back years." She seemed to age before him, the part in her hair growing wide, her bare feet wrinkling.

"I don't understand what good it does for you to see all this. It's complicated and you are unnecessarily worrying," he said.

"You should just keep the papers. The envelopes are a waste of space."

"Deepa, please." She'd defiled the bed with the papers, and he shuddered at the thought of sleeping there again. She didn't touch the cash.

When she was done, she called the caterers to arrange more cheese platters and brochettes. Through the course of the day, she made meals and tea without clearing her plates and mugs, ate granola bars without worrying about crumbs, flipped through magazines that she strewed across the couch. She avoided even the most transactional communication, loveless but constant. This was different, worse, an erasure. At night he reorganized the papers, but in the morning she took them out again. He tried to keep order in the kitchen, but the dishes piled up.

He swept and minutes later the floor was covered with crumbs again. On the morning Anu was set to arrive he suggested, joyfully, cheerfully, that they clean up and for this Deepa stared at his mouth, as if trying to figure out what it was doing there squirming about. Then she returned to her preparations, ordering tents, insisting that the whole event, in a few days' time, would be outdoors, never mind the heat. "No occasion," she said to the vendor on the phone. "A general celebration."

His lawyer asked how his wife took the news. "Oh, very well," he said. "Very understanding of these misunderstandings." The man sighed heavily, and a tickle of hate rose in Sanjay.

"We're working against the clock here, Dr. Jain. If you want to avoid a federal inquiry, and I can't promise that one hasn't already started, that at the very least an audit hasn't been launched, then I suggest you figure out how to clear up these, um, 'misunderstandings.'" Another sigh followed by a coughing fit.

"That sounds a bit croupy."

"Pay the money back. Clear your savings. Sell the cars. Jewelry. The houses. Whatever you have to do. You'll thank me."

Sell the houses? Where would they live? Did the lawyer understand that his mother, no matter how much she'd struggled to buy gas cylinders and rice and fresh fruit, always kept her earrings, her two bangles? If Sanjay had to do "whatever he had to do," then what was he paying this man for? "Yes, yes," he said over the coughing on the other end. "Make sure someone listens to those lungs."

SANJAY DIDN'T RECOGNIZE Anu at first. He'd been watching for her from the Metro North deck above the train platform in New Haven and didn't see her until she was standing in front of him. There was the weight gained, the mustache gone too long without bleaching, the unflattering tracksuit, but these were nothing compared to the hair, cropped like a boy's.

"Jaanu," he said as he hugged her and took her bags. She looked truly afraid. Her cheeks were hollowed out despite the extra pounds.

"She's going to hate it, isn't she?" Anu asked.

"Don't worry. Hair grows. Mom will understand. It must be nice and light for the summer." He'd always been the more comforting parent. Always. He'd wanted more children, had tried to be loving to make up for Deepa's gaps in affection. His wife was too hard, too strident with their daughter, while he focused on the fact that Anu was a good girl who studied hard, eager to achieve. Quiet and polite, knowing what to do at a puja, when to bow, when to touch money with her right hand. She wasn't rebellious by nature, despite the toddler tantrums early on, and even these he'd found charming. They were lucky.

If he didn't understand some of Anu's choices, he left it to a few sideways expressions. He hoped that when the time came to judge him, Anu would recognize this much, his mistakes notwithstanding. He couldn't help but think of his kindness now as insurance, not unlike the bundles of faced bills in his safe, behind the files, wrapped neatly in tongues of brown paper.

He took the scenic route that followed the craggy shoreline. But eventually they arrived at the house. "What happened here?" Deepa and Anu said simultaneously, the former surveying the latter's head and upper lip, the latter taking in the overflowing sink and dirty pile of dish towels that had accumulated on the kitchen floor in the hours he'd been away.

"Looks stylish, no?" he said to Deepa, and then, turning to Anu: "We've fallen a little behind in cleaning." Deflect, deflect, deflect. He looked from one to the other desperately.

"Mom, I can help," Anu offered, but if Deepa heard her, she showed no sign.

"I hope you at least brought something nice to wear this weekend," she said, and kicked aside a crusted tasseled towel.

THE MORNING OF the party was cloudless, the sun ready to bash them. While his wife directed caterers with fake cheer and his daughter hid in her room, Sanjay checked the safe again, kneeling on the bed, pushing aside the picture frame. The drawing had faded and blurred;

the fine details of Shiva's muscles smudged. He turned the combination lock and his anxiety eased temporarily. He pulled the stacks of bills to the front, crisp and faced, savings the old-fashioned way. He'd explain to Deepa that it was for Anu's studies, that there should be no interruption for their daughter, that her life should go on as normal while he sorted all this out.

Deepa would have to take control of the money. It could have nothing to do with him to remain valuable, and he knew she'd find the right place to hide it. He would not have to mention the Association. Donations to good causes back home, causes that looked good. Schools and medical clinics and wells in the New India, the rising India, a shining, unblemished beacon that could cleanse his transgressions. For all their failures, he and Deepa had a similar thread that ran between them, like the physical thread that had tied them together during their marriage ceremony. How maudlin he could be, a feature he knew Deepa didn't tolerate, but he also knew that she'd do anything to maintain her position, that she was too proud to let it all go, to let their daughter suffer. He took comfort in the fact, and ran his fingers over the stacks. Anu used to ask why money was valuable. Her eyes would cross as she'd bring a dollar bill to her nose, scanning for clues.

"Is it made of gold?"

Deepa had found the repeated question tiresome. "Of course it's not. You know that."

But he'd liked the chance to explain that the paper was just paper, nothing special, that its value came from their hearts, their love of it.

"So it's nothing. Not a real thing," Anu had said, her face scrunched in confusion. He should've explained that money meant she could grow up without middlemen and fixers. Without black-market ration cards for gas cylinders that arrived in unmarked trucks. Without typhoid and malaria, the fevers that had left him bedridden for months. Money was this country, this whole beautiful, awful country.

"Get dressed." Deepa was standing in the doorway, hair sliding out of her toothed clip.

What he didn't tell Deepa: Joan in Billing had said some of the insurance letters had mistakenly slipped through to a different office.

A minor indiscretion that he didn't need to worry about, according to Joan, to whom he'd given an extra bonus every year, not hush money, never that. More like the Diwali bonuses his mother used to give their small staff back home, money that could ensure you loyalty if not love. Joan would find the letters. She must.

"We should have canceled. There is no shame in canceling." His knees hurt, and he sat back on his heels. He felt naked in front of his wife, his body exposed. Her eyes were on the money.

# Deepa

## *1972–1974*

On the phone, Deepa strained to reach Ruchi's voice through the static. It was March 1972, over a year since they'd last seen each other, and the phone line was patchy at best. Ruchi was coming to America, to Connecticut, to *Vernon*. Mehta was her new last name. Something garbled about her husband's height.

"I told Naren to call you," Ruchi said. She hoped Deepa might help him get settled while Ruchi waited for her visa.

"Of course!" Deepa shouted before the line cut.

For months, Deepa's heart made plans to see Ruchi every day while her mind erased them. She was Deepa Jain now, someone new. Distance and marriage should have quelled her restlessness, rid her of the nazar that had touched them as girls. How else to think of it? But even after two years of marriage and the house in Glastonbury and Sanjay moonlighting at hospitals while he built his internal medicine practice, Deepa wasn't sure if things were right, if she was right.

She was, however, pregnant. Five months and just beginning to show when Ruchi arrived that fall. Deepa invited the new couple home. Naren had never called, and she had taken it as a slight. Now Deepa opened the front door, and there he stood. Ruchi's face was in shadow, which was just as well. Deepa might've cried.

"Welcome, welcome!" she exclaimed to hide her shallow breath. She made a show of ushering them in, laughing as they shivered from cold in thick socks and chappals despite September's second summer. "In December your noses will freeze," she teased.

She stole glances at Ruchi when she wasn't looking. Her friend was new and strange. Her part was dyed red with sindoor and four gold marriage bangles, two on each wrist, peeked out from her sweater cuffs, the kind mothers gave daughters after their wedding churi broke.

But curls still flew out around Ruchi's dark face; her brow remained thickly untamed. They didn't hug.

Deepa led Ruchi through the house, explaining that the previous owner had updated all the appliances and pointing out the sun-soaked dining room. Deepa touched the living room wall sconce, a brass monstrosity. She hoped Ruchi and Naren wouldn't notice that the house was smaller than the others on the street. Deepa scrimped and saved to appear as if they weren't scrimping and saving to the friends she'd made, wives of doctors, who mostly bored her.

"Colonial is not my taste, but we picked Glastonbury for the schools," Deepa said. She knew Ruchi wouldn't understand any of it.

"Deepa," her friend said. Ruchi's gaze caused a low throb from her throat to her fingertips. "It's good to see you."

ANU WAS BORN in a January snowstorm. Childbirth overwhelmed Deepa, the smell of her own blood and feces, the witch hazel pads that were supposed to heal her. She worried that the nurses could see the despair in her tears. She refused Ruchi's offers to visit and couldn't stand even Sanjay's presence. In the quiet of the hospital room, Deepa held the baby close.

Her mother called, and Deepa heard the insistent horns and people cursing orders on the street in the background.

"Congratulations," her mother said mutely. A girl. She was stupid, according to her mother, for refusing the epidural, for not making the most of an American hospital.

The dreams started soon after. They involved a woman with dark hair that blended into her skin, reminiscent of the monochromatic kids who haunted Dadar Station, weaving through traffic like sea creatures. The rooms were bedrooms or washrooms, or, occasionally, hospital rooms. Sometimes the woman was in bed with tubes taped to her arms, her face serene. Deepa couldn't quite make out her features.

Sometimes the dream woman was naked. Sometimes Deepa followed her legs up from the ankles to her hips. The hairs on her thighs made small *s*'s. She had the form of a woman but didn't have to be one. Could be alien. Could be animal. Deepa, in the dream, was at the foot of the bed or watching from a threshold or behind a window. At times, if she lay very still, the dream imprint remained, a faint shadow behind her eyes. And at times, the vision returned. She'd be holding Anu, trying to soothe her after a fall. Or changing her diaper. Or reading her a book. And then Deepa would see a shock of hair. A patch of flesh. A crease. And she'd be so startled she'd search for an intruder.

BY THE END of 1973, Ruchi, too, was pregnant. Anu was nearly a year old. The parallel structure of their lives both pleased and irritated Deepa. She liked having another opportunity to offer Ruchi advice, and at the same time she felt chased. She kept Ruchi separate from other friends, both in mind and in person. In part Deepa worried that, as had been the case with the nuns, Ruchi might be preferred, might excel at remaking herself. She didn't mention to Ruchi the teas and picnics and small parties.

But it was Ruchi who Deepa spoke to every week, eager for her calls, sharing advice about garbage disposals or when Stop & Shop carried bhindi or which atta was best or the benefits of lining Tupperware with plastic wrap so the turmeric didn't stain. Deepa told Ruchi to sleep on her side and to check nightly for blood in her pee. It made Deepa happy that Ruchi needed her, happy and surprised. Deep down, she knew that Ruchi was better than her.

When the doctor called Ruchi back for a second twenty-week sonogram, Deepa agreed to go with her. The appointment was a follow-up to double-check points and readings. Over the phone Ruchi said Naren couldn't take another personal day. They didn't have a second car, and anyway, Ruchi still hadn't learned to drive. In the dozen or so times Deepa had met Naren, he spoke less instead of more. She sensed he'd dislike the idea of Deepa accompanying his wife to an appointment.

Ruchi had tried to dismiss the extra test. "Silly, no, over nothing?"

"Of course," Deepa said. But doctors didn't call you back for nothing. Sanjay said every ultrasound cost the hospital more than it was worth.

Deepa packed up Anu, now sixteen months old, and drove to Ruchi's small house where she and Naren had moved two months ago. Clouds passed over the sun, giving the neighborhood an even shabbier appearance. The houses were tightly spaced, mostly ranch-style single levels with detached garages for storage. No sidewalks or landscaped islands. Broken cars lazed on the front yard across the street. The Mehtas' yard was more dirt than grass.

Deepa had been surprised, at first, that they'd bought a house so soon. Ruchi had given her a quick tour after they moved in, and Deepa relaxed. It was better than the apartment where they'd first lived, but not by much. A small house, a fraction of the size of Deepa's. The second bedroom didn't have a closet and the kitchen felt cramped even before it had a table. Maybe, someday, Ruchi could move again. Surely they must be saving. Deepa made sure that Sanjay took advantage of the best interest rates and returns. She made sure that the wealth they were building was solid. She was determined that Anu would never have cheese toasts for lunch and hunger for dinner. This precaution was the hard proof that she loved her daughter.

Ruchi grimaced as she lowered herself into the car. "I'm glad you came. Thank you," she said, her voice low and confiding. Deepa found it difficult to look at her friend's pregnant body, its fullness too insistent, too present.

"What thank you. Don't be stupid," Deepa said, though it made her both shy and satisfied to hear it.

∼

THE COLD EXAM room was cramped and smelled of disinfectant. Ruchi leaned on the table, clutching a papery robe. Machines, with their dials and cords, whirred and blew air from their bowels. Deepa took the rolling stool, which was the only seat in the room, and let Anu totter around the cords. Deepa's scans had been at a private clinic with warm blankets and soft lighting. Seeing the images of Anu on the black-and-white sonogram monitor had given her vertigo. She'd recognized nothing except the defiant skull and half listened to what was being said, though she'd fawned and smiled when the technician pointed out a hand or spine. She'd become good at making her face attentive, solicitous even, while inside she roamed her body as one might roam a sprawling house of half-finished rooms. Sanjay had watched the images with rapt attention, absently thumbing her wrist back and forth. Her mother said Deepa was lucky to have such a husband, and she took it as praise.

"I don't know why these rooms must be so cold," Ruchi said, and looked at the door. "What if we leave now? I don't want to be here."

Anu took hold of the stirrups and shook them obsessively. "It will be nothing," Deepa said. "Just see."

"How can you know?"

"Be reasonable. What can happen? The baby's kicking and growing, so what more?" Deepa said. She'd hoped for more gratitude for the effort she'd made. She'd come, hadn't she? She'd brought Anu and driven them to the hospital and forgone the child's ninety-minute afternoon nap.

Ruchi slipped out of her salwar. She hid her body behind the machine, but her legs were visible and the color of wet sand. Deepa had given her maternity clothes and couldn't understand why she didn't wear them. Ruchi wrapped herself in the paper robe before wiggling out of her cotton underwear, which she balled up and tucked under her bag in the corner of the room. "They should at least have a changing area."

"What does it matter? We're all ladies here," said Deepa, though discomfort flushed her cheeks.

Anu shook the table legs, then gurgled and turned in circles. Maybe it was wrong to bring the baby. Deepa could've called Louisa to watch the child, or one of her pregnant friends eager for practice. She didn't mind leaving Anu to go to the gym or buy groceries. In fact, she liked it. But she wanted Ruchi to see the child, and felt small and petty for it.

"She's such entertainment," Ruchi said. "Like a doll."

"I think you'll also have a girl."

Ruchi nodded, though Deepa suspected that she wanted a boy because Deepa had also wanted a boy. She didn't like to think about Ruchi having a son, Ruchi getting what she wanted.

"You should've forced Naren. He should've come," Deepa said.

"I told you he has limited personal days. There was no need." Ruchi hoisted herself onto the table, and her bangles slid up and down her arms. Deepa didn't bother to wear her own.

"Sanjay would've found a way to be here," she said.

"Your Sanjay is so good."

Deepa couldn't tell if the comment was sincere. Had Ruchi seen the stiffness that Deepa thought she was hiding when Sanjay touched her? He'd adopted the American affectation of publicly showing affection. The other doctors' wives found him charming.

"He's attentive. But his tea is horrible," Deepa said.

Forty minutes passed before the technician arrived in a gust of wind, unnaturally tall, brown ringlets buoyant around her grim face. She had the yellowed skin of a smoker.

She glared at Anu, who was now under the exam table fiddling with the wheels. "The child needs to stay on a lap."

Deepa rolled over to Anu and pulled her up, then bounced her to emphasize the fun they had together. Though it was Sanjay who spoke to her in a singular singsong, calling her "potlu" and "jaanu" and "dikri" with such sweetness that the air turned sticky around the child.

Ruchi lay down on the exam table, struggling to hold the gown closed over her belly, fiddling with the belt, bangles clinking, until the technician placed Ruchi's hands by her sides. In one motion, she covered Ruchi's legs with a white sheet and discreetly opened the gown to reveal her belly, a dark linea nigra dividing her in half. Whatever impatience

Deepa felt earlier dissolved. She wished she could offer comfort, stroke her friend's hair or whisper encouragement. It wasn't that long ago that they'd brushed against each other without a thought, spoken with their breath mingling. But now Deepa was afraid.

"Keep still so I can get my pictures," the technician said. "Then we'll show them to the doctor, and then he'll want more pictures. That's how this works."

Her name was Georgia. It was the first time Deepa had heard the name of the state used as a regular name and she felt stupid for not knowing that it was a name before it was a state. She didn't like how many times this happened to her. She pretended she knew everything she needed to know about this place and smothered her homesickness for Bombay's saturated air, its palms, Marine Drive, because to long for these things indicated failure. She didn't realize she'd arrive knowing nothing.

Deepa could see the grainy black-and-white images, the baby moving, Georgia's pupils flitting from one corner of the screen to another. With one hand she guided the stiff metal arm of the machine across Ruchi's belly, and with the other she pressed buttons. Her lipstick was a little off.

Ruchi gripped the wax paper on the bed. In fear, her face was achingly lovely, the same expression Deepa had seen in school so many times before, a stitch in her brow as she prepared for the moment after this one.

Anu fluttered her lips and rocked in Deepa's lap, precocious and big-eyed and fair-skinned, the kind of baby in commercials and films. "She doesn't know her own strength sometimes," Deepa said.

"Got to show her who's mommy," Georgia answered without taking her eyes off the monitor. "Last one. Stay put while I show these to the radiologist." She smiled for the first time, and Ruchi smiled back. But Deepa knew better.

It seemed silly now, her worry that Ruchi, with her book smarts and top marks, might overtake her. Perhaps find her footing here in a way that made Deepa's footing seem small, insignificant. The sonogram made it even more unlikely, and the thought was sad yet pleasurable. "See," Deepa said, darting her hand out to give Ruchi's cold forearm a brisk squeeze. "Any moment the doctor will be here with good news."

# Ruchi

## 1974

The radiologist sailed into the exam room with his open white coat flapping about his legs. "Mrs. Mehta," he said heartily, with a large, square smile as he helped Ruchi sit up on the table. Ruchi's legs dangled naked in the cold room. She wished this man had thought to bring her a blanket. Instead, he held out his hand for Deepa to shake, as if she were somehow in charge. Ruchi focused on a brown, rose-shaped stain on his lapel as he explained that the baby was fine. Fine in the sense that it was growing and had its heartbeat and all its limbs and organs. The term the radiologist used was "cosmetic." No, "purely cosmetic." The problems with the baby were pure. Pure problems.

"His brain is fine? What about his heart?" Ruchi asked, when what she wanted to ask was whether her baby would have a correct nose, whether his eyes would be symmetrical, whether his lips would line up. But these questions seemed petty and unimportant when the radiologist was giving them good news. He patted her hand. "Most of this can be repaired down the line," he said, and Ruchi pictured a conveyor belt in a factory. "A healthy boy."

She heard Deepa thank the radiologist for his time and then they were alone again, Anu now wearing her shoes on her hands. The ultrasound machine hummed blithely as Ruchi stood to dress. They were quiet; for once, Deepa didn't seem to know what to say. She pinched the shoulders of her delicate blue blouse to straighten it. Anu clapped the shoes together.

"I'll step out," Deepa finally whispered.

Ruchi dressed slowly. Everything and nothing had changed. Her baby's face would be different from other faces. But he was inside, tumbling. He and Anu would still be close in age. Ruchi's and Deepa's lives were still running on parallel tracks. Here they were, together. And now, a boy. Ruchi wished she hadn't hoped for it.

She stepped into the hall, where the hospital continued uninterrupted. Deepa took her purse, as if Ruchi couldn't bear the weight of it. At the nurse's station, Georgia hunched over a chart writing notes. Perhaps this chart was Ruchi's. Perhaps Georgia had seen the problems and feigned ignorance. Ruchi wanted to shake the woman for not warning her.

Naren. She should call him now from the nurse's station. She could ask this much of Georgia, but Ruchi hadn't told him about the exam. He would've taken the day to be with her had she explained. But she hadn't, and guilt pressed her chest while she resolved never to let him know the truth, that she'd chosen Deepa for the day over him. Deepa collected Ruchi's checkout papers with the list of follow-up instructions and then the moment to call Naren had passed and Ruchi was trailing Deepa, who had Anu in one arm and Ruchi's things in another, down various halls. A nurse rushed by and smiled at her belly, and Ruchi had an urge to slap her.

Once in the car, she dropped into the bucket seats of Deepa's silver Oldsmobile with a kind of tragic euphoria. She'd been holding her breath for so long. Deepa tucked Anu into her car seat while the child screamed. The sound tore through Ruchi, and when she thought she could take no more Anu stopped and gulped her breaths.

Ruchi had hoped Deepa might touch her shoulder or her hand, but Deepa was never the type of person to extend compassion when it was fished for. It made her disdainful.

In the back seat Anu turned cheerful, and her babble filled the car. Deepa loudly shushed her. Already there was something about the girl that was soft where her mother was hard, though Deepa complained that Anu was too naughty too soon. Courting trouble. Was there a touch of boasting there too? In the same breath Deepa had told her that she planned to raise her daughter as a chaste village girl. "No boyfriends!" As if boyfriends were the direst danger.

All around, sunshine peeked through blooming trees that framed abandoned mills and the decaying houses of the back roads from Hartford to Vernon and on to Crandall. Even after two months, the winding turnpike that led to Robin's Lane felt foreign. Deepa pulled up perpendicular to Ruchi's driveway and left the car running. Ruchi wished they lived across from a tidier house, not the Rolands' yard littered with junked cars and vengeful cats, but one with trimmed boxwood bushes and beds of improbable tulips and daisies.

They stared out the windshield.

"The baby is a boy," Ruchi said, just to say something.

"Lucky, no?" Deepa said. Ruchi flinched, but Deepa went on. "So many things can be done in America. Surgeries. Therapies. Were you not listening?"

Of course she was listening. "Come inside, no? Pass some time."

"Oh. I can't," Deepa said. But why not? What was so urgent that she couldn't park the car or walk Ruchi to the door, or sit with her in the kitchen? Though some part of her was relieved. She wouldn't have to worry about Deepa examining the wallpaper and deeming its sheen and yellow flowers tacky. Her stare could be brutal.

Ruchi opened the car door but couldn't swing her legs out. The small house was waiting for her with its still-packed boxes that she couldn't carry. She was frozen, and the solution was simple: just stay here. *Just stay here.*

"In any case," said Deepa, turning to look at her, both hands on the wheel. "You should rest. Sleep. Your husband will be home soon."

INSIDE, RUCHI WALKED down the hall and into the kitchen and then the living room with the paisley couches that were delivered last week.

At the store Naren had convinced her that the braided brown-and-green design was bold.

The empty second bedroom would eventually be the baby's room. The realtor said that the house was considered a junior four without the closet. "You can build one before you resell." When she'd told Deepa over the phone, her friend had scoffed, "Then nothing would be a bedroom in Bombay." But now Ruchi circled the room; the house felt like folly. Both too small and too much. The baby's care would cost more than expected. It was a wrong, but necessary, thought to have. Every day brought a new expense. She remembered two years ago, when she'd first arrived, how impressed she'd been with Naren's sleek blue People's checkbook and savings account, the CD he'd opened. He'd whisked her through department stores, Caldor and Kmart and Sears, that had multiple versions of anything you could want. She saw how this excited him. When she arrived, they'd lived in a studio he'd rented in Manchester that overlooked the back of a shopping mall parking lot. Carts clattered across asphalt at all hours, but she hadn't minded.

Naren had insisted on a house. On weekends they'd scoured for sale signs in East Hartford, Vernon, Tolland, Rocky Hill. He'd avoided the town where Deepa lived. "Those houses are not good value. Why overpay?" he said.

Only a handful of realtors returned his calls. One had said, "You don't have the financials." Naren had railed at their laziness, at how little such people worked. Ruchi had heard about neighborhoods with unspoken rules about who could live there. Unless the money was significant. Then the rules changed.

"I'll get a job first," she'd said. She'd circled listings in the back of the *Courant*, jobs that sounded both simple and daunting. Personnel Administration Assistant. Receptionist. Typist. All of them requiring "light steno" or "secretarial background" or "shorthand" or "3-4 years of experience." How would they understand her curriculum vitae with the marks she'd received in Commerce or the distinction on her SSC? When she called to inquire, she met a pause on the other end, a doubt, before her number was taken. She spelled out her name. Twice.

She'd feigned excitement about the house, the smallest they'd seen, a peachy ranch with poor natural light and a patchy lawn due to the many elms. Theirs for only $4,100, 10 percent down, for which Naren spent their CD and savings. Ruchi had wanted to inspect the mortgage packet, but Naren had insisted that worrying was no good for the baby.

Naren returned and Ruchi called out from the kitchen, "You're here." He responded, "Haan," in their usual exchange. She'd intended to tell him about the appointment right after he washed in the hall bathroom, but thought it wasn't right to give such news on an empty stomach. She'd cooked green bean shaak with chickpea and spinach dumplings that she usually saved as a weekend treat. She didn't like to waste the channa flour that they'd bought on a shopping trip to Queens. They ate side by side at the new table, their elbows touching, milky light pouring from the small window. He took seconds of the channa dumplings, and Ruchi decided not to spoil his dinner. Between bites, he told her about his new boss, John Newhouse, a hulking, red-faced man who went by his last name. "Newhouse! Because he builds new houses. Like the Parsis who have the last name Engineer. I should call myself that," he quipped and swept roti over his plate to soak the remaining masala from the shaak.

Ruchi waited for him to notice her heavy mood, the tension she thought should be visible. Instead, after dinner, he took out his new Kodak, switched on the harsh overhead light, and snapped a photo of her in profile to capture her growing belly. She stood against the kitchen wallpaper and placed one hand below and one hand above, as if everything was normal. He'd bought the camera to send photos home. Ruchi had envisioned Sarika peeking over Anoj's shoulder, smirking and jealous of their grand lives.

Naren held the camera in both hands and squinted at the small, square window on the top. "Does this mean four more left or four I've taken?"

She turned away from him, opened the faucet full force, and rinsed the dishes. She stared at the sudsy water. "There's something I need to tell you."

She explained the visit. "Small issues. Everything can be fixed," she said, as if the radiologist were speaking through her. She sprinkled Comet across the sink and scrubbed with the copper sponge that pricked her fingers. "Once he's born, we'll know more and—"

"He?"

Evenly, she replied, "A boy."

He didn't respond. She sensed his heart beating behind her, quaking through his stillness. There was nothing left to scrub, and all she could do was turn to him.

"You didn't tell me you had an appointment," he said. The camera now pendulumed from his wrist.

"I didn't want to bother you about something so routine."

She waited, not daring to look up from the speckled, beige linoleum. Finally, Naren spoke. "How did you go?"

She took a breath and looked him straight in the eyes. "Deepa took me."

He let the camera swing from the strap around his wrist. "How nice of her." He didn't like this friendship, and yet he'd bought Ruchi sleeveless dresses and high-waisted jeans similar to Deepa's. Ruchi always returned them. She felt most comfortable in her salwar sets and occasional long skirts. "But this is what people wear in this country," he'd say, and she'd nod sympathetically because she knew he wasn't the kind of man to force her. He was mild, in the end, milder than his surly nature suggested. Any anger soon evaporated to hurt.

Naren placed the Kodak on the table with the photos that would never be sent. She wiped the counters with a Bounty sheet and laid it out over the faucet to dry. She tried to stretch each sheet to two or three uses at least. There was so much she should say, all things she couldn't admit. That she'd allowed the pregnancy because Deepa had a baby. That raising the children together was one way to keep up their weekly chats, Deepa's visits. It was a childish reason to have a child, but were not all the reasons childish? The assumption that a baby was required, that it would form a complete family, a successful family, weren't these all childish fantasies in the end? Assumptions they wore to hide their loneliness? Ruchi was unprepared for the quiet emptiness of this country.

Naren tore a fresh Bounty from the roll and scrubbed grease from around the black burners that took too long to heat. Together they cleaned in silence.

# Deepa

## *1974*

Deepa called Ruchi a week after the sonogram and learned that after twenty-seven rings a phone stopped ringing. Or maybe it kept ringing for a period but stopped engaging, like blood that coursed through veins for a period after a heart stopped beating.

She hated that Ruchi was alone. Deepa should've called sooner. Just before lunch, she packed sandwiches for the two of them, snacks for Anu, and drove out to surprise her friend. She took a longer route so Anu might fall asleep, exiting early off I-84 to drive past the off-white mobile homes at the end of the ramp in Vernon with their neat flowerpots and flags. She was reminded of the crumbling flat in the posh neighborhood where she'd grown up. She drove past the strip malls and two elementary schools, one considered better than the other but neither among the top schools of the state. She slowed down to watch children chase and call to each other, stringy-haired girls doing effortless cartwheels, as if being flipped by gods.

Thirty minutes later, when Deepa pulled in to Ruchi's driveway, Anu was asleep. Deepa tried to extract her, then hesitated. Why disturb her? She'd wake up angry and irritated, and what good would that do?

It was crisp for May but sunny. Deepa rolled down the window halfway and placed a thin blanket across Anu's legs.

The doorbell didn't work so she opened the screen and knocked. Close up, the hydrangeas were limp and losing their leaves, and the roof's deep overhang gave the house a brooding quality. But it was an unfair assessment. Had Deepa seen the house as a girl, she would've been happy to live in it. Comfort was a matter of degrees; she hadn't expected Sanjay to be so enterprising, to do so well.

Naren opened the door. It was Tuesday, and he was unshaven and barefoot.

"Oh, hello," she said brightly, though she was confused. Was he unwell? How was he home if he had no personal days?

He squinted like he was trying to make out fine print. "Ruchi didn't mention."

"I came to give company," Deepa said. "How nice. You took the day."

"The day?"

"Meaning, you were able to take a day off. While last week you had to work."

"She didn't tell me about the appointment," he said. "It was supposed to be routine."

"Oh. Well." The lie made Deepa dizzy. Ruchi had asked Deepa to come to the appointment out of preference, not necessity. It was what Deepa wanted, Ruchi's need, but her knees stiffened, as if she'd been caught. Deepa held up the bag of sandwiches, her body still wedged between the flimsy screen and the doorway. Naren stepped aside to let her enter. "Chutney and cheese are her favorite," she said.

She followed him down a dark hall and past a bathroom where a towel lay on the floor. The house felt both cluttered and bare. Two oversized couches crammed the small living room, and the mantel was home to three empty vases, stacks of mail, and two clocks. But the bookshelf was empty, the walls bare except for a single batik, pink and green with embroidered mirrors, that hung above the TV propped up on boxes. Deepa had a matching one, parting gifts from Ruchi's mother that Deepa had left behind.

"I'll get her," he said.

"No, let her rest." They sat kitty-corner to each other on the pair of garish couches, probably purchased on sale at Sears. Deepa could just make out her Oldsmobile in the driveway through the double-cased windows on her left. "I see you've settled in," she said. The house smelled like coriander and rotting fruit.

"It's a small house. Not like your mansion." He chuckled nervously, folding and unfolding his hands, stealing glances at the bedroom as if by doing so, Ruchi might appear. This man who married the one person on this continent who'd known Deepa as a child. It was strange to think of it. Childhood. There was no place for it, nowhere to lay the remembrances down and relieve them of their weight. And now Naren slept next to her friend. Had impregnated her with a child. Deepa hated to think of it.

He leaned back on the sofa and crossed a foot over a knee and threw an arm over the back of the couch. "You know, of course. About the defects," he said, spitting the last word.

Deepa sat up straighter, tried to smile and then stopped herself. The bag of sandwiches sat on her lap, and Deepa worried they might leak. Naren made no move to take them from her. She said, "The baby is healthy."

There was an air about him both petulant and aloof. "I should offer you a snack. Tea."

"No need for formality." Deepa doubted he knew how but was touched by the offer.

"Apparently we won't know how severe until, well, until the baby is born."

"Sanjay says that the machines are still new and not foolproof," Deepa said, as if she were commenting on a mixie.

Naren dropped his voice to a whisper. "The problem is that she's so far along."

"Far along?"

"Too far, in fact." The expression on his face was injured, as though what he said hurt him to say. She tried to summon outrage, but anger eluded her. "In Bombay they would have sent us to family planning to make a choice. But this is not Bombay. Here there is the best care."

She nodded. It was true, everything he was saying. She did not want to like this man. He was reserved and unnecessarily grumpy. Slumped when he should take advantage of his height. She assumed that he didn't like her either.

He sat up and leaned forward, elbows on knees. "I'm not saying that—"

"But I understand." Her voice flew out. Her skin felt rubbery, the air in the room close and stale. She stood up to open a window without asking. "If it had been me. I mean, Anu. I might be thinking the same thing. You don't have to worry." She didn't know what she was saying.

She smoothed her white pants before sitting down again. His face was terrified. In this country they all seemed too young for marriage and children, she and Ruchi not yet twenty-four, Naren a year older, Sanjay, the eldest, only twenty-eight. They were caught in adulthood, unable to trace their way back to who they were meant to be. She pointed at the mantel, a photo of Ruchi on what must have been her wedding day, eyes downcast, her braid that Deepa used to decorate with picked flowers lying lazy on her shoulder, lips bitten. Naren's face was turned away from the camera, his and Ruchi's hands covered with the pundit's white shawl. The photo felt like a memory, but Deepa hadn't been there. "She looks like a child."

She wanted to explain that parenthood, no matter what, was a burden for which there was no preparation. More so here, when their children were born far from their parents' childhoods. More so when the marriage was—but there was no point to that. The room felt stifling despite the open window. She held out the bag of sandwiches. "You'll see that it will be fine. All fine."

He took the bag and placed it next to him on the couch. The bread was probably soggy by now, the cheese too warm. She thought she saw a film of tears in his eyes but when she checked again, they were clear and stony.

"What is that?" Naren pointed out the window at her parked car in the driveway. "That sound. Crying."

Deepa followed his pointing finger. She kept her voice even and carefree. "She was sleeping."

"Would she not sleep inside?"

Next to the car, a figure crouched in a long, gauzy shift. The cries, breathless, sustained, grew louder. Naren stood up in alarm.

"She's not a sound sleeper," Deepa said and crossed her arms. "At this age sleep is everything."

"Is it," he said. She hated the concern on his face and rushed outside. But the crouching woman was gone and in her place was Ruchi. A mistake of Deepa's mind. Pillowy creases surrounded Ruchi's eyes and her braid was coming undone. Through the gap in the window, Ruchi whispered comforts to the child. Fear swelled in Deepa's chest and mixed with the wild beating of her heart. Ruchi turned around.

"I didn't know you were coming," Ruchi said.

"She brought you sandwiches," Naren said, standing on the stoop behind them. The baby's cries gasped and sputtered, as if she could smell her mother.

"I'm just leaving," Deepa said. "You were resting."

Ruchi stroked her belly, up and down, side to side. "You don't have to leave." Then she turned back to Anu, whose cries had turned to whimpers. "Her face is all wet. Take her out, no? I'll hold her."

Deepa searched for something casual but biting to say, words to suffocate her rising, angry shame. She swallowed hard on her meanness and squeezed Ruchi's hand, still warm with sleep. "Don't be so dramatic. You'll see once you have your own."

On the way home, Deepa made sure to flash her turn signal at empty intersections, to wait until there wasn't a single car on the horizon before merging onto the highway. She drove in the right lane and let other cars pass. She could feel her every choice, like she was observing herself from the passenger seat, the way her driving instructor, kindly Mr. Chernick, had done. She followed all the rules. The baby had grown hoarse but still wailed dry, sawdusty cries.

She pulled in to the driveway, clicked the automatic garage door opener, and parked the Olds with the correct amount of space on both sides so Sanjay wouldn't have to repark her car to fit his own, which he did without complaint. But today he wouldn't have to. She'd been careful.

She could feel Anu's eyes on her as she collected her handbag. She clicked to draw down the garage door and it rumbled shut while the baby's cries damped to whimpers. Deepa placed the keys on the washing machine before returning to the car, opening the back door, and reaching over the child to unlock her seat belt. "Mami!" Anu called out, delighted. Her face was burnished, like a newborn's. Deepa tugged but the buckle wouldn't release. She arced over the child and pressed with both thumbs on the red lever. The garage closed in on her with its rakes and drills and shovels that menaced from corners. Anu began to fuss again. "Mami, Mami," she said over and over. A strand of Deepa's hair stuck to the child's tears and snot.

Deepa felt the scream in her throat. It tried to crawl out, but she kept her mouth closed, like resisting a vomit. Her shirt was soaked in sweat and the baby was clawing at her, crying gibberish. She could leave her there with the window open and it would be okay. Sit in a chair by the door, close her eyes, and let the sound pass through her. Sanjay would be home soon enough and would release the belt with a simple adjustment, a pressure she hadn't applied, and Deepa would commend his competence. But, as if hearing her thoughts, the metal clasp abruptly popped free. Deepa fell forward, her hip bone jamming against the hard plastic. The child stopped crying and her face shifted from distress to curiosity. She rested her chubby palm against her mother's wet cheek and laughed.

# Ruchi

## 1975

They named him Moksh, "release from the world." Ruchi gave birth on November 1, 1974, a month before her due date. Her labor was swift and painful and complicated only by a tangled cord and meconium. These mild complications, according to her OB, were unrelated to the baby's cleft lip and palate, his microsomia and twisted earlobes.

Moksh spent his first two weeks in the NICU as one of the fortunate babies. His heart never stopped. He didn't need a central line, only plastic cannulas to keep his nasal passage open during sleep. The feeding tube lasted forty-eight hours, after which he could fitfully take a bottle. He spit up the little milk she could pump before she succumbed to formula. She held him for hours to calm his bubbling reflux. "Put him down! He's not so delicate," admonished the night nurse, and Ruchi did. But once they brought him home, Ruchi made sure Moksh was fully asleep before she laid him down so her bangles didn't rattle and wake him. Though he no longer needed the cannulas, his breath made a hissing, clacking sound as if he were always on the verge of waking. She could cook only watered-down dal before he needed soothing again.

On Moksh's first night at home Ammi called. "Happy birthday," she said.

Ruchi was quiet. Ammi huffed, "What? You've forgotten?" It was December fifth.

"I don't even know what day it is," Ruchi said. November had turned to December without anyone noticing. Deepa, the only other person who might have wished her, was never reliable about birthdays.

"You should visit now, while the baby is small," Ammi said.

"He's too small."

"Ere, here he'll become fat!"

"You come, no?" Ruchi said. "Naren can't take off whenever he wants." A half-truth. The real problem: bills and more bills. First the cost of the small house, then the price of the pregnancy with its copays and deductibles, and now the expense of the baby with his extra visits and extra care. Next year, or the year after, Ruchi silently promised. Once they caught up.

After months of cajoling, Ammi finally agreed. Ruchi wrote letters for the visa and called the embassy every week. "April will be perfect," Ruchi said and persuaded her mother to stay through May for Moksh's first surgery to correct his cleft lip. She promised crisp hill station weather and flowers blooming.

But the Saturday Ammi was set to arrive at JFK was cold and unforgiving. Ruchi prepared the second bedroom while Moksh, now five months old, slept a rare long nap. The light that filtered through the blinds was milky, but Ruchi still hoped for sun. Naren had driven to the airport, and Ruchi worried about what they would talk about during the three-hour return journey. He and Ammi would run out of bland things to say. They were, after all, strangers.

By noon, the rain arrived. Ruchi cleared the bookshelf in the small room so Ammi would have space for her clothes. The shelf was full, as if they'd been living here for years. An accordion of bills, medical statements, instructional manuals.

She tried to picture her mother alone in customs, opening her bags and arguing over the yellow lentils and mustard seeds that weren't allowed. When Ruchi had first arrived, customs had taken every grain, legume, and whole clove from Ruchi's luggage. She worried about Ammi yelling at the disrespectful officials.

Ruchi placed two pillows side by side on the foldout bed. Ammi liked firm, flat pillows; these wouldn't be firm enough. With her mother there were many ways to do a thing incorrectly—fold a blanket, make toast, string a jasmine necklace for dead people—but only one right way. One.

NAREN PULLED IN to the garage, him and Ammi staring out the windshield. Their Nova was secondhand and looked especially so. Ruchi felt squat and graceless in the doorway that connected the garage to the living room. The garage smelled of sour milk and was cluttered with half-crushed boxes, a rake with broken teeth, tangles of rope that she couldn't remember why they'd acquired. Garbage.

And there was Ammi, her oiled hair and wrinkled sari and flesh-colored socks, the deep slant of her frowning lips. She placed a hand on Ruchi's cheek, calloused but warm. As if she hadn't flown through a full night for the first time in her life. Ruchi leaned into her palm; a sob clogged her throat.

"Maro baba kyam che?" Ammi said, searching for the child as they entered the living room.

"Unghamam, Ammi."

She tried to explain that Moksh was uncomfortable after a nap. Her baby was calmest in the mornings.

Ammi said, "Ere, what else is he to do but cry?"

Naren dragged in the overstuffed suitcases with gold buckles around their bellies. "We'll wake him. Why not?"

"Because no," Ruchi said.

Ammi removed her chappals and shivered.

"You'll have to buy Ammi sneakers, no, Ammi? It's too cold for chappals," said Naren.

"Don't I have socks?" She gestured angrily at her feet.

Ruchi pictured them in Caldor hunting for the right pair. A size up. A half size down. Too wide, too white, cushion there but not here.

Ammi was tired but wouldn't sit down. She'd grown both plumper and gaunter—as if her midsection were siphoning off from her face. Her hair was tied in a loose bun at her neck instead of a severe braid down her back. Had Ruchi stayed in Bombay, she wouldn't have noticed these changes. Ammi squeezed the couch. She rubbed the carpet shag with her big toe and peered at her reflection in the television screen. In the kitchen, she circled the plastic-covered table and shook the backs of chairs to test their strength. She picked up the blender and inspected the bottom, then blew her nose in a paper towel and tucked it into the top of her blouse.

"The trash goes under the sink." Ruchi offered the instruction neutrally. Her mother didn't like instructions. Ruchi's memories of her were always in motion, spitting saali and vandaro at whoever was near, stirring with one hand and slapping her with the other.

But Ammi placed the crumpled towel in the bin and followed Ruchi down the hall to her bedroom. She examined the foldout bed and shelf without comment, then directed Naren to lay her suitcase down flat. Inside were packets wrapped in brown paper. All of it there. The lentils and seeds and namkeen and sandalwood paste.

"But how, Ammi?" Ruchi asked.

"You have to be smart and act dumb," she said, as if Ruchi should've known this. Ammi directed from the bed what to do with each item. A blue salwar kameez for Ruchi and a peacock-green kurta for Naren. Both would lie in the dark recesses of their closets with other rarely worn clothes.

The outfit for Moksh was too large with tiny mirrors sewn into the cuffs. A choking hazard. Ammi unfurled a blanket, gray with pink mangoes. "I embroidered for him myself," she said, but Ruchi recognized it as one that had been rolled up in some cousin's gadda. Naren admired the stitching. The lie stung but less than it might have back home. Anything from home was now rare and precious.

There was a wooden marionette, the kind Ruchi had loved as a child. She pulled the string and its skinny arms and legs flapped around its round belly. The doll's painted suit was gray and pink like the blanket, the gloss likely toxic.

"These others are for that friend of yours," Ammi said, holding out a second female version of the doll and another outfit.

"Why bring so much?" Ruchi asked, though she was pleased that Ammi had thought of Deepa. She liked the idea of Deepa fawning over the gifts, Ammi frowning but content. "We'll take her on outings," Deepa had promised when Ruchi told her about Ammi's visit. Since the baby had arrived, Deepa had been especially attentive. She'd dropped off salty shaaks that were either over- or undercooked, and Ruchi told her she didn't have to go to so much trouble. But Deepa insisted. Each time, she held Moksh's skinny body and kissed his hands. "You've produced a boy! No one cares about his lip or ears or forehead." She talked about future play dates with Anu and the best breastfeeding and sleep positions.

Ruchi was grateful for these visits but wished for a softer, quieter Deepa who might hold her hand and pause her litany of advice. She didn't want to be reminded that he'd passed his hearing test. That his feet were fine. His fingers were fine. His trachea was perfectly unobstructed. "That's all that matters, no? The bigger picture," said Deepa. But what was the bigger picture? At night, Ruchi dreamed of the surgeries, portals through which they'd emerge, shiny and new, but during the day she knew this was false. She had the feeling that Deepa would've handled it all more capably, would've displayed gratitude over grief. Here Moksh was, her healthy child, the most consequential thing that had ever happened to her. Perhaps Deepa couldn't help her unyielding efficiency that had become more so in America. Perhaps Ruchi was greedy in her want.

The baby woke with a cry, his face covered in spittle. Dried white salt lines stretched across his jaw to his ears.

"Ravadanum bandha, baba," Ruchi said, patting Moksh's bottom. She planned to make him bilingual and spoke to him only in Gujarati.

Naren counteracted the measures by speaking only English around the child. When he was at work, she whispered into the baby's ears all the words she knew.

Ammi glared at Ruchi's wrists and asked, "Where are your churis?"

"I push them up my sleeves so they don't make noise. The baby doesn't like the sound." She hated having to defend herself for a normal thing.

"How do you know what he likes?" Ammi took Moksh and jostled him. She didn't coo or hold him or sit down to place him on her lap. She didn't offer a finger for him to take in his fist. But she looked at him. She looked and looked.

FOR AMMI'S FIRST weekend they took her to the malls. First Enfield and then West Farms with all the high-end stores, the mall they'd visited to see Christmas lights and snowflakes hung like chandeliers, never to shop.

Naren bought her a pretzel. "It's like wada pau."

Ammi pinched the bread between thumb and forefinger. "But so bland."

"Here it's all butter for flavoring," Ruchi said.

Ammi liked pushing the stroller across the tile floor. They walked past G. Fox and Sage-Allen and a store that sold only socks and a jeweler with so few items on display that Ammi said it looked poor. Like a poor jewelry store.

Each time she stopped in front of a window, Naren gave some explanation. It was nice to see him animated, to see that they had gained some knowledge. His good moods could be fragile.

At the food court Ammi wanted dumplings and french fries and pizza, and Naren agreed. "You should try it all," he said, and carried his tray to three different lines.

Ammi sat down and rubbed her calves. She was still wearing the flesh-colored socks though the weather had warmed. People scanned her mother as they walked by.

The baby began to fuss. Ruchi poked her head under the swaddling blanket and shushed him while rocking the stroller.

"What are you doing?" Ammi asked.

"He needs a nap."

"Ere, like that how will he nap? Pick him up."

"I'll walk around."

"Sa mate?"

Ammi pushed Ruchi aside, dislodged the baby from the stroller, and held him against her shoulder. His cries echoed off the high ceiling. She wiped the spittle around his mouth and the crust that collected in the corners of his eyes. Ruchi tried to cover him with the blanket, but Ammi waved it off.

"Why to hide him?" her mother asked.

"I'm not." But she knew she was.

Naren returned with fried vegetable dumplings and garlic knots and three types of rolls and a pizza slice that he cut into three, more food than they could possibly eat. Orange soft drinks for everyone.

She should not have to say to Naren, "It was Ammi's idea." She should not have to explain why their son was visible, but she did.

Naren asked, "How will she eat her food?"

Ammi balanced the child with one arm and plucked a garlic knot, but Naren's excitement had vanished. Ruchi wished she could rewind to his good mood, the baby tucked and happy, away from the attention. It wasn't embarrassment, Ruchi argued to herself. It was protection.

THE SECOND WEEK, Ammi massaged Moksh on the kitchen table. She placed him on the blanket she'd brought and swiftly covered him in coconut oil, pulling on his legs and arms, pressing his sunken chin and uneven forehead, flipping and squeezing like kneading dough.

"You can't be rough like that." Ruchi waited for Moksh to cry out, but his eyes only bulged in surprise.

"What rough? You should do it every day for any effect. It will even him out. Look how nice his skin becomes." It was true that he glowed, a baby dipped in honey.

Ruchi explained the procedure for the first surgery. "Outpatient. Easy-peasy," the plastic surgeon had said. The palate would be months later and the jaw realignment later than that. "Why not all at once? When they are babies everything is easiest," Ammi said.

"It's too much at once."

"What will he remember?" Ammi squeezed Moksh's thighs down to his feet, snapping her thumbs on his soles.

The light from the kitchen window hit the baby's face and his brown eyes appeared translucent. Ammi said she had cousins in the village with eyes like this. "Even more colorful." But Ruchi knew only that one cousin had vitiligo and never left home, and another was sweet and slow. Ammi avoided talking about either.

As Ruchi diapered her child, she kissed his forehead, and her hair tickled his belly. His face opened and a sound burst through, like a cough. She did it again until again the corners of his mouth lit up.

"He's laughing," Ruchi said.

"Is he."

Ruchi did it again, and again. The laugh stretched into a sanguine squeal. She couldn't stop. Her hair caught in his fingers, and she didn't care. "For the first time."

Ammi glared and pushed Ruchi's hip with her hand. "And so? All babies will laugh."

Ruchi blinked away the heat in her eyes. She knew better.

IN THE EVENINGS, Naren told Ammi stories about Newhouse, the crumbs that bounced in his mustache, the numerous cups of coffee he drank, his dark teeth. He didn't tell her that he was still an assistant engineer without an office of his own.

Over dinner one night, Ammi impatiently asked, "Which houses did you build?" Moksh was asleep but Ammi refused to speak in whispers.

"None of these houses. Mine are in the new developments."

"Kyam che?"

Naren dipped puri into his kadi and placed it whole in his mouth. "Not in this town. There are other towns, Ammi. Towns where fields are dug up and made into mansions. Bungalows like you've never seen."

Ammi's kadi was spicier than Ruchi's and the puri thinner. Naren was eating more; his cheeks reminded her of oranges. She waited for Ammi to ask why they didn't live in one of these bungalows. She was smarter than Naren understood, smarter than his own mother who had birthed only sons. Ammi was fifteen when she married, a village girl who learned English by copying Ruchi's Austen novels in small script into a blue form book in the middle of the night. Her mother could crush a hope, could snoop out a lie, bite without leaving a mark.

But Ammi didn't respond immediately. She slurped her kadi, sweat beading her temple.

Ruchi said, "Deepa has a three-bedroom house."

"Oh?"

"It's not so big. An old colonial. Not new," Naren said and sulked. She'd seen her husband's want the first time they'd toured Deepa and Sanjay's home, the automatic garage door, separate rooms for dining, for living. She'd been hopeful that first day that everything would fall into place, that even Naren and Sanjay, who continuously spoke loudly and cheerfully, would become friends. "Too loudly. Too cheerfully," Naren had said after. "All a big show."

Ammi asked about the size of Deepa's kitchen, did it have the same appliances, did she have a maid, did she make ghee or use flavorless butter. "What does she do all day?"

"Nakra. Shopping. Parties," Naren grunted.

Ruchi rolled a small puri into a cigarette and nibbled. Deepa should've visited by now, but she hadn't, just as she hadn't yet invited Ruchi to meet her other friends. Ruchi pretended not to notice this slight, but she did, and out of pride, Ruchi hadn't called. Deepa had promised a trip. But maybe it had just been something to say.

"We'll visit her," Ruchi said. "She wants to see you."

Ammi brightened.

"How will you take her?" Naren asked. He'd stopped eating, irritated.

Ruchi rolled another puri though she was already full. "Deepa will pick us up."

"How is she driving?" Ammi asked.

"She took the test, Ammi. She passed."

"How? She was such a stupid girl."

*Because the Jains can afford expensive lessons.* But Ruchi let the comment sit with the greasy puri that stuck to the roof of her mouth.

Behind Ammi's anger was envy, a feeling Ruchi had inherited, though she hated how it overtook her heart to stir the most basic betrayals. She wanted Ammi to see Deepa's house as an example of what she and Naren might one day own. She also wanted Ammi to find its flaws. To tell Ruchi how to guard against them.

"You don't have to be smart," Ruchi said. She collected their plates and turned from the table to hide the burn of her cheeks. "Just lucky."

# Deepa

## 1975

The cards began in earnest that year. Deepa was twenty-five. Every month, sometimes weekly, they arrived singing Dr. Jain's praises. Deepa let Anu, now two, tear open the envelopes to crush the cards inside. Then Deepa rescued them and clipped them to the fridge.

The cards proclaimed "So calm!" and "So gentle!" with "Thank you" printed in baroque scripts. Cards from mothers and sons, from sisters and uncles. All grateful to the good doctor for his kind manner and expertise. Sometimes the letters were addressed to Dr. SJ Jain or Dr. Jane or Sun J. Jane. No matter how simple the names, the Americans still mangled them.

In four years, Deepa had met many Indian doctors. Sanjay explained how many had difficulty gaining patients, were asked about their credentials, received complaints because the waiting room smelled like incense or because patients couldn't understand their accents or for the curry on their breath.

"What South Indian eats Punjabi curry for breakfast?" Sanjay railed. Railed but took precautions, washed his hair daily and insisted that Deepa make him bland cheese and cucumber sandwich lunches. No chutney, no methi masala. From the cards it was clear that he'd made himself palatable, a handsome and articulate Indian doctor who wouldn't need to moonlight much longer at Manchester Hospital.

Sanjay's private practice was taking off. Deepa talked about his successes at parties and picnics, adding her involvement, the input she offered and that he followed. She didn't discuss her hours alone at home, the house's emptiness ringing in her ears, the afternoons with Anu stacking towers, frosting pretend cakes, and flipping through the same books. All of it making Deepa drowsy and wistful. She didn't discuss the nights, how routinely she gave in.

"Do you enjoy it?" Sanjay asked on an early spring night. Deepa lay on her back, her underwear around one ankle. They'd turned the clocks forward that weekend and it was still dark outside.

"Of course," she said. "It's fine."

"Fine?"

She pulled on her underwear and tidied her pillows. "Of course."

"You're so quiet." He was looking at her, but she pretended not to notice.

"So?" She rose to clean herself and take the birth control she hid in the bottom drawer of the bathroom cabinet, behind her feminine products and sprays.

"I wouldn't mind if you made some sounds. Just some indication," he called to her from behind the door. Deepa heard him switch on the small TV and skip through channels, then there was Cher's big, deep voice that reminded Deepa of a cavernous steel pot. He switched again, and she was annoyed. "You don't have to be shy," he said.

No, she was not shy. She stripped and stepped into the scalding shower. All week, Ruchi hadn't called, and Deepa refused to try. She hated it when Ruchi didn't answer, when she was too busy with Moksh, though this was unfair because Ruchi was truly alone, no sitter for a few hours of the week, no car, no license. Deepa had tried to be helpful. She'd visited and brought meals that Ruchi thanked her for but never complimented. When Ruchi told her Auntie was coming in early April, Deepa pretended to be happy for her. She did her best to ignore her jealousy that Ruchi had a mother willing to visit.

Deepa forced her eyes open in the hot water. Maybe, had she been born in this country, if she'd been allowed boyfriends and short dresses from a young age, she'd be different now. More at ease and knowing. She appreciated how American women carried themselves, and tried to copy their swagger. Permed, freckled women brandishing friendliness, wispy ponytails, clean brows and upper lips. They looked through her. Deepa would never belong among them, which was fine. Every year more Indians arrived, a few Sri Lankans, a Pakistani family with wives who admired Deepa's flare jeans, her instinct to belt her minidresses. They'd never guess anything was wrong with her. And yet what Deepa wanted was for Ruchi to call.

The last light of day faded through the bathroom window. Deepa lay down in the tub, angled her pelvis toward the shower spray, and balled her fists in the water. She let her mind twist around useless curiosities from girlhood: a dark downy cheek, sweat drying on her skin in the shade, slivers of sun on the curl of lip she was examining, tongue. An odd sensation snaked through her at the speed of light, seconds stretched and she was in a warm, dark tunnel thrumming with blood. She turned off the faucet and squeezed her eyes shut.

ON A SUNDAY morning in March, they took Anu for a drive through the new developments, the houses sprouting up on Willow Circle and on Jasper Lane. Every month a new road or court or drive. A field becoming a plaza, a department store, a restaurant with red booths and buffets and checkered tablecloths. Great quantities of aluminum siding, fantastical, bulbous islands filled with dark mulch and hydrangeas and neat little bushes shaped into rectangles and squares ready to bloom in spring. Anu learned words like "bulldozer" and "digger," words Deepa and Sanjay didn't know themselves but adopted from a bright book about the subject. "Whole towns are coming up," Sanjay said, and she, too, felt it then. A hope, a pull toward happiness. The steel beams touched dusty pink in the morning light, rising out of leftover yellow snow like beacons. It was easy to get swept up in the perfection of it, so swept up that Deepa felt the emptiness recede, taking with it the chipped walls of the room she'd shared with her mother, the strange hunger, the father who never sent enough, gathered it all and pushed it back and back until it was a single pulsing dot. She took Sanjay's hand, reminded of how they were the same.

"We should invest in a second home. A plot of land on the shore. You must miss the ocean, no, honey?" He gripped her hand tighter.

She'd never considered it. She still thought of their house in Glastonbury as a "new house" though they'd moved in two years ago.

"I'm expanding the practice," he said. "A whole medical suite someday. Two houses and two children."

She released his hand and tucked her hair behind her ears.

"Crane!" Anu gurgled. "Cranecranecrane!" Sanjay laughed and said it was a bird and then Anu laughed. Deepa stared out the window so no one could see she wasn't smiling. The very thing that gave her comfort, the abundance, also froze her in place with fear. Whatever was gained on one side could be lost on the other. A second child would be one of these losses, another piece of herself torn out, though to say so aloud would sound heartless. Instead of a child, Deepa wanted something of her own.

That night she turned to him and said airily, "I want it in my name."

"Want what?"

"The plot. In my name." Her mind raced. "Good for taxes, no? To not have everything in your name."

He threaded his arm under her lower back, as though the arm had grown and could double loop around her if he'd wanted. "Always thinking ahead. You could've been a class topper," he teased.

"I could have. Yes," she said. "If I'd wanted." His lips found her neck, and his hands reached inside her robe.

"I'm still bleeding," she said, and lay motionless. "Next week. Better chances."

A plot of land in her name. A place to escape to. She'd take Ruchi and Moksh, show her that all would be right. She'd laugh with Anu, sand in their hair, sea salt dried on their skin.

Deepa took firm hold of her husband. She'd never done anything like it before, but she knew that this would calm him. His eyes opened wide, and she tightened her grip. "Wah," he moaned when she spat on her palm and sucked in her stomach to hold back a retch. He was too good to suspect her pills. She moved her hand faster, working a stuck appliance. Another year or two of pretending. Then she'd win. She'd wear him down. She'd read about it in magazines, how sex in marriage became stale. And the house, at least, would be hers. Partly, in name. Hers hers hers. Something to make her real.

IN LATE APRIL, Ruchi called. Deepa watched Anu play with the exercise bike in the guest room as Ruchi talked about her mother's visit.

"Ammi is asking about you," Ruchi said. She spoke in a rush, as if Auntie were listening from behind the door.

"How sweet." Deepa wanted to ask why Ruchi hadn't called sooner. Surely Auntie was helping and Ruchi had time. Deepa felt forgotten. "One minute," she said, and lifted Anu off the stationary bike. "How's Baba?" she asked.

"He's fine." Ruchi paused. "He still chokes on his spit."

Anu returned to the stationary bike, and Deepa pretended she didn't see her. "All babies choke on their spit sometimes. You have your mother at least."

"Ammi is getting bored."

"But is she getting along with Naren, with her jamairaja? You know they don't always."

"They are like fast friends," Ruchi said, bitterly. "Watching TV together all the time."

"Better than fighting." Anu turned the flywheel, her fingers ready to catch on the bike's caged spokes. Deepa resisted the desire to slap her hand off. Children learned best by doing. "You'll make yourself sick if you worry so much. The baby needs you happy."

"Ammi wants to meet Anu and Sanjay. She wants to see your house."

"I'd tell you bring her for tea but there's no time. Sanjay does so many night calls," Deepa said, though she had plenty of time. She added, "And on the weekends there are parties."

"I thought they bore you."

"Of course they do. Doctors' wives inviting me for weak chai and cold snacks. Otherwise, I'd bring you." It was true, in part. At times, Deepa wished Ruchi were at the parties to see her, but also to be with her. Both things were wrong to say.

"It's no issue," Ruchi said, but Deepa could hear the need in her voice. The hurt.

"I have an idea," Deepa said. "Let's show Auntie the ocean. An outing."

"But the ocean is an hour away. I thought there's no time?"

"Bring the whole family," Deepa said, as if she hadn't heard Ruchi. As if the busyness of moments ago had evaporated.

"Naren will complain," Ruchi said.

"Let him complain then. Auntie will love it."

Anu called for her but Deepa didn't answer. She stretched the phone cord to hide outside the room, playing a game with her daughter to which only she knew the rules. "Saturday," she said and gave Ruchi the directions, playing another game. A surprise.

AT THE BEACH property, Deepa waited behind the tall grass. She didn't want them to see her as they approached. She was hoping for a sunny day, but all she got were thick clouds. Her turquoise dress whipped around her legs, and she wrapped the thin shawl around her bare shoulders. Her pocked cheeks felt raw in the wind. She hated them. She saw the secondhand rust-colored Nova turn onto the gravel road that led past two small houses, one empty, the other abandoned. The car slowed down, and Deepa saw Ruchi with the map in the passenger seat, head turning left and right, uncertain. Deepa strode out from the grass, wobbling on the rocks in her strappy black sandals, and waved energetically, the shawl flying out behind her. She caught it with one arm.

"Auntie!" Deepa called out as Ruchi's mother stepped out of the car. "You look the same."

"You were always good at flattery. What are these clothes? Where is the bottom?" Auntie said. Deepa put an arm around Auntie, stooping to bring her cheek to her cheek. The woman stiffly withstood it. Deepa smiled at Naren and cooed at Moksh, taking him from Ruchi. She focused her attention on the child, on his small, asymmetrical face, and the warmth she felt was as real as the relief that he was not her own. At last she looked at Ruchi. Her eyes were puffy from lack of sleep, her hair ruffling around her face. She wore a pilling gray cardigan over a thin green kameez. On impulse, Deepa removed a pin from her own hair and fastened it to hold back the thick curl that had fallen over Ruchi's eyes. A gesture that could only be sisterly, just as the gooseflesh down her arms could only be caused by cold. "There," Deepa whispered and withdrew her hand.

"Why have you come alone? I wanted to meet your baby and husband," Auntie said. "I wanted to see your house."

"Next time, Auntie. I promise."

Auntie grunted, unsatisfied. "What next time? What promise?" She fixed Deepa in a stare.

"Ere, Ammi, she's invited you here," Ruchi said, but as she looked around, Deepa could see that she didn't understand where "here" was. The lot was just tall grass and rocks with trash in the seaweed. Maybe it was a mistake to bring them here. Maybe they would feel sorry for her. But only if she acted pitiful. Deepa bounced the baby on her hip, who looked all around. They had him bundled up like it was winter.

Deepa swept her free arm open. "Do you like it? It's mine."

Naren's eyes opened wide. "Yours?" He stood by the car, a sentry.

"But what is it? What is this?" Auntie asked, as if she were standing in the sludge at Chowpatty or smelling pomfret rotting in Mahim.

"Land, Auntie. For a house. A beach house for the weekends." When Auntie continued to stare, she added, "Like the film stars have in Juhu."

"So you're a film star now? Ere, Ruchi, te film star bani!"

Naren chuckled, but Ammi's voice lacked its usual bite. Deepa wasn't the girl with the strange mother anymore, the girl who people wondered: What would become of her? She gloated to the nuns in her mind and though she wanted to know if Ruchi was watching her, she felt shy about checking. She led them down the narrow path that cut through the grass to the rocky beach. She pointed out where the house would go, the deck, a carport. Ruchi continued her silence.

"Not a film star, Auntie," Deepa said. "More like the director-producer."

She turned to Ruchi, who was staring at the baby. "You hold him like he can control his neck," Ruchi said, and stepped forward to gather the child from Deepa's arm. She tucked him between her shoulder and neck, cradled his head in her palm, and turned him away from them.

"But how else will he learn?"

"I tell her the same thing," Auntie said.

"Where are you going?" Deepa called out. Ruchi had walked ahead, slipped out of her chappals, and turned toward the gunmetal ocean, the baby pressed to her as if she were shielding him, or making him invisible.

"To touch the sea," Ruchi called back, a little rueful.

"Go. Both of you take Baba. It's good luck." Auntie caught up to Ruchi, snatched the socks off Moksh's feet, and stuffed the offending things in her pocket. "Naren will keep me company."

The tide was in, and Ruchi and Deepa had to negotiate the rocks to find water that reached their ankles. Ruchi gasped from the cold. Carefully, she crouched to submerge Moksh's foot, then clasped it, like she'd burned him. A swift affection for them both threatened to draw Deepa under.

"Ruch, he'll be fine. He likes to look around."

"I don't want him to catch cold. That's all." The foam was brown. They were too close to the mouth of the river that ran straight down from Hartford.

"Someday, all this will be beautiful. With a view of the lighthouse from the bedrooms."

"Saras," Ruchi said, but in that punctured manner that told Deepa she didn't mean it.

"You'll see. Every weekend we can spend here. The kids playing in the sand."

"It will be so nice for you," Ruchi said.

Deepa laughed at the simpleness of Ruchi's resentment. "Oh, Sanjay will never have the time. He's expanding his practice. All he does is work. I'll take us with Anu and Moksh." She pointed to Naren walking with Auntie. "Look how good your husband is." Deepa felt like being daring and hooked her arm through Ruchi's free one as they walked back up the shards and sand. Through the gray cardigan, Deepa could make out the hard edges of Ruchi's bangles. She squeezed to press them into her palm, as if she had the strength to break them. Moksh rested peacefully on Ruchi's opposite shoulder. The sky brightened. Here, on Deepa's land, everything was possible, everything was right.

"You must be so cold," Ruchi said, and leaned into her. "But your arm is warm."

"Blood, Ruch. We have blood to keep us warm."

"How stupid." But at last she was lighter, and Deepa felt happy, their arms touching, their cheeks near. Deepa saw Auntie watching them return, and she pulled Ruchi closer.

The wind picked up, undoing Ammi's bun. The picnic lunch was in the car and Naren went to get it.

"Auntie, next time you can come stay."

"Next time? Oh ho! Who wants to visit this cold place?" Auntie said, glaring at them both before settling on Deepa. "Lucky you are, no? In your marriage. With your doctor-sahib."

It was the old Auntie, the one Deepa had known best.

"Very lucky," Deepa said. Naren returned with the Igloo and a shopping bag, and Auntie helped him lay out the blanket and a separate one, fraying at the edges, for the baby. She instructed Ruchi to give Deepa the bag, and her friend unhooked her arm.

"For Anu," Ruchi said, and took out a fuchsia chaniya choli and a doll with a droll little mouth.

"You were supposed to bring her," Auntie complained again.

"So lovely!" Deepa said, admiring the cheap gold thread as though she'd never been given a gift before.

"You know, my daughter could've been a doctor too," Auntie said. "She had top marks."

Naren nodded, as if he'd always appreciated this. "Too smart."

Ruchi laid Moksh down on the blanket, pretending not to listen. Deepa saw her suck in her cheeks, the little tell that showed both her anger and pride. It made Deepa sad. "She could've been," she said, opening the shiny foil of store-bought snacks. "Yes. She was top of her class. *Nearly.*"

The jerk in Ruchi's shoulder was impossible to notice unless you were watching her. She covered Moksh's face to protect against the wind and asked her mother for the boy's socks. Deepa missed their arms touching and the sharp edge of Ruchi's bangles. She eyed the rocks that jutted out of the water, the clumps of seaweed, bottle caps tangled in their fronds. The tall grass to be crushed by a house.

# PART THREE

# Anu

## *August 1992*

Why had she come home? Anu Jain, nineteen years old, wondered this as she mingled with guests on the beach and tugged at the strappy contraption her mother had made her wear for the annual beach party. It was 1992. At college, Anu had cut her hair and inked a black puzzle piece on her lower back. She'd joined a South Asian political action group that railed against fundamentalism. She'd stopped bleaching her mustache. And now she was here, wearing a blouse she hated and guiding guests to tents with embarrassing quantities of food. The house was a disaster, and her parents appeared folded and drained since she'd last seen them, which, by design, was infrequently since leaving for college. Every break she lined up an "internship" or a "project" or "community service." Whatever could keep her acceptably away.

But she missed them. She'd always miss them.

The party was bigger than ever. Friends, her mother called them. Some had known Anu since she was small—the Mansinghs, the Kashyaps. Anu mentioned her internship in New York, the premed classes she was taking, and shrugged apologetically when aunties lamented her short hair. She was a whore for approval. She liked it when the aunties and uncles called her "beti" and "dikri" and complimented her accomplishments. In between, Anu rubbed her nose to smell her fingers, hoping to catch the scent of Betina, her girlfriend, *her lover*, a term that frightened as much as it thrilled. It shocked her how cleanly she could split in two.

Her mother was still inside. Anu had spent the days leading up to the party sleeping in late and hiding in pulpy novels, afraid her mother might notice the slick of sex on her skin. As if she had an ultraviolet light to illuminate the places her daughter had been touched. But this time her mother, thankfully, was distracted.

"Why can't I come?" Betina had asked the night before Anu left. They were in bed, and Anu was tracing a line from Betina's perfect, pert nipple down to her belly button and back again.

"Oh, you'd hate it. My parents have judgmental friends."

Betina guided her hand lower. "But I love judgmental friends. And you can say I'm your roommate. You don't have to come out. Yet."

How to explain about the friend she'd had in high school? How her mother found them making out in a dimly lit basement? They never discussed it, and Anu never saw the friend again. But Betina wouldn't understand. *Her* family had invited Anu to Betina's sister's quinceañera, no questions asked.

"Your family is cooler than mine," Anu said, as Betina reached for her. Anu gently pushed the hand away and fondled Betina's nipple with more intention. She preferred to give than receive. Years later, when Betina broke up with her, Anu, in a bid to get back together, desperately explained that there was a clinical diagnosis for her condition: anorgasmia, orgasmic disorder, old-school hysteria. But these weren't it. She was simply afraid of being undone.

"Next time," Anu had said, and redoubled her efforts.

She found her father shaking a tent pole, checking for sturdiness. His limey polo T-shirt was damp with sweat. Normally, he made the rounds, telling the usual backslapping jokes, but now he kept checking on things that didn't require his attention.

"It's too hot to be out here," she said, pulling again at the straps of her blouse. "People are hopping from tent to tent so they don't burn their feet."

"It's not so bad. Heat opens the pores." He swayed on his feet, jovial. "Look, some unexpected work has come up. Nothing big."

"Like what?" She felt other people watching them, appraising father and daughter and probably assuming he was giving sage advice or clear instructions. Maybe admiring their closeness, this family that had made it with the daughter who would amplify their considerable success. Bile filled her mouth.

"Nothing, I told you. You focus on your studies, that's all."

But he stood there smiling as though he wanted to ask questions. Maybe about sex? Or her hair? The weight gain? "I like premed," she said, to head him off. "I think I might pursue it." Though in truth she didn't know if she really liked it or if she was hoping to check the right box and make up for the box she was failing to check. Over time, she'd check other boxes, too: a considerable savings account balance, a sensible 401(k), marriage, children. But not the right marriage. Not the right children. Nothing quite made up for her transgressions.

"Very good!" her father said, voice full. He squeezed her around the shoulders. Her father was the easier, more affectionate parent. Or rather, *the* affectionate parent. She recalled being twelve and her mother giving her a turquoise box of Jolēn creme to bleach her hirsute upper lip. "Never shave," her mother had said. "It will come back thick as trees." But she hadn't offered to thread the hairs the way she did her own stache. Threading meant touch, adjacent to affection, and affection was not her mother's domain.

And yet it was her mother Anu wanted to impress most, whose approval she needed to earn.

Her father swayed some more. "You can have your own medical suite someday."

"Dad—"

"Only if you want to," he said in a hurry. "It's quite a headache. Though the koi are doing well."

God, the koi. Her father had dredged a pond for her, not because she'd begged him to, but because she'd once said she liked fish. Spending money made her parents giddy. They liked to remind Anu that money never came easy, that money was its own sacred ambition. Anu asked what that meant, but no one elaborated.

The excess embarrassed her now, all that they had, how little she'd had to worry about. It was what people wanted for their kids: the beach, the austere house, the pond with its malnourished exotic fish.

"Dad?"

"Yes, dikri?"

What could she say? That she had a girlfriend? Was in love? That some part of her was happy? That she didn't think such happiness could last? Because her mother wouldn't let it. She wished her parents loved each other. That the endearments that had become habit meant something. Honey. Hona. Once upon a time, she'd hoped that a second house meant a second life. She'd helped her mother pick out bone-colored tiles and mauve blinds and chrome chandeliers, and she'd thought in this house full of details they'd chosen themselves their family would be different. Honey. Hona.

It was a child's dream. The chasm of her parents' marriage had left a hidden mark inside her, a minuscule hole in a ventricle or lung that could go undetected until it killed you.

Her father focused on the striped sea, face deep in calculations. Anu spotted Ruchi Auntie on the beach, her cheeks a little fuller, her hair still flying away from her temples. Anu smiled and waved but none of the Mehtas saw her. She thought Auntie looked less troubled than her own mother, younger. She wasn't stylish in her salwar kameez and the red tint in her part, but instead of looking out of place, she looked the most herself.

"I could've swum back," she blurted.

"What?" her father asked, searching for the memory.

But Anu remembered. The film of it rose up when she least expected it: in a coffee shop, in therapy, lying awake next to Betina.

"That first housewarming party we had. When you and Mom had to come after me in the water. I could've swum back." All this back when aunties used to tell her mother to put Anu in films, as if that's how it happened, parents dropping their children into movies.

"People always think that, Jaanu. They always think they can swim back." His forehead wrinkled and he gave her another squeeze. "Why are you worrying about this now?"

He didn't understand, and she hadn't said a fraction of what she wanted to say, should've said. How she'd played host to the other kids, inviting Moksh into the water knowing he'd refuse, luring the others in to play "underwater tag," a game Anu made up so she could graze the backs of Bhavana Mansingh's thighs. How Anu had shuddered every time Bhavana dived under. How all the while Anu kept one eye on her mother flitting through the crowd, cajoling people to eat. How Anu had tracked her with the wolfishness of the guilty. How she'd seen her mother on the shore with Moksh, seen how her mother had encouraged him, how she'd stepped into the water, how Moksh had taken off his shirt and followed. Anu remembered pumping her arms hard, out past the break. She'd been twelve.

"You don't understand," Anu said to her father, but he was already wrapped up in other worries, already weaving through the crowd.

ANU JOINED THE other young people gathered on the jetty of rocks. Bhavana had become the prettiest, a title Anu was relieved to relinquish. Beauty came with expectations of a handsome match, a quick one. Vinod was the math star. The Ravichandran boys tried to recruit kids for their culty religious camps. A minor battalion of first gen preps and nerds in Keds dreaming of scholarships and suburbia, the spawn of hard work and sacrifice.

Moksh approached. He was folded into a hoodie in the middle of August. His face had matured, easing the angles and scars. She hadn't seen him in over a year. Maybe two. He'd both grown and faded. There were photos of them as babies on this very beach. The other kids on the rocks offered obligatory cheery hellos but left them alone to sit at the end. She realized that she'd been grouped with Moksh "the mumbling weirdo" and felt both protective and anxious.

"I'm surprised your parents still have these parties," Moksh said.

Anu shrugged. Across the beach, men and women separated into their gendered groups. There was still no sign of her mother. "I'm not. Surprised, I mean."

He cocked his chin toward her. "Something about you. It's different."

"Different?" She pressed her thighs into the black rocks and prepared for the blunt riposte he'd always been good at.

"Don't get defensive. It's not a bad thing. Maybe college is good for you."

Anu swallowed. Why did the words make her want to cry? Was it not—a bad thing? Betina, her dorm room, the one-sided sex? The blatant disregard for her mother's wishes? He watched her closely, sweat running down his forehead and into his eyes, and she wanted to hug him. Sometimes they could seem like siblings or best friends.

She stood up. "Let's go inside. I'll show you what a shitstorm my house is," Anu said, and he followed. In the foyer, the cool tile underfoot was a relief. He took in the sour milk in the kitchen, the crumpled napkins on the coffee table.

"See?" she said. "My parents are losing it."

"It doesn't look so bad," Moksh said.

"Don't lie. You know it's always immaculate, like a small-town museum of little historical significance." The fruity chandelier, the floral furniture, the kitchen tile—blue sailboats and happy little anchors—normally scrubbed clean down to the grout. Betina was similar, a clean freak.

Moksh touched the rumpled blankets on the couch, outlined the cup stains, stepped over the puddles of clothes, as if taking an inventory. The house was foreign, like they'd stepped onto a film set of the house. Her parents were not okay, and this concerned her. She'd assumed an argument or a death. Never an affair. Given the frigid nature of their household, what difference did an affair make? But why didn't she consider lying? Fraud? An epic swindle? She lied all the time. Then, and always. If not lying then hiding, which fell within the realm of dishonesty.

"My parents don't really speak to each other," Anu said.

"Whose parents speak?" Moksh answered. "At least you guys have money. My parents don't speak *and* they don't have money. They don't even realize all the lies they tell."

"I'm sorry," she said. Of course, the money, the houses, the college tuition had always made things easier for her. She was a coward. The only difficult thing she'd known until then was her mother's disapproval, but it was too strong a tide to swim against. The best she could do was swim sideways.

"Are you okay?" she asked. He pressed the scar under his nose.

"I'm fine."

"Right. Yeah. But I mean, you look—" She paused, noted the set of his jaw, prepared to withdraw. "Tired," she said. Again, she'd failed to express the right thing. But what was the right thing?

"I have to use the bathroom."

She pointed him upstairs. She could've allowed him his privacy, but she snuck behind him. She hoped he might steal something expensive but of little consequence, a crystal paperweight, an expensive stapler. Where was her mother? Maybe he'd walk in on her without her game face, her makeup and perfect outfit, and she'd stumble over her words. For the first time ever. At the end of the hall was a mirror, a full-length one that Anu avoided as a rule. From the stairs she saw him square off against it, lift his sweatshirt and examine his torso. It was unbearably thin, the skin bruised from his ribs, and he ran his fingers over the purple sores with a pleased tilt to his head. She must've made a sound because he turned around and saw her, dropped his shirt, a flush of pain on his broken face. The sounds of the party faded on cue; the world narrowed to the two of them staring at each other. She realized she'd been wrong. She'd considered him oddly lucky, this kid from whom less was expected, who reneged on the fantasy his parents had created before he was even born, the fantasy fed to them all. She'd imagined that it was easier to have obvious imperfections, that it absolved him of the constant striving, but it was merely displaced. She thought of the girl she loved many miles away and wanted to be magnanimous and vulnerable; to explain to Moksh that none of them were who they pretended to be.

In the ocean that day, when she was twelve, it had been Moksh who had first yelled for help. After her parents had dragged her to shore, her mother pressing her wrist to check for a pulse, which was ridiculous because she was very much vomiting and alive, Anu had seen Moksh among the throng, and she'd hated him a little for his heroics. For knowing what she'd done, how bad it was, an unspeakable bad to falsely play the role of victim just to feel her mother clasp her arm so tight she left bruises, bruises that Anu had pressed for days.

Now she watched Moksh in the mirror and said nothing, did nothing but stare at his skeletal frame. Who is ever proud of their jealousy? No one. No one ever. In a job interview, when asked what your weakness is, no one says, "Well, I'm a hard worker but I'm a jealous person." Anu knew her jealousy was as stupid as it was fanged. She and Moksh wouldn't keep in touch, but she'd think of him from time to time, this person who had understood her.

They found their mothers sitting side by side on the floor of the bedroom. The women scrambled to their feet, like schoolgirls caught sharing secrets. Anu hoped that they might offer comfort without anyone needing to explain the need for it. All they had to do was look their children in the eyes to see what they required. It could be so easy, and for the briefest instant Anu caught a new expression on her mother's face, one she took for tenderness.

# Ruchi

## 1983

Moksh's cleft lip surgery was a success. In May 1975, a plastic surgeon stitched together flaps of muscle to fabricate her child's upper lip. Ruchi diligently cleaned out the gash as instructed. Each fix she thought of as a gash, a wound, an injury. "He'll be so handsome," Ammi said after the first surgery and again over the phone after she returned, her calls more frequent after each subsequent operation, the cleft palate after the lip, the jaw adjusted to better align with his nose, earlobes reconstructed. Then the calls fell away as Moksh healed, as years passed, as the baby turned one, then two. Then five, then six. Seven. The scars on his face faded but didn't disappear.

"Next year, we'll visit," Ruchi said, until she stopped saying it.

When she could, Deepa drove them out to the beach, to see how the second house was progressing. She laid out a blanket while Anu and Moksh played in parallel universes, lining up rocks or destroying separate sand towers. Behind them, the tall grass had been dug up, leaving a hole waiting to be filled. This, too, Ruchi thought of as a gash, or a toothless, gaping mouth. The house was taking years to construct. Deepa complained about the many permits and the difficulty of pouring a foundation into this mix of rocky, sandy sediment. Ruchi listened and hoped that the house might never be finished, that they could go on visiting the sad-looking beach on their own. Ruchi could console Deepa's disappointment. A disappointment to even things out.

WHEN HE WAS eight, Moksh found a condom in the seaweed. It was late February 1983, a rare day of above-freezing weather, the month Ruchi hated most, the longest though it was the shortest, never getting used to the unwavering cold. But the children knew only these Februarys. Moksh filled the condom with sand and threw it at Anu, hitting her upper lip.

"I'm so sorry," Ruchi said.

Anu didn't cry, despite the spreading red splotch at the corner of her mouth. She blinked and glanced at her mother.

"He didn't mean it," Deepa said. "They're friends, no?"

"Why aren't you careful, Mokshu?" Ruchi reproached. He stared at the seaweed and didn't respond. At school the children were mean. Ruchi knew this from the teachers, though Moksh never spoke of it. He told her he had many friends, though their mothers didn't call or invite him to parties. Only the pale, across-the-street neighbor's boy, Buddy Roland, ever asked him to play. Her ears went hot listening to them from the window. Buddy who won at Pitch and Toss, Buddy who declared which junked cars in his yard were off-limits and which were in play, Buddy, who himself was slack-chested and chubby, cheeks prickled with heat in the summer. Ruchi wished Moksh would speak up. Refuse. His reserve was self-protective, and a mirror of his father's.

Anu's lip had begun to swell. "I wish we had some ice," Ruchi said. She patted the girl's face with the corner of her scarf.

"She'll be fine," Deepa said. She picked up the filthy Latex weapon. "Ingenious, in its way," she said before discarding it in a pile of broken lumber. She shrugged. "He's a creative. You should encourage it."

"You'll curse the child with so much praise," Ruchi said. At night she warded off nazar, dotting Moksh's temple behind his ear with her eye pencil as Ammi had done to her. She wasn't sure what to make of

Deepa's praise for Moksh's castles and the odd collections he buried in the sand. As a toddler he'd pitched sand in Ruchi's eyes when she'd tried to teach him to swim, and Deepa had insisted he'd learn on his own, to quit pestering him.

With Anu, Deepa's attention was mixed. The child, being pretty, was more susceptible to the evil eye, yes, but Deepa treated her with both ambivalence and hawkish examination. She touched her child so little and was quick to withdraw her warmth, which to Ruchi felt familiar. Deepa decided when she and Ruchi would embrace in greeting and when they would nod, when Ruchi was allowed to lean against her while they sat shivering on a blanket on the shore and when she wasn't. At times, she watched Deepa with Moksh and felt she and Anu were relegated to the margins. Or maybe Deepa only pitied Moksh. Maybe she instructed Anu to be nice to him each time they met and wasn't worried about bari nazar or bad luck or any of it when it came to Moksh because who, really, envied him?

Ruchi squeezed Anu around the shoulders and smiled at her. "Brave girl," she said, feeling bad for Anu but not bad enough.

THAT NIGHT RUCHI lay with Moksh until he fell asleep, her head at his chest, their four feet poking out of the covers. He made shadows with his hands against the wall in the sliver of orange light from the cracked door.

"PJ always asks me to play first," Moksh said. "It's like they fight over me." PJ had spiky hair with a rattail in the back. She'd seen him at Open House, and he'd waved at her son, a limp, half-hearted wave that Moksh ignored, telling her later that if he gave PJ too much attention the other kids grew jealous of their friendship. He was that popular.

In the stories he painted himself as exceptional; that was the only difference other children noticed. He took a deep breath, performed the patience of a person weary of giving the same speech yet again. "I have to sit next to a different friend every day or else."

"Or else what?"

"Or else it's not fair. I have to be fair."

"Why is it not fair?"

"Because there's a girl who keeps track."

"Keeps track?"

"Makes notes!" he said, and kicked the sheet in exasperation. Lies, but no, they were stories. Creative stories. "Because I'm smart. The smartest one."

"Oh ho!"

Moksh paused. "Do you believe me?"

"Why wouldn't I believe you?"

"It's true."

"Of course."

He was quiet again, and then asked, "Are you angry? About what I did at the beach."

She wasn't expecting the question. "Why would I be angry? Mistakes happen."

"How do you know it was a mistake?"

Ruchi turned to her son in the dark. "Anu is a nice girl. You didn't mean it."

He considered this, then made a fist and gave it horns. "Do you have friends?"

"Auntie is my friend." It felt funny to say it like that. Baldly.

"Other friends." He ran his shadow bull in circles. "Like I have."

"Of course." Ruchi searched for something to say. What parties were any of them invited to? Besides that awkward lunch with the Rolands when they first arrived. Twice a trip to New Brunswick to meet Naren's cousin Nilesh, who bragged about his franchised gas stations.

"I have sisters," Ruchi said, though she rarely spoke to them.

"Sisters aren't friends. And they aren't here."

"I can tell you a story. About two nuns. They were such close friends that they made one person. They could step in and out of each other's skin and like that they became powerful. You never knew if you were talking to one nun or two and they terrorized us. You must be careful with friendship."

The ball of his fist he ate with his other hand. Ruchi felt silly about the story, like she'd ruined this time in the half dark that she looked forward to. She should've told him the one he liked best, a version of the three little pigs but saying "dadhi" for beard and "udavido" for blowing the house down. Moksh laughed at the words, a language he understood but didn't speak. She made the third pig sound like Ammi when she berated fruit sellers who gave her the wrong change, calling them the sons of jerks who slept with their sisters-in-law.

Other stories she enhanced. Revised. She told him how Draupadi herself made her sari endless. She told him that Radha was Krishna's aunt. She told him about the mischievous topiary in Hanging Gardens and that in Bombay Harbor the buried bodies of goddesses thrummed in the mud. Her chawl she made a castle and her father's dry goods shop an export business. Moksh questioned her but also took in every word as truth, like she'd never lie to him. Ruchi knew in a few years he wouldn't listen like this, or believe that she believed him. Every day it slipped away a little. The teachers said she must read to him but instead she did this.

"Are you and Dad friends?"

The question flew at her. That his father was "Dad" had never felt right in her mouth. At least she remained "Ma." "Yes, in a way."

"But when do you talk?"

"Nonsense. We talk." But he was right. "I can tell you another story. About him."

"Dad? Okay," he said and separated his hands, the shadows retreating to their corners. She could just distinguish the curled edges of the drawings he brought home. Boxes and triangles and menacing lines, the violence of his coloring.

"In an earlier life Papa was a fish. Like Matsya, part fish, part human."

"What's Matsya?" He stuck his finger into the space between her wrist and her bangles. When she was his age she'd known that Matsya was the avatara of Vishnu who saves the Vedas from the ocean. She thought of her form books, her beautiful script, all the things she'd memorized.

"A famous fish. It doesn't matter," she said. "A beautiful fish with a top fin like the thinnest, most precious of silks."

"Silk wouldn't be like that in the water."

"How do you know?"

"Like when my shirt gets wet it's heavy."

"Your shirt is not silk."

"Oh." He tucked his hands behind his head, a rare moment of stillness. Her foot rested on his foot. It didn't make sense because he was the shortest in his class and though she was also short, he only came up to her hip. Yet they could lie like this and magically she could put her foot on his foot while their temples touched. Just before sleep they became the same size.

"He had beautiful scales that glittered every color. He didn't know what to do with all the looks he got."

"Looks from who?"

"What? The other fish. Who else will look at a fish?"

Moksh giggled, but she'd meant it seriously. Naren was in the other room lying down and he'd likely forget to say good night, a new habit.

"He liked to wander in the darkest part of the ocean."

"Why? Why the darkest part?"

"Because he didn't want to be seen. He didn't want all that attention." They were so close and yet all she could see of Moksh in the dark was a gray impression.

"It was embarrassing for him, right?"

Was that it? Embarrassment? "A little. But also, he was protecting himself. From others. From always being noticed."

"Okay, okay." He prodded her. "So then?"

She'd intended to tell a different story, one about Birbal and Akbar and a farmer who bought a well from a rich man who didn't let him use the water. Always Birbal had answers and was witty and all-knowing while Akbar was fumbling but still king. She disliked Birbal and thought Moksh might too. But here she was telling this other story, and she'd come to a river and hadn't yet built the bridge.

"So then he meets another fish in the dark and they can't see each other but he senses that the fish is struggling to breathe."

"Injured."

"By a hook. It had gotten away but from the way the fish was breathing—"

"How can he hear this? Fish have gills." At parent-teacher conference his second grade teacher had said that Moksh tended to criticize. He argued with kids who liked Spiderman above Batman, because Spiderman was unrealistic. "He's very literal," the teacher had said grimly, and Naren had nodded as if she'd revealed a special secret about their son. But the teacher didn't understand; Moksh simply didn't want to be duped.

"You can still hear. It sounds like boiling water."

He waited.

"By the sound he could tell the fish was losing blood quickly. But Papa had an idea about how to help this fish because he didn't like seeing things suffer. He was, even then, a worrier.

"His silky fins, these he tore off and gave to the dying fish to stop the bleeding. They were magical that way, these fins. They had powers, but he didn't like to use them."

"But then Dad the fish was bleeding?" She heard the lift in his voice, a concern, a hope. His father as hero.

"Yes, now Papa was bleeding. And he let it happen, he let all the blood pour out and it did in so many colors in the darkest part of the ocean and then he died and was born as your father."

"Reborn."

"Reborn. Reborn."

The ending was rushed and nonsensical, but it folded the boy into his thoughts.

SUMMER ARRIVED, AND Buddy, their neighbor, went to 4-H, Anu to Country Kids, where they had whole days of wiffle ball and trips to ponds and yarn-related crafts. Activities Ruchi had never known as a child, a surfeit of choices, like all the different cereals at Stop & Shop that overwhelmed her. Deepa claimed camp was good for their social development, and Ruchi said Moksh was too young, though eight was old enough. It wasn't the money, though it was also that. At least at home she could feed her child; at camp he'd never eat. She liked that the summers stretched out like a blank of days, cloudless and open. She liked being a mother best when she and Moksh were alone and it didn't matter what anyone else thought of him, how he compared or to whom.

In the noon heat, she fed him while he read a creased Batman comic at the kitchen table. Moksh ate best when distracted. She cut up sandwiches into small bites, though the pediatrician said long ago that this was unnecessary. "Children at this age are finicky. It's normal. If they don't eat, they don't eat." It made no sense, American parenting with its overexuberant affection next to this lack of care. So what if Ruchi continued for a few more months? Or another year? They were not like the Americans who let their children cry in dark rooms alone. She brought the food to his lips and waited for him to part them.

"I don't like Fluff and peanut butter," he said, and hunched over a panel in which Batman pushed a man into a furnace. It was the hottest day of the summer so far, and the standing fan blew a pleading whir of stale breeze in their faces.

"Mokshu. It's so tasty."

"It sticks to all my teeth."

"You can have milk with it," she said, but he pushed her hand away.

"Water," he said, and gulped down the glass she handed him. Some dribbled down his chin and into the collar of his shirt. She couldn't tell if he was doing it on purpose.

"Take one bite then one sip. One bite, one sip," she said cheerfully.

He did as he was told before beginning the comic again. She wanted to wipe the thread of fluff from his lips but held back. In the heat, the kitchen felt smaller and the air cloying and thick. Every year she hated the wallpaper more.

"See how Batman disappears? He can't make himself invisible. He's just fast."

"Hmm," she said, and slipped him a bite of bread.

He flipped through the pages. "You don't *need* superpowers."

"No, dikra, you don't."

"Superheroes are just freaks. Regular freaks."

Ruchi's stomach turned at the words. He took two sips of water and the smallest bite. "This is true," she said to keep him talking.

She tried a corner with crust, but he kept his mouth shut and stroked the celluloid scar that ran along his jaw and refused to fade. She hated when he brought attention to it.

"Like me," he said.

"Don't talk like that."

He had eaten maybe half the sandwich. The bread had hardened, but she would make sure he finished it later after she'd given him the milk he didn't want and the cucumbers cut into gum-sized cubes. Through the afternoon, she'd serve him yogurt and raisins and crackers that he liked to soak in her milky cha until they were on the verge of disintegrating.

He mumbled, "I want more toes."

"How many more?"

"Like a hundred million."

"Oh. Okay."

"With so many toes I'll be fast."

She didn't say it didn't make sense. She didn't push him because she didn't want him to return to his habit of tracing his scars. She could hear Deepa in her mind. *Pestering, pestering.* "Yes, dikra, you'll be so fast."

"No, I wouldn't." He was watching her and deciding whether to be kind, whether to be cruel. "I wouldn't be fast. I'd still need more legs. I'm not hungry anymore."

He pushed the table with his feet.

"But you have to finish the sandwich."

"I don't want it. I don't want any more."

"Dikra, please."

"You can't make me."

"I'll make something else. With butter and jam."

But he was already running out of the room, the pads of his feet kicking up behind him.

~

ON WEEKENDS, NAREN walked around the patchy growth of their yard, sweeping his palms over the wispy stalks. He seeded twice a year, chasing off dogs and squirrels with a shoe. He complained about the trees, the lack of sunlight, but Ruchi refused to let him chop them down, for which he punished her with silence, taking to his bed, pointing out the tall grass that grew wild around the used cars and engine pieces sprawled across the Rolands' yard. "They do nothing to deserve such a lawn," he said. It was true, and still, their witchy shoots raced to the sky every spring. She didn't tell him that when Moksh pulled out rare clumps of grass she did nothing to stop him. She hurried around her husband, straining with false cheer.

Anything could trigger Naren's spells. The lawn was one. A snubbing from Newhouse another. Some stupidity in the news. Letters from Anoj, photos of Sarika looking young and plump and their two miracle children, a son soon after Moksh and a daughter two years later. Every month Naren remitted money, which Anoj never acknowledged in the letters.

This summer, there was no savings. Naren had traded in the Nova for a used blue Cutlass Cruiser with wood paneling, but with savings they could've bought a second car, a new one. They could've grown their money until they no longer had to think about it, its plenty making money disappear from their minds.

The account at People's, the account at First County, at Shawmut. Why they had to have three accounts she didn't know, but none of them had enough. The principal on the house was frightening; how much they owed. And yet he kept spending. Accumulating more items they didn't need. For months they wouldn't buy juice and then one day they had boxes of juice stored in the basement, rolls and rolls of paper towels when she'd been stretching out a single sheet by rinsing and air-drying until finally it tore. One day he came home with a back massager, an unwieldy stick like a cricket bat with lumps that rotated under its skin, and for a time they took turns using it after dinner. She understood that it was hard to know what to buy, what would be used once and never again. She didn't say anything about the many pairs of sneakers, all of them on sale, the extra milk that was half price that she knew would go bad, the costume jewelry she didn't wear, the lawn equipment that made no difference. At least the dresses she could return. Last Christmas he'd put up a plastic tree, their first, and smuggled in so many presents she'd found bits of wrapping months later in the shag carpet.

Did she prefer it to the bad moods? Perhaps. Even the freckles scattered across his nose deepened during those times. She watched how the moods overtook him and wormed through his skin. She thought of him as wired through with electric currents that crossed and trapped each other, alternating between worry and excitement. When they crashed, he snapped and slept. She was surprised by how used to it she'd become, to this marriage she thought might get her what she wanted.

"INVESTMENTS," NAREN SAID as June turned to July. "We're in our thirties and should have investments by now." They sat on separate couches watching *Three's Company* reruns while at their feet Moksh, who would be nine in November, played with marbles. They were within an arm's distance of each other in the small room, and yet unreachable. Ruchi blamed the heat, reminiscent of the heat back home, the carpet shag catching between her toes.

"What investments?" Ruchi asked. The wood frame of the couch pushed on her back through the sunken cushion. "Please don't say the lawn. You've done enough investment there."

"Ere, no, no. Real investments."

Moksh named the marbles after friends he didn't have. The light of the television bounced off his face but he took no interest in the show, in Jack Tripper or the women or the neighbors who knocked all day on their door. "What real investments?" Ruchi asked.

"We are baniya, are we not? This country is for businesspeople like us."

"Hmm." She wanted to bend down and listen to Moksh play. She was waiting for night, the dark bedroom, their stories.

"On Route 5 is a motel for sale. We can look at it."

"How would we buy a whole motel?"

"It's an investment, didn't I tell you? Franchise! Borrow the money! Look at Nilesh in New Brunswick with his stations. Doing so well. Look at your friend and that ugly land on the ocean. This will be better."

Quietly, she said, "Already we have borrowed so much. For the house." They watched the program in silence. Jack in his apron, washing dishes, Cindy's birthday. The cake a disaster. Then a commercial, a Chevy at sunset riding up a dirt road to a mountaintop. Ruchi couldn't read from Naren's wrinkled brow whether the topic was closed or brewing.

To Moksh, Naren asked, "What are you doing?" It was a question he rarely posed to their son, like Moksh wasn't made of thoughts, just body.

Moksh eyed a marble at close range. "War and destruction."

"Aren't we watching TV?"

"I'm watching," Moksh said, but he didn't look up.

"You don't look like you're watching. Come sit here. Why to sit on the floor and watch?"

"But there's nothing good."

"Leave him, no?" Ruchi said.

"You do all this with these silly glass balls?" Naren prodded one with his toe.

"Stop. You're messing up the game. That one's hiding."

The commercials kept coming. Uncle Ben's Rice then Pepsi then Wendy's. Naren prodded another marble. His toenail caught the ball and launched it toward the fireplace. "And this one? Hiding?"

She followed the arc but the carpet swallowed it. Moksh turned around, shadows deep under his eyes.

"You're mean. All you like is TV."

"It's a game, no? Now this one is hiding. Now this one is in the ocean."

She saw his eyes flicker, amused. She took his cue. "See, Mokshu, that one might be a fish in the deepest part of the ocean."

"Where it's too dark to see," Naren said.

Moksh turned to her and then him, surprised that they were playing with him together. She was ashamed by his surprise, and the trace of discomfort. The program was back on. Jack puckering up for a kiss. But Naren had also lost interest. "Oh, he must be looking for safety."

"Where the hooks can't get him," Moksh said and smiled at her.

First Naren, then Ruchi, joined him on the floor. From the corner of her eye, she watched Naren balance on an elbow, the muscles of his face moving. He took a speckled gold marble between his thumb and forefinger and bit down. "This one is real."

THE MOTEL PROPERTY was abandoned, storm pipes choked with leaves, weeds snaked through the cracked concrete, doors loose on their hinges. They walked around the perimeter like thieves, peeking through cracked windows. Fifteen rooms in all. The lobby seemed to extend into what might be living quarters.

"Are we moving here?" Moksh asked. "I could have a different room every night."

"Like a palace!" Naren said. "You'll have a palace!"

"Everything is broken," Ruchi said. She ran her fingers along a splintered windowsill. Naren straightened a porch lamp and the chipped black number five beneath it. He stood back to assess his work.

"Broken things can be fixed," he said.

"Ere, who knows how to fix all these things?" she said but watched Moksh skipping across the shared patios.

"I'm an engineer, no?" Naren said, moving on to the overgrown grass in front of the rooms. "Enough here for a pool." A foggy vision quivered in her mind, despite her effort to suppress it: Naren tending the lobby while she chatted with guests by the inground pool. The Mehtas' Howard Johnson or Motel 6 or Super 8. A visit from the cousin. A letter to Ammi and another to Anoj with photos of the property. Ruchi's karak cha served next to coffee in the mornings. She and Deepa shopping for linens and making beds. Touching. The long stretch of rooms. All the secret places.

On the way home, Naren let Moksh sit in the way back of the Cutlass and didn't complain that he couldn't see through the rearview.

When she said she needed to pick up groceries at Stop & Shop, he didn't insist on the bigger, newer Edward's with its unfamiliar aisles. He followed with the cart, his steps light, teasing her for needing to check every aisle for deals. "What difference is fifty cents?"

"Fifty cents," she said, and her husband chuckled. She hoped Moksh was watching from where he stood on the lip of the cart. His parents could be friends. Naren gave him coupons to fetch items and didn't scold him when he brought the wrong brand, just discreetly returned the item when they passed the spot.

"Pick up two gallons of milk, next to the eggs. The ones with the blue top," Naren said.

"Two is too heavy. How will he bring them?" she asked. She'd meant the question kindly but sounded shrill.

"I can do it," Moksh said, and skipped off down the aisle. Ruchi saw how shoppers, in their efforts to be polite, made their discomfort more obvious. She stamped down her anger, flames she talked about with no one.

"One at a time," Naren called.

"Go with him, no? In case he can't manage," she said.

"He'll manage," Naren said.

She didn't want to argue. The milk was in the back corner of the store next to a wall of freezers.

"I'll be back. We need one more cereal," she said.

"You're following him," Naren said. "Let him do it on his own." A pinch crept into his voice. She pretended not to hear.

She spotted Moksh searching gallons for the right one. In profile, in the flat light, his face was worn out. Skin kneaded too long. He heaved a blue-top gallon from the second shelf and stumbled. He bit his top lip and reached for the second.

"Ere, let me help you," she said.

He turned his head and dropped the second gallon. It crashed on the eggs, gold yolk and white shells spattering his shirt, his face. Milk puddled at his feet and soaked his sneakers. He stood with his arms akimbo. The lights seemed to flash, and the hum of freezers and carts halted. Everyone stared.

Naren appeared beside her. He yanked the boy's shoulder, and when the child's body snapped and bumped against the metal shelf, she felt it in the small of her back. "Didn't I say one at a time?" His voice ricocheted off the ceiling. People turned away, afraid of rolling their carts too close. Ruchi saw the shift in Moksh's eyes, saw him shut himself inside.

# Deepa

## 1984

In March 1984, an Indian grocery opened in East Hartford, and Deepa took Ruchi shopping. The weather had turned warmer overnight, and Deepa ditched her heavy coat for a checked blazer over jeans to highlight the skinny blue belt around her waist. She was thirty-four and wore the same size as ten years ago, and lately, other wives asked for her secret. But when Ruchi opened the door to step out of her house, it struck Deepa that it was her friend who really hadn't changed. Ruchi wore the same pilled cardigan over her salwar kameez, her bare feet in chappals, brows unkempt. Straightforward, unpolished toenails. Forthright and plain if not for her unruly hair that grew thicker over time. Sindoor still dyed her part and her mother's gold bangles jangled at her wrists. Deepa wanted to hug her but didn't step out of the car. They were friends who could slip out and back in each other's lives with little effort or acknowledgment. Deepa stared out her driver's side window at the house across the street. The neighbor had added more cars to their junkyard.

"Such a mess," Deepa said.

"The husband uses them for parts. Something like that. But do you see how green their lawn is? Naren is always jealous."

Deepa felt the dead headlights watching her. Making her feel small, like she didn't deserve the things she had. "Nothing there to be jealous of."

"They aren't so bad."

"Oh, there must be something."

"Marlene works at a salon in TriCity Plaza. The husband works at Pratt and Whitney and on weekends he makes his son drag all this junk onto their perfect lawn. You can smell the liquor if the windows are open."

"A shame."

"Marlene is always shouting at him. 'Ran! Ran!'"

"Ran?"

"His name." They both giggled. Marlene. Deepa had seen her once, coaxing multicolored cats to her front stoop.

They pulled in to a small lot. INDIAN PACKAGE STORE read a temporary sign.

"Could they not give the shop a more creative name?" Ruchi asked.

"In this country, naming can lead to lawsuits." Deepa learned this from Sonal Mansingh, the doctor's wife who hosted games of teen patti and then scowled when Deepa won most of the hands.

"Marlene says she'll give my name if there's an opening at the salon," Ruchi said.

"Salon? But you never learned how to properly do your own eyebrows. How will you do other people's nails?"

"Why not? I can learn, no?"

Marlene. A friend. The thought made Deepa shudder. "All those dirty feet. Chi." She wanted to say something mean, how Ruchi would never be an exacting beautician.

"I need some work," Ruchi said.

"There are so many other jobs."

"They don't want me."

"Don't be negative," Deepa said. She didn't know what to do with Ruchi's sadness except to neutralize it. She didn't know how to offer comfort except as criticism. She hated this Marlene.

They scrutinized the dusty offerings inside. Boxed masalas, Parachute Coconut Oil, Haldiram snacks. Deepa directed Ruchi's attention to the bhindi, picking through for the softest ladyfingers. Ruchi weighed the plastic bag as she filled it to make sure she didn't pay for more than a pound.

They spoke to the checkout clerk in Hindi. He leered at them like they were back home. Deepa tracked the tally as he rang up each item. She added up the numbers in her head. "All together?" he asked.

"Yes," Deepa said before Ruchi could speak.

"What are you doing?"

Deepa didn't answer. She gave the clerk her card, and he took the imprint. It was more than she'd planned to spend but she folded the receipt without reviewing it, as if she didn't care whether the total was correct. She wanted Ruchi to thank her, but no thanks came. Ruchi held the plastic bag full of fresh bhindi and stared at her feet. The money was nothing, Deepa wanted to say, but the money was also everything.

"TEACH ME," RUCHI said, loading the groceries into the trunk.

"What teach you?"

"Naren is always too tired on weekends. I should know how to drive." Of course this was true. She should. It was astounding she'd managed for twelve years without knowing. It was astounding that she'd never asked before.

"It's not so simple. There's the insurance to think of for one," Deepa said, though she didn't care about this.

"I'm sure you would be a superb teacher."

Deepa flushed. "Musca muth maar."

"What flattery? It's true."

But Ruchi was right. Deepa was good at guiding. Every month new couples and families arrived. People who needed advice. A community. How to buy a car, how to mow a lawn, how to prepare your child for picture day. Where to buy sofa sets. Dining sets. Back home, they wouldn't have known each other, all of them busy being daughters-in-law. Maybe Deepa would've liked it, distinguishing herself among the other daughters-in-law, climbing the social ladder of daughters-in-law, learning abuse from their mothers-in-law. Or maybe her father's failures and her mother's sadness would have clung to her, a long shadow at all hours. Maybe the only way for Deepa to be someone was to make herself new again and again.

She turned to Ruchi. "Here," she said, handing Ruchi the keys. "Try."

"Now?"

"Why not?"

From the passenger seat, Deepa mimed how Ruchi should position her hands, how to adjust the seat, the mirrors. She told her to tie back her hair. "You have to pay attention to every last thing around you," she said and cleared a strand from Ruchi's eyes on impulse, the hair always softer and lighter than it looked. Lightning quick, Deepa tucked the strand into a silver clip above Ruchi's ear. She was struck by her own giddiness, by the lift it gave her, this simple thing. "Oh, Ruch," she said. "You have to turn the ignition."

Twice Ruchi ran stoplights. A blue pickup honked as she changed lanes without signaling. She zigzagged and pressed the accelerator in quick spurts. It could've ended in tragedy, but Deepa maintained a steady, even-toned encouragement. She played hits from the most recent films, cassettes Sonal had recorded for her. "Har Kisi Ko Nahin Milta" and "Sach Mere Yaar Hai" and "Woh Kagaz Ki Kashti." The same playback singer, Lata Mangeshkar, from their youth, who was now middle-aged and hunched, dubbed most of the songs, though Deepa preferred her sister with the huskier, thicker voice.

*We can be together like this.* She was being kind, helping her friend become independent, fighting against what she worried she was: a nakali, a faltoo, a phony.

THROUGH SPRING, DEEPA taught Ruchi how to pull into a parking space, how to perform a K-turn. Parallel park and merge onto a highway. "No hesitation!" she called out. Her friend relaxed into the seat, deftly managed the steering, confidently switched lanes, one hand on the gear stick, her flashy bangles running up and down her arms as she turned.

They went to the library to drop off their children's overdue books, first Deepa's town and then Ruchi's, where the library was smaller, older. She saw Ruchi checking out her own books mixed in with Moksh's.

"Oh ho, still so studious, are you?" Deepa teased, but her face went hot when she saw the embossed titles. *Once More with Feeling, Come Love Me, Night of Possession.* Covers of women with half-closed eyes, romances Deepa never considered picking up.

"To pass the time," Ruchi said. The back of her hand brushed Deepa's as she slipped the books into her tote.

They took long routes that Deepa never took with Sanjay, winding, inconvenient roads through tobacco farms and cornfields. Deepa continued to pay for anything they bought, told Ruchi she should spend the money Naren gave her on new clothes but knew she would probably save it for bills. Deepa liked the appearance of generosity though in the back of her mind she kept track of each dollar spent, each tip, each school donation, a part of her always on alert for the first sign of money running dry.

When Ruchi mentioned Moksh's struggle to tie his shoes ("Should he not know by now?") or the crumbs he refused to wipe from his face or his love of disasters ("He only draws tornadoes") or the children who made fun of him, or his thinness, always his thinness, Deepa slapped her own thighs. "We are not mothers right now. We are not."

"But Deepa."

"No!" she bellowed.

Gossip was better. The anesthesiologist with the gambling problem. His wife who couldn't carry a tune. "But every time she sings! Full songs! The entirety of *Amar, Akbar, Anthony*!" Deepa exclaimed.

"Poor thing. At least she's enjoying herself," Ruchi said.

"What enjoying herself? For forty-five minutes the rest of us suffer."

Ruchi giggled. "Tejas's husband is having some problem with flatulence. She sleeps in a separate room."

"Ha! Your gori-gori sister who everyone thought would marry rich."

"Ammi says Tejas stopped eating cakes because she thinks the icing is made from cow byproduct. That his pooting is punishment for not being a good Hindu."

"Stupidity," Deepa said. "When most people are only this much Hindu." She gestured an inch with her thumb and forefinger. "At least Indira Gandhi isn't into all the haltoo-faltoo saffron flag-waving."

"She's no saint. Ammi said the one Sikh family in the chawl moved out." They were stopped at a light in front of Rein's Deli where the Americans bought too-salty sandwiches.

"Turn onto Stage Road, no?"

"It's getting late," Ruchi said.

But Deepa wasn't ready to go home. "What do you have to do? School won't be out for hours." Deepa pressed the button to roll down her window and a chill shocked her face. The sunshine was a liar.

Stage Road narrowed as it wound through the hills, past the mountain where people went skiing. Deepa didn't understand a pastime that required feeling cold. On the road were patches of white where spring buds had fallen. They rose into the air when Ruchi drove through them, then chased the exhaust, as if in celebration.

"You could take the test, Ruch. You'd pass," Deepa said, feeling generous and kind.

"You think so?"

"You drive better than Sanjay." She mimicked her husband clenching the steering wheel in two hands, his shoulders to his ears.

"Naren hardly knows how to change lanes. 'Can I go? Can I go?' 'Go,' I have to say!"

It felt good, the distance this teasing placed between herself and her shiny, cold marriage, between Ruchi and her dim, sad one.

"What happened to the salon? To Marlene's big promise?"

"Nothing," Ruchi said.

"You can't depend on them. The goras." She wanted to keep the mood, the looseness that had overtaken them, the ease. "We should have a culture center. Like what they have in New Jersey. New York.

A little South Asia. Weekly gatherings. Bollywood movie nights. Hindi lessons for the kids. A threading salon. That kind of thing."

"But who will they speak Hindi to?"

"What does it matter. They'll learn. Don't they teach Latin in school?" Deepa said. "I'll start it."

"Call it something interesting at least. Like 'Desi Spot.'"

"Or 'Bolly Masala.'"

"Or 'Chaat Mix.'"

"That's very good."

"You can join me," Deepa said casually. "Once it's open. We can be partners."

"What kind of partners?"

"A business, Ruch."

"What do we know about business?"

"What is there to know? You want a job, no?"

"It doesn't even exist, your cultural center. Your movie nights. First finish your beach house, no?"

"The house is almost done." Deepa felt the ease slipping.

"You never take me anymore."

"I want it to be a surprise," Deepa said. "In any case, you should be more enterprising. We'll make this center. You'll see." Ruchi was silent, as if cataloging all the promises Deepa had never kept.

A tight curve and the car crossed the yellow lines. "There's something else Ammi told me," Ruchi said. "Sister Braganza, the nun with the long face. She died."

"Died?"

"Ammi said she killed herself." Her voice was flat and her gaze was unbroken.

Deepa froze. Ruchi went on. Something about pills or suffocation, about how the nuns were found in the wooden house where they'd been allowed to stay despite dwindling enrollment, the body two days rotted. She didn't ask Ruchi how her mother knew this.

"And Sister Ferrao?" Deepa asked.

"The story is that she held the body until someone forced her off. That she wanted to keep a finger as a relic."

"No." But she saw the dead finger in the sister's hand. "But why—" She stopped. She didn't want to hear it. "Why do you need to bring up such old things?" The air became leaden, despite the open window. The dead nun was there with them, clambering between the front and back seats, binding their memories together.

"I miss it. The school. Home. The rains," Ruchi said.

"It rains plenty here, too."

"Don't you miss it?"

"I have no time to miss it." She sensed Ruchi's hand on the gearshift, how close it was to her knee. That Deepa could, with little effort, trap the hand. She stared out the window as if all her attention wasn't on the phantom contact, as if the skin of her knee wasn't straining to feel through the fabric. "Pull over up there," she said, pointing to the shoulder by a cornfield. Not a car had passed them.

"Why?"

"Ere, Ruch, just do it. Look, the corn is fresh." Deepa felt herself scrambling, trying to keep something alive. The corn. She pictured them trespassing, stealing cobs, shucking and eating the raw kernels. They could poke more fun at their husbands, think of more ridiculous names.

"With Sanjay," Ruchi said, her voice low and close, "how is it?"

"Oh, fine, fine. He's always busy."

"No, not that." Ruchi sighed and turned off the ignition. "I'm not talking about that."

"Oh." Deepa paused.

"It's always been strange with Naren," Ruchi said in a voice that inched closer though she hadn't moved. Her hand was still there, waiting. "Why is that? I thought it would be different. That I would feel something more. He's not a bad man, despite his moods, his spending. I thought, with time, I'd learn how to. But something is wrong. It's always been wrong."

The day could still be fine if they focused on the happy stalks of corn, the seared sky. "With Sanjay it's normal. Fully normal," Deepa said, her voice foreign in her ears. "You have to try harder."

She stepped out of the car and over the damp ground to the corn, which was just above her head. She could keep walking to the center of the field, crushing stalks until she was lost. She tore off two heads that looked young and sweet and shucked as she walked back.

"Here," she said.

"I'm not hungry."

"I don't know why you still wear sindoor if marriage is so bad."

Ruchi touched her part, the wide red road in her hair. "I don't know either. No reason."

"I don't believe you," Deepa said, hating the nuns all over again for leading their conversation astray. "Don't look so sad. All you have to do is study for the written test, make an appointment. I'll help."

Ruchi tucked a strand of hair behind her ear and turned the ignition. Deepa bit into the white cob but it was sour. They drove back to Ruchi's house, and into their silence Lata Mangeshkar sang of far-off rains.

IT HAPPENED SO fast. Deepa's body lurched forward then slammed back into the seat, followed by the crash of glass shattering.

"Oh my God," Ruchi said. "I thought I signaled."

A small red car had clipped their taillight as they pulled into Ruchi's driveway. Deepa hadn't taught Ruchi to look behind her when she was moving forward, having never understood the need to do so herself.

"Deepa, the car," Ruchi said, breathless.

"It's fine."

"How is it fine?"

"I'll say I was driving. The insurance doesn't have to know. Is this some neighbor?" Deepa kept her voice even, though she felt a rushing in her head.

The red car had reversed so that it blocked the driveway. It could've been junk from the neighbor's yard, dented and misused. A man stepped out of it, and when he slammed the door, Deepa thought it might fall off the hinge.

"I've never seen him before," Ruchi said. "But we don't know all the neighbors."

"He was for sure speeding," Deepa said. The man examined his headlight, stringy blond hair to his shoulders, delicate, thin-rimmed glasses, a sleeveless shirt meant for summer. They could see his chest through the armholes, so thin it curved like a spoon. He walked up to Ruchi's window and knocked. When she rolled down the pane, the smell of smoke wafted off his papery skin. His eyes were pink-rimmed and swimming in their sockets but still young-looking, like a new bird's.

"What the fuck was that? My headlight's bashed." He reached in through the window, unlocked the door, opened it, and stepped aside, the way chivalrous men did at malls.

"You can't do that," Deepa said, and rushed out the passenger side, chewing the inside of her cheek. "Our car is also damaged."

The man swayed a little and Deepa had an urge to steady him. "I'm not paying shit," he said. "You didn't signal."

"I was going so slowly," Ruchi said.

Deepa stepped toward the man. "I'll call the police."

"Call the cops! Call the cops!" the man hollered and whooped. "You won't. This bitch is all nervous."

"I'm not nervous," Ruchi said. "Why should I be nervous?"

"We can call it an accident. Let the insurance pay," Deepa offered.

"Fuck the insurance."

Deepa felt a kick in her body, below her ribs. She put her hand there, the way she had when Anu would kick and she'd hold her heel, a round lump covered in her skin. But this was just her own organs, blood pumping through places unknown. She looked to Ruchi's neighbor's house across the street and thought she saw a curtain rustle at the window. No, she would not let Marlene come out to save them. She began rooting around in her purse for her wallet.

But the man had fixed his eyes on Ruchi's wrists. The gold bangles glinted in the gaudy sun.

"Take these," Ruchi said. The man stared.

"Ruch, don't."

"Ere, why not?"

"I have money," Deepa said to the man.

"There's no need for your money," Ruchi said.

"How do I know they aren't fake?" the man asked but eyed the bands.

Ruchi tried to force them over her knuckles. Metal pushed against bone. The hand that moments ago Deepa had wanted to mark with her nails. "They're too tight." She held out her arm and the man cupped the bangles with his index finger and thumb and tore them off, leaving a raw, red trail. He held them proudly in his palm.

Deepa could've hit him. "Get out of here now. Go and don't bother us again."

"My cousin lives up the street," the man said. The air had gone out of him.

"Then you pretend you don't know us. You pretend we're strangers." She could smell his shame. The way his pupils jittered. The ache in the red lines, even as he placed the bangles in his front pocket. She recognized it, a person who knew he had gone too far. Her badness was a mass thumping inside her, one she tried to dress up in different clothes. A petty, slippery badness that wanted good things.

The man drove off in his rattling car. "I'm sorry," Deepa whispered, and she meant it.

Ruchi shook her head and her empty arms. "I don't mind. I never liked them."

But you could hate a thing and still mourn it. As Ruchi stepped into her house she looked lost. Lost and free.

# Ruchi

## *1984*

The Jains' first beach party, a housewarming in August 1984, was a modest affair compared to the others that would follow it. Ruchi chose the salwar kameez Ammi had brought that she'd never had occasion to wear. Sky blue with filigree up the collar and a dark-blue dupatta for contrast. Ammi used to say light colors always made you lighter. Ruchi ironed the salwar pleats into rigid sails. She'd be thirty-four in December and felt anxious as a girl.

"Ere, no one will see your pleats under your kameez," Naren said. He watched from the doorway. "The invitation said two thirty," he added.

"Don't hurry me. No one arrives on time." She plucked stray hairs from her brow before smoothing the Revlon foundation she'd started wearing over her face and neck. She wanted to look right for this first party at the new house. She was sure Deepa would ferry her from group to group until everyone in her ever-growing social circle knew her. Ruchi had made a custard salad to share.

She managed to delay until five minutes to three. On the hour-long drive to the coast, Naren took the wrong exit and drove two miles down the wrong road before turning around. In her visor mirror,

Ruchi watched Moksh stare out the window and bite at the scar above his upper lip. He was nine now, nearly ten, small and quiet and quick to frown. "I've packed you a bathing suit," she said. "All the children will be swimming."

"What swim," Naren said. "Why to insist? When does he swim?"

Moksh's heels punched her back through the seat. "No."

She kept her tone light and airy, like a rising soap bubble. "You might want to dip your feet in."

Her husband gestured to the flat gray clouds overhead. The late August day carried a damp chill. "For sure rain." Ruchi turned up the song playing in the background and sang in an off-key falsetto.

They parked last in a line of cars that hugged the sidewalk and made their way up the walk. Ruchi balanced the aluminum tray of custard salad in one hand and worried she hadn't made enough.

The finished house was nothing like what Ruchi had imagined. From Deepa's talk of color swatches and tiles, Ruchi had expected a brightly painted bungalow, blue, or maybe yellow, with a covered terrace on the second floor, like those of Bollywood stars in Juhu Beach back home. Something stout and happy like a cake. But the Jains' beach house was bone-colored with gaping windows and a severely sloping roof, just like all the other houses in the contemporary style that seemed to be what everyone favored these days. The only color came from the red crepe myrtles planted along the pathway that led to the front door. The landscape beds were filled with glossy white stones that Moksh scooped up and littered across the path. Ruchi swept them back the best she could with her foot.

A welcome mat greeted them at the door, a multicolored straw weaving of "Home is Where the Heart Is." She could smell freshly fried pakoras. Laughter and splashing drifted from the beach at the rear. Naren pressed the doorbell, releasing the first bar of "Take Me Out to the Ball Game." Inside, voices continued uninterrupted.

"They didn't hear," Naren said.

She nudged him with her hip to stop him from pressing the button again. "They'll come."

"What 'they'll come'?"

"You don't ring twice."

A woman with shiny orange lips opened the door. A block of white teeth. Probably the wife of one of Sanjay's colleagues. The woman's pink sleeveless shirt clung to her leggings. In one hand she palmed a plate with a swirl of chutneys and extended a long, waxed arm. "Sonal."

The hand was both warm and cold, like a stone heated on one side by the sun.

Two flies buzzed in and out of a frosted glass chandelier. Shoes formed a pond on the white marble floor. "Deepa's classmate," Ruchi said to explain herself.

"How lovely! School friends from home."

Ruchi blushed. She hadn't seen Deepa since the accident in May, after which Deepa said she was too busy with the beach house and the onslaught of décor decisions to give more driving lessons.

Ruchi tried to match Sonal's smile as she stepped aside and pushed her son forward. "This is our Moksh."

Sonal touched the boy's palm. She kept the smile, but her eyelids fluttered.

The house was full of strangers. Ruchi felt helpless as Sonal ushered them into the kitchen and hurried off for the host. Women perched on wicker barstools turned in their direction. Others sat in the open living room balancing paper plates on their laps, playing cards, and sipping from jeweled tumblers.

Unlike the outside of the house, the kitchen was lovely. What was decorative had a purpose: a basket for napkins, a tightly woven rug by the sink, a magnetic strip for gleaming knives. Someone complimented the nautical backsplash, a mosaic of sailboats and starfish. Tiles Ruchi would've passed over in a catalog as overpriced and dull.

Deepa took the tray and said, "There was no need." She wore a gauzy shift that showed off her teardrop calves and the outline of a lizard-green one-piece.

"See," said Naren. "I told you. There's too much food."

"Don't be silly. It's wrong to come empty-handed." Ruchi touched the wide island. "The house is so spacious."

"Enough for a joint family," Naren muttered.

"You like it?" Deepa asked and placed the salad next to cubed cheese and chutney bruschetta on glass plates. She ripped off the plastic wrap and stuck a fork in a half-moon of cantaloupe.

"Ammi's custard salad," Ruchi said. She spooned a soaked banana slice and brought it to Deepa's mouth. "Try." She pushed against Deepa's lips, leaving her no choice but to part them. Ruchi pulled the spoon out slowly, so the juice didn't drip down her chin. A smear of pink lipstick streaked the white plastic.

"Ere, just like it," Deepa said, but she didn't ask for another bite.

"Real saffron." She'd bought a thimbleful, spending so much on so little. Taste-tested the grapes at Stop & Shop. Used real sugar, not the Sweet'N Low Naren badgered her to substitute in her tea. She hated the sour film it left in her mouth.

"It's lovely."

"All this food," Naren said. "You'll have too much left over."

"Which is why you must eat. No one can leave until it's gone." Deepa handed them foam compartment plates. Ruchi fixed one for Moksh, cutting each snack into pea-sized chunks.

"Stop, Ma," he said and shrank from the food.

"A few bites."

"I'm. Not. Eating." The women on the barstools glanced at them before huddling deeper into conversation. Naren piled his own plate with pakoras drowned in coriander chutney. "Ere, let him be, no?"

"He'll go hungry." Ruchi approached Moksh with a halved grape. "Just one, Mokshu." As if one bite would make any difference to his hollow chest, his stick-thin arms.

A trio of men holding iced drinks emerged, laughing, from another room.

"He'll eat when he's ready, right, Moksh?" said Deepa. Moksh nodded, and Naren grunted in agreement. It was Deepa's usual indulgence but it distressed Ruchi, with the barstool women and their sideways eyes. Deepa squeezed Moksh around the shoulders and swiveled him toward a sliding glass door that led to the beach. He shuffled out to the patio, hugging himself as if bracing for a storm.

"They need choices," Deepa said.

"But he's small for nine. So thin."

"What nonsense. You're lucky you can gather him up. Anu is all long limbs and preteen."

"He doesn't like to be touched," Naren said between mouthfuls.

"That's not true. He's just independent."

"Better than clinging and clawing at every opportunity," Deepa said. "Ruch, you have to let go."

Always the same advice. Ruchi could offer her own. *And you should pay more attention. Not leave your daughter unattended in cars.* But to tell Deepa this would be to hurt her. Ruchi couldn't. "They're children."

"Sanjay's grilling under the carport. He's expanding his practice and has no time. He's building a whole medical suite in Manchester. State of the art with free vaccine clinics on Saturdays. He'll be thrilled to see you."

"Surely," Naren said.

"Go, no?" Ruchi whispered to him. "Here there are only ladies."

Naren left, and Deepa picked up a golden dish of pakora. Her voice dropped its false exuberance and became conspiratorial. "Have. I made them myself." A trace of vinegar tinged her breath.

"You?"

"My mother-in-law's recipe." Then, in a whisper, "That harami woman."

The crisp skin succumbed to a doughy, oniony inside. Ruchi took another that looked overcooked, but it wasn't. When had Deepa learned to cook? Ruchi had always been better at it, more patient, dicing onions to the correct fineness.

"Such a lively party," Ruchi said. The women on the barstools had left and were replaced by another group, also laughing and enjoying themselves.

Deepa shrugged it off. "Sanjay's contacts."

"He works so hard," Ruchi said. "Even Saturdays."

"Dodh dayo. He likes to look good." Deepa waved her hands in an arc. "You didn't tell me if you like the house."

"Very nice. So many details."

Deepa fanned a stack of napkins and poured juice into a glass jug. "Later I'll give you a tour. We let Anu pick out the light fixtures. It's good to get them involved."

Ruchi held back her compliments and searched Deepa's face. Her cheeks were smoother, flatter. "You've done something."

Deepa cupped her hand to a cheek. "A new treatment for pockmarks. Patches you wear at night and in seven days a fifty percent reduction." She brushed a crumb off Ruchi's lip, a gesture so brief Ruchi might have imagined it.

"Hopefully it won't rain," Ruchi said.

"So we all get wet. Remember how the courtyard would flood."

The memory warmed her. They were still friends from home, an unusual friendship, a status no one else could claim.

Deepa eyeballed the patio, guests picking at another buffet table, trays as colorful as peacocks. A restlessness crept over her face. She could never stay.

"All these people. You know their names?" Ruchi joked.

"Mostly. I'll introduce you later." Deepa touched Ruchi's sleeve. She stared in that way that told you she was judging. "I haven't seen this before."

"Ammi brought it years ago."

"Hmm." Deepa rubbed the fabric between her fingers. "Synthetic."

"Easy to wash and tumble dry."

"You must be sweltering."

Ruchi twisted the corner of her dupatta around her finger. "There's a chill."

Deepa fanned herself. "Clothes should be about comfort."

Ruchi realized that most of the women were wearing dresses, or light kameezes over leggings. She was the only one in a full salwar kameez with a dupatta over her chest. "Comfort?"

"Not that this isn't lovely. What is it? Ritu K.?"

Was that a brand or a store? Only last week she'd returned a hip-hugging maxidress Naren had bought her. "Oh, I'll be fine."

"Of course. But if you change your mind." Deepa motioned to the stairs, then waved to someone behind her. "Pick anything."

RUCHI WANDERED OUT to the patio on her own. It was silly to expect Deepa to stay by her side with so many people to entertain. She'd introduce Ruchi once she had time. Naren, at least, was with Sanjay and another man in front of a grill that resembled a spaceship. Her husband balanced his empty foam plate. She had an urge to take it from him, to relax his arms at his side, to adjust his gestures into more confident ones. Sanjay shook his head and laughed, and the other man slapped Naren on the back. She caught his eye and waved to encourage him and mask her disappointment. Sometimes he talked about the motel, as if it weren't already torn down for the new shopping plaza, and she humored him the way she might a child. "We could throw our own party," she'd once suggested, but he was always too tired on weekends. She tried to relax her shoulders in demonstration, claim her spot on the patio with more certainty. He looked away.

She found Moksh in the sand next to the deck watching Anu and the other children dart in and out of the sea. Anu, now twelve, wore her hair in pigtails but was no longer a child. In the months since Ruchi had last seen her, two mounds had formed and now curved the top of her bathing suit. Anu approached Moksh, then rested the sole of one foot on a calf, like an egret.

"You've grown so much, dikri," Ruchi said, smiling.

The girl looked at her politely but didn't smile back. Her upper lip was blonde. "Thank you, Auntie." To Moksh, Anu said, "Did you bring your suit?"

Moksh shrugged. "I don't like the water." Ruchi hated hearing it. A reminder of her failure.

"Still?"

He snarled, "What's it matter?"

"Mokshu," Ruchi said, and placed a hand on his shoulder, which the boy shrugged off.

Anu traced lines in the sand with her toe. "It doesn't. I just thought you might try it."

Ruchi added, "Look at the fun they're having."

"Please don't force me."

Ruchi tried not to frown. She saw the tendon bulge in Moksh's neck and understood he was shielding himself. She wished he could be charming, winning. Different from his father, from her. "No one is forcing you." She smiled tightly at Anu. "Maybe in some time."

Anu cocked her head and squinted. "Sure," she said, and rejoined the others.

Moksh settled at the edge of the water and wrapped a dark frond around his wrist. The whole party could see how alone he was, how separate. Naren insisted that Moksh didn't like other children, pointing out the practice packets on reading social cues that his third-grade teacher had sent home. But from behind he could be any child with an awkward bend in his elbows and a fear of the sea. Sometimes she thought that had a different, simpler girl chosen to sit with her in the hot dirt of Our Lady English Medium then the trajectory of Ruchi's whole life might have been easier. Absent of this push and pull with a friend like Deepa, a friend who resided in her, a friend in whom, Ruchi believed, she too resided. And yet she also worried that her son would never know what it was like to feel so close to someone that it was never enough. Every day he withdrew further.

THE BEDROOM SMELLED of lemon and talc. Above the bed hung a framed drawing of Shiva Natraj with Anu's name etched in a corner. Shiva tilted to the left, like he'd been pushed off-kilter, one graceless leg cocked and bent.

The bed itself was rumpled, like someone had woken in a hurry, the pillows still indented with sleep and far apart. She could tell right away which side was Deepa's. Here, among the magazines and the tennis bracelet and the half glass of water, was the doll Ammi had given her.

It was pushed to the back. Why was it hidden? Had Deepa forgotten about it? Or placed it there as a treasure?

Puddles of clothes dotted the mauve carpet. Ruchi picked up a checkered red-and-white dress, held it against her body, and peered down the length of it. The hem grazed her knee. A gray belt hung from a loop on one side, bobbing like a hook. It was the kind of dress Naren would've bought for her and that she would've returned.

Through the vertical blinds she could see Deepa on the beach, the one adult in her bathing suit. It dipped low in the back, a capital *U*. Ruchi felt a surge of longing, followed by an equally strong discomfort at the sight of Deepa's thighs.

Ruchi pressed the dress against her frame again. What harm was there in trying?

She undressed in the bathroom, where more discarded dresses littered the floor and hung off the towel rack. She could've changed in the room, there was no one there, but she felt exposed. Deepa would've called her prudish, old-fashioned—even in front of her sisters Ruchi had hidden behind a towel or a wardrobe door—but when had Deepa ever shown herself? The short dresses, the sleeveless tops, even the bathing suit weren't exposure like that. They were a dare, a diversion.

She stretched the collar of the dress to avoid staining it with her makeup. It smelled of lavender and something else she couldn't place, something bright and mean and drinkable. She threaded the gray belt and fastened it on the loosest setting. She twirled in the mirror. Her posture was all wrong. She stood on her toes and tried to pull back her shoulders, but this tensed her neck into two strained cords. She released. Better, but not right.

She remembered the nuns' dusty library that no one used. She'd told no one about the books she'd stolen, not even Deepa, and now she couldn't remember the plots. She'd read in *Reader's Digest* about women in their thirties going to night school, becoming nurses, getting business degrees. In this country thirty-five was considered young.

Outside, the party churned. From the bathroom window, she saw Moksh tossing seaweed with a stick, but it wasn't fair to assume bad behavior. He'd always loved finding treasures, which was anything found.

Something caught his attention in the ocean—Deepa beckoning. Moksh dropped the stick and unbuttoned his shirt. A few steps and he was up to his knees, reaching out for Deepa's hand. With the other he skimmed the water.

It was a sign of progress. And yet, what had Deepa done to get the boy to attempt the water that she hadn't tried herself? Deepa held him at arm's length, and though he shook his head, he continued to wade out until he was in up to his waist.

Ruchi stepped back from the window. She didn't want to be a jealous person. Deepa had chosen Ruchi's son to invite into the water in front of all these people. Later, after they'd exited the water, giggling and clumsy from cold, Ruchi would make a point of thanking her.

She stepped into the bedroom and tried to feel natural. She could only walk on her toes now, like walking full-footed would be a horrible mistake. It was not an easy dress. Not one to wear over a bathing suit; not one that slipped off easily. Was it pretty? She wasn't sure. And yet she liked it best.

She leaned over the sheets and sniffed them. They smelled fleshy but were hotel white and full of possibility.

Her custard salad would go to waste. At the end of the party, Deepa or Sanjay would wrap it up and put it in the fridge and forget about it until it rotted.

Ruchi lay down, aligning her head to the pillow's indentation. Mindfully, she straightened the fabric of the dress over her stomach and thighs. The sheets were cold, like damp wind, and she flattened her palms against them. Ten minutes passed, then fifteen, and Ruchi knew she should get up, change, return to the party.

She heard footsteps behind the bedroom door. She jumped from the bed to the bathroom, as if she was accustomed to hiding, but didn't have time to shut the door all the way. Deepa. A towel wrapped low around her hips, water dripping from her hair onto the carpet. She looked cold to the touch. She had no regard for the clothes on the floor, treading on them carelessly. She placed her hands on her hips and turned.

"I see you there."

Ruchi caught Deepa's eye in the mirror, which had a vertiginous effect, as if their reflections were close enough to touch.

"I was just trying," Ruchi said, pulling at the dress.

"Come. Let me see you properly." Deepa opened the door and stepped into the bathroom. Ruchi had never seen her like this, so much skin, so close. Here was the hint of belly, the flesh of her arms. How odd bathing suits were, that wearing them was nothing like walking around naked though it was essentially that. Her nipples, small and uneven, strained against the fabric. Only the skin of her cheeks was pocked. The rest of her was smooth.

"I don't know how you move in these clothes," Ruchi said.

"You have to be confident." Deepa picked up another dress. White with a lacy collar.

"White is for funerals," Ruchi said.

"It would look nice with your complexion." Deepa held the dress up to Ruchi's shoulders and surveyed her from head to toe and back. "Your foundation is too light. It doesn't match your skin."

Ruchi touched her forehead. Somewhere women were laughing and it felt like they were laughing at her. Through the bathroom window she could see Moksh in the water.

"How did you do it?" Ruchi asked. The air in the bathroom had shifted, like a pressure drop before a storm. Ruchi held her wrists out of habit, though she no longer had churis to fiddle with. "How did you make Moksh step in the ocean?"

"It was nothing. He's not afraid. Not really. Children don't like to do what their mothers tell them."

"Your Anu, at least, is so good."

Deepa stopped her searching and turned to her. "And look how I don't hover over her."

Was that it? Not hovering? "If I left him alone, he'd disappear," Ruchi said.

"Don't be silly."

"You should change. You'll catch cold," Ruchi said, and touched Deepa's prickled shoulder, sticky with sea. The only thing that was truly theirs were these bodies, this skin so rarely engaged.

"Did you make an appointment? For the test?" Deepa asked, her attention focused on the dress.

Ruchi shook her head. "What's the point?" she asked. "Where will I drive? I don't have a job. No second car." She didn't mean to sound petulant. She didn't want to talk about regular things.

Deepa's towel slipped off her hips and Ruchi caught it to cover her shoulders. A nipple grazed the back of her hand, as if reaching out. Ruchi held the towel in a fist, ready to pull her friend close despite Deepa's contorted lips that might've reflected her own face. Disgust.

A commotion outside stopped her. People were running across the deck. Ruchi didn't move, but Deepa stepped back and the towel dropped to her feet. In her eyes was an accusation. A high pitched "ho" reached them, like the women below had called out in a chorus.

Deepa ripped open the bathroom door and was gone.

Through the window, Ruchi saw the top of a head, a dimple in the water. There was no flailing, no struggle. Ruchi's stomach lurched at how calmly a person could go under, how little movement was required.

A group of children had gathered on the beach, but Moksh was not among them. Ruchi paused. Not more than a second or two, but it appalled her all the same, like she was watching the scene from a boat far off the coast. The dress, the fact that she was wearing it, that her legs were exposed, that her underwear was wet, that the gray belt was too tight.

She ran down the stairs, her feet thumping heavily on the patio, but even this felt not enough. The guests were spilled across the sand, and she swerved through them. She made promises to never want anything more if she was forgiven her inattention, if she could be afforded this one thing, her son breaking through the surface, her son on the shore. Her son her son her son.

"Moksh!" she yelled, but the guests seemed not to hear her. She couldn't understand why no one was moving aside, why no one made space for her. Who were these people? Why was Sanjay in the water and not Naren? Why did the coughing child not resemble her son? But it was Anu vomiting in the sand, a thick strand of phlegm slipped off her chin. Sanjay rubbed her back while Deepa took her pulse. Black liner ran down Deepa's cheeks, her eyes small and indistinct, the bruised blue deepened around them. Relief flooded Ruchi's body, relief cradled in guilt.

She spotted Moksh and Naren standing off to the side, Naren's arm draped over the boy's shoulders, both trembling from cold. Safe. Ruchi watched as he pulled the boy closer so that Moksh's face rested against his waist. Behind them, a lone gull dived for a crab and missed. She approached them cautiously, like they were breakable objects, afraid that the pause was visible on her face, that it had the power to destroy everything. She held her breath as Naren took in the dress. He said nothing, like it was the most natural thing, a secret between them.

# Moksh

## *1984*

Moksh picked through the seaweed for long fronds to weave through his fingers and wrap around his wrists. It was something to do at this party where the kids were different from the white multitudes in third grade who'd called him chocolate-tard or asked if his ass looked as bad as his face. He'd hated third grade even more than second. But here the kids weren't cruel like that, or domineering like Buddy across the street. The Perfect Indian Kids didn't need to be. They crushed you with their goodness.

"Moksh." He turned around and found Deepa in her green, skirtless bathing suit. Her legs were pale and sunless. Gooseflesh up and down her arms. He ran his thumb over the worm of his lip.

"Hi, Auntie." He didn't mind that she pinched his cheeks like they were normal, fleshy cheeks. She indulged his trash collections, his tinkering, fidgeting nature, and she'd nudged his mother to stop with the food. All those little bites. He recognized the spite in Deepa and liked it, a blade that flashed when the light hit it right. The terrain on her cheeks reminded him of treetops.

She visored a hand over her eyes though there was no sun. Fifty feet away, Anu and her friends jumped and dived at each other. The waves lifted and landed them like driftwood or trash. "Look at them. Crazies."

"They might freeze," he said.

"Oh, you are sensible. But not very much fun, na?"

She laughed at that, and so he laughed too. She didn't lilt her voice an octave like his mother did when speaking to other people's children. She had a conspiratorial way of talking that made him want to tell her things, like how his teeth ached at night, how he could feel one limb growing, the dreams of his body being torn apart, one half stretching to the tree crowns. All the stories he didn't think his mother wanted to hear.

"But you are a little naughty too, aren't you?" she asked. He'd been staring.

He buried his toes deeper until they were pointing down. "Maybe a little."

She laughed and looked over her shoulder. He hadn't yet figured out that being watched was the whole point of the exercise, like a raison d'être. "Is Anu being nice?"

He shrugged. Anu had tried to include him, and he could've been nice back. But he resisted her niceness, her wide smiles, her deferential Gujarati. All of it scratched at him. "She invited me in."

"Did your mother not teach you to swim?"

He shrugged again.

"I'll teach you."

"My suit's in the car."

"Ere, there's no need for a suit."

He wanted to ask what he would wear, but she was already stepping into the water. He had yet to shoot up and was conscious of his stomach lipping over his shorts. The water was scalding cold, and he took tentative steps through the murk, his elbows bent, hands splayed wide. He could hear Anu daring her friends to tag her. He wasn't afraid, though his mother thought he was. Just hated the feeling of wet, the feeling like slime on his skin. The sensation would follow him for years. He'd step into the shower and instead of clean, he'd feel dirty. In the ocean the water was like mud. Deepa's green bathing suit the only color against the slate ocean, the flattened sky.

"Good boy," she said. "See, the water is wonderful." She stepped over waves, and he tried to do the same. His calves were numb. He could've gone back and said he'd tried. But he was hoping his mother might still be watching, feeling proud and maybe ashamed for her excessive, stifling efforts. He knew she wished he had swum when Anu had asked. She tried to hide her wishing, but it was visible for anyone to see.

"The waves are bigger out there," he said.

"It's a cove so they're never very strong."

But he thought they curled like claws.

The salt was already stinging his mouth, his eyes. Shell shards pierced his toes. The water ballooned his shorts. He hated it but kept going. He saw how Anu watched her mother, a fiend for her gaze. Though he would've loved to have been ignored a little more, to have a mother lighter in spirit and less worried all the time.

"The real treat is to dive in. You feel fresh when you come up." Deepa came toward him and took his hand. "We can do it together."

She pulled him forward off his feet until his head was under for the first time. He'd resisted every time his mother had gently coaxed him. No, no, no. But Deepa's hand was a vise. A train roared in his ears, and the thought crossed his mind that she might hold him down too long. He hadn't inhaled enough air and had failed to close his eyes. He pictured his brain sloshing in salt water.

But the sand was right there. All he had to do was kick to break the surface. Deepa was standing several feet away, clapping. He wasn't sure when she let go. The waves were hitting her, and she didn't care.

"You did so well." She beamed, and he smiled.

"That was fun," he lied, and splashed at the sky.

Deepa applauded. "See," she said, and turned to leave him.

Salt burned his eyes, and his heart leaped from his chest to stomach and back again. But he stayed; he was too proud to get out. Deepa waded to the shore, showing no sign of having seen her daughter. Soon other kids exited the ocean too, until it was just him in the shallow and Anu in the deep.

He thought he might freeze, might truly turn into a monolith of ice that collapsed into floe. It wasn't a horrible feeling, surrendering to a force, and later there'd be other forces: hunger, anger, natural and manmade disasters. Silence, the force that defined his family. But there, in the inky Long Island Sound, he was ten and couldn't look away from Anu's figure now cutting her arms through the water, swimming still farther out, each stroke strong and desperate.

Ten minutes went by. Fifteen. Maybe more. He could've said something. Earlier, he could've pointed in Anu's direction, let Deepa know that her daughter needed her. But he'd liked that this important person, the host, was focused on him. Briefly it had felt like a stage. It meant that others were probably focused on him, that his mother was probably focused on him but without her usual worried attention. He noticed the wild force of it, of being exceptional in a usual way.

Anu kept swimming. Sideways for a bit, then treading water to course correct for the horizon. Zigzagging like this until her head went under. She bobbed up once, then under again, and the third time, he yelled for help. He waved his arms and soon others were also yelling, screaming, a gasping, frightened crowd gathered at the edge of the water. He was the hero, though deep down, he knew the truth. He'd watched Anu swim out, had watched her feel hurt, and had said nothing. He might as well have pushed Anu down himself; he was the only one who understood that she'd swum out on purpose.

He heard his father call his name and saw him gesture impatiently. Moksh scanned, but his mother wasn't there. When his father pulled him close, Moksh tried to relax into the embrace, the only one he could remember, but his body was numb and foolish.

LATER, IT RAINED. Drizzle at first that people swatted away with their hands, then undeniable drops. A frenzy to bring in all the food and lawn chair cushions. Aunties holding paper cups with their chins, bowls of tortilla chips and salsa cradled in their arms. The house was noisy, and the smell of fried food was nauseating. Moksh slipped out the door. The new turf of the front yard crunched under his feet. The rain had calmed to a cold drizzle.

Anu was there, alone.

"Are you okay?" he asked.

She answered with a question. "What are you doing out?"

"There's nothing to do inside."

"We have ping-pong in the basement."

"By myself?" He stuck his tongue in his cheek and rubbed the bulge with his knuckle.

"I could play with you."

"I hate ping-pong."

"Okay." Water streamed down their faces. He tasted it every time he took a breath. Metallic and sour.

"I heard you yell," Anu said. "Thanks."

"Sure," he said.

"I was surprised you were out there. With my mom." She waited for him to say something, but he didn't. "I thought you hated it. The water."

"I do."

"Did she force you? My mom can be pushy."

"It wasn't so bad," he said. He could see she wanted to commiserate, to wallow in feeling abandoned. He could see through Anu like the translucent jellyfish they'd once found, an ethereal mound with bruised innards. She was a nervous kid and too eager to please. Yet he couldn't help but keep track of her. He couldn't help but poke at her bruises. He was a little shit. Just a little shit with a busted face.

"I saw you too," he said. "I saw you swimming out."

Anu scrunched up her face. "What?" she asked, but he could see from how her shoulders tensed that she knew what he was talking about.

"You're a good swimmer," he accused.

"The current was strong."

"Why'd you keep swimming then?" he asked.

"I didn't," she said. And then, "Please don't tell."

Nicer. He wished he was nicer, that he hadn't strode back to the house in the light rain, pretending he didn't hear her.

# PART FOUR

# Deepa

## *August 1992*

*You could leave.* Deepa stood on the most piercing shells with the freezing foam kissing her ankles. It was a calm night with a ripple on the water and a feeble crescent moon overhead. A tent listed sideways. Another party, finally over. Sanjay had acted visibly unwell. She, in contrast, had done splendidly. No one could tell that anything was wrong.

But Ruchi's words rattled inside her. Deepa pressed her weight down harder to will the cold up her legs, to spread through her veins, pump through her organs. Sometimes, when she was feeling sorry for herself, she thought that no matter how many decades passed, she'd never feel warm in Connecticut, not even when a cruel summer sun pounded her face. And yet here she was, only wanting ice.

She didn't bother to hose her feet on the deck and left a trail of pebbles and sand on the kitchen tile. Her soles were numb. The caterers would return tomorrow to disassemble and pack, and Deepa was supposed to have the large metal trays rinsed and ready, but she'd let the oil and cream and sauces congeal and harden. Sanjay's car was gone, and Anu had retreated to her room. The house was quiet but restlessly settling.

She could see the tsunami coming for them. It was far at sea, but she knew it was gaining speed and strength, flashing their misdeeds.

But what had she done wrong?

Nothing. Nothing at all. Except that her thoughts would not stay put. They kept tilting toward Ruchi.

*You could leave.*

But Ruchi had never answered her question. What would Deepa do after she left her husband? She should be angry at the wrongness of the suggestion. She'd worked so hard to be a woman above reproach, community-minded, a modern woman, but a traditional one too. She'd worked hard not to want, not to need. They'd been girls, unthinking girls, and she'd returned home that day from Bandra Fort confused, a writhing hunger in her belly, had gone home to be alone, no sisters, no cousins, and a mother who prayed, slept, and wept, displeased with her daughter, displeased with this life, and Deepa had decided no, I cannot remain here. I cannot. She wanted to seethe at Ruchi for violating the boundaries Deepa had meticulously constructed over all these years, but she was only sorry.

Because there was this: she'd felt a slick, undeniable stirring. Her body had reacted, and the worst part was that Ruchi knew it. She always would. She'd left the party without saying goodbye, or maybe Deepa hadn't given her the opportunity.

Weariness overcame her. She lay down on the Italian marble in the foyer, dirty with sand and stray food, the cold stone a shock to the skin on her back, her legs, the clammy undersides of her arms. She stretched herself out under the chandelier, stared at the candle-shaped bulbs until her eyes closed and in her dreams the bulbs burst.

A phone was ringing. Early morning dark. She rolled over onto all fours, her lower back tightening into a ball, and thought she'd have to crawl. She placed her hand on the receiver and hesitated. Had her husband returned? She hadn't heard him. Anu appeared in the foyer, barefoot and awkward with no shape to her. That awful hair.

"Where is your father?" The phone continued to ring.

"Not here," Anu said, glancing out at the carport. "Only one car. Still out?"

Sleep and fear marked her daughter's eyes, making her look like a child again. What if the ringing phone was about Sanjay? Anu's dear father. Deepa could picture Anu's grief, could hear her sobbing for Sanjay because she thought he loved her best. Deepa forced herself to stand up straighter, ignore the stab in her spine and ready herself for whatever.

"Hello?"

A garble. A woman's gelatinous voice talking about a quadruple bypass. Thrombosis. A sudden cardiac arrest.

"Deepa," Sonal said through tears. "You don't know? Ravi Ravichandran is dead."

THERE WAS MUCH to do. Deepa enlisted the Association's events committee to organize a meal train and signed up for three meals herself. She found the most complicated dish from her Tarla Dalal cookbook, baby eggplants that required stuffing with channa flour and frying before mixing with pureed onions and tomatoes.

Her husband returned to say he was leaving again. "Sorry, Janu. Work to do at the practice," he said to Anu, as if he were on call. Connecticut Specialty Suites had turned black in her mind, a tamped-down terror that left a damp film on her brow.

She expected Anu to go with him to Glastonbury. She was used to Anu's preference for her father by now.

"That's okay. I'll stay with Mom and help her cook for the funeral. So she's not alone."

Stay with Mom? Sanjay wavered, placed a hand on his chest, but didn't protest. He could never challenge Anu, seeing only her goodness. Deepa felt a flicker of victory followed by dread. She missed Anu when she was at college, and then didn't know what to do with her when she returned.

"Is this a little fancy?" Anu asked as she sprinkled chopped cilantro over the eggplant.

"People will talk if I prepare a basic dal chawal. Grieving people need calories," Deepa said, though she frowned at the eggplants, round and buoyant, their charred surfaces announcing her efforts.

~

THE NEXT DAY, Monday, Carbonado's Funeral Home in Hamden was packed. There was Sharmila Gandhi and Vasti Bhakta, the Purohits. All the big donors of the Bharat Friendship Association. Deepa inspected the over-air-conditioned lobby, squinting in the perfumed haze, but there was no Ruchi. Disappointment clouded her relief. She and Anu followed the crowd, and Anu smiled compassionately at various aunties. She was kinder than Deepa, which was her father's influence. But an air of secretiveness clung to her daughter, to her cut hair and unshaven armpits and thick thighs, a force Deepa couldn't penetrate. When had Anu become so unknown and separate? And how to draw her back? Deepa's mind zoomed through the girl's childhood, swerving around her own mistakes.

The viewing room was even colder, and Deepa's heels sank into the carpet. Rows of folding chairs faced the exceptionally large casket for a particularly small man. She couldn't see the body, just its shadow against the fussy, golden lining. The rows had filled up fast, men left of the aisle, women to the right, except for Americans who didn't perceive the rules. Only single seats were left.

"Go," she said to Anu. "Sit with your friends."

"I could stay with you, Mom."

"Don't be foolish. Go."

How to explain that she didn't feel sad? She didn't feel anything at all.

Deepa took an available aisle seat in the back. "I didn't see Sanjay so I thought you both were skipping." Sonal touched Deepa's sleeve. How had she not noticed her before sitting down? Deepa was in no mood.

"Sanjay has an appendix surgery. Full burst." Deepa considered finding another seat, but the rows had filled and she wasn't going to sit in the men's section.

"The appendix is terrible," Sonal said, then ducked closer to Deepa's ear. "When Ravi had the attack, Pushpa thought it was indigestion from the party food," she said sweetly. "Or stress from the business with the car."

Deepa blinked at her.

Sonal tugged her sequined white shawl tight around her shoulders. "You didn't know? Someone tampered with his Jaguar. Tried to steal it! Of course, you were so busy hosting. You couldn't know. Poor Raviji. He'd done so much for your Association. For the community."

The sali had tears in her eyes, as if Ravi's death should sit on Deepa's head. This, when Sonal hadn't signed up to cook a single meal.

The older Ravichandran boy was at the podium. "My father was a good man," he began. "He was a man who cared about his community and wanted everyone to be happy. On Sunday mornings he made us dosas from scratch. Mom soaked the dal for him the night before, of course." Some people chuckled. It was meant to be funny. The boy's voice broke, and his mouth moved sideways. His younger brother, the high school tennis star, joined him, propped him up by the elbow. Both boys were shining examples of NRI children with broad, muscular American chests. Deepa was glad that they were too young for Anu; she wouldn't have to endure the humiliation when they passed her over. Or when Anu showed no interest.

There were more speeches. A good man. A community man. A cousin brother who had flown the red-eye from California called the Bharat Friendship Association "Ravi's temple." Deepa bristled but kept her face serene. Blasts of cold air pumped through the vents overhead. Intermittently, the cousin brother chanted. He asked for others to say a few words. These speeches, like at a wedding. When had that started? In Bombay or Mumbai, whatever they called it now, were people giving speeches at funerals too? She, the director of the Association, could've offered a speech. She had many things to say about Ravi Ravichandran.

A long line formed to see the body. She did not feel guilty. Not for the death. Not for her husband's misdeeds. Not for the temple she hadn't wanted, for the concessions she'd made. Not for Amal Syed, who was now standing in the back, who smiled cordially when their eyes met. Deepa was surprised to see her; the Syeds had stopped coming to the Bharat Friendship Association years ago, but then business was business.

The only guilt, real guilt, Deepa felt was for Ruchi, who wasn't here, who Deepa hadn't called. Ruchi who lived in the sad little house on the sad little road. She had taken for granted that Ruchi would remain forever inhibited. Deepa had counted on her hesitation, her insecurity, her fear, her discomfort. She regretted that she needed it, that she couldn't wish for her friend every happiness.

THE CREMATORIUM WAS off-site. Deepa and Anu returned to their car, and a cloud of chili and garam masala from the eggplant stung their eyes. Deepa drove several cars behind the hearse, headlights on. Anu ribboned a tissue in her lap and wove it between her fingers, then wove it out. In and out, in and out. Dispiriting.

"Stop fidgeting. Please. All your nerves make others nervous, too," Deepa said. Someday her daughter would appreciate her advice; Deepa still believed this.

"It's horrible, to lose someone so suddenly," Anu said. "The boys seem broken."

"Hmm." But the boys had their college funds, their father's life insurance. She'd told Sanjay that it would be his responsibility to prepare Anu, if the time came, to fill out the FAFSA, to explain that she'd need a scholarship, that his "mistakes" would probably be in the local news, that they'd have to sell things, many things. "Everything passes," Deepa told her daughter. The new mall construction appeared on the left. The top of a crane shot into the blue sky. "They'll be fine."

"There's something I need to—"

"Please, Anu, stop with this tissue." Deepa reached over and snatched the shreds out of her hands.

"I've met someone at college," Anu said.

"Oh, good. You have a friend." They passed a laundromat. A Cumberland Farms. Here the trees were closer to the road, the canopy darker, sunlight speckled across the asphalt, leaves flashing silver in the warm breeze. The sun made shadows short on the road.

"A good friend, actually."

Deepa waited for a name, some indication. "Good friends are important."

"That's not what I mean."

Deepa kept her eyes on the road. "You must be careful with friends. They change. Even good friends."

"Mom, I'm not—"

"Your studies are what's important. I'm sure you're being sensible." Deepa's voice, too shrill and false, bounced off the windshield. She went on with whatever gossip she could: who had gained weight, who was going to good schools, who was going to bad ones. Her words had the intended effect. Anu was quiet.

The crematorium was a concrete box set back from the street, no sign, no windows. A chimney at the back painted to match the concrete as if to camouflage it. Against the saturated sky she could see the thinnest trail of smoke.

Two attendants in dark suits, clearly unaccustomed to hosting so many people, ushered them in. The room, not much cooler than outside, was speckled tile and wooden walls with a single opening in front of a large metal tray, the casket on top. "Mrs. Ravi—" the bigger, meeker looking attendant said. He slipped out a card from his shirt pocket like he'd sheepishly forgotten a line. "Mrs. Ravichandran," he said, this time with a hushed finality that he must've perfected over months or years at this job. His colleague stood by the opening and pressed a button. A whooshing captured the room, a stereo reverberation that reminded Deepa of prolonged thunder, which itself was reminiscent of the time she'd traveled with her mother to a hill station where women, saris tied between their legs, balanced luggage on their heads and ran through the red dirt streets warning that they had no intention of stopping, that they would, if you stood in their way, run you down.

"Yes," Pushpa said. "Yes, okay. Yes." The attendant opened the shaft to reveal a Crayola-orange interior. Together the two men took hold of the sides of the casket, ready to hoist it, but the sweaty cousin brother stopped them. Deepa saw the irritation in the attendant's brow.

Well, what were they expecting? The sons, stripped of all courage, their torsos wilting, were summoned forward. Pushpa was relegated to the back with the rest of the women, the men having found some purpose at last.

"They're good boys," Deepa whispered to Pushpa. The woman didn't answer. She'd kept her tortoiseshell sunglasses on. They were too fashionable for the occasion. They slipped down her shiny nose. "But of course, you know that. They'll take good care of you."

"They'll grow and they'll leave," Pushpa said in her grainy voice.

"Ere, Pushpa, they'll look after you."

She gave a crisp, gaunt laugh. "They'll become doctors and marry doctor wives who will someday put me in a home. Some American home."

"Nonsense, Pushpa. Nonsense."

"What do you know?" She spoke through clenched teeth. Deepa had thought this woman admired her, that they were at least on a level field. She was wrong, and she let the knowledge sting.

The boys struggled against the casket, as if some life might yet be left in the man inside, and soon the cousin brother was pushing too. The attendants stood back and waited. When it was finally in, one attendant moved to shut the door but was stopped.

"We need to see the body catch fire," the cousin brother explained.

The attendants blanched. "But once it's inside we can't open the door again. It locks."

The furnace roared. Could that not be evidence enough? But the cousin brother continued to negotiate until the door was raised just a fraction so you could peer inside, see the charred wood.

A love marriage. A good man. The things that faith had delivered to them but hadn't delivered to her. What she'd never told Ruchi, never really admitted to herself until just now, was that she knew about Ferrao and Braganza long before, before Ruchi even arrived at the school, not because she'd caught them in an illicit embrace, not because of her spying, though she had done so several times. No, Deepa knew because she was good at observing, at staring, at watching closely. She was good at catching what people didn't want you to see and like that she understood how the sisters needed each other, how, despite their square jaws and battle-ready countenance, when they locked eyes, when one came near the other one, a warmth flowed between them, a force field, like nothing she'd seen in any film. She'd been frightened and repulsed, and worried she'd never feel it herself, anything close to ecstasy.

Deepa receded further until her sore back met the wall. She rested against it. She was surprised she still remembered the shloka her mother had taught her for such an occasion. At first she sang to herself until some of the women caught on around her and she pushed her voice over theirs. Somewhere she heard Anu's voice, too, and together, all of them made the song beautiful, maybe the most beautiful song ever sung. Pushpa didn't turn around, but Deepa saw her shoulders tighten, and it made her sing louder still, so loud she might drown out their deceptions and jealousies and petty competitions, all the things that made them small and tired and worn, all the things that held them in place, stopped them from being themselves.

# Deepa

## *1984*

The dress looked terrible, that had been Deepa's first thought. It was the wrong shape for her friend, and in the bathroom light the color had done nothing for her. There were so many others to choose from. But she was surprised to find Ruchi there at all. Deepa hadn't believed she'd take seriously the invitation to try on her clothes. And Deepa had been too happy to see her.

She couldn't escape the sensation that she'd been warned. Anu had almost drowned at the housewarming while she and Ruchi were being stupid. Nazar didn't care if Deepa had intended to slap Ruchi's hand, berate her, make her feel small. If back home people went overboard, thinking the evil eye was every other eye, Americans didn't worry about it enough. Here, nazar roamed around unfettered.

In the months after the housewarming, Deepa tied a black thread around her wrist, the kind she used to tease Ruchi about, and forced herself to stare at her home temple for a few minutes every morning. It was nothing like her mother's. Deepa hadn't stuffed it with cheap amulets, just like she didn't spend half the day mumbling over mala beads. No, Deepa's temple was spare. Ganesh for good luck, a photo of Krishna, of Vishnu, the collection perched on a corner of her dresser next to a mirrored tray full of polishes and lipsticks. She'd set it up and mostly ignored it until now. She felt ridiculous standing in front of metal figurines, but she refused to send Anu to school with kaala teekas all over her face to get teased. American children were nothing if not mean in their ignorance.

It was up to Deepa to take the necessary precautions. It was up to Deepa to fend off the nazar from Sanjay's perpetual doting, nazar from the teachers' constant praise. Which was why, after Anu's vomiting had abated, after her exhales and inhales had steadied, Deepa had laughed at the commotion, expertly wiped her running eyeliner with a towel, and ushered the party along, which was otherwise a great success. She'd received calls about the food, though she herself hadn't touched a single pakora.

Ruchi had changed out of the dress and back into her filmy salwar set before leaving. The Mehtas said goodbye a little after the rain started. Late to arrive but early to leave. When Ruchi apologized, Deepa had taken both her hands and dug her nails into Ruchi's palms. "Anu is fine. It was nothing. Nothing."

This was true, though that night Deepa slipped into Anu's room after she was sure her daughter was asleep and pressed the warm underside of her wrist, trying to pull the girl's rapid, insistent pulse into the pads of her fingers.

THROUGH SEPTEMBER AND October, Ruchi called, and Deepa didn't answer. She forced herself to step away from the ringing receiver, reminding herself that she was doing them both a favor. Each avoidance was a sacrifice, and a reward. This would not be forever, just a cooling, a brief separation, long enough to keep them safe. A necessary, if difficult, kindness, reeling them in from the horrible shame of it.

Diwali arrived on the last Sunday in October, early this year, and Deepa lit scented candles, bought chocolate frozen yogurt, made pakora again but with less care, burning half of them. A sad, insufficient festival season. She was left with a swift longing; one she hadn't felt in years. The air singed with crackers, Auntie fixing their saris before they delivered sweets to the neighbors, then lit sparklers on the balcony, daring a burn.

Sanjay's expanded practice was set to officially open after the new year, which in 1984 fell on Halloween, that stressful holiday. Deepa insisted on making Anu's costume every year, though Anu would've preferred something store-bought. "You have to be unique," Deepa had explained ever since Anu's kindergarten teacher had suggested she wear "something cultural" to the class party. Anu had gone as a ballerina, and the teacher had called her an "Arabian dancer," for which Deepa still hated her.

This year Deepa had decided on a butterfly, and the night before the ribbon cutting she alternated between preparing wings for Anu's costume and coconut and rice for the Vastu ceremony, all of it spread out across the dining table. Sanjay occupied the kitchen island with his files and documents. They were an industrious couple.

"Isn't Anu too old to be a butterfly?" Sanjay asked without looking up.

"How is she too old? She's twelve," Deepa said though she, too, had a doubt.

"Fine, but at least stop all this vastu fastu nonsense, Deepa. Why are you bothering, honey?"

"It's custom. Keeps bad luck away."

"People will think it's strange."

She understood his worry, though it was different from the office smelling like curry, from incense in the waiting room. Vastu could be done secretly, an invisible protection. "I'll do it before anyone is there. Then we can cut the ribbon. You can make your little speech." She dressed the coconut with rust-colored leaves and store-bought carnations. Anu's wings, shaped out of hangers, she painted teal and purple. "If you want me to be your office manager then you have to let me manage it."

"It was you who wanted something to do. Some job."

She stopped and examined him. He was nearing forty. She had liked that he was five years older when they'd married, but now he seemed too old, too tired. He was forever shifting through files and documents, fielding calls from his billing department, adding and re-adding numbers. She noticed a touch of gray at his temples. She liked him best when they were around other people who admired him, like at the housewarming. Alone, they'd made a habit of being short with each other once they realized nothing would happen, that their marriage would grind on and on.

"What are you saying?" She registered his wince.

"Nothing, nothing," her husband said and left for bed.

She caught sight of her reflection in the kitchen window, the shadows under her eyes. She wanted the role, any role, more than she let on. Her heart was always beating in her throat, waiting for the moment when someone—the fawning girls in school, her mother, the lunch wives, Ruchi, even Anu—would call her bluff.

THE NEXT MORNING Deepa fussed with the butterfly wings she'd hung in the bathroom off the shower door. Anu had argued that most butterflies were brown. "Those are moths," Deepa had said, as if she knew anything about it. The wings were too plain, too simple. They needed some chamak. Anu would have to wear a black leotard underneath, though in the last month, she'd begun to hide her developing body, caving her shoulders into her chest in that posture Deepa hated. A good girl to a fault.

In the kitchen, Sanjay had turned on the TV. "I don't like TV in the morning," Deepa said as she came down the stairs, but he seemed not to hear her. Maybe this was it, the moment he'd had enough of her instructions and comments.

"Look," he said at last, and she did. Ted Koppel. In the morning? Why so somber and tired-looking? A photo of Indira Gandhi flashed on the screen and Deepa coughed a chuckle. How absurd. A profile shot that emphasized her nose and shock of white hair, the sari over her head. Why to bother with the sari at all? It did nothing to soften her.

"She's dead," Sanjay said.

They'd been asleep when the prime minister had strolled into the garden. Some thirty-nine bullets fired. Her son would be sworn in, that stupid boy who no one respected, who would get himself killed, too.

"They keep calling her Mrs. Gandhi," Deepa said.

"What else should they call her?" They didn't usually talk in the morning, having formed a comfortable routine that required little interaction.

"I think of her as Indira or Gandhi or Prime Minister. This 'Mrs.' feels wrong. Go. Get dressed. We can't be late."

A photomontage ensued. There she was as a teenager with her father, meeting Jackie Onassis, how small she was next to Reagan, how skeptically she looked at him. Mixed in were scenes from Delhi, burning cars, mangled bicycles, men running down streets.

Deepa allowed the TV to remain on through breakfast. She allowed Anu to watch with her cereal. Outside AIIMS Hospital people were dressed in white. The body was still there and the next day it would travel to Teen Murti Bhavan where her father had lain in state years before. Ted Koppel talked about the Golden Temple, its holiness, the attacks the prime minister ordered in June.

"Her bodyguards. They were Sikh," Sanjay said.

Of course. This was why they were showing photos of the bloodied temple, its sagging awning, walls cut up like paper dolls.

"What's a Sikh?" Anu asked.

Did she really not know? "See the men in turbans? They are Sikhs." She wasn't supposed to answer questions with annoyance; Deepa knew this from the many articles about mothers and daughters. "But not all men who wear turbans are Sikhs."

The guns were from England, Ted Koppel said. He spoke to a woman reporter on the phone. The reporter explained that the crowds on the streets were growing, that a bus was burning, that nightfall had increased the day's chaos. No one was paying attention to the curfew, she said, as if recounting a torrential rain.

Anu watched with milk-coated lips. "What are they running from?"

"They might not be fleeing," Sanjay said. "They might be chasing."

"Who are they chasing? Why do the streets look so dirty?"

It struck Deepa that her daughter was regarding the scenes from a completely different angle, that what she saw had no reference point, no memory to challenge it, to block it out or shape it or fill in the bleeding edges. "The streets aren't so dirty. It's the poor quality of the video," Deepa said.

"You didn't say who they were chasing." Anu spoke through her cereal. "It's like a mob."

"It *is* a mob," Sanjay said. Deepa tried to catch his eye as he sat back in his chair. "There are always people who will take advantage. The country will burn." He turned off the TV and dropped the remote on the table.

"Do you think they'll cancel school?" Anu asked.

Deepa turned the TV back on. "Of course they won't cancel school. Don't be stupid." Deepa could see how it would be: for a night or two, the evening news would carry the story, perhaps lead with it, though the death would be overshadowed by violence and the country would be summed up in this way, backward and embarrassing itself. She looked over the brown paper bag she'd prepared with the coconut, the scissors for the ribbon. She thought of the black suit she'd bought for her first day as office manager. Everything should be canceled. Everything should go on. Her eyes snagged on the blue phone. She knew Ruchi's number by heart. But she couldn't call. Not yet.

And in any case, what would she say? It was a disorienting grief. The prime minister had been a cold, calculating woman. She'd had a love marriage and had sat cross-legged on the floor at her wedding, eyes downcast like a properly forlorn bride, though there was nothing wifely about her. When Feroze died in his forties, Indira had shown no signs of crying, hadn't worn dark specs, eyes clear as glass as she floated next to his body, swept up with the swarm that carried him through the streets, supervising the priest's last rites the way she might the laying out of an expensive tea. Deepa rubbed her eyes. Light filtered in through the sunroom painting the walls silver. It was going to be a beautiful day. Crisp but not biting.

"I'm sorry, Mom," Anu said as she rinsed her bowl and placed it in the dishwasher. She never had to be told.

"Why are you sorry?"

"You're upset—"

"I'm fine. Turn the TV off." She winked back the sudden tears. Sadness was a luxury. A luxury to feel hollowed out, to let her daughter feel hollowed out, too. To let the assassination follow them into their day, not dismissed as something that happened "over there." They couldn't. No one here would care.

THE COCONUT TOOK several efforts to crack on the concrete. A sign that it was old, had probably been sitting in the grocery bin for weeks. When finally it broke open, water stained her new red leather-upper pumps.

"Quickly," Sanjay whispered. Cars were arriving at the adjacent Kmart. It was not yet eight o'clock. Deepa shivered in the shade of the office building, a squat two-story brick structure, while Kmart's enormous blue and red sign basked in golden southern light. Deepa dipped her pinky in the small tin of vermilion, careful not to touch her black slacks and blazer. She made a tiny dot on the brick above the coconut, then a faint Swastik on the ground, which she covered with a vase of blue lilies. She felt her mother with her, repeating the same motion but on an endless loop, blind to Deepa, her hunger, the empty table.

Sanjay shifted back and forth from his heels to toes. "Stop looking like we've done something wrong. We aren't dacoits," Deepa said.

"The flowers make it look obvious we're hiding something."

He was right, but she didn't move them. She unfurled the blue ribbon, chosen to match the lilies, and waited for people to arrive. The cutting was hasty, the applause muted, the two Indian doctors speaking in hushed tones, as if at a funeral, while the Americans followed along politely. Everyone tucked their chins into scarves, cold in the October shade. Sanjay made his speech, clapping his hands in front of him, his smile apologetic as he spoke about efficiencies with a shared billing department and the dream of a "one-stop shop" for patient care. The free weekend vaccine clinics. But no one was in the mood. Kmart shoppers peppered the lot behind them.

The doctors and their staffs filed into the new suite. Its ten offices were at capacity, a good sign. A group of internists next to orthopedists. Pediatricians next to OBGYNs. All of them had waiting rooms and receptionists with their own desks and chairs that they'd set up with photos of their families.

"Can I help you?" Sanjay's receptionist asked.

"I'm Deepa." All the chairs behind reception were occupied. "The office manager."

"Is that right?" the woman said without looking up, and pointed to the closet.

Deepa had envisioned a desk, perhaps a separate office. But there weren't even hangers in the closet, and she had to lay her coat on top of her bag on the floor.

For the next hour, she milled around the waiting room. A nurse in lavender scrubs scooted in and out between the reception area and exam rooms, a place that felt forbidden to Deepa, like she wasn't qualified to enter. *But I'm the office manager!* She'd picked all the furniture, the landscapes that hung on the walls, and an aquarium that she planned to fill with tetras as colorful and delicate as small cakes. She'd let Anu pick them out, a perfect mother-daughter outing. Fish were meant to be soothing. And yet, of course. Of course, it was unessential. Frivolous.

She wandered down the hushed hall to the first floor. She wanted to know how insurance was handled, the way money came in, details Sanjay refused to share as things she didn't need to worry about. The office was tucked away at one end. Three women in cubicles, a small window with a view of Kmart.

"Hello," she said. They looked up in unison. "I'm the office manager."

"Excuse me?" one of the women said. She reminded Deepa of an owl.

She clarified. "Dr. Jain's office manager."

Their expressions brightened. "Oh, Dr. Jain! We love him, don't we, girls?"

"Yes, well. He asked me to learn more about the good work you all do."

A coder, a biller, and a filer. Each woman had her own role. The chargemaster listed the prices for different services. A well visit versus a sick visit. An X-ray, a blood draw, an injection, each item had its own code depending on the part of the body, the purpose, the aspects to be examined. So many codes. Towers of binders already filled the shelves. A fax machine seemed to beep every hour. Deepa listened to their gossip, their haggling with insurance companies.

"Your mind must be swimming," Janice, the owly woman, said, as if Deepa were only an accumulation of lunches and parties and lessons for Anu.

"Not at all," Deepa said. "I was quite good at maths." She could see how some codes added up faster than other codes. She'd been quicker at calculations than Ruchi, though Ruchi could spout all the formulas. Deepa thought of the dead prime minister, how she, too, had been undermined as a petite lady in saris. A dangerous misjudgment, the nuns used to say, and they'd been right, but also wrong. They'd assumed that the Iron Lady of India would be good. Not a brutal woman.

There was little for Deepa to manage. The ladies in Billing didn't need her, Sanjay's receptionists didn't need her, his nurses mostly ignored her. Deepa left early and drove to the costume store at TriCity, the storefront that changed each season. She wanted to add glitter to Anu's wings. Inside the store, the aluminum balloons screamed their happiness, and the costumes were disheveled, missing wands, axes. Seasonal stores always highlighted the absurdity of existence. There was so much of everything and yet the pumpkins on display had already started to sink and soon they'd be thrown away, becoming homes to squirrels and mice.

The cashier was a man in a papaya-pink shirt with the name RUBEN over his heart in block letters. The scent of smoke pulled off his skin. He rang up the glitter, his mouth working a piece of gum. He looked Goan or Sri Lankan, but Deepa was often wrong about these things.

"A tragedy," she said, and shook her head. She could feel the smoke as much as she could smell it. "Her bodyguards." Ruben paused, a packet of glitter in his hand. She swore his hooded eyes were yellow and green, and they gazed at her blankly.

"Excuse me?" he said. The accent was American.

Deepa forced a sheepish grin and placed an apologetic hand on her chest. It was astounding, the ignorance. "I was just talking to myself."

Loneliness rattled her limbs, a rushing river in her ears. It was all a poorly constructed film set of home. The mediocre Bharatnatyam teacher in Windsor. The children who couldn't speak their home language. The mindless parties, including her own. And now here, this clerk, had no idea what she was talking about.

A shop was for lease two doors down, next to the Coin-O-Mat. A former nail salon. Deepa peered inside. Tiles were missing in places, and the furniture had been ripped out. Deepa wrote down the number on the poster. The plaza, only ten years old, was already crumbling. Perhaps the space would be cheap. She understood that Sanjay had no intention of letting her be useful in his office. She understood that it was punishment for the coldness she'd cultivated as protection. But she didn't need him. She could create a life that no one expected of her; she could erase the slights of childhood on her own.

SHE WAS PLEASED with how the costume turned out. The glitter would catch the streetlights at dusk and her daughter would shimmer and hate it. Underneath Anu's goodness, water eddied and churned with no outlet. Deepa twisted the black thread around her wrist. What good was it when it came to daughters? What protection could it possibly offer? But she didn't break it.

"I'll stay home," Deepa said that evening. "To pass out candy."

Anu stood in the hall, frowning at the feathers in the mirror. "Don't we always leave candy in a bowl?"

"Dikri, your mother wants to watch the news," Sanjay said, and threaded his arms through a new coat.

Deepa said, "And you don't want to watch the news?"

"But there's nothing new to see. Didn't you tell me that?" he said. She hated how he lowered his voice to swipe at her. "Already there's a new prime minister."

The latest thank-you card preened on the refrigerator, held in place with a fruity magnet. Deepa used to think the cards made her life enviable. At the housewarming she'd let slip to Sonal that the construction of the house had required no financing. She'd whispered this, feigning a secret, as if she didn't know that Sonal would tell everyone by the end of the afternoon. Deepa liked the admiration for all they had, but it wasn't enough. Worse than that. Under the money, she smelled a trace of rot.

She had to find a way to keep Ruchi nearby, if not close. She had to make their friendship normal again. She missed her too much. And didn't Ruchi need her, too? Hadn't Deepa taught her to drive, taken her to important appointments, cared for her child? Her friend who needed something to do, who needed a job more than Deepa did. Deepa was nothing if not helpful.

She watched Dan Rather and learned that twenty-three bullets remained in the prime minister's body after she died. Deepa imagined the casings dropping out of the fire, someone sorting them out of the ashes. What would the nuns say about Indira now? That she'd become power-hungry and fueled her own demise? What would they say about the killing in the streets in her name? The henchmen? There were rumors about the former prime minister's appetites. Her yoga teacher lay down with her during their morning exercises, massaged her full body. Her father's secretary was in love with her. Feroze was often in England, and no one paid attention to his mistresses. Deepa had always found the photograph of Indira sitting at Gandhi's bedside odd, the way he angled his emaciated body toward her and laid his bony hand on her forearm. Her hair tented out the way thick hair on little girls tended to, and she smirked at the camera. Though maybe the nuns still would've loved her. Who was without their faults? Some hard part of Deepa resembled the woman, which frightened her, but lifted her too.

~

IT WAS AN unseasonably warm evening. Her daughter was almost her height, and by next year Anu wouldn't be interested in dressing up.

Kids rang the bell and asked for candy, and Deepa allowed them handfuls of Twix and Mounds and Life Savers. Teenage girls wore high heels and fishnets and aprons to indicate they were waitresses and boys dressed in sports uniforms. They stared at her, unsmiling, as they took more than their fair share. She preferred this to performing small talk with parents who had run into Anu and commended Deepa's craftmanship. "Just like a fairy!" Deepa nodded but the compliment brought her no joy. None of these people knew that the world was burning. It wasn't burning for them.

When Anu was younger, she and Sanjay helped her count her candy at the end of the night, sucking on Fireballs until their eyes teared. A nice memory. But now Anu took the bag into her room and closed the door. Deepa had allowed Anu a subscription to *Teen* magazine and on her walls were posters of Vanessa Williams and Ally Sheedy and Michael J. Fox. Men soft as boys and girls hard as women. Soon Deepa would explain to her daughter that she couldn't date, couldn't kiss, that she needed to save herself for marriage, and because Anu was obedient, more obedient than Deepa, she'd listen and learn that a good life required sacrifice.

Sanjay joined Deepa on the couch to watch the news again at eleven thirty. The prime minister's face floated next to the local anchor's, world news squeezed in before weather. Maybe a thousand dead. "We should do more charity," Deepa said.

"Every year I send money back."

"Not just that." She let her hand fall close to his. "Here, I mean. For the community."

"Property tax is our charity here."

"Ere, listen. You see how the Mehtas struggle." She let him tickle the nape of her neck, wrap his arm around her shoulder. She felt a surge of conviction. "Give Ruchi the job, no? I don't need it."

"There's not much to do in my office."

She'd been right, then. The position had been bogus. But it didn't matter. "With another doctor then. There must be something she can do."

"What does Ruchi know about office work?"

Deepa pretended she didn't notice where his hands were going. "She was almost top of her class." She clucked her tongue in pity. "Bechari. At least give her something."

The dreams. They were harder to access, like boats across a lake shrouded in mist. In another life, maybe she'd have lived inside them. Without them she felt cleaner but also emptier. Maybe the two were the same.

"And you?" her husband asked, shifting her how he wanted. "What will you do?"

Deepa was quiet, as if she didn't hear. On TV, Indira stared at them, her eyes as bright as they were mean.

# Ruchi

## *1985*

Though Ruchi needed the job, any job, her first impulse when Deepa finally called was to say no. Deepa talked as if no time had passed, like she hadn't avoided Ruchi's calls since the housewarming in August, like it wasn't now January 1985. Deepa went on about Sanjay's medical suite, the new lady OBGYN. "A Wellness Center, she calls it. As if it's something fancy," Deepa said, and Ruchi thought "suite" also sounded fancy. Deepa explained that Dr. Sharma needed an office assistant. Someone good at filing and organizing. Someone fine with a little extra work on Fridays. "It was Sanjay's idea," Deepa added. "He gave your name."

"I called," Ruchi said. "You never called back. I tried so many times." She hated the obvious hurt in her voice.

"Don't become upset," Deepa said. "I wanted to call. I did."

And yet she hadn't. "I'll have to think about it. I'll have to see."

"What do you have to see? Did that neighbor give you some salon job?"

Ruchi considered lying just to hear Deepa cajole. "Nothing like that."

"You'll learn quick. You always have."

It was only flattery, Ruchi reminded herself. It meant nothing. "Why don't you do it?"

"Sanjay begged me to manage his own practice," Deepa said with a laugh. "You know I was never an office type. You'll be much better than me."

Empty flattery. And yet it warmed.

FOR WORK, RUCHI bought long accordion-pleated skirts in geometric print that she thought looked smart with the lab coat Dr. Sharma gave her. The doctor showed her the three exam rooms, the nurse's station, and the small storage closet that she used as her own office, all of it as flat and unadorned as the waiting room with its bare walls and cushionless chairs. "You can use my Mercedes," Dr. Sharma said, since on some days Ruchi was expected to deliver samples, collect medical files, and fetch results from other labs and hospitals. "You do know how to drive?" The doctor spoke in an upper-class accented English that reminded Ruchi of Cathedral Prep girls with their hemmed skirts and buckle shoes. Girls who became doctors and actresses, housewives with staff. Dr. Sharma wore fabric bangles on her wrists that didn't make a sound.

Ruchi nodded. She'd be very careful. "Yes, yes."

Dr. Sharma didn't ask about a license, which Ruchi still hadn't gotten. After the housewarming, she'd hoped Deepa might still follow through on her promise to help her study for the driving test. The activity could've restored their equilibrium. The housewarming remained raw in Ruchi's mind, the rough grain of Deepa's towel in her fist and the cold that rose off Deepa's body like steam. The thoughts hurt, wrapped as they were with what came after, which Ruchi blamed on the dress. She'd felt clownish and wrong-footed until she'd washed and folded the ugly dress and tucked it in the back of her closet.

Ruchi drove Dr. Sharma's Mercedes with care. The seats were navy leather and the windows automatic. It smelled of spiced lotion. She enjoyed handling the samples, urine that sloshed in the biohazard bag, rows of blood vials pressed into a foam case. She double-checked the labels and made sure the black marker was legible, though it wasn't expected of her.

When she wasn't delivering or collecting, Ruchi worked at reception. She always wore her lab coat to distinguish herself from the actual receptionist, one Mrs. Gerb, a prim white woman of indeterminate age who sat at the opposite end of the long desk and took her time with every task. The wall behind their desk was a puzzle of pastel green and yellow file cabinets that Ruchi neatly labeled her first week, just as she organized the pamphlets on the counter above their desk where patients checked in. Glossy trifolds about pap tests and period management and polycystic ovaries that Ruchi read cover to cover because it was her job to know more than their patients.

"Aren't you a thorough one," Mrs. Gerb commented after two weeks of observing Ruchi's tidy corner, the ordered stack of patient files, the model ovaries regularly dusted. Mrs. Gerb had offered to drive her to TriCity after work where she waited in front of People's Bank for Naren to pick her up, but Ruchi preferred to walk. "Call me Pauline," the woman said. Ruchi felt it too informal, so she used "Excuse mes" and "Ums" and questions that required no direct address.

Because Naren dropped her off before heading to his office Ruchi was perpetually early. Sometimes she'd see Sanjay in the office lobby, though he didn't see her. He was generally in a rush. She thought she should speak with him; they were, after all, connected. His office was on the second floor, a corner suite with a mauve color scheme, a shelf of miniature cactuses, and ocean landscapes on the walls. Deepa's touches. Ruchi made a mental note to tell Dr. Sharma about her green thumb and the benefit of plants in the waiting room, or maybe a succulent rock garden, objects pleasant for staring.

"I'd like to speak with Dr. Jain," Ruchi said to the woman behind the desk. She noticed the quantity of folders not yet filed. Handwriting illegible.

"Do you have an appointment?"

"No. I'm sorry. I'm not a patient." The woman blinked at her. "His wife's friend."

"His wife's," said the woman and frowned.

"I'd like to say hello," Ruchi said. Ruchi had left her lab coat behind and wished she hadn't. It was early, the waiting room empty. She could've said she wanted to thank Dr. Jain for recommending her, but she had no intention of doing so. She didn't want him to feel overly important, overly helpful. She'd never asked for charity. No, what she intended was to make her presence known, to show that she could speak to him, that he was no better than her, that she was someone of consequence in his life, regardless of whether he thought so or not. She knew his wife. Even now she cared for her.

"I'll let him know." But she didn't get up. She stabbed at a ledger with her horrible handwriting. Ruchi had time. She sat in one of the chairs that Deepa had picked out, both plush and sleek, though it wasn't as comfortable as it appeared. At last, the woman rose and went to the back. She stayed for several minutes and returned alone.

"He'll be out in a moment."

Ten minutes passed, and Ruchi almost left. Then Sanjay burst through the doors with his characteristic smile, a stethoscope draped elegantly around his shoulders. He stood over her with hands on hips, the way he might stand over a patient. "How nice of you to stop by, Ruchi," he said.

Ruchi stood, but he didn't invite her to chat in his office. This was both a relief and a slight. She'd only ever seen this man with Deepa, and she realized now that they'd never spoken beyond forgettable pleasantries, though she'd observed him enough to find Naren lacking in confidence and style in comparison. Bitterness coated her throat, though Sanjay had done nothing but what he was supposed to do, and had done it well. He'd made Deepa comfortable, if not satisfied. "Thank you," she said in a small voice. "For the job."

He laughed. "No need! Deepa made the suggestion."

*It was Sanjay's idea.* Deepa had lied on the phone. A small, unnecessary misrepresentation that proved that Deepa needed her. "Give her my thanks, then."

∼

DEEPA AND RUCHI's phone calls became regular again after Ruchi started working. She didn't understand why but accepted it and fell into a routine of calling Deepa from the bedroom after dinner while Naren watched sitcoms and Moksh retreated to his room. She lay on her bed, lights off, as she told Deepa about the improvements she'd made with new plants and magazines and the special forms patients had to fill out to qualify for free services, which many grumbled about.

"It's ungrateful to be so bothered about filling out an extra form when Dr. Sharma gives the best possible care," Ruchi said. "It's not Trivedi's Government Clinic where they didn't even use gloves." She'd had her first exam a week before marriage. Dust motes cascaded from the ceiling as she lay on the rubber gurney and a clerk-like doctor inserted the cold metal clamp. No, Dr. Sharma's patients didn't know how lucky they were. She was the kind of doctor Ruchi might have been.

"I hear you're diligent," Deepa said. "Hardworking."

"Did Sanjay tell you that?"

"Sanjay. Some friends."

Always some friends. "How can they know?"

"You think people don't talk? Everyone here is connected."

Were they? Ruchi had no idea. Mostly, she felt alone. She picked at the flaky, dry skin of her heels, a habit she warned Moksh against though she couldn't break from the sensorial comfort herself.

"It's all good things, Ruch."

"I wish you worked at the office. It would be fun to have lunch together sometimes. Gossip properly." She said it as if coaxing a shy child out from behind her.

"You'd outshine me at office work, and I'd be jealous."

"Don't be silly," Ruchi said, but she knew it was true.

"I could do nothing all day and life would pass."

"Don't say that."

"You take everything serious. I've found a place for our little project." Deepa described the empty storefront. "Just a dream," she said, as if that were true. Maybe this was the plan. Ruchi would learn about administration and budgets while Deepa designed and decorated the space. They would have something together, and it mattered less and less what it was.

Ruchi brushed the dead skin off her bed. "We have to name it something good."

THE LAST FRIDAY of the month, Dr. Sharma performed abortions. "I assume you don't have any objections?" Dr. Sharma had asked during the interview. "We follow the law." Ruchi saw no reason to object. "We keep this part of the practice quiet. No need for Dr. Jain to know," Dr. Sharma said, and Ruchi honored the secret, though she wanted badly to tell Deepa, because she considered the work important, perhaps the most important work she did at Wellness. The women, both young and old, cried quietly or twirled their hair on a finger or shared tips with each other. The loud talkers had done it before and tried to reassure the others, but it came out like bragging that put no one at ease.

In the time they were with her in the waiting room, Ruchi offered them care. She fanned out the newest magazines. She clipped brown leaves off the weeping fig and trimmed the spider plant. She spoke in tones meant for theaters and funerals. When it was time for the ultrasound, then the counseling session, then the procedure, Ruchi called names in a low, tender voice.

The skittish men, the ones who came, had to stay behind in the waiting room. They relaxed in the women's absence, then tensed each time the door opened. Even the meanest-looking ones who smelled of old grease and syrupy cologne were vulnerable then, their faces lost on themselves. The women returned limp and bowed, though Dr. Sharma said that the pain was minimal. "It's the mind that makes the pain." Ruchi thought of another office, brown, no windows, and the split second, a second broken in half, less than that, when she'd not wanted her baby. She looked at the women with daya, becharis emptied of what they'd brought.

∼

ON PAYDAYS, RUCHI deposited her earnings in their account at People's. A month later, it was gone, like throwing her money down a well. This summer they would need to pay for camp. Ruchi didn't like to leave Moksh home alone, not just for the usual dangers of home invaders and exploding toasters she'd seen on the news, but also because he would bury himself in solitude.

"You need your own account," Deepa said. "All women do." But the minimum balance was too high, and Ruchi feared the fees. She cashed the next paycheck and received hundred-dollar bills. The quantity seemed meager so she exchanged them for twenties, adding a satisfying weight to her purse.

She hid the money in batches in her drawers and behind large glass jugs of rice and lentils in the pantry. She kept careful track of her hiding places and the growing amount in a slim yellow notebook. If Naren noticed that she was no longer making the deposits, he didn't let on. It was so little, much less than his own deposits. Though that, too, wasn't much. He remained an assistant despite the new developments that continued to crop up everywhere, as if farmland were in endless supply. Summer came and Ruchi was thirty-five, Naren thirty-six, in the prime of life, living in a still-growing economy. Ruchi read about 8 percent raises and investments that doubled one's money and felt far outside of it, like she was staring at a wall with rows and rows of identical buttons making it impossible to find the one that might let them in.

But her bundles of cash grew. She paid for camp and dreamed of a second car. After five months of working for Dr. Sharma, Ruchi told Naren, "I need to be able to drive." They were walking in the summer evening, a new habit, silent but together with their arms pumping and armpits wet with salty crescents.

"You need lessons for that," Naren said. They walked briskly around a cul-de-sac where the houses were bigger split levels that cut off their view of the setting sun.

"You never have time for lessons."

"Don't I drive you to your job? Don't I pick you up?"

She hated to spend one more minute waiting for him outside People's at TriCity. The tellers leaving for the day gave her odd looks, like she was there to steal. "Should I not have a license? Deepa got one right away."

He walked faster to leave her a step behind. "You don't need to be like Deepa."

A twinge of satisfaction tickled her skin. No, she didn't need to be like Deepa, but that wasn't the point. "I can drop you and pick you up. No need to deal with the TriCity traffic. It's too much hassle."

Naren didn't speak for the rest of the walk, but that weekend, he made a show of driving them to the empty school parking lot and explaining how to reverse and the different speeds of the windshield wiper. Ruchi feigned confusion and did better than anyone expected. She could've told him about the lessons with Deepa. He wouldn't have stopped her. But she hadn't wanted to.

"Not bad, Ma," Moksh said and met her eyes in the rearview.

"It's much harder when there are cars everywhere," Naren said, but he let Ruchi drive home in the dark. They hadn't had dinner, and Naren called for pizza, not minding that he had to pick it up, not minding the sudden thunderstorm. Moksh was hungry for once, pleased with the pizza, and Ruchi took pleasure in being the source of his enjoyment, that she had succeeded in making their lives lighter.

SHE GOT HER license on the first try and a warmth settled into the house. She dropped off Naren at work and Moksh at camp through the summer. She felt more at home among the Cutlass's detritus than in Dr. Sharma's Benz. When her piles of money grew too fat, she made new piles. Summer turned to fall in a single day, but she didn't care. She bought a new Revlon foundation in True Beige that was a better match than her usual, cheaper Maybelline. She surprised Moksh and Naren with sneakers from the Foot Locker in Manchester. Moksh had wanted Nikes that weren't on sale, and she said it was fine. There was enough. For a full day he wore them in the house, hopping up and down to break them in. At the start of fifth grade he was as tall as her, which neither of them had expected. Tall and wiry. She made plans in her mind—the promotion Naren would ask for next year, maybe a trip, or a trip back, which they'd never done, which they never discussed anymore.

At night, Ruchi checked the piles like they were seedlings. Then she cradled the receiver to her ear in the slatted moonlight, and it didn't matter what Deepa said or didn't say. Ruchi wrapped one arm under her breasts as Deepa described her future business with the same energy she'd had about the beach house. On and on she went about the special permits that a commercial space required, the teen patti tournaments they'd play while their kids took Hindi classes, the garbas around Navratri, barbecues for the Fourth with separate grills for meat and vegetables. "Once the place has a full renovation, of course," Deepa said. "I'll even add one room for threading and waxing." She sounded girlish and sweet and Ruchi didn't ask when she could join, when they'd become partners, like Deepa had promised, like she'd promised so many times before. But it would happen. This time was different. This time was what mattered.

In bed, once she was sure Naren was asleep, his body sinking into the mattress, Ruchi took out her new novel, skimming until she arrived at the part where the hero touched the heroine, taking his time with his fingers. Ruchi let herself imagine the fingers as separate entities detached from the hero on a real woman with uneven breasts and fat deposits in her belly. She let herself think of Deepa in the shadows of a bamboo grove, her tongue flicking at Ruchi's lip.

She reached for herself tentatively. First through the cloth before stretching it aside. She thought she wouldn't know what to do, but she did, she knew herself, she knew where she needed to touch, how much and how fast. The simplicity was shocking, a simple act of imagination, though she stopped right in the middle, afraid Naren might wake or that some djinn might be watching. Or because of the old shame and misgivings, a disgust she couldn't help. She tiptoed to the kitchen where she scoured the offending hand with Comet and hot water. She got back in bed and rolled to her side and tucked her arm under her cheek.

~

EVERY DAY, DR. SHARMA depended on Ruchi more, trusting her with urgent blood samples and the handling of complicated, last-minute schedule changes. At the Manchester lab Ruchi removed the neat trays of cold blood from the bag with its peeling orange hazard symbol. "We never have problems with yours," Nurse Magda said, as if the samples were Ruchi's own blood, her own urine. "Don't tell me you have nothing to do with it," the woman said slyly. Ruchi knew better than to accept the compliment too readily and tempt bad omens.

Dr. Sharma added billing to Ruchi's responsibilities. "Pauline can do more at the front desk," she said. "I know you cover for her." She sent Ruchi down the hall to learn about coding from the central billing department. Central billing was one of the unique perks of Connecticut Specialty Suites because it supposedly saved paperwork, which meant it saved time and money. Three women showed Ruchi how to code services to get the most from both insurance and the government. "Make sure you've done it right before you send it off to us. Corrections mean time, *my* time," one of the women said, her wide, freckled jaw tensed, her blue eyes scowling at Ruchi's lab coat. "We'll take it from there."

"I can also do the filing. To save you the work," Ruchi offered.

"Oh, what a dear. But what would we do if you did our jobs for us?"

"No, no, not possible," Ruchi said with a smile. "You are specialists." But even these women she'd prove wrong. Even these women would realize she was valuable.

On some days, Ruchi took her time delivering samples, driving through soupy black puddles with her window down. She meandered through errands. Images to pick up, mail to be sent, reports to be dropped off. She dialed through stations before switching to AM and listening to traffic reports, the cadence not unlike the priest who had performed her wedding. Each word ran into the next.

After Labor Day, she ate her lunches—chutney and cheese sandwiches that she cut into crustless triangles—in the courtyard behind the building where Sanjay supervised the digging of a pond. She sat on a bench at the far corner and assumed he didn't see her. Otherwise he would've said hello. Over the phone, Deepa judged the pond a ridiculous expense. "All because Anu mentioned she likes pretty fish," she sneered. "That girl will be spoiled."

"You'll never allow it."

Ruchi drove by Deepa's cultural center. *Their* cultural center. Ruchi still imagined they'd name it together and unveil a large sign to hoist in the air and stick over the faded outline of #1 NAILS. She liked seeing Deepa's Lexus, the taillight fixed, parked in the lot. The Whiskey Store, Coin-O-Mat, and Dress Barn had their own boldfaced signs, happy children shouting their names. Deepa had decorated the windows with orange marigolds and white carnations.

One day a Volvo and BMW were parked next to Deepa's. Ruchi hesitated before pulling in to the lot. She walked down the concrete plaza that smelled overwhelmingly like detergent. The windows were taped up. Ruchi opened the door without thinking. Inside it was dark and a chemical smell stung her nose. The space was bigger than the outside suggested, a wide, raw space with rows and rows of speckled taupe tile. Light came from a room off to the side, the door ajar to what might have once been a waxing spa. Deepa sat behind a desk talking with her hands. Two women sat across from her, their backs to Ruchi. No one had noticed her. She approached slowly, as if they were a flock that might fly off. At the door, Ruchi cleared her throat.

"Ruchi?" Deepa said, eyes wide, hands in midgesture.

Could it be that they hadn't seen each other for a year? Since the housewarming? The phone calls made it feel like less. The other women turned in their folding chairs and appraised Ruchi.

"I was in the area," Ruchi said.

"You haven't bothered to stop by." Deepa stood up but didn't make a show of air-kissing as she had at the party. There was an expression on Deepa's face that Ruchi couldn't place. Unsettled, perhaps. Her hair was swept up into a banana clip, revealing the delicate lines of her neck. A thick, hot nostalgia made Ruchi light-headed.

The two women wore crisp kurtas over jeans, one with a stylish headscarf. Ruchi recognized the other as Sonal who had answered the door at the housewarming, that long, creamy arm. "Sonal and Amal are helping with the center."

Deepa had never mentioned them, not once in all their calls. Ruchi waited for Sonal to recognize her, but she knew it wouldn't happen, just as she knew that Deepa would fail to introduce her to Amal.

"We're looking for donations," Sonal said. "We're asking all the doctors."

Deepa pulled at the sleeve of Ruchi's lab coat. "Oh, this!" It was playful but Ruchi flushed, sweat beading her upper lip. She worried that her new foundation was still off a shade but also noticed that Deepa's cheeks were pink with irritation. Maybe she'd been using the patches too much, or too little. Or maybe it was shame. Sonal and Amal cocked their heads in curiosity, and Ruchi was reminded of footage of the queen on a dais inspecting an elephant tusk carved into the Qutub Minar.

"I'm not a doctor," Ruchi said. Though both she and Deepa knew she could've been. Once upon a time it had been possible.

"But one of the best receptionists," Deepa said.

"Office assistant," Ruchi corrected.

Deepa knew the difference. Of course she did. It was just her habit of belittling, of pulling Ruchi down, a habit that would've made another friend angry, another friend turn away. But Ruchi forgave her too much. She was too loyal in her unspeakable need.

"I handle the files and specimens. And billing." The women continued to smile, but Ruchi could feel their interest waning, sapping her own energy. "I should go," she said.

Deepa sat down again. "How nice you stopped by." She didn't ask Ruchi to stay or join them for lunch. Ruchi couldn't, regardless. There was work to do, and she hadn't wanted to hear about donors who gave money like it was sport.

She tried not to let disappointment and anger taint the evening and spoil her husband's extended good mood or Moksh's old sweetness, newly returned. But her own family seemed lacking to her now, which in turn heightened her rejection. Here they were striving, but for what? They could only just make their mortgage payments and clipped coupons for groceries. How silly it had been to dream, not one dream but many, the multiplicity of dreams that she'd gathered over years into piles as meager as her piles of cash. She'd always lack something, brutality perhaps, a willingness to pursue an end at all costs.

When they spoke that night, Deepa talked about her usual frustrations with the Coin-O-Mat, the pungent, citric detergent they used, her plan to buy it out once she had enough funds, as if Ruchi's visit that day had never happened. As if it had never been "our project." Ruchi wasn't surprised.

"Can't Sanjay pay for the renovation?" Ruchi asked. "Can't he buy the Coin-O-Mat? Like he bought the beach house?"

"We aren't made of money," Deepa said, but Ruchi could hear a twinge of self-consciousness in her voice, a twinge that only Ruchi would understand, that same twinge she'd known since the day the nuns picked her over Deepa, like her throat was full of paste. It betrayed her doubt and fear.

"Are you not? The medical suite is doing so well. Sanjay is building a pond. I do Dr. Sharma's billing," Ruchi said. "I see how everything is handled."

"Not everything is about money, Ruch. Many things, but not everything."

It was true. And also it was not.

THE END OF September brought a second summer, and weather anchors tracked a hurricane over the Atlantic. Gloria, they called it. On slow days, Ruchi listened to the radio while she arranged the magazines and snipped the baby shoots in the pots. Mrs. Gerb pored over *Cosmo*, licking her thumb between pages. It was unnecessary to keep her for the phones. A waste, really. Ruchi could manage on her own; often she had to remind Mrs. Gerb of what to say, which insurance they took, which needed referrals. The woman was always thankful and smiled solicitously. They were probably paid the same.

Ruchi thought there'd been some mistake that Friday when Sonal appeared at the check-in desk with her daughter, the girl as tall as her mother with an open face, like she would show you anything if you asked. She held her mother's hand. Mrs. Gerb fiddled with her collar and gave Ruchi a sideways glance as if to say that these people were Ruchi's responsibility.

"Ruchi, hello," Sonal said in her cool South Delhite accent. She peered down at Ruchi sitting at the desk.

"Hello," Ruchi said.

She leaned on the counter and the cord of her neck tensed enough to break. "We have an appointment."

"We?"

"My daughter. We are here for my daughter."

The daughter, whose hand was now clasped to her mother's chest, was glass-eyed. Ruchi could see the veins pulsing along the underside of her forearm, blue like the robin's egg shells around the dogwood, the last flowering plant still alive in their yard. The hydrangeas had died years ago from too much shade.

"How old is your daughter?"

Sonal pulled at Bhavana's hand, and the girl startled, as if woken abruptly from sleep. "Tell her how old you are."

"Fifteen."

"I see." She was three years older than Moksh but it was as if Ruchi had never witnessed so young a girl in her life. As if she herself had never been that age. The girl wore shorts that revealed scarred knees.

Sonal slid her insurance card across the counter. It was not one they accepted, and the daughter certainly wouldn't qualify for federal assistance. Ruchi had learned that the government knew nothing about what the money was for. Dr. Sharma had Ruchi code the procedure as antepartum care or postpartum care or post-hysterectomy care. Reagan had decided that the government should never give money for the procedure. Which meant Dr. Sharma hadn't been completely truthful about following the law, though Ruchi considered such deceit smart rather than willful. Helpful rather than harmful. The lie of a good person.

Sonal and Bhavana conferred over the confidentiality agreement and the waiver that wouldn't hold Wellness responsible for future scarring or excessive bleeding, uncommon side effects. Bhavana had to let go of her mother's hand to sign. The two men left in the waiting room stared at their laps.

Ruchi prepared to turn Sonal and her daughter away. She'd find them somewhere else to go. She, too, was good. She, too, was smart. There were other places that offered services like Dr. Sharma's. No one saw anyone for free.

"I'm sorry but we don't accept this," Ruchi said.

"No?"

Bhavana slipped off her shoes and pressed her heels onto the lip of the hard chair. She had long, veined feet that didn't match the rest of her. "I can help you find another provider—"

"No need. How much is the service? I'll pay cash."

A slim, quartz-colored purse hung from Sonal's wrist. She opened the gold clasp and took out her checkbook. Ruchi told her the amount, and Sonal wrote it in small, perfect cursive with glossy blue ink.

"We will need to call the bank to verify the sum," Ruchi said. Sonal Mansingh had her own account at People's and the bank was happy to verify, like it was such a small sum when compared to the balance that its absence wouldn't be noticed. A sea of money that could swallow whole any eventuality and return to its original, placid form. A sum that Ruchi would never carry in her purse, a sum she could only stow away and keep safe.

Sonal smiled at Ruchi. "I'm sure you'll not mention this to anyone. Deepa is a dear but a gossip."

"Of course not. By law it's confidential," Ruchi said, but there was something she didn't understand. Everyone talks. "Why come here? There are other clinics that—"

Sonal reached across the counter to take Ruchi's hand. "Because," she said, squeezing hard, "we want the best."

# Naren

## *1985–1987*

A change was overtaking his wife. Naren watched her at night from his place in bed. The bathroom door was ajar and through it he could see Ruchi's vigorous tooth brushing followed by tongue cleaning until she gagged. The violence of it unnerved him.

He did like to watch her applying lotion to her hands. It brought him comfort. She cupped her palm and, with two fingers, lightly fluffed the jade-green pillow of Vaseline Intensive. This she worked into the top of her cupped hand, her fingers moving in a lulling circular motion. She worked from the back of her palm up to her knuckles and between her fingers.

Gloria was scheduled to make landfall tomorrow. All the seed he'd spread across the lawn with the spreader he'd borrowed from the red-faced neighbor who never had to seed, whose grass grew beautifully no matter how many car parts he burdened it with, all of it would be washed out.

"They say we should tape up the windows," he said.

She emerged in her floral housecoat and said with a forcefulness that surprised him, "You should ask for a raise." She held her two smoothed hands together above her navel. "How else will you get one?"

She placed her rings in a brass tray on her nightstand, her fingers now too slippery to wear them. In the morning, the first thing she did was slip them back on. She'd stopped wearing the bangles some years ago, and he was pleased. They used to make a racket when she shifted in bed, waking him from half sleep. He hoped she might sell them. "I, too, will ask for a raise after one year," she continued.

"Who is asking you to ask for anything?" he said. Though it was true that since she began working, some strain had eased. Less argument, their tones lighter. And still he resented the Jains, their good deeds and charity, how small they made him feel, as if they were especially deserving of their good fortune. At times he worried that had he and Ruchi traded places with the Jains, had they had more money, more status, the texture of their lives would be no different. His family would be no happier, still struggling to remain in orbit while Deepa and Sanjay continued to the bright center. It surprised him, the hold Deepa had on his wife, given how it disturbed Ruchi. Early on he had compared the two and might've even wanted Ruchi to be more like her friend if it wasn't so clear that Deepa thought Ruchi had made a mistake in marrying him.

Unfortunately, they would need the money even more now, though he saw no need to explain this as yet. He was certain that the move to Accounts would be temporary.

He felt Ruchi's feet moving under the covers, a familiar rotating of the ankles, her body settling into bed. He did not want to bother it.

"I told Newhouse I'd do a half day."

Again she was quiet. He felt the room glare at him though he hadn't quite lied.

"School was canceled. It won't be safe to drive," she said.

"It may only rain," he said hopefully.

"So why tape the windows?"

Her quickness irritated him at times. "Newhouse has asked to speak with me."

"Ask him then, no? About the promotion," Ruchi said.

"It is not so simple!" He hadn't meant to raise his voice.

"Then don't spend on more lawn nonsense. All that netting."

He'd purposely left the materials in the garage so he wouldn't have to explain. "With new seeds you have to protect them. If you let me do the work in fall then you'd see."

"Who is stopping you?"

"Lawn takes investment." He was always trying with the lawn, always working to make it grow. He'd see an ad or a display, and it was an opportunity for improvement. A tool to apply fertilizer, a shed for the new tools. All it required was time and money. He wished Ruchi appreciated these attempts. Though the lift he felt after a spree never lasted. He had come to expect the crash, the floor rushing up to meet him. The expenses couldn't be blinked away, instead infecting whatever good feeling he'd achieved.

He switched off the light. "The Cutlass needs a tune-up," Ruchi said. In the dark, her voice reached him through a tunnel. "And Moksh could use braces."

Sometimes he encountered Ruchi's savings, rolls of bills tucked into neat buns behind the hairdryer in the bathroom drawer, stuffed into an empty photo album, and though he'd never skimmed a single note, their presence both eased and irritated him.

"We'll be fine," he said, flexing his legs under the winter blanket, which Ruchi had spread across the bed too soon. It was a warm September. She turned to face him.

"That brother of yours. Does he thank you for the money?"

He made sure to hide Anoj's letters these days; Ruchi couldn't possibly know about the extra money. "Why worry about everything? Every family sends money." He turned away before she could say more.

His mother had requested the additional remittance. Just one time, she'd said, but Naren made the transfer every few months, which became every other month, then monthly visits to Western Union. In response Anoj sent more photos of his improbable children given how long they'd taken to arrive, a son and daughter, the latter good-looking. He was a boasting brother, even as he struggled to meet his gambling debts and keep the bank clerk position. Early on, Naren wrote letters about the

Cutlass, the quiet streets, the different compartments of their fridge, department store sales. Later, he focused on the new things he bought, the weedwhacker, the sandwich maker for toasties. Sometimes he was poetic and described a first snow that painted the elms and how, if you looked up, the flakes became visible just before they touched your face. Anoj made no comment about these observations. Naren told him to visit, even offered to sponsor him and his family, but his brother said he wasn't interested. "Mumbai is my darling," he said. What was this Mumbai-Shumbai? What happened to Bombay? Anoj sent more and more photos—the girl could be in films—but never thanked him, which was fine. It made the giving more satisfying; even in generosity Naren was superior.

But lately the letters, which came faithfully in a blue aerogram, talked of saffron flags, a movement to restore the nation's pride, a new fervor Anoj had found for his country. As a child, Anoj used to make sly jokes about the goddesses and their bosoms, but now he performed daily darshan. Naren could visualize his brother's forehead with a faint red splotch where vermilion from too many blessings had seeped into his wrinkles. It made Naren nervous that Anoj was finding some purpose.

Naren heard the creak of a drawer opening, the crackle of pages turning. Ruchi thought she read her romances in secret, but Naren had seen the covers. Anoj would've told him to forbid the books with a firm hand, but Naren felt only a sharp, wistful sadness. Maybe the problem was rooted in their wedding night. His family's flat hadn't been configured for privacy or conversation. He heard Anoj's voice in his ear, taunting him, but he wouldn't know what to do if he touched Ruchi now. He couldn't force her to want when he himself was uncertain of what he wanted. It would've embarrassed them both to speak of such things; talk meant for films.

At last, he heard Ruchi's soft snore. In the morning he'd tell her about Accounts.

But the morning came, and he left before anyone rose. Sunlight angled through his windshield before disappearing behind the oppressive gray. No one was in the office. The move to Accounts required

Naren to pack a cardboard box and shift to the other side of the office, a task he wanted to perform alone. Newhouse had been kind when he'd given Naren the news, asking Naren to sit down. Naren generally stood while talking to Newhouse, staring at the slap of hair reminiscent of masking tape. "Look, downsizing is happening across the board," Newhouse had said, and Naren had nodded heartily. Already they were down to one floor instead of two. Newhouse proclaimed that the decade of development was over, though it was only 1985 and Naren saw more construction than ever. He had not asked why him, why not Tim or Ryan, why not Farhand Syed who was junior, a more recent hire. A Lucknow man who went to school in Delhi and wore striped shirts tucked severely into his pants and saw no reason to hide that his wife, Amal, an investment analyst in Stanford, made more money than all of them.

Naren packed his paper clips and thumbtacks, his unused notebooks and sticky notes, though technically these items belonged to the office. Newhouse had already been by for the project files. Naren suspected that Farhand had inherited several of these. The new subdivision in Glastonbury. The remodeling of Green Hills Shopping Center. He also suspected that Newhouse had not considered moving Farhand to Accounts, where one fielded calls from upset clients about the accounting. He suspected that Farhand approached each project with what Newhouse described as "an eye to efficiency." His desk was intentionally cluttered to suggest constant productivity. Yesterday, when Naren was preparing for the move, Farhand had leaned against Naren's cubicle, fingers hooked into belt loops, and asked if he'd been given a timeline.

"Timeline?" Naren had asked, confused, both by the question and the dizzying stripes of Farhand's purple button-down.

"Did you ask how long you would be needed in Accounts?"

He had not. "Not long."

Farhand had shimmied his legs and recrossed his arms on the verge of song and dance. "I would ask for a timeline. We are not day laborers, after all."

Tim and Ryan had chuckled.

"Newhouse said a few months at most."

Farhand's whole torso had stretched forward, and Naren had instinctively leaned back. "You can never know with these people, yaar."

Naren still wasn't sure who "these people" were. Newhouse was just one person. Unless there were other people who had decided to send him?

He hugged his box close to his chest and walked down the hall. Though the cubicles were empty, he felt watched. He placed his box on a long table with three phones arranged in a line, each station with a headset to make call taking easier, like telemarketers. It was a phone and data job, far below Naren's education. He placed the box at the end of the row, as far away from the rest as possible. The one woman in Accounts, Martha, wore jeans and old sneakers. But Naren would continue to dress in slacks and polished shoes and a collared knit shirt in case he was urgently called back to Development. He sighed, and his bowels turned to sand. He ran to the bathroom, only to pass gas, a pointless indignity.

THE RAIN BEGAN as he drove home, first a patter over the constant replaying of "Gloria" on the radio. Then, as he turned onto Turnpike Road, a road he'd once loved for its red barns and dandelioned fields now dotted with developments and gas stations that he should've had a hand in building, the patter became a downfall, no, a deliverance that drowned out Laura Branigan's dry voice, the kind of rain he hadn't seen even after thirteen years in this country. He pulled in to the driveway and saw the eyelets of grass seeds poking through the dirt, mocking him.

He found his family in the basement, slurping tomato soup and listening to the radio. He cringed at the thought of their disappointment. But sometimes you have to say a thing to make it true, and right there the plan arrived whole in his mind, an orb that floated up from his bothered bowels and gave him some peace. The homeowners loan money. Ruchi's savings. Together they'd be enough to get by until he returned to Development. Enough to continue the remittances to Anoj and the outsized pleasure it gave him. Because of course he'd return to Development, of course he wouldn't remain in Accounts. All of this was a blip. The lights flickered once and then steadied. He descended the stairs.

He switched on the bare bulbs, startling them. "What's the use of playing the same song over and over?" he complained, as Ruchi hummed along. Through the small window the tops of elms whipped about to parody his new resolve. He felt jittery about the lie he was about to tell. But, like the storm, the lie gathered force and hurled him forward.

"A tree might fall on the house," Moksh said. He'd hardly touched the soup. Naren had wanted to cut down some of the trees, to let in more light for the lawn, but Ruchi had stopped him. "The expense," she'd said, and he could've brought it up now, the expense they'd incur for a new roof, the high deductible on their homeowner's insurance. But he wouldn't be deterred.

"I spoke to Newhouse."

Ruchi tugged her thin gray cardigan across her chest. She never kept any of the clothes he bought for her, preferring long, shapeless shirts that mimicked a kameez. All he'd wanted was for them to blend in, but each passing year they became more separate from the Americans and the Indians both.

"What did you say?" Ruchi asked.

"Nothing. Newhouse himself said he was considering it. A promotion. See? I didn't even have to ask."

He kept very still as she folded her arms, then slid her weight to one hip. "Considering," he repeated, and then to fill the air, added, "a small raise. At first."

The radio announced that the worst of the storm had moved north and would downgrade to a tropical disturbance by evening.

"Very good," Ruchi said at last, a smile touching the corners of her lips.

THE LIE MADE it all bearable, the call taking, the supervisor who went by "Kirk" and took little interest in his work, the fluorescent lights dimmer and harsher than the ones in Development, the black rolling chair needing oil. Except for visits to the bathroom, there was no reason to get up and walk anywhere, but Naren periodically made his way around the area, walking briskly, as though he had somewhere important to be. Still, each morning his bowels tightened as he entered the building and didn't release except on days when he visited People's to transfer money from the loan account to his checking account, a process so routine and simple that his favorite teller, Janina, began asking him, warmly, with no judgment, "The usual transfers, Mr. Mehta?" As if recognizing the great work he was doing.

A YEAR PASSED, then two. He wasn't returned to Development, though by 1987 business was booming again. At fourteen, Moksh became as tall and thin as a reed, his frame swimming in his hoodies. On weekends, Ruchi took to making rich foods, covering the counters in thalis of chickpea flour, frozen peas, and jeweled vegetables that she tied into katoris and dropped in electric pools of oil. She made fresh sev when she could've bought ready-made packets from the Indian Store. It was pointless when Moksh refused to eat anything fried.

Sometimes they went to the Jains' parties, and next to Anu, who had become a hulking girl, Moksh appeared even thinner. It always struck him, seeing his son next to other children. The parts of him Naren got used to were thrown back at him. Moksh's face, his thinness, his coldness. He generally didn't smile or look people in the eyes. It used to bother Naren when he saw his child at a playground struggle with equipment and refuse to play with the rare child who approached, as if Moksh was purposely making life harder for himself, though at times Naren's chest constricted into a dull ache of recognition. He, too, had been reserved and never saw the point of going through the day always smiling.

Anoj's son was also ugly, but in a normal way. On Sundays he went to a special camp to chant shlokas and do what sounded like military-style exercises. Bodybuilding, Anoj called it.

Ruchi asked about the promotion from time to time, whether his title had changed, whether his raise had taken effect, and Naren deflected.

"Tell me, where is your promotion? Why hasn't your doctor ma'am given you a raise?" he said, raising his voice to hide his nervousness. Ruchi didn't bother to argue, didn't meet his irritation with her own irritation, just turned over in bed and curled around her ridiculous book; he knew then that she didn't believe him.

One early morning in late February when winter was at its worst, he received a rare phone call. The line stitched with the faint murmur of other phone calls. Naren, still in bed, held the receiver a little away from his ear. His brother tended to shout. "Boss, you should move back!" Naren had always hated when his brother called him "boss."

"What for?" Naren asked. He kicked off the covers and stretched the receiver cord to shut the door.

"This is your country, no? Amrikan bani gayo?" Anoj shouted.

"We've been here fifteen years," Naren hissed. But also the number shocked him. How had it happened?

"So what?"

The background murmur turned into an airy singsong.

"Boss, you could live in Navi Mumbai where the flats are bigger!" Anoj said.

"Then how will I send you money?" Though he couldn't help but picture the sleek flats with no confounding lawn to maintain.

"I'm going north with the sevaks. You know enough is enough. Ram's birthplace is his birthplace!"

"And what, you'll stand outside the masjid screaming for Ram?" Naren chuckled, pleased with himself.

"Laugh if you want, but in ten years there will be a temple there. Everything will be different. All these foreigners living here taking our jobs."

Naren didn't say that he'd heard the same thing said about Asians in America. Anoj's voice bobbed with grave excitement as he told Naren about the other sevaks, their chants and their flags, the roti they shared on the train. All seva, working for free. Naren had read about it in *India Abroad*. Bricks were being laid around the mosque, some of them with gold-encrusted SHREE RAM in coarse letters. He strained to understand Anoj's fervor for a faraway temple. Instead, he yearned for an old Bombay evening, golden light picking off the waves, a burnt smell in the air. Here only a milky gray sneaked through the crooked blinds.

"You could increase your help, boss."

"Increase?" Naren sighed, and a whistle formed in his throat. The phone line had cleared, the silence heavy. His bowels burbled.

"Money is the biggest thing."

A FEW WEEKS later, after the first day of spring, the Connecticut sky no less gray, the air no less damp, a second conversation jarred him. This time Naren was in the bathroom stall at work when he heard Newhouse with Sanjay Jain. "This cultural center. It's my wife's pet project," Sanjay said, followed by a synchronized stream. Naren crouched in the stall, not wanting to sit on the toilet but also not wanting the top of his head to peek over the door. He could smell the remnants of his shit. His quads burned.

"I'd recommend a different approach," Newhouse said. "To minimize costs."

"Always good to minimize costs. The wife thinks money falls from the sky. You know, I have a friend. One of your structural engineers."

"Great guy. A real cost cutter."

Naren coughed and shuffled his feet. The fake cough turned into a real one that he couldn't control.

"All okay?" Sanjay called out.

Naren nodded ineffectively. He tried holding his breath to stifle the cough but that made it worse.

"Water?" Sanjay offered.

Tears began to form from the effort. "Fine, fine," he muttered in as low a register as he could muster.

The men on the other side were silent. Naren clung to the hook on the door.

"Mehta, is that you?" Newhouse said.

His cough subsided and he stood up straight, unlatched the door, and stepped out. He caught his flush-faced reflection in the mirror.

"Naren!" Sanjay called out with ridiculous cheer. "Perfect timing. I told Deepa, 'Use the beach house,' but no, no, she wants a center-shmenter. At least Ruchi is reasonable, not so demanding. She's a very good receptionist."

"You know each other?" Newhouse asked.

Sanjay looked at him quizzically. "Of course. Isn't this the cost cutter?"

A tap dripped and the HVAC system clicked into the next gear. "Sure." Newhouse cleared his throat and pulled at his waistband.

"We should not mix business with social," Naren said. He couldn't stomach the suggestion of pity.

"Don't worry, SJ, we have someone else who'll be thorough," Newhouse said. "I think you'll like him."

SJ?

"Good, good."

Naren approached the sink to signal that they should leave now, that all was fine. He could see that Sanjay—SJ—and Newhouse were relieved and offered tepid farewells. He ran the water over his hands as hot as he could stand.

That evening, Ruchi dumped Moksh's leftovers into plastic containers and stainless steel compartments, as if he might eat them later. Naren admired the simplicity of her worry, how it could be poured into a container, refrigerated. At night, she spent extra time on her skin-care rituals, washing her face and sweeping a cotton ball over her skin to remove the foundation that gave her a ghostly pallor. It had always bothered him; he preferred her skin in the morning before any makeup when it shone at its deepest brown. His mother had been disappointed by her darkness, but he was darker. He wanted to tell Ruchi he liked her natural color but didn't want to embarrass her.

It was a pale night, and when he was sure Ruchi was asleep he tiptoed through the sliding door and then down the porch steps that needed staining and into the backyard where nothing would grow but stubborn elms. The full moon was a disk in the sky, its light cutting through branches. The cold air punched at his chest, but soon it would truly be spring, a season that made him lonelier than was normal. He'd be approaching eighty by the time they paid off the house.

He walked to the edge of the yard where it became woods. The neighbor told him the elms were invasive. Theirs was the only house with so many. Dirt and leaves poked at the thin soles of his chappals, acorns dug into his arches. The play gym with its rusted swings and slides, the clearing in the woods where Moksh used to spend hours among stumps he'd named, characters in his head, friends he didn't have. He never could indulge his son's make-believe the way Ruchi had, not because they were lies but because each one was too bright, too painful a longing. Still, Naren wished he'd paid more attention then, when the boy was sweet and full of hope, unknowing. Ruchi thought he was hard on the boy, distant, detached, but he was none of those things. He loved his son, and as with most things, the feeling lived too close to fear.

Tomorrow he'd distinguish himself in Accounts. He'd rise to the top, force Kirk to notice him, to praise his diligence. Someday he'd tell Ruchi the truth, someday when it didn't matter anymore and they could laugh like old friends. He'd pay back every cent he'd withdrawn from the loan, as if borrowing from their borrowing had never happened. He blinked into the dark and saw bricks through the trunks, each one etched with someone's name, someone's seva, someone's good work. Maybe his.

# Deepa

## *1989*

Deepa was tired of smiling. It had taken her two years to acquire the dilapidated storefront, and now it was almost 1990, she'd turned thirty-nine, and the renovation was still pending. Ravi Ravichandran sat opposite her desk, blathering on about his two oversmart sons and their overachieving achievements, their tennis and badminton, their Ambassador Clubs and honor societies, their Vedanta lessons and Indian-bornness and cultivated American accents, his back to the sad space that needed renovation, the folding tables that lined the walls, the cracked floor tiles, the chemical tang that still clung to the air no matter how many times Deepa had the space cleaned. But she was stubborn; she wasn't one to give up.

She'd unrolled the blueprint across her desk, a plan that included the Coin-O-Mat next door, a storeroom in the basement, a small kitchen and separate lobby. An office with a window, all of it in the service of an open event space with skylights and chandeliers and a square parquet floor for dancing and wall sconces and an accordion divider for weekends when the women might play cards while children took classes. Deepa ran her hands over the paper while nodding along to Ravi's monologue. She needed this little man and so she would show interest in his little life, his charitable works, his "share and care" attitude.

He skirted his pinky finger through the fragile folds of his ear, then investigated his findings, as if expecting gold. "If we buy out the Coin-O-Mat then you can have a whole section for cultural events. Big raas garbas!"

"A cultural center," Deepa said, trying to meet his exuberance. "For the children, so they don't become Americanized."

"Very nice. Very nice." His mustache wiggled as he spoke, the air circulating in the hairs. "And my point exactly, Deepaji. The mandir is essential. Everyone will donate for the mandir. No need to drive to New York and New Jersey for basic darshan."

Who were these people driving to New York and New Jersey? Did they not have home temples? "Of course, of course. We also are tired. And we've been here longer."

"Then what is the problem? We can decide today." He thumped her desk.

Deepa folded and unfolded her hands, smoothed the blueprint again, then again, but Ravi ignored these gestures, as if she had no hands. This was the nazar she'd tempted: Ravi in her makeshift office demanding gods.

"For the community," Ravi went on. "A place to pray together."

Deepa's cheeks ached from maintaining a cheerful expression. "But the mandir will be secondary, of course."

"Secondary?"

"To the cultural center. The main space. Like we discussed."

Ravi polished his nails and examined them, before returning his pinky to work on the ear. "No problem. But it's all one space. People will think it is all one space. People will come because of the temple. You'll have so many people. From all over the state."

"I see," Deepa said.

"We can have camps for the kids."

"Camps?"

"You don't know about the camps? The lovely Hindu camps?"

She'd received a saffron-colored brochure in the mail with photos of unsmiling children in red T-shirts holding sticks, junk she threw out with the circulars. "Yes, the camps."

"Who wants to send their children for so many weeks to Rochester or Edison? We can have Hindu camp right here, where the children will learn shlokas and mantras, and not just popular ones like Gayatri mantra. Rare bhajans. Correct history!" For this he thumped his thigh.

"Just one thing, Raviji," Deepa said with sickening gentleness.

"Separate ones for girls and boys, of course."

"Yes, yes."

"Too bad your Anu will go to college."

She signaled to the blueprint with her chin. "One thing."

"Next year, right?"

"Yes, but—"

"She can be a counselor."

Deepa inhaled deeply and pressed her hands to her thighs under the table. "Raviji, we have received sizable donations from the Syeds." Unlike other donors, Amal and Farhand made no suggestions for how their gifts should be spent, no specific requirements, the money speaking for itself. But there weren't enough people like the Syeds who made sizable contributions, wrote thousand-dollar checks, asking for nothing in return. There were far more Ravichandrans.

"Yes, the Syeds. Farhand is very good at tennis. Always enjoying himself."

"Yes, and his wife, Amal. I would like to—"

Ravi licked his lips. "No one makes laccha paratha like Amal."

"Yes, yes. But what I'm saying—"

"And her kheer."

"Of course." She took another breath and focused on the ends of his mustache that flicked out like fishtails. He was her peer, an unhealthy, older-looking peer, and yet here she was, talking to him as if he was some venerable sir. "I've asked Amal to help with the opening. To oversee it," she said with what she hoped was finality.

Ravi's pinky went still. "The Diwali celebration? The Syeds?"

"The *opening* celebration," Deepa corrected. "Amal herself is a singer. Lovely voice. She might do backup with the group."

"Where is this group from?" Ravi asked. The ear had turned red from his fiddling.

"Toronto. They are top on the East Coast. Amal has wonderful taste. Sophisticated."

"Very nice."

Deepa exhaled. She'd tape god posters in the lobby as a concession, a nod to Ravi's generosity. She could even rename it Bharat Bhavan or Masala Heritage, or some other vaguely pious nonsense. That much she could manage. It would bring them luck. But she was not in the business of temples.

Ravi stood up and Deepa stood with him. He adjusted his pant waist over the bulge of his stomach, then sat back down. Deepa didn't know what to do. It seemed silly to sit down when she'd just stood up. And in any case, it was time, was it not, for him to leave?

"Deepaji, there's one problem."

"Problem?"

"We need a pundit."

Her stomach tightened. "Pundit."

"For Diwali. And Amal, well. I don't think a Muslim can find a pundit." Ravi blinked innocently. "Of course, you don't have to take the donations. Sanjayji's medical business is doing so well. Pushpa visited her doctor the other day and said he's built a small bridge over the fishpond so you can be with nature while you wait. Genius man, your husband."

Deepa drove the nail of her thumb into the opposite palm. She did not want her husband's money, his endless generosity. She thought of the decorative tricolored koi, the new diagnostic imaging machines and waiting room armchairs, the free bottles of water in minifridges, the new fax machines for the billing office, the catered sandwiches for receptionists. She thought of his nighttime nudgings, infrequent but insistent. No. She was determined to keep this one thing separate. Clean. "But Raviji, who is saying we don't need a pundit?"

∼

THE RENOVATION WAS set for summer. The Coin-O-Mat owners grumbled but were quick to take Ravi's money. Deepa also grumbled—Ravi's budget forced her to acquire cheap floor tiles, varnish that would scratch—but refused Sanjay's offers to make up the difference, which were empty offers at their core. She saw his relief at her refusal, his constant worry about money, even as he earned more of it.

Deepa avoided talking about the project with Ruchi. She didn't want to answer Ruchi's questions about the temple or hear her assessment of the name Deepa had settled on. The Bharat Friendship Association was just fine. Most of all, she didn't want to hear Ruchi's disappointment at not being included. It was best to talk about other things.

Though during their phone calls, Ruchi also withheld. She stopped talking about her problems with Naren, her constant worries about Moksh. Deepa had heard about Naren's job difficulties, of which Ruchi made no mention. Their talk became mutually evasive. Of course Ruchi knew about the mandir. Of course Dr. Sharma would've gossiped. And yet Ruchi said nothing, kept up her stories about ungrateful patients, her pride in her competence, how deftly she navigated insurance codes, how meticulous she was. In the late evenings, Deepa took the cordless into the empty living room where she tucked her legs underneath her on the vast white sofa and lay with her ear pressed against the receiver so Ruchi's voice could pour into her. Now and then Deepa murmured assents that might substitute for intimacy.

Until one July evening, Ruchi called as usual but wouldn't talk. Deepa stretched her legs down the cool leather cushions and filled the sullen silence with complaints about Anu, Sanjay's indulgence of her, how it made the child needy. "Teenagers in this country are too delicate."

"Why are you complaining?" Ruchi finally said. "Moksh goes to his room, shuts the door." Her voice was thin and ready to fight.

"There's nothing wrong with reserved."

"Anu does the same?"

No, Anu wouldn't dare. Anu was forever watching her, wanting to tell her something. It was Deepa who wanted to hide in a room and close the door. "Of course," she said, "you have to leave them be sometimes."

"You're always saying that."

The words aimed to throw Deepa off-balance, to reach through the phone and tip her off the sofa. "No one is saying do nothing, Ruch. That it's not difficult. But what can you do, right?"

"You're mocking me."

"Don't be silly," Deepa said.

"Sometimes I think, had I never come to this country—"

"You'd have nothing. And you'd be so far." Deepa sat up and placed the phone on speaker. She'd said too much. "Don't be stupid."

"I'm not being stupid."

"In Bom you'd be cursing your mother-in-law all day."

"Maybe. But children don't hide from their parents in Bombay. They eat. They talk." Ruchi spoke with an energy that made Deepa afraid. "I only came to America because—"

"I should go. It's late," Deepa said. She refused to hear Ruchi say it. And yet of course Deepa had always known Ruchi had come for her. It had been Deepa's intention.

"You must be busy with the renovations," Ruchi said, her voice swerved low.

Deepa went to the kitchen and placed the phone on the counter next to the stove. She boiled a pot of water. She'd started drinking a cup right before bed to aid digestion. "You have no idea." She took a sip that burned her mouth but held the water on her tongue until it cooled.

"Are you on speaker? I can't hear you."

"I'm calling it the Bharat Friendship Association!" Deepa yelled. The word "Association" was Ravi's idea. Deepa swallowed her disgust at the name.

"Bharat? Association?"

Deepa held the burning mug in her hand. "Associations get more donations."

"I keep forgetting to send."

"No, no, there's no need." It felt wrong to take Ruchi's money. "Some Hindu groups have given. In exchange for pujas now and then."

Silence. Deepa made a racket with the pot to preemptively drown out Ruchi's judgment. But when Ruchi spoke again, her voice was seeped of sharpness.

"I can help, if you need. With any planning," Ruchi said, beseeching again, which made Deepa swell with pride and meanness. She picked up the phone.

"No need," she said.

WHEN SHE AND Amal met at the office to go over plans for the opening, Deepa intended to mention the mandir. Diwali. The now-and-then pujas. The gods. It wouldn't affect the mission they'd crafted with Sonal: "To promote awareness of Indian cultural life and festivities." Deepa liked the word "festivities," how it formed in her mouth and on her tongue. They would still have festivities.

The place was a construction site. The floors stripped, walls demolished, the stink of laundry detergent still present, but Deepa insisted they meet at the dusty office where she could sit behind a desk, act as if she was in charge. Had she invited Amal home, she worried she'd feel small and nervous. Amal was good at details. She was quick to organize the program and outline how the evening should flow. "By the end, everyone should be dancing," she said. Deepa admired her stylish headscarves, her undernourished, aloof accent. It was more than posh, an accent that begged imitation but then left the imitator feeling unworthy and insecure. It was hard not to compare her to Benazir Bhutto, her long face, the way her cheeks hollowed when she spoke. A beautiful face in composite, each feature a little too strong by itself.

"It will be wonderful, the new space," Amal said. It was warm in the room and her headscarf had slipped so that strands of her hair swept her brow. She could be unnervingly lovely. "I've already spoken to the other analyst at work. A Bengali." Amal had a habit of mentioning work here and there, a reminder of her stature, her education. "She said she's bringing her children who refuse to eat desi food. We'll make sure there's English translation."

"You're lucky yours were born back home. They're not so Americanized." Deepa was hopeful that Mirza, the Syeds' daughter, a freshman at Mount Holyoke, would be a good influence on Anu. The girls were spending the afternoon together. Amal said Mirza had been a gangly thing when she was little with bones too big for her face, but her features had settled into something demure and smart. Anu had good bone structure but was a slouch of a girl who let her eyebrows caterpillar together, refusing to do anything to depress the follicles. Mirza must have scrubbed between her brows, her upper lip, and her sideburns after showers, rubbing the skin with a rough towel until it was raw.

"We were right to leave," Amal said stiffly. "Mummy says everything has become worse. The flag-waving and saffron-wearing."

"All politics."

"Politics? More than politics. At least here we can try to not copy that tamasha."

"There was hardly anyone here when we came. Not even an Indian store." Like the Ravichandrans, the Syeds were newer immigrants, arriving ten years after Deepa. None of the newbies fully appreciated how much easier it was for their children not to be the lone Indians in their school, for their grocery stores to carry frozen pita to function as naan, for the woman in Avon who offered threading in her basement. How hard Deepa had worked to keep up Anu's Gujarati when most, Ruchi included, had given up. Though Anu's filed-down pronunciations grated on Deepa just the same. "Now at least we have enough people for proper functions."

"Unless everyone breaks into their own groups. The Tamils and Gujus and Bengalis." Amal wrote out a list of how many aluminum trays they'd need, how much food they should order, her script precise like everything about her, a precision that Deepa worried she'd lost from being in this country so many years, a manner both soft and firm, whittled to an edge. Around Amal, Deepa felt so typical.

"The Pakistanis and Indian Muslims," Amal said. "As if I have anything in common with a Pathan." Amal twirled the pen through her large fingers. For all her elegance, Amal was also animal. Her feet, too, were wide and muscled. A scent that carried a trace of decay, the scent of rainstorms.

"It won't be like that. Not here." Though Deepa knew it was already happening in New Jersey, where there was a Gujarati Samaj and a South Indian support group and a separate organization for Muslims. And now her center, skylit and newly carpeted and with a renovated kitchen, would have gods. "You'll see."

THE GODS ARRIVED in October, just as the renovation neared completion with the place stinking of paint and wood polish. The large boxes boiled over with foam peanuts when she opened them, but inside Lakshmi was smaller than Deepa expected, the size of a car seat. She was draped in cheap green cloth and had a tangled nest of hair. Some assembly was required for the lotus, the sun disk. Deepa had chosen lightweight plaster statues as opposed to stone ones, both for the cost and to facilitate installation because she insisted on doing it herself. What could it take? There were instructions.

She'd ordered eight. The statues had a manic blaze in their painted eyes as they lay on the parquet. They had upturned mouths. She avoided their faces, but not out of reverence. Even these plastic molds could carry nazar. She saw what gods had done to her mother, how they'd trapped her. She remembered being nine and going on a pilgrimage to Nathdwara and clinging to her mother's hand. She remembered the expanse of her mother's back, women with rice dripping from their foreheads staring at her mother's overly made-up face, kohl tinting purple-blue the papery skin under her mother's eyes. Bells rang. The intertwining of sweat and incense. Old widows in white saris with the strength of beasts, heavy and chanting, pushed forward, while guards swatted bamboo sticks at lumps in their backs. But the women couldn't be stopped. A priest watched from his platform, a curled, cruel smirk as he lifted the sheet to reveal the glory of Shrinathji. Deepa had been too short to see. Her hand slipped out of her mother's, and Deepa frantically tracked her until she was consumed, carried forward in a sea of bodies that didn't care who fell underfoot. Afterward, her mother, radiant, bathed in devotion, had shown no remorse for their separation, offered no comfort as Deepa, bruised and crushed, trembled.

Technically, Deepa was no longer Hindu. Sanjay was Jain, though the Hindus thought of everyone as Hindu, a great, wide tent that required no forcing. A somewhat monstrous canopy that even the Christians, unbeknownst to them, were part of. Her mother had had a tiny figurine of Jesus, a shy-looking white man dressed in blue robes, on her home altar. Everyone included. Except the Muslims, never them, an exclusion that Deepa found perplexing, if not downright childish. She'd been naïve to think that such demarcations would matter less in America, that this country did anything to heal divisions.

But to interrogate her beliefs now felt foolish. Here was Lakshmi, and she deserved better clothes, jewelry that looked less fake. Deepa would pick from the saris she wasn't saving for Anu.

She was supposed to hire a priest to set up, but why needlessly spend money? She had created a budget for puja-related activities, but who was watching her? Just like who was here now to pull the gods out of their musty packaging? Plump with chipmunk cheeks, long-toed and the color of flesh never exposed to the sun. She was surprised that the goddesses had breasts, though the cloth and jewelry had a flattening effect. She suspected that none of them had genitals and resisted the urge to check.

They were not well made. Ganesh arrived with plastic rhinestones missing from his crown. Shiva wobbled like the uneven restaurant tables that Sanjay found especially noisome. Parvati's lips were poorly painted, the color slipping over the lip lines like madness.

They were a means to an end. Once she put them in their places, dressed them up, bought the puja kits, strung garlands around their necks, hung a bell in the middle of the room, it would all feel better. They could be there, and she could forget them.

She arranged the gods against the back wall. As a Shaivite, Ravi had requested that Shiva be the largest deity with the coveted center position. The statue was larger than the rest, and she heaved him from his armpits, bore the weight in her hips, and pinned Shiva's forehead under her chin.

She'd barely elbowed Lakshmi, but it was enough to topple her, chipping her nose. "Oh, fuck shit." The English curse surprised her; it made her feel pleasantly outside herself. Lakshmi's plaster nose was now pocked and discolored. Deepa rubbed the area and more paint flaked off. Lakshmi's eyes, Deepa realized, were asymmetrical. One bulged wider than the other. She turned the statue to face the wall and drove to CVS for foundation to fix the mess.

THE RENOVATION FINISHED in late September after Navratri, and Deepa still hadn't said anything to Amal about the statues. They weren't so close that she couldn't feign ignorance. But ignorance about what? When had Amal said she herself was religious? She wore headscarves, yes, but she also wore form-fitting jeans, spaghetti-strap dresses. Let Amal see that the gods were a sideshow, a decoration.

"So much light," Amal said when she walked in. A tailored button-down shirt, the cream of skin at her collar. "It's a lovely space." She scanned the room, first the high ceilings, the separate kitchen, the office door with Deepa's name under DIRECTOR. Her eyes settled on the gods lined against the back wall.

"For the opening the stage will go in front," Deepa said. She stood with her arms outstretched, as if she could cover them.

"It's a Diwali event. You think I didn't know? Ravi's asked for financial advice. Farhand even signed off on the structural plans."

Farhand? Deepa felt like a fool. Amal paused at Lakshmi, cocked her head. With the light shining on the plaster face, you could see where the makeup hadn't been blended, but only if you wanted to find fault.

"Next door we can create a masjid," Amal said.

"A synagogue, too."

They laughed at their imaginary world. Deepa had always been good at conjuring such things. Was it her fault that Ruchi had believed in them? Her friend was smart, and also foolish.

Amal left to check the sound equipment in the basement, measure the dimensions for the stage. Deepa had not yet told Ravi about the stage, or the curtains she would install to hide the gods. She was growing to hate the little man.

THE EVENING OF the program, Anu seemed happy to attend. She wore a mint-green lengha and tasseled earrings without complaint. She tugged her blouse to cover her thick waist, squirming with the cumbrousness of a small child. When Mirza was in town, she and Anu took to making plans independently of their mothers. It pleased Deepa that the girl was having an influence on her daughter, maybe teaching her how to be pretty. When Anu returned from these outings she had an aura about her reminiscent of Amal, a raw sheen. Deepa gazed at her daughter's neck when her back was turned, trying to see inside.

The space was resplendent. White and yellow carnations festooned the stage and fairy lights hung from the walls. She'd made this happen. Deepa, who the nuns had taken for a dunce.

She had worried about the previous businesses' misfortune leaving a mark, but Ravi had done a Vastu, broken a coconut on the threshold, painted a small rice and vermilion Swastik on the door that was quickly wiped off. "The thieving Nazis," Ravi had complained. Deepa scoffed at his piety but appreciated his forethought. Nazar could rise out of any common jealousy, and at the first sign of good fortune. What did it matter that she was driven by fear more than belief? What was belief if not fear?

She could hear the singers inside, a woman testing the mic in a high, shrill soprano. Mirza in the doorway, a vision in blue chiffon. Anu running up to her; the girls hugging. They walked into the hall hand in hand, skirts trailing, tiny sequins winking under the lights. The scene overwhelmed Deepa, an enchanted place scraped clean of loneliness.

Inside, the singers, a couple, strutted across the stage, though the woman was the star, luminescent. Amal in a twilit sari surveyed from the middle of the room, surrounded by white dinner tables speckled with yellow petals. The statues lurked behind stiff navy curtains, like they were at the theater.

She and Sanjay had to sit with the Ravichandrans. Pushpa was livelier than her husband but still a bore. "Very lovely, Deepaji," she said, chewing on her cubed paneer. The vegetables were bland and the rotis tough, but the guests were eating, filling their compartment trays with a little of everything. From across the room, she saw the Mehtas hunched over their plate at a table by the exit, Moksh sulking and swimming in his kurta. The boy was too thin. Ruchi caught her eye and waved a plastic spoon in her direction, but Deepa pretended to be too engaged in conversation to notice her. She'd explain that Sonal had made the seating plan and had placed Ruchi farther from the stage than Deepa would've liked.

Ravi waved over a small, stern man dressed in a dhoti, his skinny, hairless legs bare to his knees. "Punditji!" he exclaimed, which did nothing to alter the man's expression. Ravi leaned toward Deepa. "He's come all the way from Edison."

Deepa nodded a hello to the man, and the man answered with his hands in prayer. During the day he was an anesthesiologist.

Deepa asked Ravi, "But didn't you do Vastu puja last week?"

"Deepaji, every occasion needs blessing."

Ravi led the pundit to the stage and the singers stood aside, heads bowed. The two men fumbled with the navy curtains until they managed to pull them back. The gods stared out at the crowd in their mismatched finery, their plastered grins. The pundit incanted and anointed while Pushpa and Ravi muttered lispy prayers. It went on too long, and Deepa's expression glazed into neutrality. She felt a pulse in her chest that wasn't her heart.

At last, the party started, and the singers were even better than expected. If Amal was bothered by the puja, she didn't let on. She danced with Farhand, her arms circling above her headscarf, the pins artfully concealed in her hair. A finger's breadth of skin showed between her blouse and the pleats of her sari. Meanwhile Ruchi stood at her chair, clapping. Deepa guiltily wished she wasn't there. Her presence felt like an omen, a sign that Deepa had done something wrong, a reminder that she'd been too bold and besharam as a child, wiping off her kaala teekas, smiling at the once-a-day barber, playing silly games with Ruchi on the balcony.

"Garba time!" the singers shouted, and the tables were pushed back, the folding chairs propped against the walls. A chaos of half circles formed. Deepa was too busy to join for long, attending to the caterer, fetching more plastic cups, arranging the meethai into geometrical patterns on silver trays. Off to the side, Sanjay taught the Syeds, two steps forward, one back, spin, clap, again.

In the center Ravi clumsily tried to follow some new sequence all the big raas garba groups were doing. Sanjay stuck to the outer circle with the older women who liked to fawn over him, dancing with a little shake of his head. Ruchi hovered at the edge, waiting for an opening, when she should've just jumped in. The girls were nowhere to be found, which was fine. Her daughter garba-ed like an ostrich.

There was a whoop for dandiya, and Deepa hurried to the basement to fetch sticks. She admonished herself for not having them ready. Later, she'd have to reorganize the pairs that had been strewn about the hall. Next year, she'd make a rule about this and ask for a nominal deposit to drive a message home about orderliness. It was not, after all, their father's kingdom to wreck.

It was early, not quite ten, though already she felt the end of the evening approaching. It had all gone so well, the pundit departing once the dancing started, the guests forgetting the mediocre food once they began moving. Tomorrow she'd call Ruchi to go over it all, because Ruchi would listen and enjoy the gossip. Whatever strangeness between them would recede. Deepa would explain her plan to raise money for an addition, maybe buy out the seasonal store so the gods could have their own wing, and she too would pray there, thank them for staying out of the way.

She opened the door to the basement, the vast storage space barely filled. A light was on in the corner. Odd. There was no reason for anyone to come down here. Or had it been on all this time? She scolded herself. Think of the bill.

A rustling. She stopped halfway down the steps, careful not to make herself known. She'd made sure the cellar door was bolted shut and bound in chains. No one could've gotten in from there. Or did the Coin-O-Mat owner still have a key? Was he angry about selling? No, it could only be vermin. She calmed her heart and stomped her feet.

"Hello?" she called and switched on another bulb.

A swish of skirts, gasps, bangles falling down arms. The girls stepped out from behind a beam, flushed and full-looking, their chunis askew. Mirza with her hair slipping out of a loose bun. A heat behind her daughter's eyes that wouldn't dissipate.

"Hello, Auntie," Mirza said. But how composed, in seconds. As though she'd done this before. "The music was paining my ears."

The color drained from Anu's face, leaving her gray in the light from the naked bulb. "You too, Anu? It was paining your ears too?" Deepa asked, but Anu was frozen. Deepa wanted to hold her and beat her simultaneously. The music thumped above; the crowd restless for their sticks. Deepa searched for a definitive action to take, anything to quell her rising shame. But Mirza was taking her daughter's hand, like they were skipping schoolchildren, pulling her forward, pretending it was nothing.

"Anu!" Deepa's voice cracked and betrayed her. "I need your help with this." She dragged two bags from the corner, the metal jingling.

The girls continued to hold hands, but Anu's had gone limp, until finally Mirza dropped it. Despite herself Deepa's anger flashed at how quickly the girl discarded her daughter. "You can go," Deepa said to Mirza and wished the sky could suck the girl up, like she'd never happened. But in the dim light Deepa couldn't help but recognize Anu's longing, a frayed, painful stirring as she watched Mirza's feet on the stairs. She straightened Anu's disheveled chuni, tucked the end roughly into the girl's waistband, and felt a tremble under her skin. A whole crescent of water threatened to overflow from her eyes, to pull Deepa in. But she steadied herself, resisted. Deepa dropped her daughter's arm. "Take these."

"Mom."

"Take." She thrust the bag at her chest, and Anu stumbled from the force. A great bellowing cry from upstairs and a quake of music. She made her daughter hand out dandiya, made her smile and look happy until every last one was handed out and then let her slump in a seat in a corner. Amal sang onstage, a hip artfully jutting out and back in. Deepa saw Ruchi picking her way through the crowd toward her and wanted to whisper it all in her ear, to burden her with the heaviness she felt, and blame her, too.

"What a nice voice she has," Ruchi said.

Deepa shivered. She kept her eyes on the dancing crowd that moments ago had seemed so lively, such a reflection of her own abilities, a scene that made Deepa feel she'd done something important. Something good.

"You're too easily impressed," Deepa said. "She's off-key."

"You're so critical, always."

No, Deepa wanted to say, not critical. Smart. Careful. Elegant. A woman who knew better than to dismantle her life over momentary desires. In a breath, she prepared to shut Amal out, a gentle but precise distancing, carefully worded so as not to seem unkind. She'd work harder, steer the events toward prayer, an annual puja that would grow so large and so devout that Amal couldn't help but see that her money would only lead to more expensive statues, gods for Deepa to dress in finer saffron silks, then tuck her desires into their folds and pleats, and snuff them out, like a solid act of love.

# PART FIVE

# Moksh

## *1989*

Moksh realized that by eating less, he could eat even less. At night he kept track of his bones, radius and ulna, the manubrium of his sternum, marked the portentous outline of his ribs. Diwali came just before his fifteenth birthday, and at the grand opening of the Bharat Friendship Association his mother pulled him into the long buffet line where trays of food lined up like soldiers ready to trap him.

"Sonal," his mother said to the woman ahead of them. "Happy Diwali."

"Ruchi. How nice you've come. Happy Diwali." He remembered her from other parties, how she greeted them down her nose. His mother poked him.

"Happy Diwali," he muttered.

"So tall," Sonal said, as if it were both an achievement and an affront.

"Bhavana is well?" his mother asked.

"Very well, yes. College visiting already. All top schools," she said. As she turned, her mouth dropped into a scowl.

They reached the head of the line, and his mother passed him a foam compartment plate. "Take properly," she said. She touched the back of his arm, and he instinctively pulled back. He'd developed a habit of withdrawing from any contact.

"I don't like the food to touch," Moksh said. Palak paneer and makhani dal and fried papadam and yogurt thick as bread. He spooned palak without the paneer. Exactly five pieces of iceberg lettuce. One puffed bread. A bare minimum of rice that he'd chew grain by grain.

The band wasn't loud enough to cover his mother's sigh. Raspy Bollywood standards over speakers that reverberated with too much feedback.

They sat at a table far from the stage. His parents looked terribly alone. They ate side by side in silence, seemingly the only family eating side by side in silence. His father sulked into his food, and his mother smiled at nothing. She caught Moksh's eye, and he looked away. A regular dream of his at the time: his mother, because of some mean thing he did or said, transfigured into a crow or a squirrel that he chased through the backyard, flinging his father's clumps of grass to catch her attention and stop her from escaping into the woods that he used to think was a forest but realized was just a scrim of privacy from the house on the other side that you could see through well enough in winter anyway. No, no eye contact. He convinced himself he was protecting his parents from seeing the full, blunt force of his discomfort, even as he also knew he was purposely hurting them, especially his mother. Not because she was a bad mother, but because he could. Because she made such a thing possible. He'd turned into a clear-eyed and steely teen, but steelier than he wanted to be.

"I wish we were closer to the stage," his mother complained.

His father knocked the wall to his left and shook his head. "Could've gained four feet if they'd taken this out."

A couple a few years younger than his parents approached with their plates. After looking around for a different table, they sat and offered a stiff nod. The auntie next to him plowed through her four compartments piled high with paneer and makhani and when she thought he couldn't tell, she examined his face. He assumed he made her uncomfortable and nervous, as he did most people. To complete the picture, he frowned and stared slack-jawed at his food, then worked on his bottom lip, scraping off the dead skin with his front teeth and working the scabs in his mouth. He almost felt bad for this auntie and her yellow-toothed husband stuck out here in Siberia with them.

"You think they could have proper tables that don't shake," his father said through his food. The uncle across the table grunted, maybe in approval. There was no telling.

"Ere, it shakes because you keep moving," his mother said. She turned to the auntie.

"Ruchi," she said. "Naren."

The auntie asked, "Surname?" like she was filling out a form.

"Mehta."

"Minal Shah."

"Gujarati cho thame!" his mother exclaimed. It was always a surprise to her that anyone else was Gujarati.

"From Ahmedabad," Minal said and motioned to her husband. "Varun. Engineer." The uncle smiled dyspeptically.

"Naren pun engineer che," his mother said. His father continued eating as if she hadn't spoken about him, rolling his tongue over his teeth.

"Very nice," Minal said.

"Civil engineer," Varun the Engineer snorted. It seemed he spoke in grunts.

His mother answered, "Naren is structural."

"Must do well with all the development."

"Oh, very well," his mother said, and his father harrumphed. Moksh was certain everyone knew she was lying. Minal and his mother traded generalities about Bombay and Ahmedabad: what school, what road, what did your father do. Moksh counted his mother's inconsistencies, telling Minal the story version of her life that she'd once told him as a child, that she grew up near Churchgate, not Bhuleshwar, in a flat, not a two-room chawl with a single toilet for the whole floor. Her father a merchant, not a dry goods vendor. Sitting with these strangers, Moksh wished his mother would stop, wished she'd speak in her normal voice, tell the truer version of their lives. That his father slept through Saturdays, that she still organized coupons into aisles at the supermarket, that they watched too much TV.

"Moksh is in tenth. In India he would be taking his SSC or maybe even ICSE," his mother said, connected to nothing. "Mokshu, you're lucky you don't have to take those exams."

"I don't know what those are, Ma." The belittling came out too meek. He wasn't good at brash, American-style disrespect that rolled easily off the tongue.

His mother appealed to Minal. "Here the system is so different. High school for four years. In India it's two years and then junior college."

Minal turned to Moksh, as if he'd just appeared next to her. "In India there are also American-style high schools. If you have the money. We'll send Stuti back when the time comes."

"India is rising," Varun said, with orange food in his mouth. "Good time to invest."

"You must sign up for the Hindi classes the Association will offer next month," Minal insisted.

"Who will he speak Hindi to?" his father asked, but no one paid attention to him.

"Wouldn't that be nice, Mokshu?" his mother asked. Minal turned to him again, expectant that he might tell them about his extracurriculars.

"I don't know," he muttered to everyone's disappointment. He spooned rice into his mouth and twirled it around with his tongue.

A little man guided a priest, clad in a button-down shirt and wrap skirt, to the stage. The little man took hold of the microphone, which screeched. The room went grudgingly quiet. He made a self-congratulatory speech that went on too long. "All this"—he drew wide, emphatic circles with his arms—"for the next generation. For their cultural heritage and full success." Cultural heritage and success, as if the two were linked. Varun grunted again, and Minal nodded along. To be Indian was to be enterprising. Nothing less would do.

Then, like two fumbling magicians, the men wrestled back the thick curtain to reveal the heads of gods, their bodies hidden behind the stage.

"Wah!" Minal clapped.

"Since when are the Jains religious?" his father grumbled.

"Shh," his mother said. "Fold your hands."

Minal politely ignored them. Varun grunted again. The little man onstage muttered alongside the priest, hands pressed in prayer. Moksh, with nothing else to do, folded his hands in his lap and thumbed the bony knuckles.

LATER, EVEN HIS father danced a little among the aunties and uncles in the outer circle. "Come, Mokshu," his mother begged. Though part of him wanted to, he slunk down in his chair, and she left him. She had her eye on an inner circle for the more advanced dancers, more complicated steps that went backward to move forward. But the circle was fast, and she couldn't find a good opening. When he was a kid, he'd spied on her from between the legs of the secondhand console where his father stored magazines and playing cards and accordion folders and a whole drawer of small change, his mother dancing to ABBA and the Pointer Sisters and Donna Summer, her floral housecoat that hit just below her knees gliding among the dust motes and skimming the furniture, a little on her toes, hips swinging, pretending she didn't see him, pretending she was alone.

He searched for Anu. Normally, she would've invited him to join her group. But he couldn't spot her in the crowd, and he felt abandoned.

Hunger snatched at him as the night wore on. He wanted to go home and followed his father out to the lobby where a box sat by the front window on a plastic table surrounded by shoes. A red metal box with a silver clasp and a yellow sign with DONATIONS written in bubble letters. Inside, cash mingled with envelopes and checks, like a tray of disorganized desserts. His father picked up one check different from the rest, with green tint instead of blue and a customized paisley border. Moksh peered over his father's shoulder. A thousand and one dollars, the one for good luck. "Wow." A bold, capital *F* signature at the bottom. He thought his father might stuff it in his pockets, and silently he cheered him on.

"Why wow?" His father tossed the check into the box, pulled out his wallet, unfolded his own blank check, no border, no gold thread, and used the blue pen taped to a string to scratch out "one thousand one hundred and one." His hand shook.

"That's a lot, Dad," Moksh said.

"Shh. It's nothing. Why are you spying?" his father said.

"Don't worry. I'm not going to tell anyone." Across the lobby, aunties shuffled in and out of the restroom, their skirts jingling like coins.

"Ere, why would I worry? What am I doing wrong?"

"Nothing, Dad. I just thought we didn't have—"

"We have," his father said, raising his voice. "We have plenty." An auntie stepped out of the bathroom and hurried away from them.

"Okay. Okay."

"Find Ma and tell her we're leaving."

"She's dancing," Moksh said and hoped it was true. "You find her."

But he wasn't good at being alone with his father and so he went back inside. There was enough chaos that he could avoid finding his mother if he didn't look. The music was on pause as people rushed to make new groups, find partners, teach kids the routine. He spotted Anu moving through the crowd with a bag of dandiya, aunties and uncles swarming around her to grab a pair. His mother had once taught him the steps with her roti belans. "Tap your sticks, then your partner's left, partner's right, tap yours again, bye-bye." He'd tried to mimic the bounce in her step but tripped over his feet and fell behind. He wasn't quick like that.

He wished for an earthquake. A meteor to tear through the roof. Any disaster that might shake his loneliness, disturb his fear that if he tried to join in, no one would want him. Even these people who were supposed to be his.

There were other stories his mother used to tell him, stories about kings and goddesses and nuns. She tended to muddle the lessons, to add strange little animals, sarcastic princes who didn't mind smelling like garlic, who took baths in baking soda, nuns who could tear a person right open. That was how he remembered them. Outwardly, he dismissed them as stupid stories, even as the fanciful part of him wished the statues peeking over the stage might raid the buffet line, scoop koftas into their mouths with their bare hands, grab Anu's dandiya and divvy them among themselves to twirl overhead with their many arms ready to bash each and every—

But something was wrong. The usually cheery Anu, the Anu who would go to the best colleges and earn the best honors to become the best pediatric endocrinologist she could possibly be, that Anu wasn't cheery. That Anu was lumbering about in her heavy skirt, eyes squinting, a hand on her stomach as if she were sick. Maybe she was.

The bag was empty in her hands, but instead of joining the teens making their own exclusive dance circle, Anu hugged herself into a chair.

He sat down at an adjacent table.

"Hey," she said. She was focused on one girl, older, prettier, a better mover than the rest.

"Who's that?" he asked.

"No one. Some family friend."

"Why don't you join her? Clearly you want to."

"I'm no good. I end up whacking people's hands and apologizing the whole time."

"Yeah." They were quiet. Their mothers were across the room, talking, arms crossed.

"You think they're arguing?"

Anu shook her head. "My mom is probably complaining about me."

"About you?" he asked. "What could she possibly have to complain about?" He'd meant it sarcastically but his voice betrayed tenderness.

"There's plenty. I wish, sometimes . . ." But she didn't finish. She sat there slumped, looking both hungry and lost. In contrast, the pretty girl, the good dancer, was having a great time.

His bowels emitted a liquidy gurgle. He could tell no one that every shit he took, every expulsion, every purge, gave him joy. Less of himself made him feel more.

"What do you wish?" he asked.

"I wish I could hate her. I wish I didn't care what she thought of me. I think I might be adopted, like a mail-order child, like those Sally Field ads with kids who can be your pen pal. I think there's something wrong with me."

He couldn't accept her sadness when she was the perfect one, when her family had money, when her mother seemed happier than his mother, when his father seemed better suited to life than his father. It wasn't right for her thoughts to mirror his own. "Nothing's wrong with you," he said. "Don't be so melodramatic."

"You could be nicer, you know."

"I'm being honest." Though he wasn't. The truth was that her sadness made him less lonely.

Silent tears rolled down her face and neck and into her glittering, pale-green top. He felt bad and weak for feeling bad, but he and Anu were bound, whether he liked it or not. Both caught inside their parents' sacrifice, all they gave up in coming to this country so their children could lead great lives and strive without pause. He and Anu were supposed to be grateful.

"You don't know," she whispered. "You don't."

His father found him. "Why are you taking so long?"

It was time to leave, though the dancing was beginning to speed up and his mother had just found a group to join. Anu wiped her face with the heel of her palm and smiled at them in goodbye, as if she'd turned her head around to present the correct, sunny version of herself. She let some auntie pull her into their group and tripped over her skirt as she performed the right steps. She didn't look back at him, as if they hadn't just spoken about honesty.

Out in the parking lot, the cold late October air slapped him hard in the chest. His mother gave him the passenger seat, and his father drove. They passed the gas pump and Panda Express and Denny's and Town and Country Store and signs for I-84. His mother's face flashed in the side mirror every time they passed a streetlight, and for the first time Moksh thought she looked old. She was thirty-nine, and later, when he was the same age, he'd gape at photos from this time at how young she was, how much like a girl. She stared straight ahead, her tongue massaging the inside of her cheek, while his father tapped the steering wheel, a sign that he was in a good mood.

"Aren't we going home?" she asked.

"Why the rush? It's a nice night for a drive."

The shops petered out and were replaced by fields. His father turned onto a winding, hilly road, and Moksh was lulled by the grain of the pavement, by the dark dome of sky above them, the elms and pine black and still against the expanse.

His father slowed and parked the car on the shoulder.

"What are we doing?" his mother asked.

"We're going for a walk."

"It's, like, night," Moksh said, though he was the first to open his door.

"What, you don't use your legs at night?"

"Where will we walk?" his mother asked. His father beckoned her to the other side of the road where tall grass carpeted a field, which might have once been corn. Moksh followed them down a path along the edge. The path turned a corner so that it cut the field in half. Tall stalks lay flat across it, as though they were sleeping and would wake in the morning. "I'm not wearing the proper shoes," his mother said, but she continued, and Moksh felt they were traveling a great distance.

He couldn't see the end of the path and assumed they'd turn around, except that they came across another path, one that was mowed down to the dirt, the stalks and tall grass cleared to make a road, what would be a driveway, and at the end an unfinished house. Despite the darkness, the blond plywood walls shone, large squares cut out for windows.

The house was surrounded by piles of gravel and discarded blocks of wood and orange machinery prepared to come alive at any second. His father picked his way through and pulled himself over the foundation and onto what would be the ground floor, his footsteps echoing against the planks.

"Stop! What are you doing?" his mother called out.

"This must be the kitchen," his father said, testing a beam.

His mother hesitated but then turned to Moksh and said, "Come, Mokshu." She needed no help to climb up and gestured to say she'd found the living room. Next to that the dining room with a veranda. French doors. His father insisted on a sun-drenched porch. Double granite vanities. A finished basement. They moved from one end to the other adding rooms where there were none, rooms inside rooms; doors that led to tunnels that led to a wall of ornamental waterfalls. Hunger coursed through him, zipping through his ribs. He pointed at the sky. "Over here the stairs that lead up," he said because he'd never get this chance again, all of them lying at once, tiling bathrooms and cutting windows, a view to the turquoise pool, speaking over each other until their voices were a single, uninterrupted sound rising and falling in the circling night.

# Ruchi

## *1990–92*

The Bharat Friends Association was nothing like what she and Deepa had discussed. It was a *temple*. The gods along the back wall made the space feel smaller than it was, the way the courtyard at Our Lady English Medium School shrank when either of the nuns watched over them during break time. At the Diwali opening in October, Ruchi took refuge in the small, squalid satisfaction of seeing Deepa's plan compromised. She dragged this meanness into the new decade. Ruchi didn't feel the renewal that the magazines she laid out at Wellness said she should've. *Time* featured a wooden sculpture of a frowning woman in a skirt suit holding a naked wooden baby and briefcase and the title "Women Face the '90s." Women were sick of trying to have it all. They were supposed to shed the eighties like weightless shapeshifters. But was "having it all" the briefcase and the baby? It didn't seem like much.

And then in February, that short slog of a month that Ruchi never got used to, Naren was laid off. He came home with a cardboard box of belongings that he taped and deposited in the garage. He and Ruchi walked up and down their driveway while Naren railed against Newhouse. It was too cold to venture much farther, but she didn't want

Moksh to hear the news. "I was going to leave anyway. They've become a faltoo developer. All their houses leak and shake," said Naren. Ruchi knew it was all talk, he'd had no plans for leaving, but she was too weary and cold to poke at his bravado. Her gloves needed mending.

THE FIRST WEEK he was home, Naren coughed and stayed in bed, and Ruchi drove Moksh to school and got to work earlier than usual. But the second week, as she turned onto Lake Drive toward the high school, Moksh broke their usual silence. "Why isn't Dad going to work?"

"He's tired, Mokshu," Ruchi said.

"If he can stay home when he's tired then I should stay home too."

They descended the hill toward the school, past a raw dirt road that cut through an empty lot for yet another subdivision. "He'll go tomorrow," she said. "Or the next day. I wish you would let me drop you at the entrance."

"He's not going back, is he?" Moksh asked. His brown paper lunch bag was balanced on the gear shift between them so he wouldn't forget it, which he sometimes did. She couldn't pinpoint when he'd become so thin. At fifteen a boy was supposed to fill out.

"It's temporary. The company downsizing. I'm sure they'll call him back. Or he'll find something better."

"Maybe he'll open that motel," Moksh said and snorted. Ruchi pulled up to the curb a hundred yards from the entrance.

"We didn't want to worry you." She held out the bag as Moksh opened the door. "Your lunch."

"Don't you think I should know that Dad lost his job? Don't you think I would've found out eventually?" He snatched the bag from her hand. "You can't pretend I won't notice."

The swiftness of his anger surprised her. He generally showed displeasure through silence. Distance. The torrent of words was both better and worse, a provocation requiring a response from her. "Mokshu, please, don't leave angry. It will be fine. You're making a big thing about—"

He slammed the door and pulled his black hood over his head when he should've been in shirt sleeves. He clutched the brown paper bag in his fist, likely crushing the sandwich inside. She realized that she'd sounded like a poor imitation of Deepa, her breezy advice playing in Ruchi's head: *Let them be, stop worrying, don't be so dramatic.* Ruchi never knew the right thing to say. The crushed sandwich that Moksh would likely throw out was her fault, as if she herself had crushed it in her hands and made it unappetizing to eat.

NAREN SLEPT THROUGH the spring. He rose in the mornings after she insisted that good luck came when you prepared for it. But when she returned in the evening, she'd find him in the room again, rolled to one side on the made bed. He didn't work on the lawn or take walks in the mall, and perhaps she should've been grateful for the latter, a sign that he understood his spending problem, but his tiredness confounded her. She was reminded of her chawl and the men who lay head to toe on charpoys down the long balcony on hot Saturday afternoons while women stepped over them to hang wet sheets and wring out rags.

"Downsized," Naren muttered from time to time, as if he'd lost his job through no fault of his own, as if he'd been going to work every day as normal, performing tasks he was asked to perform, as if he wasn't leaving the office to wander around the adjacent strip mall until it was time to pick him up at the end of the day. As if she didn't know he was borrowing from what he'd borrowed, as if she hadn't been paying the bills herself, tracking the bank, mortgage, credit card statements. Once a week she opened the file cabinet in his closet with a suitcase key, rattling the lock until it gave. His cotton cardigans smelled of peppermint and vinegar and she didn't mind sitting among them, poring over papers. She'd found the letters from that ungrateful brother who went on and on about his "great project" in Ayodhya and his obedient children, their monkish commitment to seva. She'd read about the "project" in *India Abroad*, plans to restore the birthplace of Ram, as if Ram were paying all these people a living wage, or had sprinkled them with fairy dust to make them believers. Anoj was proof of its hollowness: a man who would do nothing for free. But then, what did she know anymore about people back home?

And yet Naren had been sending him money they didn't have. The debt stalked her. She realized that they would owe forever. Money, money, money—the word ricocheting until rendered senseless.

At dinnertime the phone rang and Ruchi picked up the receiver with her wrists. She was rolling rotis by hand at their yellow Formica counter. She'd seen the ready-made frozen variety at the Indian Store but justified waking at five to knead dough and the forty-five minutes after work to roll fresh rotis as a necessary thrift. A bag of atta was cheaper than buying someone else's labor. She cradled the receiver between her neck and shoulder.

"Do you need money?" Deepa asked.

The roti on her makeshift tawa puffed and she pinched it off the heat before it blackened. Ruchi was the one who called. For years now, Deepa was always busy. "What are you saying?"

"Ruch, I heard."

Ruchi froze. "Heard what?" Ruchi whispered, but she understood. Friends are always talking.

"A loan would be no issue. And Sanjay can recommend Naren for—"

"No," Ruchi said, her voice rising. "Don't be silly. Already he has prospects."

Deepa said, "If I'd known I would've insisted he take the contract."

"Contract?"

"For the Association renovation last year. Instead of that Farhand Syed. Pushy like his wife. But Sanjay said Naren declined it. Some stupid reason about not mixing business and pleasure, except how else does business happen? Sanjay is too mild to insist, but I would've made sure." Deepa paused. "Did you not know?"

She didn't. "Of course I knew. Naren is also too mild." She rolled roti as expertly as Ammi used to. When had she become her mother? Though Ammi would've been angry, finding someone to beat with her belan or berate with her tongue. Ruchi's anger simmered but didn't explode. She wasn't sure if that made her an improvement.

"For the best, maybe, rather than work with an ingrate like Farhand," Deepa said.

"Aren't the Syeds big donors to the center?"

"The *Association* has many big donors," Deepa said. "Ruch, if you need help, you know you can ask."

"Who said we need help? I have my job, don't I?" A surge of adrenaline cut through her fear. She had an income, whereas Deepa did not. Ruchi would manage because of Ruchi, an enormous weight that steadied her as much as it held her down. "I can manage it," she said, then added, casting for a tender spot: "Is Anu coming home this summer?"

But Deepa showed no sign that the question bothered her. "A full ten days in August. Better she stay busy than start some boyfriend-smoyfriend business."

"Anu houshiyar thai gai," Ruchi said, then whispered, "Like me," and hoped Deepa had heard it.

BY SUMMER'S END, Naren returned to the lawn and the television and found work as a clerk at a candy and magazine shop in Hartford. Every night he brought home Mars and Mounds and Skittles that Ruchi stored in jars lined up on the counter, as if to buoy her husband, to show that his work had a product, as though the jars might form pillars and walls of the large developments he'd never been assigned. Meanwhile, Ruchi's piles of money dwindled to a single bundle she hid in her purse.

For Moksh's junior year, Ruchi decided he could drive them to work, first dropping Naren off at a bus stop in Vernon, then Ruchi at the office in Manchester. She hoped her son might enjoy having the Cutlass in the afternoons to do what he liked until it was time to pick them up, like the American teenagers who roamed malls in packs. But Moksh spent his afternoons alone at home. On weekends he worked at Dairy Queen, and when he returned, he said he'd drunk shakes all day and was too full to eat, which was a lie that Ruchi pretended was true. He left his paychecks in her nightstand drawer, next to the novels

Ruchi made sure to place facedown. She wanted to refuse the money—children should not pay for their parents—but couldn't, both because of the shortfall and because the checks, endorsed to her in Moksh's careful script so like her own, stood in for the boy's affection. She cashed them and made new piles, smaller now and quickly used up.

Moksh turned sixteen and became even thinner. One Friday in late spring, as he drove her to work, Ruchi decided that something must be done. "I'm making an appointment for you with Dr. Shark," she announced. "The first available."

"My pediatrician?"

"And so?"

"I don't need a doctor. Especially not a kid doctor. I'm nearly an adult, Ma."

"But until then a child," Ruchi said. He pulled up to Ruchi's office, maneuvering to the curb with ease. His confidence as a driver mirrored her own.

At Wellness, Ruchi plucked the ficus's yellowed leaves and trimmed the overgrown ivy hanging from the ceiling. She freshened the magazines and dimmed the lamps that she'd purchased to counter the fluorescent lighting. She ordered the files for the day into a neat column with names visible. The work was, always had been, too easy, and on some days, after the lab samples and files were delivered, when the patients had thinned out or canceled, boredom threatened to overtake her, stuck as she was with Mrs. Gerb's endless thoughts on the latest turn of events on *Dallas* or *Dynasty*. Ruchi made sure to keep a novel in her purse next to the carefully rolled stack of fifty single dollar bills. Mrs. Gerb would've kept talking if Ruchi didn't explain that she was trying to improve her English. "Always a good idea," Mrs. Gerb chirped, and Ruchi was relieved that she didn't offer to teach her.

That year Ruchi had received a small bump in her salary and at last a promotion to "manager." She should've asked for more but was no better at that sort of thing than Naren. She worried that what was given could easily be taken away, chiseling a small but sharp resentment toward Dr. Sharma. The doctor who accepted Medicare and Medicaid, who used government funding meant for contraception to offset the cost of abortions, who never turned anyone away, also drove a new Acura and wore expensive shoes and rarely repeated an outfit under her white coat. Dr. Sharma adhered strictly to inflation to calculate her staff's yearly increase and gifted scented candles instead of cash at the holidays. These things did not escape Ruchi's judgment. Had the good doctor been first in her class? Or second? Perhaps third? Dr. Sharma, too, was a Bombayite, but posh Cathedral Prep was not the same as low-fee Catholic. It didn't matter how hard Ruchi worked, how meticulous she was with prefilling patient forms, how much efficiency she built into their filing systems or streamlined their insurance process. She was an office manager, a sign that she hadn't worked hard enough. A lie, but maybe a lie Ruchi would've also believed if she was in the good doctor's place: that prosperity followed those who deserved it.

Would she have liked being a doctor? She would've enjoyed being called "Doctor," the visibility, the assumption of smartness. But was it only vanity? Or might she have enjoyed other things: depressing a tongue, feeling for lymph nodes or a protruding spleen, counting the vertebrae of a back, divining a person's insides from light touches. Comfort, soothe, offer warmth through a clinical eye, warmth that didn't require love. She might have been good at that.

ANOTHER MANAGER WOULD'VE thrown the envelopes away after seeing that they weren't addressed to Dr. Sharma; Mrs. Gerb certainly would have. But Ruchi filed them in her desk drawer to study later. Over the course of weeks, three arrived, all in the same envelope, all from the same insurance company addressed to the suite's billing department down the hall.

On a slower than usual Friday, she remembered them. She'd forgotten to bring her novel and searched for anything to occupy her to avoid a Mrs. Gerb monologue.

"I'll take the mail down the hall," she said by way of explanation. She took two of the envelopes with her and left one behind.

Joan in Billing glared at her. "These are dated from weeks ago."

"I thought they were junk pharmaceutical offers," Ruchi said.

"These are all of them?"

Ruchi nodded.

She opened the third envelope at the pond, carefully unsticking the seal in case she needed to seal it again. At the top: IMMEDIATE ACTION REQUIRED. She skimmed through quickly and then read again more slowly, examining the attached invoice for which the company was "demanding reimbursement." Payment for vaccines. Tdap, MMR, Hib, rotavirus, polio. Ruchi thought of Sanjay's Saturday vaccine clinics, how they served "the most vulnerable." But why this demand for reimbursement? What heartless insurance company didn't cover vaccines?

The puzzle turned in her mind for the rest of the slow afternoon. Dr. Sharma had never received a letter like that, threatening to report her to state authorities. Ruchi always double-checked their billing codes, called to verify coverage far beyond the scope required. A way to keep busy, yes, but also an unwillingness to allow a single extra penny to flow in the good doctor's direction, and so out of pettiness, perhaps, too. But a pettiness that spared Dr. Sharma scrutiny and allowed her Friday scheme to continue, a worthy scheme, but still a scheme, to offer special procedures at reduced cost. Preventive medicine.

Most people were careless. Most people didn't pay attention to details. If Ruchi were working in central billing, she would've done things correctly.

The day passed and she realized she hadn't made the appointment with Dr. Shark. Tomorrow. But tomorrow came and again she forgot, and again. She spent lunch hours checking vaccine schedules and codes, searching for answers. Finally she walked to the pay phone outside Kmart and called the insurance company that had sent the letter, saying she was new to the billing department and didn't have the full account details, no, but if someone could help her understand, she would work to fix the mistake, because of course, there was some mistake. These were vaccines that should be covered, and Ruchi would clear it up on her own. Her blood jumped with her duplicity. Someone would thank her in the end.

"Fix the mistake? I'm sorry, who am I speaking with again?" the woman on the phone asked.

"Janice," Ruchi blurted. "Roy."

"Well, *Ms. Roy*, our records show that we've been sending these letters for over a year."

A year? Had she heard the woman correctly? What did the ladies in central billing do all day?

"But this must be a coding error. These are scheduled vaccines. Surely your company covers scheduled childhood vaccines?"

"Not if your office obtains the vaccines for free from government programs." The woman spoke in the measured tone of a parent to a tantruming child.

Free from government programs. Ruchi considered the million minisoaps and packets of Tylenol and boxes of Actifed that passed through Dr. Sharma's office, pharmaceutical freebies that they took for personal use but never sold. That would be ludicrous, not to mention dangerous. Like billing for vaccines obtained for free.

The fraud rose in front of her, large and bloated and obvious. Both beautiful and stupid in its simplicity.

"No, of course not. Nothing is for free."

RUCHI SLOWLY CROSSED the parking lot, lightly populated at that hour, to return to the office. For the rest of the day, she performed rough calculations in her head. About three hundred dollars for all vaccinations in the first year of life, times an estimate of patients based on Dr. Sharma's daily load, times two because administering shots was quick, times an estimate of all the other insurance companies that had been paying the medical suite for vaccines obtained for free. It was enough for new cars, new houses, second houses. Enough for a child's college tuition with money left over. Enough for renovations and vacations. Enough for life lived twice.

The amount sank from her mind to her throat, belly, thighs, landing in her feet. Everything the Jains had was built on a scheme, a cheat, thievery. Sanjay, who, like most powerful men, seemed generally unworried, was a dacoit.

She hoped Dr. Sharma would know what to do and take the choice out of her hands. Ruchi casually left the envelope on the doctor's desk while collecting the day's files scattered throughout the exam rooms. "I thought you should see this," Ruchi said.

Dr. Sharma studied the paper longer than it took to read it. Ruchi explained about the government vaccine program, the incompetence of central billing, Dr. Jain's Saturday clinics. When there was nothing more to say, she adjusted the stack of files pressed to her chest. "We should inform someone, no?"

"One invoice would be a mistake. Two, three, twenty, is a pattern. A crime," Dr. Sharma said. "The whole suite could be shut over this kind of thing. Any authority would investigate us all." Dr. Sharma sat back in her chair, her face lined and weary.

"But your practice has done nothing wrong."

"What codes do you use for the Friday procedures?" Dr. Sharma asked, placing the envelope and its contents in a drawer.

"That's different. No one is getting rich from—"

"What codes?"

Ruchi was silent. Routine ultrasounds, pregnancy care, contraception.

"Central billing means we're all attached. One ledger leads to all the ledgers. No, there's no one to inform. Let it be an internal matter."

Ruchi nodded, feeling she'd done something wrong while being right. She left folders on her desk to file tomorrow, something she never did. Moksh picked her up, and they made their way to the bus stop where Naren was waiting with a bag full of candy no one would eat. On the drive home, Ruchi, too, wanted to be silent but didn't dare remain alone with her thoughts, so she filled the car with made-up stories about dead koi in the pond, patients who spelled their own names incorrectly, Mrs. Gerb's bad breath. Mean things to force a chuckle. But the silence was waiting for them when they returned home. She had yet to call Dr. Shark, distracted as she was by a situation she should leave alone.

At dinner the sound of her chewing rang in her ears. She felt hemmed in by the kitchen's floral wallpaper, the raisin-brown cabinets and outdated electric appliances that crowded the counters. Without thinking, she placed an extra roti on Moksh's plate.

"If you don't eat, your acidity will get worse," Ruchi said, what had become a regular refrain.

"I don't have acidity," Moksh said.

"We'll go to Dr. Shark next week. He can prescribe an acid blocker."

"Did you not hear him?" Naren pushed back his chair, shaking the table. "He doesn't have acidity."

"Why are you getting involved? He's growing too fast. Needs too many calories."

"All he does is waste your food. Don't you see it?" Naren said.

"Please, Naren, be quiet." She pivoted around the kitchen, hoping to drag the silence back.

But Naren leaned toward their son and snarled, "What is stopping you? Why not eat this food?" He picked up another roti and slapped it onto Moksh's plate. Then another, and another. "Perfectly fine food."

"I'm not hungry," Moksh said, his voice unbothered though he clutched his spoon, his hand shaking.

"Can't you be normal?" Naren said.

The word hung in the air. Ruchi thought it too at times, a thought she beat back into shadows.

"Sure, Dad," Moksh said, his voice hoarse. "I'll be like you."

THAT NIGHT RUCHI was far away from everyone. She washed off the foundation and swabbed Clinique toner over her face. She lotioned her hands and lay awake. Her husband was turned away from her with a clenched fist resting on his shoulder. They did not talk of the evening. Her parents had slept on separate charpoys, an arrangement Ruchi would've suggested if it didn't mean more solitude, when what she wanted was less.

She should've called Dr. Shark. What else was more important? But a terrible tremble disturbed her skin. Did everyone wish for things they couldn't have? She thought it would pass, but her feelings had festered even as Deepa locked hers in a vault, even as she didn't visit, made sure they were never alone, reduced their interactions to calls, the phone an instrument of longing. Could closeness live amid fear, amid resentment and regret? Could it fill and empty you at the same time?

She could've made other friends. Friends who were warmer, kinder. The lab tech who praised her work, the librarian who brushed her sleeve while suggesting titles, the cashier at Stop & Shop who met her eyes and smiled every time. JEWEL read her bronze name clip. Women hungry, like her, to touch and be touched.

And yet her mind circled back and back. Deepa had chosen Ruchi in a dusty courtyard when no one else would, had whispered in her ear. Sometimes Ruchi could still taste the blood in her mouth. To forget, to not taste it, would be far worse. Fear was nothing next to the stark pain of absence.

Again Deepa called. She and Ruchi talked about weather, and Deepa mentioned a sale at Filene's. They flitted around safe topics that meant nothing. Ruchi told her Naren had a good job and Deepa acted like she believed her. Weren't they all, each one of them, fakes, cheats, frauds in one way or another?

"You'll come, no?" Deepa asked. "To the party?"

The beach party had become an annual August affair. Ruchi hadn't planned to go this year. But she saw an opportunity.

"We'll stop by," she said. "Promise."

NOW HERE THEY were, sitting side by side against the bed. Ruchi trying to tidy the papers. Deepa catching her wrist and asking her, daring her, to say what she meant.

"And?" Deepa asked again. "I leave my husband and then what?"

But Ruchi didn't have an answer. Not one she could say out loud. The bedroom walls were closing in, though the door was still ajar. She understood that nothing was simple, that Sanjay would be caught, maybe even go to jail. The medical suite might go under. Ruchi might lose her job. She understood the repercussions; she wasn't a fool.

But wasn't a truer life still possible? A house, this time by the sea, she and Deepa on their own, casting incantations to protect their faraway children from the nazar clamoring at their windows, perhaps even performing rituals to snatch their husbands out of harm's way too, but mostly they'd keep their interests narrow, protecting only themselves.

Ruchi's hand was on Deepa's downy thigh. Presumably Deepa had placed it there, but when? How could Ruchi have missed the exact moment? It could be nothing. The way two bodies touched in a crowd. Or the two of them as girls. That one memory, like a song you hear for the first time but have always known, that becomes clearer with time, the fog dissipating until the two figures were no longer blurred. Hardly a breath between their faces.

Except. Ruchi pressed Deepa's thigh. Not casually, not accidentally. She felt awkward, but not ashamed. She moved her hand up until her thumb grazed Deepa's thin underwear and the tiny hairs that poked through. Deepa's voice was small and chiseled: "Ruch. Ruch, please." Was it a protest? An invitation? Both? Ruchi still had nothing to say. She expected that in seconds, the moment would end. She expected Deepa to push her off, pull her hair, kick her in the ribs. Call Ruchi crazy and unwell and proclaim her own innocence. Disgust, green as bile, would pour out of her. But Ruchi didn't want to think. She didn't want to place herself in the moment beyond this one.

Gently, adeptly, she pushed the fabric aside with her middle finger and found Deepa's smooth nub, wet and ready.

Deepa's lids fluttered, then shut. The exclamation marks between her brow softened, her throat swallowed. She squeezed her thighs together and trapped Ruchi's hand at the wrist. Ruchi held her breath and flicked her finger as seconds, then minutes passed. She watched Deepa's nostrils flare, her mouth part, and Ruchi understood. She pressed her lips to the corner of her friend's mouth. Inexplicably, Deepa's breath smelled of rain. She shuddered, and Ruchi held her.

# Ruchi

## *1992*

There was a knock at the door. "Ma?" Moksh said, and Ruchi's body jammed, a key caught in a lock that didn't catch.

In a single motion, Deepa stood and smoothed the designer dress down her thighs while Ruchi rose clumsily, stepping on the scattered papers. For the second time in her life, Ruchi wanted to run from this place, but her legs were leaden. She could do nothing with her hands except let them hang.

"You there?" Moksh pushed the door open.

Anu lurked a step behind Moksh, her frowning, pained mouth and dimpled brow, a face still pretty despite the cropped hair. "Dad doesn't look well," she said. "He says he has a fever."

Deepa ignored her and gave her attention to Moksh. "I was having a good gossip with your mother, na, Ruch?" she said with a sly wink, face serene as glass. There had been nothing to see, nothing to catch. Whatever it was lived in Ruchi's mind. Deepa was already fussing. She exclaimed that no one could leave until all the food was gone, then pulled Moksh into a hug, which he endured without complaint. Deepa stepped back and inspected him. "What's all this growing and thinning?"

"I eat, Auntie," Moksh lied.

"Come. Everyone is waiting," Deepa said and filed them down the stairs, a flock of obedient pigeons. She waved her hands cheerfully at the mess as she made her way outside.

"But Mom." Anu tried to grab the flesh of Deepa's arm. Ruchi wanted to reassure the girl that her mother couldn't help being how she was. If Ruchi could peel back the hostess bravado and the hot-and-cold eyes, Anu would see that her mother was afraid. In some other universe, they'd commiserate over their rejections, help the other accept that none of it was their fault.

Deepa hissed, "Your father is fine," and added to salt the wound: "Why do you always need to be his pet?" How easily she could spread her hurt, her shame.

Out on the sand, guests formed around Deepa on cue, praising the tents and the food and her dress. In return, Deepa laughed and feigned embarrassment about the spicy dishes in the heat. She teased and complimented while Ruchi's stomach lurched from her reckless hope that Deepa might change.

AFTER THE PARTY, Ruchi was certain that this time, the silence between them would be prolonged until it was permanent. That's how her friend was. How she'd always be. Ruchi was free of her. At last.

Except. Deepa called. The day after Ravi Ravichandran's funeral, which Ruchi had heard about at work, and so she listened to Deepa gossip about the poorly prepared body and the very basic foods people made compared to Deepa's exquisite baby brinjal. "I stuffed them by hand."

"Did you fry the channa flour with dhana giru first?" Ruchi asked.

"Of course. And fresh garlic."

The receiver was hot against Ruchi's ear. She sat at her kitchen table skimming the hairs growing back between her brows. She traced a path through the florid yellow and brown wallpaper that she'd always hated.

"You should've seen how Ravi's boys were crying. It wasn't their fault that their father died too young, didn't watch his salt and sugar, that he liked all those fried naasta in the morning. Hot Mix every breakfast. No, the children shouldn't suffer. And I swear on my head that Pushpa didn't shed a tear."

I'd forgive her, Ruchi thought. If she says anything. I'd forgive.

"Someone tampered with Ravi's Jaguar at the party? Sonal had to tell me this, as if the stress of it had killed him."

IF RUCHI WERE braver, she'd tell Deepa this story. At the party, once they'd rejoined the crowd, Ruchi had needed to be alone. She'd intended to sit in the Cutlass, the oldest car in the long line of cars. She'd passed a green Jaguar and noticed the window halfway down, the keys left in the ignition, a plush orange key chain screaming FLORIDA hanging off it. It had seemed natural to reach inside and pull up the lock. She'd sat in the scalding leather bucket seat and then turned the ignition to see what it felt like. Then she was easing the car into reverse and driving to the lighthouse. All those years, and she'd never been. The interior smelled faintly new and faintly like feet. She'd driven right up the rocky hill like in pickup commercials. She'd watched the tents and people on the beach, knowing Deepa was there, somewhere.

If she were telling this story to Deepa, this is where Deepa would try to interrupt, but Ruchi would go on. She'd stun Deepa into a rare quiet. She wanted Deepa to know that while she gazed from the party to the house to the sky she'd thought of ugly things: a finger inside her mouth, her mouth on a nipple, lips sweeping her ankles before running up her legs and between her thighs to take the shape of her. She wanted Deepa to know that she'd untied her salwar, reached into her underwear, and stroked herself with care. That she'd arrived at an agreeable pain. And here she'd ask Deepa, had she felt the same? Had her mind also arrived at a perfect blank? Ruchi had strained to keep her eyes open. The sensation had radiated and threatened, and this time, for the first time, she didn't stop. Though she'd wanted it to be over at once she didn't stop, and when the pleasure arrived, she was awed that it was hers. *Mine, Deepa.* It had no purpose, served no aim, did nothing to change the material facts of her life except that for some seconds, she could live inside herself entirely, needing nothing but her own body, her own love.

After, she'd wiped her finger on the steering wheel. She'd wanted to sleep, but an agitation in the back seat had startled her. Briefly and without reason, she thought the dead nuns had stowed under the seats, waiting to scold and applaud her.

At this point in the story, Deepa might even laugh.

It had been a large moth. Its silvery, veined wings caught the light and made frantic attempts at the window. What was it doing there in the daytime? Ruchi had twisted herself around, the gear shift pushing against her stomach, and had caught the insect in her palm. She'd felt it suffocating against her hands, a gasp of wing flutter. She'd rolled down the automatic window and released it, but it fell to the ground.

And then, this side story: for a single summer, Moksh had collected dead moths in jars that he'd lined on his windowsill. Ruchi had complained they were dirty but grew to love the ones with delicate wings and mourned when he'd lost interest in their rotted exoskeletons, dumping them in the woods one afternoon. Or maybe he'd done it for her, and she was sorry now for not finding beautiful what her son had found beautiful, as if that one mistake had changed everything. What if she brought this moth home, delivered it as a gift to soften the air between them? Though it was possible that he'd regard her coldly, or worse, choose not to remember the jars, or just not remember, worst of all. How had their children become these people? She'd ask Deepa, but wouldn't wait for her answer. She'd explain that when she'd opened the car door and bent to scoop up the creature, the moth had hopped and flown off in a crazed zigzag toward the sea, off to die elsewhere.

She'd returned the car exactly where she'd found it, expertly paralleled into the same tight spot. She'd rolled up the windows and hidden the keys under the floor mat to make them hard to find. She, too, could be mean.

On the phone, Deepa continued talking. Anu had decided on premed. Wasn't her hair horrible? The girl had no fashion sense. On and on, without a single mention of anything important. As if the fraud didn't exist. As if her husband weren't a criminal. As if she and Ruchi were just school friends. Just school friends from home.

"But Deepa," Ruchi interrupted, "we never finished our discussion."

From the kitchen table, Ruchi could see her black purse on the counter. Gold plate had chipped off the clasp.

Ruchi had slipped back inside the beach house. Others had also entered, loitering in the kitchen. She'd seen Dr. Sharma in a spaghetti-strapped sundress and low-slung heels. Ruchi hadn't said hello, thinking it was best not to be noticed. She'd made her way upstairs. Ruchi could explain to Deepa that her body had continued to move without her mind, had reached into the safe and taken a bundle off the top. Did Deepa notice it was gone? Ruchi's hand had slipped the bills into her purse next to her own small bundle. And when she'd returned to the party, the extra weight had made her feel light, unreachable. Then, finally, she'd made a plate for herself, plucking food off trays at random, licking her fingers and listening to Deepa's exuberant voice crawl to the top of the general hum. A consolation prize, Ruchi would say, as a joke.

"You left without saying goodbye," Deepa said now.

"Did I? I don't remember." But of course she remembered. She'd found her family and Naren had strode happily ahead of them past the Jaguar to the Cutlass. She and Moksh had been alone, and she had wanted to explain that she was different now. No one could see it, but she was.

"It was a nice party," she'd said instead as they passed the line of expensive cars. "Though the food was bland." Moksh hadn't answered, but it didn't matter. "I'll make a full rasoi tonight. A feast."

Moksh had absently run his finger along the cars and avoided looking at her. "I'm not hungry."

"Of course you are," she'd insisted, despite Deepa's clipped voice in her head. *Let him be. Let him be!* "You have to admit it."

"Stop. Please."

But she hadn't. She couldn't. Even now.

Moksh muttered under his breath.

"What did you say?" she'd asked, though she knew it was just more foolishness, this desire to know.

"Nothing."

"Say, no, Mokshu? Say what you mean." She had wanted to show that she could understand anything, and he'd stopped to meet her eyes. A rare direct hit.

"I wish I had a different family."

The brazen sun was behind him, but she could make out his mirthless smirk that pinched the scar. "Different how?" she'd asked.

"Easier. Better. Like Auntie."

The words had been quiet and calm, but she'd crossed her arms and contracted her body into a shield. "You don't know Auntie," she'd said. "You don't know her at all. She wouldn't be nice if you were her own." The one true thing she'd said that day. But he'd moved past her, opened the back door of the Cutlass, and folded his long frame inside.

AND NOW DEEPA whispered, "Ruch," the nickname Ruchi had never liked. If she could be honest, she'd explain that what had hurt her most was the thing Deepa didn't know. The money, the fraud, the rejection, all of it was secondary to her son's confession. *Like Auntie. Like Auntie.* Ruchi had played it over and over again. She played it again now. Any onlooker would say Deepa had only been kind to him. It wasn't Deepa's fault that Moksh preferred her. It wasn't her fault that the boy had turned brittle and hungry. But it was a betrayal nevertheless.

*Even this I'd forgive.* She'd fold it into the years that bound them if Deepa acknowledged some shiver of *feeling*, an affirmation, a sign, a tiny avowal, anything more than this empty talk.

But she laughed at Ruchi's silence. "It's all going to be fine," Deepa said. "You'll see."

AT WORK THE next day, Ruchi made the call without thinking. An anonymous tip to an 800 number, a fraud hotline, like she'd seen on police procedurals.

Yes, she had evidence.

No, she was not a patient or an insurance company.

Yes, there was more than one document. More than ten. More than dozens, probably.

Yes, she could mail the documents. No, she hadn't made copies. Yes, she would.

She would, yes.

Had she been personally harmed? The woman on the other end waited. Ruchi could hear her tapping her pen, impatient and bored.

Personally? Harmed? "No," Ruchi said, trying for the truth, but when she hung up the pay phone, she stood with her throat full of cotton, daring Kmart's automatic doors to close their jaws on her remorse.

BY NOVEMBER, SHE'D spent the bundle of money. She paid for new clothes, for college applications that Moksh half-heartedly filled out, for Cutlass repairs, and stored whatever was left in her old hiding places. Each day felt heavier than the day before. For the first time in her life, she didn't call Deepa and didn't take her calls, though her friend left breezy messages poking fun at Ruchi's silence and wondering aloud whether she'd become the queen of England.

Time accumulated, then slipped away. At work, no one showed any sign of trouble. Dr. Sharma continued to praise her. The ladies in central billing continued to regard her suspiciously. Ruchi told herself that the phone call she'd made and the invoices she'd sent probably made no difference. Likely no one was investigating at all. Or maybe Sanjay had paid back the money. Maybe a deal had been struck. The one time she saw Sanjay rushing down the hall, he pretended not to see her but seemed himself again, unruffled and unfazed, a man who could bend the world to his will. People with money could do that, while for Ruchi, the credit card companies were sorry they couldn't forgive the fees, the mortgage company apologized that they couldn't wait another month. Outwardly, she, too, was fine, the same, but inside, debts mingled with guilt, which mingled with regret. She'd done nothing wrong.

December arrived. On her forty-second birthday, she found a card from Moksh on the speckled kitchen counter next to the empty glass with white film, milk he'd poured down the drain after a single sip. This he did because he knew she checked the rim and thought he was fooling her. On the green envelope he'd written, "To Ma," and her heart leapt with the curl of his handwriting. "Cool Moms Are Hard to Find" on the cover, a melting ice cube against an orange backdrop, a hand-drawn heart around the *M*. She traced these smallest of efforts, his hand there, his eyes searching the drugstore shelf, signs of being remembered, of a thaw between them. On the drive to work she thanked him for it, and he dismissed it as corny. No, she wanted to say, no, it's not.

That night, she made a show of using the heating pad Naren had bought her, noticing the rainbow of settings and the softness of the blue-green fabric. She set aside her anxiety—gifts meant less money. She would've preferred something to make their mouths sweet. The pizza arrived cold, and Moksh refused to have his reheated. He ate a single slice, leaving the crust and a thick rim of cheese, but Ruchi forced herself not to cajole. After, they watched a *Rescue 911* episode about a baby who choked on a Christmas bulb. They sat in a line on the faded couch that faced the TV and watched the doctor pull out the bulb. There was a knock at the door. "One of those pranking kids," Naren said as he peeped through the hole. "They should get frostbite." But there was no one on the stoop, only a cake box and a note.

Ruchi unfolded the note. Inside was Deepa's miniature script: "You will never be younger than today!" Ruchi felt a bulge in her throat like she, too, had swallowed a bulb. She opened the box. It was a stone-cold grocery store cake with a glow of dark frosting and whipped cream skirting the bottom, not the kind Deepa would ever serve, but Ruchi still turned away to hide her trembling lip.

She cut three neat slices and insisted on feeding Naren and Moksh heaping bites with her hands. She felt their lips through the cold cake and smudged their faces with icing, as if they were the type of family that touched naturally and all the time. Moksh chewed and swallowed with the delicacy of sparrows organizing seeds that dropped from the feeder. All his bones worked together.

A squall of flurries arrived the next day, a Saturday, and it made the house feel like a cocoon. Ruchi resolved to call Deepa to thank her for the surprise. She could do it. She could patiently withstand their chatter about weather and holiday sales if she held on to the bit of happiness from the day before, the card and the cake and the heating pad that she'd enjoyed on the highest setting.

The phone rang, but it wasn't for her. Naren took the cordless into the bathroom, like he did whenever his brother phoned collect. Why did Anoj have to call today? It irritated her.

Naren looked unwell when he returned. "What is it?" she asked.

"Nothing, nothing."

Outside the squall swished from left to right, flakes dying on the windowpanes. Naren switched on the TV, but it was only football and hockey, the white noise of constant cheer.

"What is it?" she asked again, more insistent.

"There must be some news of it," Naren said, speaking to himself.

"News of what?"

"Anoj said to check the news. To look for something big."

Ruchi stuffed her feet into an extra pair of socks. "Is he still following that silly man riding around in a Toyota chariot?" She'd seen grainy photos of it in *India Abroad*, L. K. Advani and his clowns on what looked like a Thanksgiving Day float. Years ago, during one of their regular calls, she and Deepa had laughed at the photo of the scowling dada with an orange pagadi tilted on his head. But Ruchi was no longer sure what Deepa thought of it all now.

"That 'silly man' has millions of followers," Naren said. He checked the news that night and the next day and flipped through the morning talk shows for some mention.

On Monday, she found it, page 2 of the *Courant*, a two-column story with the headline HINDU MILITANTS DESTROY MOSQUE. Thousands stormed the sixteenth-century mosque and tore it down with axes, hammers, and their bare hands. Some brandished swords and iron pipes, others tridents. Loudspeakers carried speeches and a makeshift well had been dug in front of the destroyed building, though the article didn't elaborate on what this might be for, why people had gathered around it, whether the well had water, what would happen next. Around the country, curfews were declared.

At dinner, Ruchi switched on the *Nightly News*. Naren moved to shut it off, but Ruchi hid the remote behind her back. "What if I want to watch?" she said.

A cacophony of men jumped over fences. Some chiseled industriously while others pumped their fists in the air. Some wore saffron headbands, bright and sunny against the billowing dust. A group of men covered the masjid dome, packed so close together they seemed a many-headed hydra. Here they were, Naren's extra remittances.

"Dad, are you seeing this?" Moksh asked.

"Western news always covers the drama," Naren mumbled.

"Drama? This is a bit more than drama."

Tom Brokaw narrated over the images, describing the division of "British India," the same way someone might say "British English" or "British cookies."

"From here how can you know who is right and who is wrong? You don't know what's happening," Naren complained.

"And you do?" asked Moksh. Her son had spoken her thought.

"Eat, no, Jaanu," Ruchi said weakly.

But Moksh stood up without a word and left, his plate untouched. Naren switched off the TV. He fetched the *Journal Inquirer* from the other room and shook it ceremoniously in front of her.

"'Doctor Defrauds Free Vaccination Program,'" Naren read. Words reached her in fragments. "Prosecutors are refusing a settlement" and "years of illegal reimbursements" and "hundreds of thousands of dollars" and "bail met."

She thought nothing had happened after she made the call. She'd been wrong.

"'It is the first time a charge of this kind has been made in the state.' First time! Ever! Well done!" Naren slapped his thigh. "But this part sambhal lo. 'I never cheated my patients.' He says he never cheated his patients!"

"Please, Naren."

"What please? Everyone looks good from the outside."

The rubble on television, the men and their saffron bands, their slogans and whoops, faded into the background. She stared at the photo in the paper. Sanjay smiled for the camera, Deepa a step behind him.

THE FEDERAL INVESTIGATION into tax evasion carried a ten-year prison penalty. A fine of $150,000 was to be paid back to Medicaid. $350,000 to private insurers. Deepa's voice messages became clipped and brief. "Call me, please." Sometimes Ruchi dialed her back before hanging up. She argued with herself that her guilt was irrational. She'd only reported what she'd discovered. Her single anonymous tip couldn't result in such a big case, such large sums, by itself. Ruchi wasn't responsible. And yet, at work, she noted a stiffness in Dr. Sharma, a clipped professionalism from the ladies in central billing. A broader investigation would cost them all, which could mean that reporting the fraud made her selfless, thinking of the greater good, except Ruchi knew too well that she was fueled more by pride than by goodness. Goodness was always in question.

Ruchi suffered through a gray winter of debts and chores and Moksh's stubborn refusal to eat. She laced their food with extra ghee so each bite he took was loaded with calories. The more she fixated on eating, the more Moksh resisted, but she saw no other recourse. Persistence had always been her secret weapon. She was not like Naren who gave up too easily. She felt sorry for her husband who emerged from his calls with Anoj confused and drained of purpose. Sometimes she caught herself wondering whether if, had they stayed in Bombay, Naren would've been one of those men, not the ones screaming on the masjid's dome, but among the crowd below, body tensed in fervor.

Maybe it would've been easier, if not better, a cosmetic improvement to his sunken, increasingly stooped existence. Tenderness still flowed beneath her frustration with him, tenderness and more guilt. He, too, was a casualty of her misplaced desire. She wished she could name the competing urges inside her, separate them into sensible, discreet curios, clip their excesses. It would've made for a simpler life.

Eventually, Deepa stopped calling; the last message simply stated, "It seems you will never call back."

# Ruchi

## *1993*

In the spring of 1993, four unconnected events happened that Ruchi would link in her mind. First, on March 12, a dozen bombs blasted across Bombay, retribution for the Babri Masjid demolition in December. Ruchi and Naren read about the attacks and watched them on the news and went to work. Ammi called to say they were safe, and Anoj called to rail against the violence, and Ruchi and Naren realized that they didn't know either of them very well anymore, if they ever had.

Soon after, Dr. Sharma stopped her Friday clinics as the authorities expanded their fraud investigations. Ruchi brushed aside her guilt. An anonymous tip was just a small piece of evidence, nothing more than that. If Dr. Sharma blamed her, she kept it to herself, just as Ruchi remained silent as Naren continued to send Anoj his small, inconsequential remittances.

Third, after the bombs and the closure of the Friday clinic, Wellness received an uptick of miscarriages. Every week, women arrived looking hollowed out, red veins jumping in their eyes. Ruchi tended to them in the hushed librarian tones she'd mastered.

One woman felt the baby melting inside her. Her braids were pinned back with an aluminum barrette, and her pastel-green skirt, too thin for the weather, swept the floor. Light shot through her brown skin; her eyes flickered topaz. The kind of beautiful person it was hard to look at directly. She held her middle and grimaced.

"This is my fourth," she whispered.

"I'm so sorry."

"All of them, it was like this. Melting. No blood. Just this warm feeling inside. Like dripping wax." The woman closed her eyes and, without warning, laid her head on the desk. Ruchi's eyes watered from the scent of the woman's hair.

"Let me get you your forms," Ruchi said. When the woman didn't move, Ruchi gently nudged her head straight. She felt the waiting room watching them.

"Have you ever lost one?"

Why did the question confuse her? Besides being too personal—Ruchi could forgive her that—she had the feeling that any answer she gave would be imprecise.

"Let's get you checked in," Ruchi said. Like Moksh, the woman had an insubstantial quality to her. Her arms and legs were too thin. Ruchi handed the woman a clipboard of forms, took her ID and insurance, and gave her a glass of water, which the woman drank slowly but with determination. Ruchi watched the water move down her throat.

Ammi used to say coincidences were best in threes. But that spring, a fourth thing happened. As the woman drank water, the phone rang. Ruchi felt it in her bones. She hesitated to answer it, fearing a spirit on the other end.

"Moksh couldn't stop vomiting," the school nurse said. "We didn't have this number and we couldn't reach your husband. That number said he no longer works there."

"Yes." It had been years since she'd filled out the blue emergency contact form. Years since the school asked her to update it. Every September, they used the one from the year before. Her hand shook as she took down the name of the hospital, as if she wouldn't remember. She moved in a calm haze and organized the afternoon's files so Mrs. Gerb wouldn't make a mess of them. She got her coat—never warm enough—her purse, her water bottle. Her lunch she left in the fridge. She called a number for a taxi; Moksh, of course, had the car. She moved methodically but felt separate from herself, her mind out of sync with her body.

The patient—her name was Merl and she'd written on her form that it rhymed with "twirl"—began to moan. She clutched her hips, tucked her chin to chest, and howled. Ruchi's mind pushed past her, but her body rushed to hold her by the elbow. Merl was warm, as if she were truly melting. She was more solid than she looked. Other pregnant women formed a wall around them, and Mrs. Gerb called for Dr. Sharma through the door. Ruchi helped Merl to the ground, to all fours. Another howl poured out without breath, unending, until Ruchi noticed blood trailing down Merl's green skirt, as though the sound and the blood were connected. She saw the future Merl, a mother twice over with exhausted eyes, thinking how odd it was that she'd once been in such pain in the arms of a stranger. A pulsing premonition. But the taxi had arrived. Ruchi had to leave.

At the hospital, she gave her name and insurance card and filled out pending forms and felt caught in a loop of cards and clipboards. "My son?" she asked. "When can I see my son?"

"He's being seen. They're giving him fluids. We'll call you from the waiting room."

"What kind of fluids? He's vomiting."

"Intravenous."

Ruchi detected the woman's impatience. Nothing was so serious when you were sent to a waiting room, she told herself, but the waiting was interminable. Everyone hunched in their coats, the air inside as bitter as the air outside. An elderly man was reading the *Journal*, and Ruchi caught the headline: MANCHESTER DOCTOR TO APPEAR IN COURT. Had the man read the story? Had he shaken his head at the Indian doctors who were everywhere nowadays? Ruchi felt that the headline was pointing at her, singling her out. She was supposed to feel grateful for this country and its safety and good roads, its clean hospitals and supermarkets and cars and lawns and summer fairs and malls, so many malls, and breathable air and drinkable water and good TV. But how?

How to feel gratitude? Time passed through her. Even if she'd given Moksh a name like Michael or Mark, even if she'd called him "Mo" like Naren once suggested, the kinds of names found on decorative license plates at checkout counters, the days would be no easier for him.

She glanced at the intake desk. She'd dropped off samples to this hospital's lab before, but she recognized no one and no one recognized her.

"Ms. Mehta." At last, a nurse. A tall man in blue scrubs waved her to the desk with a chart. Ruchi worried she'd fail to reach the desk fast enough, just as she'd failed to call Dr. Shark.

"My son."

"He's this way."

"Okay."

He led her through the emergency room, past empty gurneys and beds with curtains drawn, past a child wearing a patch over one eye, down a hall to a windowless exam room with another set of curtains around another bed.

"The doctor will be with you shortly."

"Okay."

"Ms. Mehta, you're shaking." The man placed a hand on her hand to confirm this. The touch was startling. His mask was pulled down under his chin, the straps bending his ears in half. It looked painful. The nurse waited for Ruchi to step inside, but she paused, unable to move, as if all the hesitations of her life had gathered and made her stiff and immobile. The nurse exerted a solid but kind force on her back. She wanted to stay with him, to let him guide her through the rest of the day, and the next and the next.

"Your friend is already here."

"My friend?" But she knew. She could feel Deepa's electric presence before the nurse explained. She hadn't seen her since the party, hadn't spoken to her since the phone call a few days after.

"The emergency contact. The school must've called everyone on the list."

The curtain was a seafoam color with flecks of blue. The nurse pulled it back. "They've given him a sedative to help him relax. He's taking the fluids well. He'll be fine."

"You made it," Deepa said, her hand on top of Moksh's.

"Hello." Ruchi's voice stuck to her throat. She avoided looking at Deepa, but she also couldn't look at the tube in her son's arm or the oversized hospital gown or the protruding collarbone. What had she been doing while her son withered away? What was the aim of all her worrying if it wasn't to avoid this very situation? She'd been blind. Or rather, she'd chosen to be blind. She was a fraud of a mother.

And still a petty, jealous thought tapped her skull: Deepa, the favorite, was here with him before she was. "He's—"

"The vomiting stopped with whatever they gave him," Deepa said, as if she could read Ruchi's thought. "He was asleep when I got here."

Ruchi trained her eyes on his face. He looked peaceful. The scar above his lip was almost completely faded, and his jaw aligned in a way it didn't when he was awake. A rough, thin blanket covered his legs. It couldn't possibly keep him warm.

"Oh, good. Good," Ruchi said. The corner of her eye twitched. In the nine months since the party, Deepa had aged. The natural shadows under her eyes that Ruchi had always admired had grown both darker and duller. The craters of her cheeks were ashy and without their typical glow. She looked old and this tore at Ruchi's heart.

"Ruchi, he's not well," Deepa said, a gentle punch.

"Yes, yes. I see that. Maybe something he ate."

"No, Ruch. This doesn't happen from food. But I guess I should've told you that before."

"Told me? What would you have told me? I'm his mother. You were always telling me to leave him alone." Ruchi steadied herself against the bar of the bed. The monitor, the tube, the bracelet on his wrist. All of it had a cost. Another petty thought she blinked fast to erase.

"You didn't understand what I meant, Ruch."

"Please don't call me that. I never liked it."

Deepa sighed. "You could've called. You could've reached out."

"I didn't want to bother you. I thought you'd be busy."

"Other friends called. Offered support. It's what Moksh needs now. Not your obsession with food."

"To feed my child is an obsession now? Your daughter, too, wants support, no? What do you give?"

"Anu isn't here," Deepa said. "Anu isn't lying here."

Ruchi leaned over her son to look directly into Deepa's eyes. She gripped the bed rail with strength she didn't know she had. "You think you are perfect when you are not. It was always me reaching out to make the effort. I only wanted to stay close." Ruchi was amazed with each word that came out of her mouth.

"Close?" Deepa laughed. "You wanted to stay close? Who has helped you here? Who tried to guide you? Do you not remember anything?"

She did. Ruchi remembered every last detail together. "Do you?" she asked.

Deepa blinked down at her lap. Her shoulders slumped uncharacteristically. Ruchi released her grip just as Deepa looked up. Her expression was sad and mean.

"The lawyer says that the evidence against Sanjay includes internal documents," Deepa said. "Strange, no? Documents only the practice could've had. The lawyer suspects it was an anonymous tip from someone who worked at the suite."

Ruchi stared at her son's hand, the one closest to her that she could've easily taken. "Strange, yes."

"It makes no difference now, but who would do this?" Deepa's voice had turned sickly sweet. "Who would have provided this information?"

"It was wrong, was it not, the stealing? You would never have stolen," Ruchi said, as if it were true.

"Would I never? Would you never? Who is to say? Who hasn't made mistakes? But what can you do, right, Ruch?"

"You can stay with me. With us." Ruchi took a deep breath. "Moksh will like it."

Deepa waved the idea aside. "I'll go now that you're here."

A panic scalded Ruchi's belly. No. She couldn't leave. She didn't have the right. She was always leaving. "Stay. You have to stay. Please."

She felt like a child after making a promise she'd failed to follow through on—soak the dal when Ammi was out, press Dadi's legs, teach Tejas sums. She'd tried to fend off the jitteriness in her chest with lies. Here it was again, her failures, one lying in this bed and the other sitting across from her.

"I'm needed at home," Deepa said. She looked tired, like the argument had sapped the last of her energy. As she stood up, Moksh's hand slipped from hers and lay on the bed disembodied, the protruding knuckles and taut tendons attached to nothing.

"I don't want to be alone," Ruchi said. Truth should make a person feel lighter, but the words weighed her down. "I should've called."

"Don't be stupid," Deepa said, as if her own hurt were a thing of the past. "What does it matter now?" Ruchi saw a glimmer of the girl she used to be, sharp-tongued and cruel, but also kind. Also beautiful. Deepa's hand hovered in the air as if to reach for her. Someone cried out in another room and it could've come from Ruchi's own heart. It's okay, Ruchi wanted to say. *Whatever we are is okay.*

But Deepa spoke first. "I'm sorry, Ruch. I am." Then she moved through the curtain and out the door.

Ruchi took Deepa's seat in the over-air-conditioned hospital room. She nested her son's free hand in both of hers and pressed hard, but he didn't wake. When the doctor came, she watched words slip through her lips, like her mouth was a slot in a door. Distortion. Restriction. Control. Disorder. Ruchi nodded as she tried to gather the terms, keep them from escaping and crowding the room. She'd do it, whatever it was. She'd make it better.

# PART SIX

# Moksh

## *1993–2000*

The hospital light bounced off his mother's curls. Moksh watched her sleeping and spied a small tear in the collar of her brown blouse. She was slumped over in the chair, her hand warm and heavy on his. He didn't know what to do with it. Though now it seems obvious. Hold her hand! Hold it! But at the time, he could focus only on the tubes disappearing into both his arms and his aching stomach, bruised from the inside. A machine whir buzzed in his ears. He was afraid of waking her, of the tears that she wouldn't be able to restrain. He wanted her to go on sleeping so that he'd never have to face her. He was naked without his hoodie, and the room absurdly cold. Why would a place of care keep a room so cold?

But she didn't cry, not at first. "Jaanu," she said when she woke. "They made me do paperwork. Insurance and all that." She patted her chest with her free hand. "I was here. You'd fallen asleep."

"It's okay. I'm fine." He heard shifting from the curtained bed to his right, the side that had a window. The room door was open; gurney wheels clattered across tiles. His mother's warm hand pressed on his limp one.

"How long have you been up? You should've woken me."

He looked around. It was just her. "Dad's not here."

"He knows. They'll release you once you go to the bathroom."

Moksh lifted one arm to demonstrate the tube. "How can I do that like this?" He saw a bedpan leaning against the side table. "No."

"You're too weak to walk right now."

"I'm not. It's a bug. It'll pass."

Behind the curtain the roommate grunted once, twice, before flinging out a long series of staccato coughs. Tat, tat, tat, tat. His mother squared her shoulders. "No, Mokshu. It's not. It won't."

The weight of her hand on his lightened, about to pull away.

"You can't force me to eat. You can't just put food in front of me and make me eat," he said. His face was wet.

"Okay."

"No more of that. Please."

"Every mother wants to feed her child. But okay. Okay. We will do things differently."

He succumbed to the bedpan, a humiliating, prolonged trickle, his mother, and presumably the coughing roommate who Moksh would never meet, listening behind the curtain. They signed a treatment plan, what his mother called "the Treaty" because it sounded sweet. He agreed to be weighed, to log his eating, to ask for help. The latter he'd never do, but he signed. When he was finally allowed to stand up, the room swirled and blackened and he had to sit down again. At discharge, he was lowered into a wheelchair, his mother's hand circling his upper arm for support. He has no recollection of how they returned home. Likely he slept the whole way, his body stupidly heavy, bloated with the fluids they'd pumped into him. Jelly clogged his veins. His father was home, but how? Had he spent a hundred dollars on a taxi? His mother must've organized the retrieval of the car at school, a ride for his father, who followed as he climbed the few steps to the garage door, stood by him as he brushed his teeth, not speaking.

At first, instead of eating, Moksh drank. Protein shakes, fruit smoothies, juices, teas thick with jaggery. Interminable sips of dense liquids. Then came the rich foods, small portions that made him gag, even more ghee on every roti, more bang for your buck, a sale. His mother made everything from scratch, returning from work to fry mustard seeds or cumin seeds or curry leaves, stuff okra with channa flour, grind white lentils and almonds into a paste.

She watched closely. A laser focus, unflinching and unapologetic. She didn't cajole. She didn't plead. When he refused one dish, she briskly removed it and offered another, as if her feelings no longer mattered. Sometimes he cheated, binged on weight-logging days, jotting down fake calories. But the reflux improved; his limbs filled out. He still touched his stomach too often, still searched for his ribs in the shower, but some days he barely did it. Some days he could let it go.

His mother drove him to therapy, during which he sat mute on a brown couch in a brown room with a leathery Dr. Jules for forty-five minutes. But the doctor didn't force him to speak, and his mother didn't ask him how the sessions were. After a few weeks, he began to talk, and Dr. Jules nodded and then said it was all normal. His face, his body, his feelings. His family. Nothing about them was wrong, though he might feel otherwise. They were just people being people. This was true but how could Dr. Jules know what they felt like? How could anyone know how anyone else felt?

"Parents say things they don't mean," Dr. Jules said of his father, and Moksh wanted to believe it.

His mother waited for him in the car. One day, on the ride home, Moksh said that Dr. Jules suggested a group session.

"What is that?"

"She wants to talk to you, too."

"Me?"

"And Dad."

His mother took the exit and they drove past the Gerber plant that had shut and the trailer park, then the small ranch houses, then the big developments that used to be fields, contemporary houses with siding they couldn't afford, houses his mother still longed for. He hated all of it: the developments, the hedge that tried to hide the trailer park, the emptiness, the longing.

"The sessions are expensive," his mother said. "We'll see." A tendon in her frown throbbed with fear. In a group session they'd have to speak of his father's problems, about money, about her unhappiness. They'd have to give their silence a name. They'd have to face Moksh's questions, the ones he didn't know were in the back of his mind until he said them aloud to Dr. Jules, the words surprising him. Did his parents know what he looked like? Before he was born? Did they know and still want him? Or was he a disappointment from the start?

But how could he ask? How could they talk about these things and return home and watch sitcoms? How could they allow words to run around in the open without destroying them?

HE ENROLLED IN an associate degree. He relapsed. Got better. Relapsed again, but each time a little better until he finished school, which was two years of a bachelor's at Central Connecticut State before moving as far as he could, which was forty miles south to New Haven the first year because the only job he could find was writing copy and handing out event postcards for a militant environmental group, paid according to the number he distributed in a shift. He could've thrown the postcards away and said he handed out all of them, but Moksh wasn't a cheat.

He took a Greyhound to Hartford for his mother's fiftieth. She picked him up at the station, and they hugged lightly. The decades-old Cutlass rattled, and the heat vents whistled. He asked her about work, and she said it was fine. She'd been laid off when Dr. Sharma moved her practice and downsized to a smaller office, but his mother never talked about it, never discussed her new job as a cashier at a nail and threading salon in Wethersfield except to say that now she could have a pedicure and do her brows whenever she wanted.

They arrived at the house. It had shrunk, the walls closing in as if he could stretch his arms and reach from the batik in the living room to the glossy kitchen wallpaper. The scalloped yellow and brown petals reminded him of cabbage.

The jars had multiplied. Tomato sauce jars and mango pickle jars and plastic Jif canisters stuffed with Skittles and Reese's and Mounds, some of it nearing a decade old, a noisy piling up of silent disappointments.

But he'd come wanting to be kind and lighthearted and suggested they go out to dinner. He wanted to give his mother something besides the cards he'd gotten into the habit of giving, the ironic ones with the cataracted old woman on the cover because she made his mother laugh. He was twenty-six now and thought he was different.

"But you are the gift," she said, and he couldn't look at her.

She reheated dal from the night before and chopped green beans for a simple shaak. He tried to be helpful, washing dishes until she insisted that he stop.

"Anu is in fellowship now. NYU," his mother said casually.

"Huh."

"You're so smart, Mokshu. You could also be a doctor."

"Not everyone wants that, Ma," he said, and knew then that he'd leave for a long time, that he couldn't stay close, that he couldn't be whoever he was if he stayed. But it was his mother's birthday and so he said, "But yeah, maybe." In his heart he asked for forgiveness.

His father, watching reruns in the living room, called out, "Did she tell you Anu has to help with the legal fees? That Deepa has become like a pujari? Every weekend she goes to her haltoo-faltoo temple. I'm sure all the donations they collect for this festival and that festival are paying down their debt. Ha!"

"You can't know that," his mother chided.

Moksh thought of the check, his father's slanted handwriting signing away money he didn't have. He thought of the destroyed mosque on TV, the hush after a distant prime minister's death, the letters his parents fought over, events that he could understand only as events, not as emotions. Would it have been different if they'd gone back every few years, like other Indians? If he'd kept up with Gujarati? If he'd grown up in Jersey or California or Texas where Indians had formed entire towns for themselves?

"Deepa and I talk sometimes," his mother said to him quietly. "How would I know about Anu otherwise? They had to sell the Glastonbury house. She lives at the shore now."

"Lucky she has any house at all! Sanjay should've gone to jail!" his father shouted. "Always these people are finding loopholes!"

They ate with their plates balanced on their laps in the living room with the TV on. Reports flashed images of Y2K: people pushing carts full of water bottles and flashlights and lamp oil and canned goods to their cars. "I knew it would happen like this," his father said. He leaned over his dish toward the screen. "You can't rely on computers for everything."

"You just want to go shopping and buy too many things," his mother said. She wasn't as gray as his father. Only a couple short, frazzled strands peekabooed through her waves. "I wish you'd come home more, Mokshu. You need home food."

"We should've gone out tonight," he said. "My treat." It struck him how small a gesture it was, coming home, and yet how much it cost him, how much it sank him back inside himself.

"Children shouldn't pay for their parents," his mother said. "Come for New Year's." She glanced at the screen. "In case."

He collected and rinsed their plates, which she rinsed again. She was wearing the blue salwar she used to save for parties. It was shiny with wear but unstained. She was lonely. He could see it in her posture, in the squint of her eyes. The phone rang and she shot up, cupped her hand over the receiver and took the cordless into the hall. But she was back in moments, unchanged.

"Who was it?" he asked.

"Nothing. Telemarketer. They have recordings now to make you think it's a real person. Ere, where are you going?"

Moksh saw worry gather around her mouth, the desire to stop him, to keep him where she could see him. "I've got an errand to run," he said. "I'll be right back."

His father followed him to the garage and slipped him a list of items to pick up. Electrolyte drinks, water, tins of peas and carrots, vegetable seeds. "Don't tell your mother. She gets all worked up about any expense." Moksh had seen the patch cleared in the backyard surrounded by netting meant to keep out raccoons. His father reached for his wallet.

"It's fine, Dad. I've got it."

"No, no. Take." He thrust twenty dollars at him, which wouldn't be enough. Moksh took it, resolving to leave the bill on the counter in the morning. The dim garage light obscured the Cutlass, the boxes and hoses and rakes and clippers, the broken mower and paper bags of tools that had lost their purpose, but Moksh thought he could hear them chattering and wondered if his father could too.

"Ma won't say but I read in the *Journal* about the deportation." His father's voice dropped, conspiratorial. "Sanjay Jain, that crook. He agreed to go back to India to avoid jail time. The daughter will have to manage their debt for years. Poor thing. But who knows, maybe she'll be a big-time crook doctor too."

"I thought you all were friends," Moksh said.

"What friends? Your mother calls but Deepa only picks up now and then. That woman always thought she was better than us. Your mother complains I spend too much money, but at least I'm not a cheater."

"Whatever, Dad," Moksh said, opening the rickety Cutlass door. But a pang shot through him for Anu. She'd never be a crook. A liar, for sure, but never a crook. They were similar that way.

HE WENT TO the new mall in Manchester for an ice-cream cake with a crunchy middle that his mother favored when he was a kid. Enormous silver Christmas ornaments hung from the ceiling that could've crushed someone below.

He wasn't sure it was her at first. He hadn't seen her in seven years. The navy pea coat looked too big and her hair was shorter than he remembered. But he recognized the walk, shoulders thrown back, an upturned chin. He thought that maybe she was there for the same reason, to buy a cake at Baskin Robbins and surprise his mother with a visit. He followed from a distance. He remembered the cake on their doorstep, how his mother had tried to hide her elation.

She passed the ice-cream shop. Two stores down, at the Express, she paused at a display and caught his reflection in the store window. Their eyes met in the blur. She hesitated, then spun around.

She said, as if expecting him, "What a surprise after so long!"

"Hi," he said. He couldn't call her Auntie but was too shy to call her by name. A trio of teenaged girls in cropped tops passed between them. Deepa stepped closer until she was beside him, as if they were people-gazing together. "I heard you live on the coast," he said.

"I was nearby and thought, why not finish some shopping? There are no good malls near Guilford." Her voice was too slippery, too sure. Her face a study in shadows, her pitted cheeks a little sunken. "All you kids leave home and never come back," she said. "Come to temple. It's good for you."

He'd once wanted to tell this woman his secrets.

"I'm leaving tomorrow," he said. "Been busy with grad school applications."

"Graduate school. How nice."

He could tell she didn't believe him, but she joined him in line at Baskin Robbins. She talked about the rise in gas prices and the mild winter they were having, as if his mother didn't exist. Could it really be that she didn't remember his mother's birthday?

"I'm sorry about Uncle," he said, hoping to embarrass her, to exact revenge on his mother's behalf.

"Uncle? Oh, he's fine. Living like a king, I'm sure."

"Lucky, then."

She pretended to search the air before letting her eyes settle on his. "You're still so skinny." He admired how quickly she deflected from her own misfortune, how seamlessly she could call up the kid he'd been. The version of himself he'd worked to escape. He recognized her grin, one he used to find alluring, as smug.

"And Anu? Probably working all the time."

Her smile froze. He'd inadvertently landed on a soft spot. They locked in and waited for the other to attack or retreat. Sales screamed in bold block letters about two-for-one discount cakes, a special butterscotch vanilla crumble. Overzealous lighting and Bing Crosby's baritone bore down on them. They moved up in line, and he noticed that her boots were frayed.

"You don't know?"

He didn't.

"Anu's engaged. We found a good boy. Almost a love marriage."

Engaged? "My mother didn't mention it."

She squinted, stung by something, a reminder. "Did she not? We don't get time to talk these days."

"Congratulations, in any case," he said.

"Twenty-eight is too young in America, but maybe not. Anu wants a long engagement."

Then she touched his elbow, and he startled. "Look at you," she said, and he tensed his shoulders, preparing for the bite. "All grown up and making your way. And your mother had worried so much." He turned to her and wasn't expecting the film of kindness in her eyes. "All for nothing. Look what you've become."

# Anu

## *2004–2015*

Anu remembered that the ceremony had been lovely—a few close friends and Betina's sour grandmother, aunts, uncles, and a dozen catty cousins—in a barn in Massachusetts, the first state in the union to make such things possible. It was the summer of 2004, and Betina looked like a mermaid in the pale-pink sari that was Anu's mother's one contribution. Her mother attended and left before the reception. "At least she came," Betina whispered in her ear. Anu danced and kissed her wife while feigning disappointment, when in fact she was somewhat relieved.

After five rounds of IVF, Betina had first Jambi, then the twins, all over the course of a decade. They lived in a small apartment filled with warmth that Anu didn't know she was capable of. It was what she'd wanted. More than she'd ever wished for. And yet every August, Anu drove from their Brooklyn two-bedroom to Connecticut for her mother's annual summer puja where she played the role of dutiful daughter, and her mother pretended it was true.

Betina and the kids weren't invited, though Anu had never needed to state this explicitly. She and Betina had a setup: once a year, they allowed each other a weekend to walk out of their lives—work, kids, money, chores. They had rules: no STDs, no indiscriminate spending, fix whatever you break. Anu went faithfully to the puja every year.

But children complicate things. Jambi was eight and filming a Dracula spoof on her phone, forcing the twins to hang upside down from their beds, tongues lolling. He was a struggling reader, and Betina insisted he needed a specialist, while Anu assured her that he just needed time. It should've been a cause for joy when he appeared in the narrow opening of their kitchen fluently reading aloud a string of texts. "Nani is asking what time you're arriving tomorrow."

"What was that?" Betina asked. She stopped moving, letting Jambi know he had her full attention.

"'Do not wear ugly clothes. After poo-ja is lunch.'"

Anu continued scraping undercooked garbanzos off a plate as if she hadn't heard.

"You're visiting your mother?" Betina asked.

A deep-bellied animal sound came from the other room. Lana said something about Dev's head being fine.

Anu exclaimed, "Jambi! You're reading!"

Silence.

"What's a poo-ja?" Jambi asked.

"Jambi said poo!" Lana called from the bedroom.

"It's a religious ceremony," explained Betina, who had gently taken the phone and was scrolling. "Apparently your mother goes every year."

ANIL VORA, ANU'S imaginary husband, was her mother's creation. It was her mother who conjured him for the benefit of her vast network of "friends," donors who kept afloat her beloved Bharat Friendship Association after her father's downfall. Her mother fabricated a small destination wedding and frequent business trips to explain Anil Vora's general absence. Anu thought of him as Mr. Vora, a presence not unlike an austere but essentially harmless piano teacher, someone she could hide from Betina with impunity.

Over the years Anu contributed, giving Mr. Vora hobbies and promotions, food allergies (wheat and chocolate) and phobias (spiders and large gatherings). He loved pujas and was always so sorry to miss them. Anu assumed that in time she'd divorce him or become a tragic widow. Then, hopefully, she'd never fake marry again.

It was a path not just of least resistance, but of the least harm done. Her mother took her acceptance as a sign of doubt about Betina, about her life. Though her mother was wrong. Anu was a coward, but a compassionate one. A coward who lied out of love.

"THIS, ANU? THIS?" Betina sat cross-legged on their mattress, a foot on the opposite thigh, posture impeccable. "All these years and *this* is how you use your weekend?"

Anu tried to summon outrage. "You're breaking our rules! No questions asked!"

Betina lunged forward over her open hips, and Anu, twice her size, flinched. "Don't be cute."

"I'm not cute," Anu said, wincingly.

If she could explain what she should've explained years ago, at the beginning. But how to explain without appearing pathetic? Being closeted was so 1998. In 2015, people got on with it. *But I'm afraid to hurt my mother.* That wouldn't do. Anu pigeoned a leg onto the bed and sat on it, as if she were flexible. "You don't understand, Bets. You know how obsessed my mother is with her pujas, her work. It's what keeps her mental health intact. After, you know, the Bad Thing with my dad and—"

"Anu, I'm not telling you not to go." Betina reached for her hand.

"You aren't?"

She squeezed Anu's knuckles together. "No. I'm telling you we're all going."

Good god. Her mother's face appeared as a cloud above Betina's head.

"You're hiding," Betina said.

"I'm not."

"You're hiding us. You don't want me there," Betina said. Her hand was now a vise. "You never have."

For the first time that day, hurt glowed in Betina's eyes, so luminescent and pure Anu thought it might jump out. "Of course that's not true." Her folded ankle ached under her ass. "I always want you everywhere. It's supremely boring, you know. All that chanting. Aunties droning on too long with their nasal singing. The incense will bother your contacts. The fundamentalism will irritate you."

"Then why go? Aren't you irritated?"

Of course she was. Of course she didn't like the religiosity, the weird camps, the "charities" that the temple supported in India, dubious organizations that built schools and clinics, all with vague, orthographically challenged mission statements about *Hindu* empowerment. She didn't think her mother liked it either. But what could she do? It was best not to look too closely. "The priest gives out sacred sugar cubes."

"Anu."

"Believe me, you'll hate it." The pain in her ankle tugged at the pain in her gripped hand, the two sensations at war. The sound of educational apps wafted in from the living room. "It's not like my mother doesn't know you're my wife and these are our children. She's the one who matters, right? We don't need to parade around her people."

"But I love parading around."

"Really, I'm sparing you."

"Oh, that's what it is. I didn't realize." Betina exhaled forcefully through her nose. It flared. "Do you remember the years we were broken up? How you entered and exited relationships like clothing at the Gap? Never getting past the basics? This is the same."

"Betina, please. At the very least I moved on to business casual." Anu chuckled hopefully.

Betina tipped her chin and looked down her nose. "What should I wear?"

"Oh, come on. That was funny," Anu pleaded. It was not.

"One of your mother's saris, perhaps? She can help me fold it. Lana will love it."

Anu stared at her wife and tried, again, for outrage. "But I've never denied you *your* weekends!"

Betina leaned in close. The hurt had solidified into resolve, and she smiled. "Take the kids tomorrow and pick me up on Sunday before the ceremony." A metallic taste filled Anu's mouth like an afternoon hangover. She tried not to move. Betina kissed her good night, a dry, mirthless kiss.

BETINA WANTED TO *know her.* It had always been the problem. She wasn't satisfied with vague stories about family estrangement and exile. She never gave Anu enough credit for attending all those quinceañeras. Or for the fact that Anu had shared newspaper clippings of her father's arrest. She'd kept them in a plastic report protector folded into her copy of *Zami* under her bed. At the time of the arrest, her mother had kept it secret, not wanting to spoil Anu's studies. Years later, Anu found the *Courant* article on microfiche, the grainy photo of her father being led down their manicured, fake-cobblestoned path. A short-lived, symbolic arrest with lights but no sirens. Discreet. He would've been smiling and polite to the officers for protecting his head as he ducked into the backseat of their patrol car.

They were in bed, and Betina had fanned the clippings over their naked laps. "Your father's a criminal?" she'd asked, holding the folded article with one hand and absently stroking Anu's stomach with the other.

"Yup," Anu said.

Betina scrutinized her. "Are you okay?"

"Okay?"

"Your father. He went to jail."

Anu laughed. "Jail? Oh, no. My mother bailed him out."

Betina whistled. "I didn't know you came from money like that."

"I didn't know either. Anyway, my father's being deported in a few months."

"What?"

"It's fine!" Anu squawked and quickly gathered the clippings and tucked them back into the clear plastic. She hoped this prized piece of vulnerability was enough to show Betina that she was not emotionally constipated.

But it wasn't. A week later, Betina left her. In a heartbroken miasma one evening, Anu stupidly called her mother. She was supposed to be applying to residencies but instead was in a fetal position on the mildewed bathroom floor of her graduate housing, pretending not to cry. The landline cord stretched to its breaking point. "Working hard?" her mother had asked, forever worried that having a thief for a father would diminish Anu's outlook.

"Yeah, sure."

She was angry with her father, but her mother made her saddest, how she expected them to rise above and move on, disassociating, doubling down on gods and faux righteousness, as if money hadn't tainted them all.

The last time her family had been together was at the airport, the day of her father's deportation. He was as affectionate as ever, but they'd traded places, she the parent and he the child who struggled to take full responsibility for his actions. The TSA agent regarded their farewell while picking his teeth. Her father whispered in her ear, "Visit, Potlu. I'll have a nice flat," as if he were leaving by choice.

"Great, Dad. That's just great."

"What? You want me to be punished forever?"

At one of the hearings, he had cried, his voice wobbling in high octaves of remorse. Crocodile tears. "No, Dad. Not forever."

"It wasn't easy here," her father said, grimly. "Just understand that."

And she did. She understood. They'd been stunted despite their success, displaced despite the opportunity. Languageless when it came to their interior.

Her mother tapped her foot impatiently, a vision of cold sturdiness, the tearing apart of their family rolling off her.

Outside the terminal, Anu payphoned Betina. She cried and words poured out about her fatherlessness, her mother's denial, the delusion she'd been raised within and was just now grasping the depth of. It seemed she spoke for hours. When she finished, the airport had emptied, as if it, too, had been spent.

Make-up sex lasted a week, lush and dirty and mean, then settled into something kinder, Anu letting Betina explore a little further, touch her to a point.

But to demonstrate that she'd really changed, Anu let Betina invite her mother to dinner.

Her mother arrived with a stricken expression, her mouth a clamp. By way of greeting, she evaluated Betina from head to toe, while Betina complimented her taste in footwear, fed her overly salted palak paneer, smiled through the silences. Anu wanted badly to take Betina's hand under the table and feared Betina might take hers. In a grave voice, the one reserved for inappropriate questions, her mother asked, "So, you are roommates?"

In bed that night, Betina held on to her sleeve. "Why didn't you tell her?" she asked.

"Believe me, she didn't want to be told."

"But she asked! You're not giving her a chance. She deserves honesty. We could've cried together."

"Honesty? Ha! Her game is denial, hiding behind some fantasy of who I am. It's why we talk about the weather. Don't you see? It's obvious that she knows."

"That's not the same as telling." Betina's voice was quiet. Anu took a deep breath and prepared herself for the end.

Instead, Betina kissed her, sweet and slow, the way you kiss a person you care for. "It's a step." Anu moved closer, promised to take more steps, all the steps in the world, and Betina nodded sleepily. For once, Anu forced her mother out of her mind until she receded and there was only herself and Betina, floating in a bubble.

ANU PULLED UP to the beach house. The boxwood bushes were weed-choked and the azaleas were long dead. Each year the untidiness startled her anew. Jambi burst from the car. "Nani!" he said and disappeared into her mother's blue kaftan. Above his head, her mother glared at her. The twins clamored for attention.

"You should have called."

"What's wrong with spontaneous?" Anu said. "A surprise."

"I don't like surprises." She smiled at Jambi. "I would have made the thin roti you like." To the twins, she gave a sinking look. She knew, without knowing, that Jambi was Anu's egg, the twins Betina's. Though they all looked more like their ethnically ambiguous sperm donor. It should have incensed Anu the way it did Betina, her mother's thinly veiled preference for their eldest, but it mostly made her tired, like she was pushing a heaving object uphill without knowing why.

"I have to make two hundred kati rolls before Sunday," her mother said.

"We can help?" Anu offered.

"That's unlikely." The kids ran into the house, and they followed. "You'll have to tell them not to talk about it."

"You can say her name, Mom."

"Or a sitter can stay home with them."

"But they've never been to a puja."

"What? Now you are religious? Take them to the temple in Queens." Her mother was calling her bluff. She'd never let the kids wreck the house with a sitter.

"Fine," Anu said. "Call a sitter."

Her mother strode to the kitchen as if she hadn't heard her. "You also don't have to come. Be sick this year."

Anu was surprised by the gut punch. Maybe no one thought Mr. Vora was real. At best they probably considered her an unmarried spinster. But the pretending made her feel safe, a fact she abhorred but couldn't change, a vestigial tail she couldn't hack off.

Anu sighed and made herself a smoothie. Power greens and chia. Frozen blueberries and fresh strawberries. She composed the beverage carefully: washing and using spinach leaves that fell in the sink, taking just enough blueberries and then twirling the bag into a tight bun. Her mother fished the strawberry tops out of the trash, shifting around crumpled plastic wrap with her pinky finger. She cut the minute slivers of red berry around the green stems, rinsed them furiously, and popped them into her mouth.

They went to the temple to help set up. No one was there except shirtless Birju, the priest. The annual puja was the Association's biggest fundraiser, the proceeds of which contributed to Birju's upkeep, the procurement of additional deities, and the Bharat Fund. It all made Anu uncomfortable.

The kids scooped up handfuls of the cubed sugar that served as god-anointed food. Birju fussed over the mess, frowning with an air of resigned condescension, like a teenager weary of explaining technology to parents. He seemed to hate children.

"Madam," he said. "No more ghee for diyas."

"What about the puja kits I ordered?"

"Useless! Not enough to light a birthday candle. We need a big fire!"

Her mother had upgraded the gods over the years. Invested in Jain tirthankaras, twenty-four of them. Lakshmi and Ganesh got their own vestibules, and Vishnu and Shiva competed for attention. All were decked out in crowns and Christmas tinsel.

Through the course of the afternoon, everyone seemed to have something to do. Birju took stock of the sacrificial legumes among the altars. Her mother set up folding chairs in perfect rows across the wide hall at an alarming rate. Jambi placed programs on them. The twins raged and settled and raged again, like parabolas.

Anu followed uselessly behind Jambi. The chairs were endless, and she was grateful when her phone buzzed and gave her something to do.

*Now is better than later.* Followed by a clock emoji.

"Is Mama coming tomorrow?" Jambi asked.

Up ahead, her mother unfolded a chair and slammed it to the ground.

"She's teaching," Anu said.

"Not on Sundays."

"Sometimes she does."

"No. She doesn't." Two defiant black orbs peered up at her.

"Yes, she does."

Jambi fidgeted with a program, dog-earing the corners. "I hope she comes."

It was essentially a gift. A chance to come clean, to break the cycle of lies. Mr. Vora be damned. He was a burden, a weight in the back of Anu's mind, and had taken on the proportions of truth. Sometimes she fantasized about revealing it all to Betina. The depth of her cowardice. The insurmountable obstacles to overcoming it. How funny it all was when you took a step back. She'd point out Mr. Vora's poor taste in clothing and his emphysemic laugh. Isn't he so silly? Perhaps there was a time when Mr. Vora could've become an inside joke, their personal Apocrypha. But they were well past that.

Jambi was waiting. Her mother kicked open a chair. Nothing Anu said would be the right thing to say. "Someday, Jambu. Someday she'll come."

ANU WENT ABOUT the rest of the day with surprising equanimity. Meals were had, fights were mediated, sets of teeth were cursorily brushed. After the kids went down, she restuffed the duffel bags and Ikea satchels. The sea was a restless patter. With the window open the smell of salt and seaweed wafted in, mildly fishy. Twice a year, the beach flooded, no matter how many dunes were dredged. She felt an unexpected tenderness for the place, as though it too had succumbed to its fanciful self-deceptions.

After the children were asleep and her mother closed her bedroom door, Anu dragged the duffels down the steps and out the back door and across the cracked walkway to her car under the carport. She was careful with the trunk latch, pushing rather than slamming it shut. She rid the back seat of pistachio shells and ribboned tissues and crushed Goldfish. They'd leave right after the puja, run out like bandits.

"Where are you going?"

Anu jumped. Her mother was at the top of the stairs that led to the house, blue kaftan billowing around her. A moment later she was at the carport, like she had wheels for feet. She made her way around the car, as if on official business, while Anu stood with her arms by her sides and trash in her fists.

"Why are you loading the car now? You could do it in the morning." She opened the trunk just to slam it shut. "So many bags for one night."

"You never know what you'll need."

The moonless sky was swept clean. They faced each other, her mother backlit by the house lights.

"You don't pack sensibly. Come inside now. You'll catch cold."

"In a minute." Anu held her breath. She couldn't move, couldn't step closer or further away. There were questions she needed to ask. "What happened to Ruchi Auntie? She never comes to the temple."

Her mother's mouth parted, then shut. "Sometimes she comes. You don't see her."

The lighthouse at the end of the cove was even blacker than the night sky. It was silly to push, but Anu couldn't stop now. "I wish I'd kept in touch with Moksh. He's not on social."

"I hear he's fine now. It was a long time ago. Not everyone can keep in touch. Now come inside." She snapped the blue kaftan at her legs and turned to leave.

If Anu went inside, it would be years before she'd find the courage again, if she ever did. "She was your best friend."

Her mother stopped but didn't turn around. "We were school friends. People become busy with their own lives."

"What was it like?" Anu asked. She had a desire, inexplicably, to growl, though what she felt was much gentler. "When you were younger, I mean." Had she never asked her mother for stories? Or had she tried and been dismissed?

"What a nonsense question. Come in."

But Anu caught a hesitation, enough to manipulate. "I will, but tell me something at least."

Her mother turned around. The tendons of her throat contracted, then relaxed. "We liked films. On special occasions we went to Metro. Ruchi's favorite was Madhubala, but I preferred Meena Kumari. Or maybe she also preferred Meena Kumari but wouldn't admit it. We were like that when we were younger, challenging each other. We could walk to Marine Drive, eat hot fafda and roasted peanuts in paper cones. Sometimes we had to follow my mother to temple and—" She traced her upper lip, then dropped her hand. "Why are you asking about stupid things? It was so long ago, I can't remember."

Anu kept very still. "The kids would like to know you more." *I would like to know you more.*

Her mother grunted. "I sent you those books."

"You mean the *Mahabharata* comic books? Those aren't the stories I meant." They were silent. Anu stared at the dark, unrelenting sea. "Why Vora?"

"Why not? It's a good name."

"It's ridiculous. The name. The lie." The Goldfish in her palm had turned to a creamy bisque. "If you'd told everyone from the beginning, they'd be used to it by now. People can be conditioned, like pigeons." It was Betina's line.

"People are not like that. They talk and gossip."

"So?" The carport had no walls, being a carport, and yet Anu was stuck inside it. Had she tried to step off the concrete slab, she'd have bounced off an invisible force field. "Eventually, we'll have to say something."

"Let them think you're divorced. Who cares?" her mother said.

"Then why? Why the charade? What are you avoiding?" Anu blurted all at once. "You don't believe in any of it. Not in the gods, not in the prayers. Not the charity. You know it's not charity. You know it's some warped Hindu fantasy."

Her mother twisted the end of her kaftan around her index finger. An effort traveled across her features and converged on the two worry lines between her eyebrows. Anu rubbed her matching one. Her mother's lips quivered, the slightest shake that another daughter might've missed. Another daughter also might've steadied it, might've said it was okay, whatever it was her mother was ashamed of.

But now Anu waited too long. Her mother had found an opening. "It was for you. Everything. Everything was for you. Coming to this country. Before you were even you, it was for you. Making a life."

"I'm grateful."

"You are not."

"We're thieves."

"That's your father."

"Us too," she said. Her mother's eyes seethed. Anu could never take it, those eyes. She spat out the words. "Betina wants to come to the puja."

"Take her to Queens."

"That's not what I mean."

"What do you mean then?"

Anu felt like running around the carport with her head thrown back, laughing and crying. "I mean, she's coming. Tomorrow. On Shore Line East." Her face was hot, but her ears hurt the way they did in the cold.

"Bhale. Your friend can sit in the last row and leave you alone."

Her friend. "Leave me alone?"

"You must explain it to her. Make her understand. Why make it everyone's business?"

"I can't. I can't make her understand." Anu's eyes flooded with tears.

"Don't cry! You married who you wanted." Her mother shook her head. "Is that not enough?"

"It's not enough," Anu said in a voice that was too small. Her mother laughed in response. "You can't stop it, Mom. Betina is coming."

"You have no regard for my wishes?"

"No, I don't." It was a salty lie, and her mother saw through it. She could see how it hurt Anu to say, she could see inside as much as she could lock her out. With effort, Anu swallowed her tears, and she liked to think that with equal effort her mother swallowed hers. They were probably still there inside, swimming upstream. Her family wasn't like other families for whom sincerity came naturally and easily to the tongue. Her mother's lip quivered again, then settled. The kaftan shimmered under the flood light of the carport. She held it closed at the neck with a fist and hurried up the walk.

Anu texted Betina good night and placed her phone in the glove compartment. In the morning, she helped the boys struggle into their silk kurtas tight in the armpits. She tied Lana's jeweled skirt that was an ankle too short. They stood in front of her, her children, expectant, their faces as new as the day they were born.

"You can have candy all day with the sitter," Anu said.

"We can't come?" Lana asked.

"There's been a change of plan," she said, as if she weren't hiding them from view. She ignored the hurt on their faces, turned away before it could punch too hard. At the temple, Anu sat crisscross with her mother on the floor in front of the chairs they'd arranged the day before, while Birju chanted shlokas over an assault of incense. Her mother closed her eyes and sang out louder than usual. They were sitting so close that Anu could see the pixels of rouge in the shallow craters of her cheeks, each pock a time when her mother couldn't resist the desire to scratch and pick and squeeze a pustule. Her arm brushed Anu's as she swayed. Anu leaned in to keep touching accidentally. She waited for her mother to shift out of reach, to search for a program or scoot her hips or fold into prayer, anything to maintain the necessary distance between them. But Anu felt the pressure on her arm returned, and she, too, closed her eyes, knowing that her phone was ringing, that the messages were coming in rapid succession and then less rapidly, like someone bleeding out, the gush followed by a trickle. Any second now she'd stand up and be gone. Any second.

# Moksh

## *2004–2015*

Moksh sent money home, whatever he could, Western Union cash, checks in letterless envelopes addressed to his mother. She rarely mentioned these gifts, and he was grateful to be spared the awkwardness. Years he'd spent fighting his body, and now he worked with it, became sturdy and agile, flipping houses ruined by flood or fire, contracting for a company down south, out west. He called from pay phones on Saturdays and told his mother about a canyon he'd slept in, the fierce red of the rock walls at sunrise. He wanted her to be astonished by these things, to see them too. "Jaanu, come home. You're alone," she said every time, and he laughed, though it made him sad. He didn't mind being alone. He wished she understood that, wished they could've started over. Known each other better.

HE WANTED TO tell her things she didn't know. How when he was ten, he'd slipped out of the house the morning of the hurricane to hide with Buddy Roland in the enormous junked Buick in the Rolands' yard, seats ripped out, floor mildewed, the smell tangy and sweet, like oranges on the verge of rot. His mother had been busy taping up windows last minute. His parents hadn't believed the weather reports, didn't understand the fuss. "What is a hurricane next to Bombay monsoons?" his father had said. Moksh lay flat in the Buick while Buddy took a marker and traced the hypertrophic scar above his lip, the angle of his forehead, the bulb of his nose. Buddy said he'd seen uglier kids on TV who'd had hundreds of surgeries, whereas Moksh had had only six. "You're just medium ugly," Buddy said. But when Moksh saw Buddy's handiwork in the rearview, he wished the marker were permanent and that his face could just stay this way, a structure imposed on another structure. Buddy said the storm would wash their cars down the hill, floating like heifers until they reached the algae pond and drowned. School canceled for a week. Buddy said his parents fought most nights, that his father drank in the garage, that he was building a bomb in the shed where no one was allowed. All these stories, and Moksh had no good ones. His parents didn't drink. They didn't fight in that way. They didn't build secret weapons. He was ashamed for feeling ashamed. The hurricane, he'd hoped, would change everything. He'd made plans to float out on the blood-red snow saucer his father had bought on sale the previous year, the one that cracked after a single use. He'd planned to hand out provisions and rescue animals stranded on mailboxes and low branches. Moksh had wanted to stay in that Buick while Buddy was being nice, but he'd seen his mother all alone with the tape. "Fucking wuss," Buddy called after him as he scrambled out the car door.

 He'd snuck into the house and washed his face until there was only the faintest trace of marker left. His face. He'd pressed his nose against the mirror until his eyelashes skimmed the surface. His ugliness had disappeared into the dark. The house was storm-dim, and later, in the basement where they took shelter, his mother couldn't make out the vestiges of black ink on his skin. He wished he'd known to miss her eyes on him, her searching, her vigilance. He wished he'd known that it wouldn't last forever.

 He remembered those hours before his father came home as happy ones. They didn't turn on the bare bulbs hanging from the ceiling so the only light came from the slit windows, the white sky. They heard the house go still as the power flickered. They sat on a cratered sofa bed, listening to the radio talk about the storm of the century, the hundreds of thousands evacuated, the storm surge on the seaboard, and when the announcers ran out of things to say, they played "Gloria" and nothing else. Moksh and his mother sang along, absentmindedly, sweetly. She was strangely at ease. She didn't point out that he hadn't touched his soup, was picking at his sandwich. He remembered it as peaceful, like they were the last two people alive, until his father returned and spoiled her good mood.

"A promotion," he'd said, and she'd nodded like she believed him. But worry flooded her body. Her hand gripped the edge of the sofa and her leg stretched straight and dropped. The storm had passed with not a single fallen elm, and Moksh liked to believe that his mother had been as disappointed as he was.

HE TURNED THIRTY-FIVE. A sunset in Colorado. The standing trees dark against a cerulean sky. Moksh took SLR photos of their branch tips that looked like molten fingers poking at a blue sheet. It was weird and beautiful, but not the photo he wanted to send. His mother liked vistas, so in the early dawn he climbed to the highest point he could find. The valley fog swirled through the tree branches. His thumb blotted out the bottom fourth of the photo. He developed the roll and found an internet café where he scanned the photo and rotated it 180 degrees before sending it to her. The black rounded edge that was his thumb became the top so that it looked like a photo taken from outer space, the instant a rocket left the earth's atmosphere and the pilot could see the planet curve. He added a caption that read "Look where I am!" along with a dozen punctuation emojis in that time before real emojis.

Weeks later, she still hadn't responded and he was on the deck of a ferry wending across the Pacific's cobalt waters, as far away as his feet could get from where he was from. In school he'd learned that "Connecticut" was a Mohegan-Pequot word meaning "long tidal river" or "upon the long river" and that where he'd grown up was probably Podunk land. They learned the names of different tribes and had to spell them correctly though no teacher made them pronounce them. "Indians," the teachers said, and Moksh sensed the whole class's attention turn to him.

Though later, when he told people he was from Connecticut, their expressions became tentative, like the expressions of well-meaning people who couldn't pronounce his name, the *o* either too much like "toe" or "rock," though even he was too American to say his name the way it was intended. He clarified that he'd grown up outside Hartford, nowhere near New York, hoping to convey a small, dying town where the fields were tobacco and strawberry and pinched between strip malls, where the Town and Country Store became a needle dispensary when he was in high school, where his family was never on the inside, always watching and aching, like seeing a band of friends in conversation and realizing you'd never have anything to contribute.

On the ferry, the salt spray dotted his face, and he pressed down on his pulse like the captain had advised to fight back the already churning nausea. He pressed until he could almost feel his fingers meet through his wrist. Across the sea was an island with million-dollar homes that needed clearing. "You'll have to guard against mosquitos. It's a bitch," they were told at headquarters. "Too much standing water."

When Moksh was very small, his mother's hand on his stomach used to soothe the ache. Sometimes he could recall its coolness and dampen the urge to vomit. Things had changed. In some circles, he was beautiful. Where people wanted him because of his asymmetries rather than despite. A woman once took photos of his face in every light. A man had watched him sleep. There was no way he could've known any of this as a kid, though it would've been helpful. He wished his mother knew. He released his wrist, tried to shake the numb from his fingers. On the island, he found a place to check email. Finally, a response. "Stop your foolishness," his mother had written. She'd returned the photo, set right. Ten sideways smiles. He placed his head between his hands and gave in.

IN THE ISLAND rubble, Moksh found toasters, crutches, packets of soy sauce still intact. A single rubber boot with the sole ripped clear off.

Once, the paw of a dog. The mud gurgled and sucked. They had to lay down boulders for places to step or get sucked in, too. He slipped after a twelve-hour day, his leg up to the knee. It took two crewmates to pull him out.

He found books, some with familiar covers. When he was thirteen, he'd wake in the middle of the night, his room as still and dark as a tomb, and sneak into his parents' bedroom to steal the romance novels his mother borrowed from the library. He'd skimmed them from under his covers with a flashlight. Embossed serifed letters, illustrations of half-clad bodies. Their house was given to moths in spring, and one would find its way under the covers, bouncing between the light and his page, its wings tapping sharp and accusatory. He'd skim through until arriving at a paragraph-long description of sweaty embraces. He'd earmark these pages and read them over and over until the words lost their power. It made him feel both sick and elated, like he'd stepped out of the haze of childhood, his mother transforming into flesh and blood instead of his mother. He'd find a moth lying flat on his arm, clinging to life, and he'd stare at it until it gave a last gasp. He'd collected their bodies in jars that he placed on the sill, jars that his father threatened to throw out but his mother protected despite her disgust.

He'd always returned the books before she noticed they were gone, though she must've seen the earmarks, she must've wondered if it was him. She must've read the passages, must've known that he'd read them too. Did she think that the way he looked precluded desire? He eventually realized that they were dancing around each other, speaking in a secret language, a language of inefficient gestures, a language that tried to serve as affection, that required no direct contact. People asked if he was close to his mother. Was he? Could you be close to a person you love, to a person who loves you, and not know them at all? Maybe you could.

HE DIDN'T GO home. Not that year. Not the next. There was the work, a constant demand in every direction. Fires and floods and landslides that offered employment, people who needed him. He assessed the detritus in destroyed beachfront homes, the remains of cliffside abodes. A wearable sleeping bag, a dented but usable Keurig machine, a leather ottoman. Treasures he saved from landfill to ship home, gifts in addition to the money, the unaffordable extravagances that his father used to buy. He felt virtuous in his repurposing until he discovered that the leather was sourced from the Amazon or the Keurig model used #7 plastic. In the end, they were all culpable for their want by degrees.

"We don't need all this," his mother said. "Why are you sending, Mokshu?"

"Why not? Dad always wanted expensive things."

"What will we do with a sleeping bag? Where do we use it?"

"It can be a blanket on the couch."

"Your father, he was asking about you." It was a lie; they both knew it.

SOMETIMES, AFTER SEARCHING hours for a gas station pay phone down an endless road on a moonless night, he'd call to find his mother far away. Perhaps she hadn't thought of him in days. The effort it took her to engage, a weariness in her attention. "Mokshu, dikra, we'll talk later, okay?" she'd say and forget to ask him, implore him, to come home. Ruthlessly, he'd withhold a phone call for weeks. He hated how cruel he could be, how quickly he could regress to childhood, to the one time, he believed it was only one time, he told her he wished he'd had a different mother. He'd wanted her to laugh it off, to make a joke out of her hurt, to forgive him on the spot, but she didn't know how to be glib. She avoided his eyes for the rest of the day and the next. He couldn't apologize, couldn't overcome his shame and pride, and in his heart he was lost.

"I NEED HELP with your father," his mother said. He was outside Olympia where the temperate rainforest was burning. There were no more houses to clear, and Moksh was on watch rotation tracking the direction of the smoldering blaze, monitoring the camera stations, overseeing the sensors and wind shifts, the shapeshifting plumes. For a week the blaze chased its own tail without burning out.

"What kind of help?"

"He hardly leaves the house. Mostly sits on the sofa talking to the TV. His fingers hurt."

"Ma."

"I think it would help if you came home for a few days."

He could've. It was a windless August night, orange embers forming vertical lines. Not a single cloud graced the sky. The fire towers were relics, the monitoring could be done from anywhere, but Moksh chose to spend watch rotations in the forest, a dying breed of ranger. He hadn't taken a break longer than a day in years and had become known for his stamina. He was thirty-eight and felt far younger than his parents had seemed at that age.

"I'll think about it," he said. He wanted to climb down the ten flights of stairs, tell someone his family needed him, that he was heading home, doing the right thing. No one would've begrudged him. He could've done it, but he didn't.

His mother didn't ask again. She said that his father's fingers were arthritic. His mind at times foggy, at times sharp. Fluid in his knees needed draining from time to time. She took him to his appointments. Said his father did puzzles, that he still railed against the news, the clowns who kept getting elected, the nonsense of the Dow. Moksh listened like a good son.

SUMMERS PASSED. FIRST one, then three. He was nearly forty-one and it was the fall of 2015. A hundred miles outside Durango in a wooden office, he heard Deepa's voice on a beat-up landline of all things, a miracle anyone could find him.

"Your mother," she said as greeting. She sounded exactly like herself, like no time had passed.

"What is it?" he asked but didn't want to hear it.

"Your father couldn't call. He wasn't able—"

He asked, "What is it?" A woman sitting at a desk looked up.

"She met with an accident," Deepa said as if the accident was a person his mother had encountered.

Moksh scanned the posters taped to the walls: faded trail maps, an aerial view of Durango, A GREAT PLACE.

"She'd taken a backroad with no shoulder. The rain, how it pours these days. In sheets."

Deepa waited, but Moksh couldn't speak. He couldn't take his eyes off the little houses all facing the sun. "She spun out and ricocheted through the forest."

It sounded almost beautiful. "Tell me again," he said.

"Moksh."

"Again," he said and so she did, using different words with the same ending. "I'm coming," he said. "Tell me which hospital." His mind raced. He'd pay for rehab. He'd get her onto disability. She'd been at the salon close to fifteen years. That must mean something.

Time stopped with a crackle in the line.

"Beta, you don't understand."

"Can you pass the phone to my father? He must be there."

"Beta, he's not here."

"Please stop calling me 'beta.' Please."

"Your mother, she was my friend."

"You abandoned her. She was alone."

"We spoke every day."

"That's not true. She never mentioned that you spoke every day."

What was this tremble in her voice? "Maybe not, but we did. We started speaking again."

"I remember you wouldn't take her calls."

"That was wrong of me. I wasn't ready."

"Ready?"

"She was coming to see me when—"

"Please," he said again. "Don't."

"Dikra."

"She never mentioned you at all."

He squeezed his eyes shut to call up the last time he'd seen his mother, a palpitating smile playing on her lips, a pale-green housecoat, one hand holding the other, ready, worried. But the memory was already fading out of focus into a vague impression. The heat in the room was stifling, but his hands were cold.

"We were close," Deepa said, and here a choked sob, at last. "I want to tell you that we were always close. Even when we weren't talking, she was"—and here the line crackled again. "She was beautiful, your mother, my Ruchi." Her Ruchi. Hers. But he realized that deep down he already knew this, just as he always knew his mother was beautiful. What none of them told her was that she was loved.

He flew. Spoke words that needed speaking to get taxis, tickets. Meals were put in front of him that he didn't eat. The flight attendant placed a hand on his shoulder. "Sir, we're here." The attendant had a baby face with salt-and-pepper temples, white clouds reflected in his black eyes. Moksh wanted to grab his hand and beg him to let him stay, to let him ride the plane to wherever it was going next.

The house was misted in fog. A fine mist, like a gauze filter to induce a fake glow. The door unlocked. His father was in the living room on the tea-stained paisley couch, his feet raised on the leather ottoman, his soles webbed with cracks. He was staring at the blank TV, his chest bare, pajama drawstring tied at his waist. Moksh hadn't yet spoken to him. He hadn't yet spoken to his father after learning of his mother's death. This should've struck him as odd. His father's lids were heavy, skin dried out, ashen, thinner, a crease between his chest and stomach, as if any second he might crack open.

"Dad."

His father's eyes followed his voice. "I see."

"Dad." Slowly, Moksh moved from the doorway to the middle of the room where the mist was thickest. He wondered if his father saw it too. The room was as it had always been but indistinct, smudged. He was expecting a clutter of pill bottles on the coffee table, half-eaten breakfast bars, crusted plates. But it was empty except for a *National Geographic* that he'd read as a kid, open to a photo of a yellow-eyed bird of paradise, an outrageous crest against a blurred forest. Photo of the Year, or something like that. The mantel with plastic flowers in a souvenir vase from Niagara Falls, a jar of old pens, the yellow highlighter he'd used in high school, the batik with missing mirrors. The only wedding photo he'd ever seen of his parents—his mother's eyes cast down, his father staring at their clasped hands covered in a white cloth. A sturdy braid resting on his mother's shoulder.

"Dad," Moksh said again. He thought he might sink to his knees. He thought he might run. "Please."

The air changed, grew luminous, like the seconds after a flash. He wasn't sure what he was expecting, what he wanted from his father. Over the years, he'd created memories from his mother's descriptions: his father's lips moving in a constant whispered monologue, his obsession with old documents and bills and files, the piles he made in every room. "His good cholesterol is excellent," his mother had told him again and again, as if to prove a point. A picture of health.

But what he thought of now was Matsya and the story his mother had told him. He wanted his father to slough off a scale or unfurl a fin. He wanted his father, this faded man, to guide him to the deepest part of the ocean. Even if it was only a story. Even if only that.

"Dikra," his father said at last and stood up, recognition flooding his face. He swayed and Moksh steadied him with a hand on his bent elbow, the skin oddly smooth like a waxed apple. In another life they might've embraced, clasped each other around the shoulders and held on. Made unspoken amends, curled together in their grief, seeing each other, as if for the first time, in the clarity of mourning. But in the middle of the afternoon, dust glittering in the sun-slabbed mist, his father shrugged him off. "Come, dikra."

Moksh followed him down the dark hall, past the pantry filled with jars of different-colored lentils and candies, into the kitchen that someone had finally painted a blinding white. They opened the fridge and took out everything she'd left: kadi a few days old, undhiyu with turmeric dumplings, pulao with peas. They weren't hungry, either of them, but they filled their plates, filled them past the blue borders until they spilled over. When his father pushed his away, the sun falling behind the unbroken trees, Moksh took the plate and ate what was left, ate until finally it hurt.

# ACKNOWLEDGMENTS

I'm grateful to everyone who has supported my writing life and the long road to this novel.

To the incomparable Iwalani Kim—I've never met such a fierce advocate in so calm a person. Many thanks to Sanford J. Greenburger Associates, especially Madeline Wallace and Dorothy Vincent.

To Grace McNamee, my supremely talented editor, for asking all the right questions and guiding me toward a much better novel. To the entire Bloomsbury team, especially Jillian Ramirez, Kenli Manning, Barbara Darko, Callie Garnett, Nancy Miller, Valentina Rice, Sarah Rucker, Laura Phillips, Eleanor Peters, Rosie Mahorter, and Lauren Moseley. Special thanks to Jaya Miceli for the gorgeous jacket, Emily DeHuff for the sharp copyedits, and Megha Jain for the proofread. Here's to independent publishing!

I am and always will be a writer in training. Many thanks to the teachers who believed in me before I knew how to believe. To the Michener Center for Writers in Austin for giving me three glorious years to work and learn, and especially Holly Doyel and Blake Lee Pate for their constant support.

To Elizabeth McCracken for her generous, and numerous, readings of this novel, her peerless precision, and so much more.

To Bret Anthony Johnston, for his sage advice and endless care.

To Edward Carey, Deb Olin Unferth, Maya Perez, Stuart Kelban, Megha Majumdar, and Charles Ramirez-Berg for their mentorship and knowledge.

To my talented peers at the Michener Center and the New Writers Project who inspire me daily: Ashley Moore, Anika Jhalani, Anindit Dutta, Kion You, Sarah Berry, Carrie R. Moore, Stephanie Macias, Brynne Jones, Megan Kamalei Kakimoto, Adithi Chandrashekar, Pathikrit, Eileen Chong, Sanjana Thakur, Stephanie Morris, Sophia

## ACKNOWLEDGMENTS

Emmons-Bell, Zhenglong Yang, Cristina Herrera Mezgravis, Will Watkins, Hannah Fritz, Avery Lin, and many more.

To Kumudini Lakhia, my kathak guru, who taught me that persistence means doing what you love no matter who tries to stop you.

I would've never become a writer if it wasn't for three teachers, Patricia Davidson, Steve Foley, and Alan Ziegler, who saw potential in my first attempts. Thank you.

To the Cuttyhunk Island Residency, the Sustainable Arts Foundation, Millay Arts, the Steinbeck Fellowship, and Tin House for providing invaluable support, and to the teachers, writers, and mentors I've met at these places, especially Ben Shattuck, Ethan Canin, Kimberly King Parsons (the first to see I had a novel on my hands), Rion Amilcar Scott, and Lance Cleland. A special thanks to A.L. Major at Tin House for the many opportunities and steady friendship.

To the readers who offered invaluable feedback on this book in all its incarnations, especially Megan Kamalei Kakimoto, Jinwoo Chong, Carrie R. Moore, Stephanie Macias, Brynne Jones, Kion You, Parul Shah, Adithi Chandrashekar, Parthikrit, Camara Garrett, Roohi Choudhry, and Dhwani Yagnaraman.

I'm grateful to the editors who have championed my work at various literary magazines fighting to keep literature vibrant in this big, bad world, among them Malinda McCollum and Jonathan Bohr Heinen at *swamp pink*, Preety Sidhu and Erin Bartnett at *Electric Literature*, and Tara Isabel Zambrano at *Waxwing Literary Journal*. Thank you to *Third Coast Magazine*, the *Masters Review*, and *Joyland Magazine* for publishing early versions of several chapters.

A big thank you to the editors at *The Rumpus* with whom I've had the privilege to work alongside: Stephanie Trott, Alyson Sinclair, Aram Mrjoian, Rebecca Rubenstein, Vonetta Young, Kelly Dignan, Katie Quach, Chris Santantasio, Liwen Xu, Allison Field Bell, and W. S. Gong.

Thanks to the friends who have sustained me over many years. You are many and mighty: John Allgood, Mauricio Valverde Arce, Marcos Avila, Roshni Bhakta, Symeon Braxton, Dionisio Bustillo, Manuel Ceano, Richa Chinoy, Katy Chrisler, Sonia Cifala, Sonsoles Cifuentes, Camara Garrett, David Gavril, Katie Giordano, Vandana Goyal, Mitra

Feldman, Winthrop Han, Juju Hattangadi, Sahaan Hattangadi, Grace Hunter, Deyanira Jiménez, Mohip Joarder, Euriphile Joseph, Frank Joyce, Rashmi Kashyap, Kayla Keller, Tasha Kosviner, Chris Krantz, Francini Leon, Mike Locker, Raul Ayuga Loro, Kenna Manos, Vanessa Muncrief, Nalini Nadkarni, Paula Nijamkin, Edda Pacheco, Elizabeth Piper, Pallavi Raisurana, Jane Renaud, Siva Ramakrishnan, David Romero, Raj Soni, Amol Sharma, Anastasia Shown, Arturo Sosa, Kanchan Thadani, Karen Valby, Héctor Valera, Ammr Vandal, Katy Van Dusen, Mara Washburn, Anandhi Yagnaraman, and more.

To Kim Lewis, my first real friend and to whom I return again and again.

To Parul Shah, for immeasurable friendship in art and life, thirty years and counting.

To my grandmothers, Jaswanti Sangani and Taraben Shah, and my uncle, Shantilal Shah, who sacrificed so much to make everything possible.

To the Neidls: Phoebe, Paul, Jess, Bill, Ben, Cyndy, Linda, and Tom for continuous cheer.

To my family, near and far, especially Nutan Desai, Nisha Desai, Jayshree Shah, Pravin Shah, Pankaj Shah, Manish Shah, Pooja Shah, Dimple Shah, Sejal Shah Miller, Ranjan Vaidya, Mehul Vaidya, and Preety Vaidya. Special thanks to Nimisha Shah and Jignesh Shah for their knowledge of Gujarati. And to Hasmukh Shah who told me long ago, with great confidence, that I would one day write a novel.

To my mother, Madhuri Shah, who is very often right. To my father, Dinesh Shah, who taught me how to live with grace and humility. To my sister, Ami Shah, who always has my back, and who will forever be the smarter one. To my brother, Rajiv Shah, his wife, Kaitlyn Piper, and my nephews, Kiran and Kairav, for much laughter, warmth, and boundless support.

To Tuki—you deserve your own line, even though you are a stubborn dog!

Lastly, but really firstly, to Chris, Som, and Haroun, who are my home. You bring me every happiness, for real.

# A NOTE ON THE AUTHOR

REENA SHAH is a writer, editor, and teacher. Her work has been featured in the *Masters Review, Electric Literature, Joyland,* the *American Prospect, National Geographic,* and the *Guardian,* among other publications. She has been awarded fellowships and residencies from the Martha Heasley Cox Center for Steinbeck Studies, Millay Arts, Tin House, Sustainable Arts Foundation, Cuttyhunk Island Residency, and the Fulbright Program. She received an MFA in fiction from the Michener Center for Writers, where she won the Keene Prize for Literature. For many years she was a kathak dancer in New York and India. She now lives on Roosevelt Island, New York, with her family and teaches in a public school.